the backstory of a guy

Laura Ross

Staten House

Staten House

Copyright

Printed in the United States of America

First Printing, 2022

ISBN 979-8-89686-905-4

Staten House
447 Broadway

2nd Floor

New York, NY 10013

www.statenhouse.com

CONTENTS

Go and open the window to
Let the air in
And your God.
Feel that wind on your face?
I told you I'd come back to
Love you and
Hold you and
Make you
Pay.
So, go ahead,
I see you.
Finish making your meal.
Soak in those last bites and
Savor the lush breeze of freedom in
Your hair.
Come and rely on me when
Nobody is watching.
Well, I am Nobody.
And I see you.

To my readers,
For always keeping it REAL with me.

Love and light,
Laura

"It really is a pity that you're dropping out of school, young man. Is there nothing else we can do to set you up for success?" Counselor Riviera asked cautiously between small bites of her fish bagel.

Well, it looked and smelled like fish, my nose auto-detecting the pink flesh poking out from the sides of it as something belonging to the sea. Fucking nasty is what it was, no doubt about it.

I shifted in the seat opposite of the fat Spanish lady, being careful to hold in my breath a few precious seconds before responding.

"Uh, yeah," I sighed. "The best way to move forward is letting me drop out. Peacefully. And without my parents too deep in the process."

"Peacefully? Any trouble at home? I'd be glad to follow up with your parents if—"

"Not necessary."

Flustered, she took another bite from her smelly fish bagel before lamenting, "Shamel, son, please understand this is a serious matter here. You've exuded nothing less than academic excellence since you began at Marlton High, and it's just my job to counsel you about this possibility."

I tried really fucking hard to keep the barf from coming up, and hardened my face as I stared at her crumby one. "Like I said, Counselor Riviera, that's not necessary. There ain't no problems at home. In fact, my

Old Man been nagging me to drop this school shit for a minute now."

"Surely, that isn't true?"

"Too bad it is. And I been fighting it, but now I think it's time I go. Just show me the paperwork necessary to start the process."

"Shamel," she extended her hand to me, her eyes sympathetic. "Can you not hear the problem in that statement?"

"What's the problem?"

"More like, *who's* the problem? Surely, your father is not encouraging you to withdraw from high school. That's unethical."

"Well, I ain't exactly his pride and joy." I respond, my tone flat and withholding. I was more like his shame and fury. And it was true, I thought, as I considered his permanent frown and shitty disposition when it came to me. "But if it's his approval you need, gimme a sec."

"Okay." She agrees as I slide the newest edition iPhone from my denim jean pocket. I dial one of the three numbers saved in the contacts and place the trilling phone on loudspeaker as we wait for it to connect.

"Fuck you want, man?" My old man demands in his usual setting of pissed off.

"Trying to drop out of school. Counselor's giving me a hard time, saying I need your permission, or some shit. You on loudspeaker and I'm in her office."

I anticipate the fury behind his next retort. "Tell that bitch I said you want out. Yesterday. And to send me any paperwork needed to make that happen. Understand?"

"Yep." I met her eyes, which were round with shock.

"I'm talking to your teacher, not you boy. Do you understand what I'm saying?"

"Y-Yes, Mr. Masters," she stammered in embarrassment while wiping the crumbs off her face. "Loud and clear."

"Good." he sneers. "Now don't call me again unless it's an emergency." He hangs up without a goodbye, Commander style, and an action I've long since stopped getting in my feelings about.

"So." I begin. "We good here?"

"Shamel, I really wish—"

"I'm trying to play this shit nice!" I stood up, pissed at her protests but also unable to be in the presence of that nasty fish sandwich she devoured minutes ago. "Gimme the papers, or I'll get them myself. I ain't come to you for counseling. Or your pity talk. Or your disappointment. Fuck all that."

"Excuse me?!"

"Nah, excuse *me*. I gotta find somebody who actually can do their job without all the fucking condescending ass, gentle ass, third degree."

She's sputtering and hurling threats my way as I turn to the door.

Somehow, her enraged scolding puts me in mind of my old man whenever I returned home with the unsold product he placed in my charge to move, and a dark smile curves my lips as I exit the office. Waste of talent, she calls it? A pity? Nah, I operated with ease in the shadows and took pride in people's general lack of faith in me. Maybe my ties to the real monsters on these gritty Camden streets was my downfall, but if I went down, at least the fall wouldn't be alone or in vain. I had a mission, and I dedicated my next few years to seeing that shit through for a change.

Was it a pity to be dropping out of this underfunded dank ass school? Maybe.

Was it a waste to be leaving the only home and family I ever knew to start this mission? Possibly.

Was it worth it? Hell fucking yeah.

Pity played a huge part in me dropping the "L" in my government name so that I could live and profit comfortably from the shadows.

Ain't that a shame? Yeah, that's me, and you'd best learn not to forget it.

PART ONE

SHAMEL

ONE

YESTERDAY

Sad to say, I've seen more bullets in my childhood than cupcakes and playdates. After all, there was nothing cushy about growing up as one of Jersey's finest dealer's kids. In fact, it was him who got me my first real gig, except, it was kept entirely secret from everyone.

I adjusted my eerily still position in the dark. In the silence, where I worked most of the time, I recollected the black chunk of metal I received as a birthday gift from The Commander.

"This here is your birthright." Quincy, my ex-military father we fittingly referred to as 'The Commander,' told me the morning of my tenth birthday after barging into the small room I shared with my older sister.

He wore his usual espionage black attire: black jeans, black turtleneck sweater, with a designer trench coat over top.

I stared at him in open confusion as he unsheathed the black felt box from his inner trench pocket.

"What's this?" I asked, still groggy from the sleep he interrupted and stunned by his unexpected presence.

He tossed the slim box at me and grunted, "A gift from Santa."

"Santa?"

"Yeah." He answered wryly. "Open it up."

"Okay." I muttered, opening the black case to reveal the menacing looking firearm: a Colt Single Action Army gun.

"A gun?"

He nodded, his long shoulder length dreads spilling over his eyes. "Finest piece around. We'll try it out at Remy's later on."

Remy's was technically a bar, but its owner, Remy Shelton, was who you went to to get unregistered and under the table weapons like this. His underground level functioned as our makeshift shooting range, where Dad and I would go to fire off rounds for sport. I started shooting officially at age nine, and had since never missed a mark or practice target laid out for me. A gift, they called it. An assassin in the making, were the remarks I'd hear after blasting off several rounds of silent bullets into the paper silhouette target. While only a hobby of Dad's, shooting had become my obsession. In fact, it got so bad, I found myself studying gun types and bullet variations during classes and after school at the cost of making my grades suffer.

After a firm but loving scolding from my older sister, Shayne, to "straighten them grades the fuck up before I whoop your ass," I paid the attention needed in class to turn those F's into high C's. At least, Tierra Sales turned my grades around by "accidentally" revealing a little too much of her exams, worksheets, and other assignments for public view as I cheated off her in class. She wanted me, and I knew it, and just like most girls in my grade when I asked them to help me out a little over the promise of a few seconds beside me in the halls or a seat at my table at the lunchroom, her blush was automatic as I shot her a playful wink and kiss as payment for her services.

Pure joy crashed through my then-scrawny body as I surged forward with the urge to embrace my reticent father.

"All right, all right." He said, blocking my outstretched arms from even attempting the hug I nearly gave him. "I think after a couple more sessions at Remy's, you'll be ready to Put in Work."

"What you talkin bout, 'Put in Work?'" I demanded, slighted, and eying him suspiciously as I grasped the gun.

"If you need to ask, then you sure ain't ready for it." Dad said while turning his heavily clothed back to me.

"Be ready in ten minutes. We're heading over there now to practice some shots."

I frowned. "Now? But I got school in like an hour."

He shrugged. "Well, then I'll leave it to you. Just remember, both choices will dictate the rest of your future."

"Hmm." I considered, still savoring the feel of cold metal in my hands. Dad would always come up with the most philosophical shit at just the right moments. The moments he either wanted you to do something or get out of his face.

Assuming the former, I shrugged, already accepting the ass-whooping from Shay later about missing school. "All right, I'm down. I'll roll with you."

"Good choice, young man." He praised, as if knowing what my choice would be. "Downstairs in ten."

"Where you goin?" I drawled while watching his large frame slip through the door.

"Going to the corner store to get some Loosies. I'll be back before you finish getting dressed. Keep an eye on your little cousins while I'm gone." He answered without facing me before leaving as silently as he came. Predator style.

"Cousins–" Before the question fully leaves my lips two toddlers rush inside my tiny room with a probable sugar-filled energy.

"Mel-Mel!" The chubby faced little girl who had eyes like mine and two thick puffballs in her head mused.

She climbed my bed to get to me, same as the little boy with her face.

"Mel-Mel, let's play!" He demanded with the biggest grin on his face.

My heart swelled with a love so pure it froze me in place. Nobody had ever been just happy to see me. And while irritating as hell, I always looked forward to my cousins visiting, as they occasionally did with The Commander's bimonthly visits.

"Big Mike and VonVon!" I exclaimed, scooping both three-year old's in my scrawny arms with ease. They giggled and began to wrestle over who got to hug me first.

"Mikey, stupid!" My cousin Yvonne complained, swatting at her twin brother Michael in a furious motion. "*I* hug Mel-Mel!"

"No!" Michael pushed her off of him. "Big Mike hug Mel-Mel."

"Hey, hey!" I caution them, pulling the fighting toddlers apart in my lap. Tears pricked both their eyes as I continued. "I have room for both of y'all. Always. Okay?"

"No!" Yvonne protested, swatting Mike again. "No share."

"*My* Mel-Mel!" Michael screamed at her.

Hugging them both tightly to my chest, I shushed and rocked them until only my hums could be heard in the small room. They soon settled into a quiet so peaceful I anticipated the light snores a few moments later. Being here, in this place and time while cradling my favorite cousins off to snooze town filled me with a tranquility that was hard to explain. Being there for them like this did the opposite of what The Commander's presence did: steadied me. I'm not compelled to bite my nails to bloody stubs as I listen for their breaths and ruminate on some shit.

As I'm rocking and humming, my mind turns as I consider my father's words. I'm immediately aware of his meaning of "Loosies" as single cigarettes he purchased from Reyes, the corner store he often went to whenever he was in town visiting us.

"Loosies..." I whispered, my mind separating the actual slang meaning of the word to a story we learned in my AP History class.

A fallen angel from God's grace came to mind as I recollect the evil personified later in Milton's *Paradise Lost*. What was his name? I queried inwardly while settling the snoozing toddlers onto my bed. Pulling my t-shirt and jeans on, I remembered he fell to the bottoms of the earth and remained there as a forever reminder of God's imperfections. He was evil and darkness personified who morphed into the Devil.

"Lucifer." I breathed, remembering the sinking feeling in my bird chest as I resonated with the flawed character.

I gripped the gun tightly to my chest, reveling in the protective powers filling me as I did the same thing God did to the fallen angel.

Gave it a name. Luci.

She'd become my longtime companion in these cold Camden streets and my greatest savior in the heat of a moment.

Even now, I grasped her tight and angled the silencer attached to the nozzle at the Latin Crip's head from a distance.

The stench of the abandoned building I hid inside was nearly enough to distract me from my mission. My purpose. But I choked down the smell and positioned the gun just right to prepare my aim for the kill shot.

Once positioned correctly, I pulled the trigger, allowing Luci to do her thing and anticipating the crash of lifeless body against the cold ground.

I didn't linger to make sure the job was done. I knew it was, since I never missed my mark.

There was so much about this bloody job that I knew all too well, could expect like clockwork after Luci and I completed a contract kill.

However, the shrill scream from the alley takes me by surprise and turns my warm blood into icicles in my veins.

"*¡Dios* – Hector!" The guy hollers in complete terror as he rushed to the scene. I don't recognize him, but curse myself for allowing my daydreams about Luci to infiltrate my rationale and distract me from securing the area before pulling the trigger. That was Rule One, after all. No witnesses. Ever.

"Who the fuck did this to you? Hey!" The tall Hispanic guy called before running down the opposite end of the alley.

I used his frantic departure to creep back down the street. There was a crowd a couple of blocks from the crime scene I created, and I used that to strategically slip into the busy New York hustle-bustle and camouflage my existence.

NYC nightlife just hit different, I thought as I waded through the corporate coke heads and professional junkies I recalled selling product to. There was always a vibe that embraced me like a warm hug when I entered this part of sin city, and for a moment, wonder replaced the panic in my chest as I made it towards the slate black Cadillac tucked into another alley The Commander let me use during deployments.

Deployments, he used the term reserved in layman's-speak alluding to war to name the contracts that slid across his desk. Maybe he was right to name it that, I considered as I fumbled with the car keys in my black denim pockets. So much about this life, the hiding, scoping out targets, and clean sniper kills from a far-from-comfortable distance was a war. And I often compared myself to a soldier, existing day-to-day and surviving as best I could until my next orders from The Commander.

Before I'm able to twist the key into the ignition to peel out of there, to lick my wounds from a failed covert operation, the windshield shatters.

"Fuck!" I hiss, ducking down from the bullet that pierced through my car.

The crowd stirs from the sounds of someone aiming at me and shooting in rapid fire, but it's not the shots that make my blood chill.

It's the voice behind it.

"Pendejo!" The gruff male's voice I recognized hollering frantically over the dead homeboy I eliminated from earlier calls. "Don't think I didn't see you, *puta!* Do you know who you just capped?"

His voice is inching closer, I know it because of the clarity of it and the sound of him reloading.

My hands are sweaty vessels that somehow fit the key into the razor thin ignition.

Soon as I'm able, I speed out of there and weave through the night traffic with easy precision, though I'm driving like a psycho at nearly twenty over the speed limit. Though only thirteen, I'm no idiot. Quincy, my father and Commander, taught me early on about Rule One: operate in the shadows and never get caught. I made it my priority to follow his orders, to stay on his good side for fear of being on the receiving end of his wrath and sacrificing my spot as next in line to run his empire, but raw disgust fills me at the realization of my own failure. My insolence for breaking his most cardinal rule.

And not only was I seen for my mistake, but nearly gunned down in the process. In fact, I'm more afraid of The Commander's reaction to the shot-up state of his favorite whip than the state of me: Shaken, sweaty, and...bleeding? I ponder curiously at the feel of warm liquid oozing down the side of my arm. In fact, it's heavy as I race across state lines into the Garden State and eventually reach the parking lot of Jefferson Heights, the twelve story, twin tower, apartment complex I used to stay at. My family moved into a two-bedroom house a little larger than the cramped one bedroom we lived in a couple of years ago in the Heights. While rich, my family often lived in safehouses, which were in rotten conditions, but necessary to live in to ensure our safety, according to The Commander. This meant sharing a space with my annoying ass older sis, who often left home with no clear explanation of her destination or reason why she'd always sneak back in all sweaty, afraid, and begging me never to tell our parents her whereabouts. We both had our secrets, I thought as I climbed the steps to the fifth floor, secrets that had no business coming to the light.

I pounded on the worn door of apartment 506 and offered a lame smile to the shocked weathered face of my Project Granny.

"Shamel!" Miss Pat exclaimed, her eyes darting around the outside before pulling me into the cramped two-bedroom apartment that smelled constantly of Pine Sol and whatever food she was frying.

I licked my lips as I collapsed onto the tattered blue couch. "Damn, Miss Pat. You fried chicken?"

"Pork chops." Grumbled the heavyset old lady I monikered as my "Project Granny," considering our tight relationship we formed throughout the years I grew up here in the hood. "And boy, tell me what happened to you! What's with all this blood leaking out your arm like you just got out of a fight or something?"

"Ah!" I winced, only now noticing the damp cloth rag she used to staunch the wound. It stung like a bitch.

A knowing look lit in her eyes as she leaned over to stare into me. "Mmm. More of that gangbanging mess, huh?"

I nod slowly. "You know I can't go into particulars, but I got into some trouble. Real bad."

"I ought to kill that daddy of yours." She groused, bringing a surgical kit to my field of vision just then. "This gonna sting a bit, but I got to sew this up before the bleeding gets worse. Okay?"

"Just get it over with." I breathe, the pain making my head swirl but overall deciding to trust the former registered nurse.

"He didn't see your face, did he?" Miss Pat asks an hour after finishing my homemade stitches over dinner. We're sitting at the dining room table amongst a sea of bookshelves, Knick knacks, and family portraits and I'm all but shoveling the fried pork into my mouth as my stomach whined from emptiness after the pain diminished.

"Nah." I answer her worried glare from across the table. "I ain't fuck up that bad. But he saw my ride. My plates."

She nodded, worry etched in her face but not an ounce of fear. Miss Pat was fearless in that hard way that single moms had to be when faced with too many bills and not a dime from their baby's fathers. Outside of my Pops, she was the only one who'd had any in-depth knowledge of my dangerous job. She was privy to more info than my own mother, as I made sure to keep Miss Pat stocked with medical supplies for events like this. This surely wasn't the first time I'd come home with a boo-boo too difficult and too bloody to explain to my willfully ignorant mother.

"You were right to come here." She added. "Don't want you followed home."

"I wasn't." I said.

"You can't be too sure either, Shamel. Now, who was using you for target practice?"

"Hard limit, Miss Pat." I warn between bites of macaroni.

"You know I can't tell you all that."

She waved my words away. "Oh, shut up. You come here injured from them missions of yours and I'm not allowed to ask questions? This the third time now, and this is the worst it's ever gotten. If you hadn't gotten here when you did—"

"Deployments." I cut in, correcting her. "And I know. My bad, Miss Pat. I don't mean to keep putting you in these situations. Don't mean to keep involving you in this business."

"Boy, I know all about this life and yours ain't the first bullet wound I sewed from my living room." She responds, wistful and despondent for a second before tacking on, "I can handle it."

"It's not a good idea. You already know too much."

"And you're just a child. Barely a teenager at that. Don't make me keep you here and raise you as my own, now."

I chuckle at that. "Now you know you can't keep me anywhere I don't wanna be."

"Little asshole." She mutters, crossing her arms petulantly across her chest. "Fine. Don't tell me then. But you can at least stay here and rest a while before heading back home."

"Thank you, Miss Pat. I owe you."

"Sure as hell do." She growled under her breath while standing to collect our empty plates. "A goddamn explanation next time and more sutures!"

TWO

DISTANCE

"Where've you been and why do you smell like shit?" My older sister, Shay, asked as I trudged silently inside our shared bedroom in the middle of the night.

I froze at the sound of her lilting voice.

"Shay?" I cautioned. "You up?"

Her grunt answered the waiting silence, and I un- froze enough to make it to my bed at my corner of the room. Fucking weird, I know, the reality my sister and I lived through that forced us to share a space. We were actually rich, well, at least The Commander was, but his paranoia didn't allow us to occupy the nicer neighborhoods in the upper East Side or even a nice high rise in Manhattan. No, we lived in this squabble of a fucking house that doubled as one his safehouses he kept around New York and Jersey.

I couldn't see the eye roll, but heard the sucked teeth and felt her attitude as if it was an actual presence outside of her.

"Where you been at?" She demanded.

"Nunya." I barked evenly as I laid back against my bed.

"Yeah, well, you've been somewhere you ain't have no business all right. Seeing as you smell like you just walked out of the shit factory."

"Shut up, Shay– damn!" I roared in an aggravated whisper, chucking a pillow over at her and praying it hit its mark.

Shay, at fourteen, was the most loving but aggravating older sister a dude like me could ask for, as if I had any choice in the matter. Even so, it was her who disciplined me when I got out of line or did something stupid like skip school or come home looking every bit the hitman I was getting groomed to be. She stood taller than me and was thicker than most girls at our middle school, and this often made her the target for a lot of bullying when we first moved to East Camden.

However, that was shut down after she cold-cocked the mouthy girl in her homeroom for whispering insults about Shay to her clique of bitches. Shay gained a reputation since then as one of those gorgeous light skinned chicks who took no prisoners. Besides the one guy I put a bullet in, I didn't do much sticking up for her. She was a real boss, more like The Commander in that lethal way she had of conducting herself. You'd never guess a kind looking girl like her would be out here blackening eyes, but appearances didn't mean shit. Rule Eight.

A waft of sour air assailed my nose and I'm immediately envious of Miss Pat's obvious strong stomach to be in the presence of it; I really did smell like that dirty ass abandoned house I staked out at.

"He needs to ease up." She hissed, and I'm not all the way sure if she's talking to me or herself when she adds in the darkness, "Need to keep eyes on the goal. To get outta here."

I scrunch my face at that. "What you talkin bout?"

"Nunya." She shot back. "Go take a shower before Mommy bust in here with questions you can't answer."

My sis had a lot of mysteries about her, and I'd often catch her beautiful voice singing idly as she went about a task like studying or washing dishes. Not singing catchy tunes from the radio, but sorrowful chants with haunting lyrics that make me wonder about exactly where she often escaped when I came home to find her bed empty. I'm tempted to press her about one of those mysteries but think twice about it.

I waved that away. "She won't. I'm sure she already took her Night Potion."

I almost laughed when I thought of our mother, a gorgeous ex-model and British native, who changed her passion from beauty to mix and matching roots. An herbalist, she called herself, much to The Commander's chagrin, but I think it was that same out-of-the box wackiness he adored about her. And boy did she love him. Her love for my father was an understatement, considering the successful top tier career she abandoned when she met him during a thirteen city tour she'd booked that had her North America bound. Apparently, they met and married within a week of knowing each other.

Mommy's 'Night Potion' was a strong blend of sleep herbs she infused in her nightly tea. There was a potion for every circumstance, according to Sommer Masters, who rubbed herbs in our wounds since young children.

A thought entered my mind, so immediate and astonishing it made me blurt, "Why are you here this time of night anyways?"

"I don't know what you're talking about, but last I checked, I lived here." Shay groused in rapid fire again.

Shay was never home when I came back from deployments, but always seemed to be here at just the right times, like when The Commander was due for a visit or when Mommy needed to speak with one of us.

"I better not find out you been out here creeping around with TuFace." I growled, not even trying to withhold the menace from my words.

TuFace was a cold street head a couple years older than Shay. This age gap was not the reason our father had me put a bullet in his leg, however. He'd been an all-right dude, serving as one of my dad's most loyal foot soldiers and phenomenal at selling huge drops of product in a short amount of time, but shit changed. Changed for the worst when he started partying with The Commander's dope. Instead of selling, he started using, burning a Jersey sized hole in my dad's pocket he couldn't leave unpunished. That was probably one of my most memorable contracts, recollecting the sissy whimpers he made after I pumped metal into his upper leg. That shot was meant to send a message, one that rang loud and clear after he nearly lost the limb. Rule Three: traitors got the cross. It was a rule I lived by and gave me intense pleasure to give him a permanent limp he was now known for on the streets.

He got jumped into the 8Roadz last month, or so I heard through the vine of talk on the streets. That didn't make him an official enemy, but we could never get too comfortable with it. Never get too comfortable in this line of work.

My normally saucy sis stays quiet, which sort of weirds me out but heightens my suspicion as I rise grumpily from the bed to trail over to her.

It's so dark inside, I'm not all the way sure she sees me standing by her bedside, but her panicked chirp assures me she's still awake.

"Mel, back the fuck up off me, please!" She laments, shifting into an upright position from what I can decipher from the rustling of her sheets. "And stay out of my business. If I'm messing with TuFace, or not, is no concern of yours!"

"It is if I say it is." I snarled, "The Commander would kill you if he found out you still creeping around with an 8Road. You remember the rules. Rule Twenty-Three?"

"We deal drugs, not with gangs." She recites, same as she would have if our father demanded the recitation. With attitude.

But the usual temp of her anger doesn't flare like it normally would've at my invasion of her space, and concern enters my chest as I regard her with a head nod.

"You good?" I probe.

"I'm fine." She whispers. "I'm not messing with Tu-Face, we deaded that after The Commander caught us the first time. I swear. It's…just been a hell of a night."

"You don't gotta tell me exactly what happened, but if I can help, I will. Just shout me. All right?"

"I appreciate you, Mel. But nah. Just know I'll be in the house a lot more than I usually am. No more late nights for me. Especially not with school starting tomorrow."

I sucked in an irritated breath. "Shit."

"You forgot, didn't you?"

"Nah, nah. I ain't forget, I'm on it." I lied.

"Course you are."

"I am."

Laughter erupts between the both of us, replacing the quiet whispering we'd been doing so as not to wake up our mother.

Before I could turn around to make it back to my bed, her bedside lamp illuminates the small quarters.

I anticipate the horrified gasp from her all too much when she growls, "Mel! Look at you!"

"I know, it looks bad, but–"

"But what? You got shot?!"

I turn to face her and throw a subconscious hand over my bandaged arm. "I'm good. Okay?"

She shook her head, standing, with horror in her brown eyes. "Who did this to you?"

"Nunya."

"Shamel!"

"Shay, just chill out!"

"Shamel! Did Quincy put you up to this? Is that why you won't shower, to keep the water from wetting this huge ass bandage?" She barked, real close to me and accusatory.

A fierce bout of protectiveness heated my chest as I glared at her. "Shay, I said chill out. He had nothing to do with this. This was on me. Stop trying to blame him for everything."

I knew I was stepping on her triggers, knew her hatred for our father all too well and just the right things to set her off. I didn't like throwing her hatred for our father in her face like this, but I had to get her to stop asking questions.

The little she knew, the better I could keep her safe. So, queue the outburst in five…four…three…two…

"You dick!" She shrieked, shoving me back so I stumbled back onto my bed. "I 'blame him for everything?' Why you always gotta defend him like he's God's gift to the Hood or something?"

"I don't." I grumble while twisting to an upright position in spite of the pain shooting through my arm.

"You do." She thundered. "You always do. Stop protecting that psycho. He's doing what he always does. Using you to get what he wants."

"And what's that, huh?"

"The reason he's got us in this shitty house. The same thing that keeps him terrorizing everyone in the neighborhood. Money."

A tense silence befalls the room as we glare at each other from our respective sides. Neither one of us, like the Mount Stubborn kids we were, are willing to concede.

"What's the two of you going on about?" A groggy British voice asks from the doorway. I curse under my breath at that, at our utter carelessness to keep our voices down enough not to awaken our mom.

I groan as I study the slim thick woman at our door frame with irritation clearly written on her face. I'm immediately dreading the painfully fake interaction as

I study Shay's face changing from a boiling glower to a pleasant grin. As if she hadn't shoved me mere seconds ago.

"Oh, hey Mom." She said nervously, freezing in place. "Sorry to wake you up. Mel stole my good pillow again and it sort of pissed me off."

"Oh?" Mom asked, her tone light but suspicious as she stares us down.

"Yes." Shay supplied evenly, stepping in front of me to block Mom's view of my bandaged condition on the bed. "Go back to bed. Sorry to cause a ruckus."

Even though I spot Mom eye my bandaged arm with momentary alarm, she forces a large smile before readjusting her gaze to Shay.

"The pillow, yeah?" She asks, her voice tight and quavering with restraint.

"Yeah." I answer her, keeping my eyes trained on the floor. "It's...a comfy pillow. I'm sorry, Shay."

Shay turns sad eyes to me, and I brace myself for the sorrowful melody that usually follows one of those mournful stares, but all she says is, "All good, Mel. I'm sorry, too."

"So, everything's sorted?" Mom asks, still with artificial airiness yet mild concern.

At that moment, I wanted to spring from the bed and stand in front of her. To force the truth of my gunshot graze and lethal underworld into my mother's face. But I...can't bring myself to. Can't bring myself to ruin her small world of blissful ignorance and blind faith in our father as I return my gaze to the floor.

"Get some rest, Mom. Besides, isn't dad due for a visit tomorrow?" Shay adds. This was the only time I'd ever heard my big sis use the term 'dad:' when she was speaking to our mom.

An honest glee sparks in her lovely hazel-colored eyes at the reminder of our father's twice a month visits.

"You're right!" Mom squeals, as if she's won the lottery and not blatantly overlooked the mysterious bandaged state of her teen son a couple of feet away.

I can almost hear Shay's gag of disgust at her reaction but clock our mother placing a gentle kiss on her eldest daughter's forehead before turning around.

"Night darlings," she calls before disappearing from the doorframe and back down the hall to the tiny room she shared with The Commander when he was in town.

Shay and I don't speak after that, and I soon find my eyes sagging shut as a dreamless sleep overcomes me.

When my eyes peel open the next day, I notice the clothes on my bed first. Except, they're carefully placed and color coordinated with a piece of paper on top. From Shay.

SHAY: *I woke you up, but I know you probably fell back to sleep. I set your alarm for thirty minutes from when I'm writing this. Get your ass up, wash down, and be in that uniform by nine. I'll see you in school.*

I shook my head, smiling a little as I rose from the bed to do as she instructed. Today was the first day of eighth grade, and while I secretly enjoyed learning and all that came with literature and stories, I couldn't deny the dread in my gut as I heard the giggle from outside my room.

A giggle.

Shay truly never laughed or had a reason to show any merriment in this house, so the feminine chuckle could have only come from our mother. I try to remember the rules I lived by, set by The Commander, as I start for the bathroom to wash up, but what I see in the hallway blocks my path.

Or, rather, who I see.

It's my father, Quincy, The Commander, beaming unsmiling eyes on me.

"Hey, Pops." I utter coolly, as if his presence doesn't terrify me.

"Shamel." He grits out, digging in his pocket for something. "Here."

"What's this?" I ask, palming the slim black folder in my hands. There's a picture of a buff black dude leaving what looked to be a club.

"Contract." He bit out. "Be there tonight. He'll be at Shookie's Nightclub in Queens."

"A contract?" I query, eying the folder worriedly. "And in Queens? Pops, I got to be in school today. Today is the first day and my teacher's gonna ask questions if I ain't there."

"This joker is paying us a lot of gwop for this contract, boy: Twenty-K upfront. Be there. Make it clean. And don't get noticed."

I opened my mouth to protest but knew better at this point. Knew better than to defy him or his rules. My mind drifts to the one time I'd defied a rule, the only painful blip in my history of living by his rules I saw more as street law. There was so much pain...so much blood...but I don't go there. I don't allow my brain time to linger too much in the past for fear of repeating a mistake, so I just nod my head.

"Yes, sir." I respond dutifully much to the chagrin and aching pressure on my heart.

"All right, cool." He says and begins to reenter Mom's bedroom before pausing. "Oh, and I seen them bullet holes in my car, boy."

Fear freezes me in place as I fight not to tremble all over. "Sorry, sir. Last night got kind of intense and–"

"It's big easy to replace that." He snarled coldly. "But I can't replace you. Whatever happened is in the past. I can't afford to lose my best shooter because he got emotional."

I gulp before reciting, "Rule Twenty-One: Pussies cry. Bosses make things happen."

"That's right." He agrees with more satisfaction than I'd heard from him in a while. "Now, take my car and get a head start to New York before it gets too late. I left details in that folder where you'll need to stake out for the night."

"Yes, sir." I repeat in a hollow voice. This was right. This was my reality. The very thing that made me happy and gave me purpose. I chant this to myself with obsessive familiarity as I fold the school uniform, tuck it into the worn dresser, and prepare for the dark descent into my second underworld.

THREE

TAKER

It takes all the strength I have inside of me not to moan as the warm marinara meets my tongue and assails all my good senses. I mean it when I say that I died the best death and went to food heaven as I polished off the remaining bites of pasta on my heavily sauced plate.Unable to help myself, I rise from the wooden dining table and place the gentlest kiss on the middle-aged Italian woman at the end of it.

Giana Ricotti returns my forehead kiss and embraces me in her thin arms. "You act this way every time I make my *pasta al forno!* Shamel, you're a gem."

"Yeah, and a hog, too." Emilio Ricotti, her son and my longest-time homie, grumbles as he scoops an extra portion of the pasta onto his empty plate."You just mad 'cuz your mom loves me better than you." I said with a menacing taunt before placing an extra kiss on Ms. Ricotti's powdered cheek.Milio shoots to his feet from my action with fury in his eyes and murder on his mind, I'm sure.My chest swells from the call to fight I recognized from the way his fists are balled and face reddens. We face off with about a foot's worth of distance between each other in the large dining room."Say that again, pussy." Milio challenged darkly as we circled each other.I chuckle at that. "*I'm* the pussy?""That's ri ght.""Don't think I ain't clock you making love eyes at your phone all through lunch. All blushing and shit.""I was not." He bites out, his pale skin turning a deeper shade of red."That girl you texting got you looking like a whole vagina with sneaks on. With them fake ass J's you wearing.""Fuck you!" Milio hollers before slamming into me. We crash into the dining room table, effectively thrashing its contents all around the room. The remainder of Ms. Ricotti's *pasta al forno* covered the pale-yellow walls in the dining room as we wrestled. "Boys!" She scolds, standing with her hands on her hips as she peers down at us. "Take that outside. Go. Now!"A piece of chipped wood from the broken table pierces my side and I wince as another piece scrapes my fresh gunshot wound."Take it back!" Milio grunts in my ear, ignoring his seething mother as he puts me in a headlock. I feel all the breath in my lungs evacuate and the room fuzzies as I'm pinned. The logical thing would be to accept defeat, tap out and take my loss belly up like a sane person. But The Commander's voice drifts like an acid cloud in my mind, reminding me of his rules. Rule

Ten, in particular: Win, by any means.Keeping those commandments in my brain, I reach over and grab the broken table leg and smack it against his head from behind.The action disorients him enough for me to scramble out of the chokehold. He's cradling his head and whining at the same time, and I rise to study the destruction I knew The Commander would be proud of."Cheating prick." Milio mumbled petulantly as I helped him to his feet.I grinned, my lip bloody but chest full of satisfaction as I added, "Don't hate the player."We're both groaning from our newly inflicted wounds when we notice the small Sicilian woman glaring at us.

"I apologize, Ms. Ricotti. I take the blame for all that." I tell her, but she still looks peeved as she studies us with disappointed eyes.

"That's the third table you boys ruined in the last year. Ease up or keep it outside, no?"

"All right, Ma." Milio regarded her halfheartedly, both he and I, cognizant of the fact that it would happen again but not wanting to upset the loving woman who'd welcomed me like a second son.

After digging through my jean pockets, I flipped through the fat wad of clean bills before rolling them and taking Ms. Ricotti's hand in mine.

"Get yourself an even sturdier table next time, okay? On me."

Her face changes from irritated to mildly flippant amusement as she envelopes me in her arms. "You're a good boy, Shamel."

"And you're a fine woman, Giana." I say, licking my lips in admiration of the shorter woman's curves as I embrace her.

"You trying to go for round two, or what?" Milio warns, making me nearly fall out in amusement.

"Nah, man. It's all good." I say, as we pull apart.

"All right, then come with me around the block some-wheres. To get some loosies."

"Solid." I agree before setting off outside. That's just how things were between us. One minute we burned hot, fighting tooth and nail or until we drew enough blood for one of us to claim victory. And the next, sharing a smoke outside as we appreciated the fine girls walking by with thick thighs and asses we could drool at for days.

"Yo, I'm banging one of these real thick jawns I met last weekend in NYC." Milio says between puffs of his cigarette as we occupy the stoop of the abandoned house around the block. We often chilled here whenever I came to his side of town to hang. He'd been the best friend I had when we both lived in Jefferson Heights. After his dad left his mom for a younger woman in Italy, he and his mom ended up moving to Ms. Ricotti's sister's house in Queens. Even though his aunt died last year, they continued to live in the place and offered it as an extension to me when I came to this side of New York for deployments or to kill time. Like now.

"Yeah?" I responded between coughs of my blunt. "Shawty got it like that?"

"Hell yeah, dog." He chortled, nodding his head appreciatively as if the girl stood before him now. "Got that good throat, too. Gobbled my shit like a demon."

"Damn!" I laughed, passing him the joint I rolled earlier. "That the same chick that had you smiling at your phone like a simp?"

He punched my arm as I nearly collapsed in laughter. "Nah, bro. That's another girl I'm messing with."

I frowned. "Nigga, who?"

He flexed his jaw, considering, before taking another drag off the blunt. "We keeping it lowkey, know what I'm saying?"

"What you out here keeping secrets and shit for, bro?" I demand, incredulous.

"Ain't no secret." He counters.

"Then tell me her name."

"Dead that."

"Wait, she's probably somebody I know. Or ugly."

"Shame!" He spat my street name, serious now. "Chill on that shit. She ain't just anybody to be talkin about."

My eyes widened, shocked at what I'd been piecing together since witnessing him giggle at his phone. "Is it Nita?"

He frowned at the mention of his crazy ex. "Hell nah! You know she ain't right in the head. Crazy bitch tried to kill me last year."

"So, it's not Nita. Hmm..." I mumble thoughtfully, tryin to make sense of the breadcrumbs he'd given.

Milio suddenly shot me a look. "What you doing here?"

"What you mean?"

"I mean." He bleated. "Why you over in Queens? You mad far from home. Don't you got like school or something today?"

"Nigga, shut it." I growled, waving him away. "You barely be in school yourself to be lecturing me."

"Damn." He guffawed a huge cloud of smoke. "You ain't wrong. But for real, what's up?"

I halt for a considering second before answering him. Before checking whether or not the truth was best to rest on his ears.

I shift on the cold slab of concrete we occupied before taking the plunge. "I got...a job out here to do. You know, something slight. No big deal."

"Mmm." He says thoughtfully, studying me with a knowing look. "Who dying tonight?"

"Nigga!" I warn, looking around in fear of eavesdroppers and onlookers. "Don't be airing' my shit all out in the open. How you know anyway?"

He shrugged, real easy, as if I asked him about the weather or who won the World Cup this year. "Streets talk. I heard a few things."

"From who?" I hissed, trying my hardest to hide the panic blooming in my chest.

"That chick I told you about with the good throat?"

"Yeah?"

"She opened her mouth like she opened her legs: easy-peasy. Apparently, her cousin is TuFace's new girl. He told his girl, his girl told her, and *voila*." He snapped his fingers with wry emphasis. "Said TuFace admitted that he suspected it was you who gave him that limp. That he'd give you one to match as soon as he got the chance. But I just thought the ho was lying. But seeing that look on your face when I accused you...I'm not so sure."

"Yo, what the fuck?" I breathed, not fully believing that TuFace outed me in spite of the possible comebacks for even breathing that suspicion out loud.

"You need to let me in on that. I got a few jobs you can help me with." He offered in that mafioso dialect that sounded more like a deal for him than me. "I could help you; you know?"

"Shut the fuck up."

He straightens, his face turning serious. "No, for real. There's somebody I might need taken care of in the future. Don't trust him."

Infuriated, I take a hard hit off the blunt before squaring off with my mouthy homeboy. "Bro, chill. I told you I came for something else. I had an unrelated job to do. That's it. Fuck whatever the streets been tellin you. Trust what I'm saying when I tell you I'm just moving some work around."

He sort of chuckles/grunts as he stomps on the cigarette. "We'll just leave it at that, Shame. Let me know if you need my help with cleaning some shit, *capiche?* You never know when we might be in need of your services, too."

"I'm good." I declared with finality, already done with the direction this conversation was taking. Milio, while my loyalist homeboy, was a blueberry Crip, through and through. My friendship with him should have been deaded after he joined them, considering it broke The Commander's rule to deal with gangs. But he was solid. An emotional, poetry-reciting motherfucker, but still one of the most down dudes I knew who would back me no matter what. That type of loyalty was golden in this life, this underworld, and so I kept him around.

"Yeah, okay." He agreed. "Let my offer marinate, we pay good, and we always got you. You fam, for real."

"Word up." I muttered, dapping him as we stood.

***

Like clockwork and despite the pain radiating through my wounded arm, I kneel before the dirty window of the abandoned crack house to study the lowkey nightclub on the east side of Queens. Shookies was a real swanky joint I only ever saw older adults hang, like The Commander, but it was sort of a hidden hangout nestled between the corner store and an alleyway. That alley existed as an ominous tunnel with smoke from the club's kitchen ballooning through the dark space.

At Milio's house, I took the time to review the papers in the contract The Commander handed me earlier. Besides dozens of pictures of the man performing mundane shit like taking out his trash, mowing his lawn, or getting into his car, there was little else that belayed his crime. Usually, the pictures showed the contracted person's wrongdoing, like cheating on a spouse or snorting some product, but this guy looked...normal. Like, was I supposed to kill this guy who looked more like a college professor than a crackhead? More lawyer-like than thug-like? The only other information I saw in the folder was details about his schedule, noting exactly what the events in his calendar were like as if it was stolen from his fancy office's secretary. He was due to go to Shookie's tonight, but apparently had another undisclosed event that happened about two hours after he arrived at the swanky nightclub.

Even his name was square and strait laced. Stanley True. How was I supposed to unleash Luci's wrath on a man with honesty for his name? Why was he doomed to die?

I shook my head to rid it of the question. The forbidden question I wasn't supposed to ask myself or The Commander regarding a contract. I had to get through this, to honor the family name. I took pride in being a Masters, pride in wielding this weapon as an extension of my father's wrath. I had to keep reminding myself of my destiny, that it was all destined to be mine one day and to toughen up and hold back the voice screaming in my head to turn around.

I poise the rifle, Luci 2.0, aiming it at the entrance where the juiced-up bouncer stood. This Stanley guy should be leaving the club any minute now, if my predictions were right, and my trigger finger wiggled with apprehension and indecision.

However, after the second hour turned into the third, I placed the gun at my side. Nobody matching this dude's description left the club. From my vantage point, there was only an Asian looking guy and some drunk white chick exiting the front. They didn't appear to be walking together, since the drunk chick wobbled around the corner and the Asian guy made a beeline for the ominous alley.

Was there a back entrance I didn't account for? Or, maybe my apprehensive "pussy-thoughts" as The

Commander would call them, permeated my logical thinking so much that I missed the chance to complete the contract.

Doubt and shame weighing me down, I wiped the dust off my all-black attire before gathering myself to leave the crack house. I shot across the street with predatorial ease, disappearing into the same dark alley as the Asian man did moments earlier.

The killer quiet I expect isn't what I stumble into, however, since the groans and whimpers greet me first.

The darkness enshrouded the scene, causing me to approach quietly and in short, silent steps.

"Please don't hurt me!" A man whined from the dark.

Minor scuffling leads me to believe the man who uttered the plea was being roughed up. No one answers him, but the panicked man adds, "I promise I'll have your money next week! I just haven't had the chance to pay it. I've been working overtime, but my daughter's school is so expensive. It's impossible to pay y'all with interest and her schooling without being in the negative at the end of the month. Rent still needs to be paid, man. Please understand!"

A hard thump I recognize as fist pounding against flesh makes me stumble back a little.

"Deadline was yesterday." A smooth, but quiet voice utters in the dank dark, and I'm almost sure it came from my imagination until it adds, "Today, you die."

"Hang on, man!" The beaten guy pleads. "Just give me a little more time. I said I'll get your money next–"

His words abruptly end after the muffled shoot and squeak of what I know to be a silencer firing off. Curiosity plagued me at the interaction, and I can't resist the pull to investigate the identity of these people fully.

My eyes bug and fear grips my heart at the scene, however. The Asian dude with the long-ish hair I saw leave the club earlier is standing over the bloody, beaten, and dead body of no other than my intended target.

Stanley True.

"Kid." The Asian guy calls, despite my lame efforts to be a dark fly on the dank wall. "Did you see any of that?"

I nod, barely able to reconcile the terror in my heart. Except, the fear is not coming from just witnessing a murder.

Nah.

It's from not completing the contract myself. Whoever this Stanley guy was had a lot of enemies. The worst kind that had more lethal looking dudes like him hunting for him. The Commander couldn't get word of this, I think, lost in my own tornado of fearful thoughts.

Wiping the blood stains from his cheek with a gloved hand, he does exactly what I pegged he would.

Aims the bloody gun at me.

Four

GRIMY

I expel a huge gust of wind as I eye the Beretta the Asian dude's aiming at my forehead. Somewhere in the middle of my doubtful thoughts I was able to calm down enough to face the killer, no older than maybe six or seventeen, with the anger flaring in his half-moon eyes.

"You gonna kill me?" I asked, ensuring to lace all the boredom in my tone that I felt.

Instead of a verbal response, he bows his head in a tight answering nod. Even under the scant lighting of the street lights, his snake tattoo is visible. There's also a gold ring on his index finger that sort of gleams in the low light and makes me wonder at how much money he's from. That ring strikes me as vaguely familiar as I alternate my gaze between him and the dead body.

I shrugged. "Go ahead. Take your shot."

A confused expression twists his face. "What?"

"You heard me." I countered, my tone arid and drained of all amusement as I raised my hands. "Take your shot."

"You should be cowering for your life, kid." He replied, readjusting his hold on the gun I'd been considering purchasing from Remy last month.

"Cowering?" I queried.

"Yes." He answers dryly. "You know, afraid? Pissing your pants?"

I shook my head at that. "Nah, I know what 'cower' means. Just a very strange moment to use an academic word like that."

"Understandable coming from a little brown kid like you. But this is *proper* English. One should use their best language at all times. Whether interacting with princes or—" He gives me a displeased onceover with his tiny eyes. "Paupers."

"Paupers, huh?" I demand, pissed as fuck at this Asian douchebag for attacking my intelligence but careful at not letting it show. "This ain't exactly the first time I've been held at gunpoint by scary-looking motherfuckas like you."

He nods again, switching the gun to his left hand.

"Can you do me a favor?" I say.

"What?"

"Kill me now or move the fuck on? I ain't too fond of lectures, so either put the bullet in my brain, let me go, or hand me the gun so I can end it myself."

An admirable grin cracks his face. "Hmm. So, you really aren't scared then?"

I shrug, letting that be my answer as I observe him lower the gun at his side.

"You accept your impending demise with honor." He began. "I admire this."

"Thanks?"

After a heated stare down, one which I'm good at since having to practice staring into my father's empty eyes,

Asian dude seems to concede with a capricious head nod. "I've decided not to end your life tonight."

I raise a skeptic brow. "Is that right?"

He turns his back on me, a stupidly fatal move on his part on a typical day, but not now. Right now, I had a plan in place to get out of this blemish free. "Carry on, be fruitful, and of course, speak of tonight's events to no one. Understand?"

"Hey! Wait a minute." I called after his disappearing form in the dark.

"My conditions are not adequate?"

"No. That's not it. I think...I think you could help me. And maybe I can help you."

He chuckles. "How can you possibly render me aid?"

This dude reminded me of Milio's poetic ass, but I dismissed it with a shake of my head as I continued.

"This guy's death is gonna be all over the news today and tomorrow. Not sure if it was your intent to murder him, but I was sent to off him tonight."

"Were you?" He narrows his eyes at me, disbelieving.

"Dead ass."

"Really? You? A kid?"

Grunting, I reached into my back denim pocket to unsheathe Luci, my main girl. He retreats a step as I present the slim metal Colt Action to him.

"Just who are you?"

"They call me Shame." I say, pocketing my gun.

"Shame..." he mulls my title over as if running it for a coding diagnostic. "An armed child was sent here to execute this man. One who calls himself Shame."

It isn't a question, nor is it directed at me, but I reflexively answer, "It ain't my job to get you to believe it."

"Oh?" He queries, more intrigued at this point than angry.

"Then please enlighten me as to your purpose for interfering with my business. You must be certifiable."

I chuff, a dry sound escaping my mouth. "I'm a lot of things. But crazy ain't one of them."

Asian dude nods, as if digesting the information to store and use for later, which makes me hesitate for this next part. There's only one way I can think to get myself out of this unscathed. I don't trust the criminal fuck as far as I can throw him, but maybe– just maybe–I could use him. Gulping, I straighten my back before taking the stab in the dark.

"I got a feel for who you are." I continued. "I clocked you when I saw that gold ring on your finger earlier."

He inches towards me with slow predatory focus, as if he's hunting for something that'll take off if he doesn't approach with caution. "You know nothing of me."

"Kobayashi, right? I know that's some sort of family ring y'all always wear."

He only stares at me through soulless eyes. Eyes that belay a certain level of distrust I identified with in this line of work.

"Who sent you?" He demanded in a cold menace.

I sighed, hating the thought of having to share the reality

of this underworld with someone else but take the plunge. "I was sent here to complete a contract. To kill this Stanley True dude. I don't get reasons why, only locations and orders to kill within forty-eight hours of an assignment. So, here I am, except, you did my job for me."

"Hmm." He vocalizes in consideration while training an unflinchingly glacial stare into my eyes. "I sense no deception in you, Shame. Now, tell me where you are from."

"I...operate outta Jersey." I admit with no fear for him abusing this information at all. There's something in his eyes that I recognized within myself and it makes me pity and respect him. "My, uh, Commander gives me the contract and I act on them. That's it."

"Wait a minute." He breathes in mild suspicion. "I've heard wind of this, but didn't think it to be true. Quincy Masters has a lucrative operation in New Jersey, New York, and a few areas in D.C. There was a rumor that he was ruthless enough to enlist his own children to do his wet work. Now I think about it...this makes sense."

I knew the streets spoke volumes and could mean the success or downfall in this underworld. I knew about these rumors, but kept sure to ignore them and avoid suspicion by working in the dark.

"Sounds like a cold motherfucker." I say, an odd feeling in my chest as I remember, "one who'd only sent his best to take care of that Crip who'd had the nerve to cross a Kobayashi."

His face scrunched in a silent question before mute terror filled his eyes. "No. Wait. The service my family contracted to kill that bastard...was Quincy Masters'?"

I smirk, remembering the two shots I blasted into the towering guy's neck before peeling out of there in The Commander's shot up caddy. "I think there's a way we can both help each other out. I have a solution that'll keep both our bosses pleased."

"Why should I trust you? Enlist the aid of a child in my business? You mistake me for a fool."

"I don't make many mistakes. Not when I killed that LC for that Kobayashi contract. Even now, as I look at the panic in your eyes, I see what I know to be true. You weren't supposed to kill that dude tonight. But you did. Now you're going home with empty pockets."

He bites his bottom lip, a depleted expression marring his face as he sinks to the ground. "Hector Ortega murdered my brother in cold blood. Shot him and left him for dead in a back-alley trashcan. He had to pay for that. I...my family owes you a great debt. Now I know the identity of the man behind the job, I can pay you my humblest of gratitudes. Especially since I never forget a face."

"Come on, man." I mutter with heavy emotion in my chest. "Stand up. It was just an assignment–"

"An assignment that brought great peace and vengeance to my family."

Suddenly, he bows low to me. "Takeo Kobayashi of the Kobayashi Clan. Please share your plan."

Five

PRIDE

Two years later

"I have your shit, Shame! I'm waiting for you in the parking lot whenever you get here." LaDawn's aggravation was tangible as she yelled through the phone.

The blazing heat and blinding powers of the sun caused me to squint some real effort into locating the girl. I crossed the busy city streets to make my way to Cooper Hospital, the same hospital from which I was born after nearly killing my mother during a grueling thirty-hour labor. I didn't have the typical entry into this world, since I was never my parents' pride and joy. My accidental creation and nearly deadly birth made me somewhat of my mother's shame and father's fury.

"Earth to Shame!" The cantankerous teen shouted into the phone as I entered the parking lot. "Bring your ass on before I pull off. You know my baby's daycare closes in an hour."

"All right, all right." I sighed as I surveyed the spacious lot filled with cars that looked too much alike.

However, it didn't take glasses or rocket science to point out the faded red SUV with chipped paint. It was parked amidst a sea of luxury vehicles that emphasizes its dilapidated state due to its over a decade lifespan. There's also a smoke cloud floating above it that makes me cough as I near the half open driver side door.

"Finally!" the seventeen-year-old harrumphs as she climbs to a stand. She's a few inches taller with golden skin and a wide gap in her teeth that adds to her overall sex appeal. Her forehead is drenched in sweat as she wobbles to her full six feet under the sweltering sun.

"You feeling okay?" I hedged, concerned for the girl who's normally energized by the sweltering summer heat of Camden. She would always brag about her increased stamina in warm weather, speaking as a former track star for our high school, Marlton High.

She takes an exaggerated drag off the blunt in her left hand while the other flies to her pregnant belly, "I'm good. Feel like this baby bout to drop any day now, though."

I can't resist the urge to touch her, to soothe the evident discomfort written all over her face.

However, I predict like clockwork the angry swat that prevents me from making physical contact with her shoulder. "Don't touch me. Just get your shit and go."

"Should you even be lighting up while you like this?"

She rears back, exhaling another smoke cloud and rolling her eyes. "Oh, hell no. I know you ain't over here tryna play Super Daddy when you ain't been with me to one appointment. Now you want to pretend to care after I been begging you to come see me after all these months?"

"Dawn." I grit out, irritation bubbling to the surface by the second. "Chill. It was just a question. You ain't have to go Fatal Attraction on me like that when all I wanted to do was check on you."

"Yeah, well check your mammy. Don't try to check me. Grab your little medical supplies and go."

Remember the rules, I tell myself as I suppress the second urge to strangle this ho. Stay in control no matter what and don't get emotional.

I wiped the sweat trickling from my short dreads from getting into my eyes as I stared at her. "Don't make this difficult. We can be civil, you know? I'll try to swing by tonight to visit, all right?"

"Lexus misses you." She said. I caught the guarded glint in her eyes as if she was daring to hope, but too accustomed to a certain level of disappointment. From me. Which isn't entirely hard to believe. "But if you think you coming over after dark to "swing by," then you can just stay home. I can do without another dude sticking his dick in me after dark and leaving me with another mouth to feed."

Sighing, I pinched the bridge of my nose in resignation from dealing with her usual setting of pissed off. It seemed like there was never anything I could do to help her. Nothing I could do or say to prevent the usual argument that erupted between us like merging tornados. She was the kindest girl a guy like me could ask to run into when Milio first introduced us two years ago. That stormy tension that crackled between us was magnetic when we first met at that house party. Not only was that some of the best pussy I had, but our undefined relationship post-fuck was cool for a while. Since her mother worked as a housekeeper at Cooper Hospital, she soon became my connect for medical supplies that I ensured to keep my project granny stocked with.

However, mixing business with pleasure was a mistake I was still paying for.

She jabbed a thumb towards the backseat. "All she could snatch was cotton balls and alcohol this time. My mom's boss is starting to ask questions so that's all you get for now."

I nodded, reaching low to retrieve the trash bag filled with items from the rundown backseat. "Thank you, Dawn. I appreciate you for real."

She tsked. "Whatever. You done?"

I frowned, feeling the familiar flares of anger rising as it typically did during our interactions. "What I do now?"

I could practically hear the ticking bomb explode between her ears as she crossed her arms. "What *didn't* you do? Always out here tryna use me for some shit."

"Using you?" I spat, cornering her into the driver side of the hooptie. "I ain't using you. We had an agreement, and I thought you was helping me out?"

She rolled her hazel-brown eyes. "You always tryna step over people looking for a come up. How many times did I beg you to come to my track meets? Or meet my family? You never do for me like I do for you. And I know you ain't gonna be shit as a father either."

LaDawn had a unique way of knowing all my sore spots and sticking in the knife real deep. I didn't reveal to many people about my arrangement with her. She wasn't my secret, but she was definitely a problem I couldn't bring home. Not to Mommy and sure as hell not The Commander. I let her in a little during one drunk night of spilling all my daddy-issue-bullshit and this is where it got me.

With LaDawn. My irate babymoms and perpetual instigator. Even though I knew guns better than algebra at sixteen, she was well versed in stepping all over my triggers. Like now.

I expelled an aggrieved sigh, exhausted from this conversation and livid on the inside from being toyed with. "Dawn, my bad. I ain't tryna take advantage. Just need you to hold me down for a little longer until I sort some shit out. Till I can get the supply coming in at a cheaper flow. Nah mean?"

Her honey brown cheeks flame a deeper color red as she regards me. "I hear you. You need to make sure you be there for the birth of your daughter, too. My induction is in two weeks and I finally found a babysitter to watch Lexus."

I glare at her, hating her thinking the worst of me. "You don't gotta tell me. I'll always be there for my daughter. Yours, too."

I made it a point to reference the three-year-old she birthed before we met.

A tender look crosses her face for a brief flicker of a moment before she says, "All right, Shame. Cool. I'll text you the details."

"Thank you."

"I mean it!" She hollers as she reenters the car. Once she's fully inside, she screams behind the rolled-up windows. "You ain't never been there for me, but you better show up for *her!* Luxury ain't gonna need a deadbeat for a daddy."

I roll my eyes and sigh deep as I watch the raggedy SUV pull off into the street. I hate this feeling, this uselessness that blooms in my chest as I consider the truth and weight of her words. After Dawn told me she was pregnant a couple months back, I reacted straight out of character by accusing her of fucking her baby daddy, insinuating that it was his second mistake instead of my first. Well, the sweet girl I'd met died after I threw those ugly words at her, and in its place blossomed this embittered teen who sat on the sidelines of her track meets now instead of participating as the team's star runner.

I apologized after watching her watch her track meets from the shadows with watery eyes. Who the hell was I kidding? It was me. I was the blame for robbing her of a future, and like I did my Mom, it was a sin I couldn't take back. Could only move forward and deal with the shame of my existence and actions by swearing to do better by the daughter my fam didn't know about.

The vibration of my phone makes me yank it out of my jeans and study the screen with irritation.

> **SILENCE:** *Got a cleanup job in D.C. tonight. You bringing the mop?*

Much of that shame and uselessness arose when I thought of my father, who'd spent more and more weeks away than his usual bimonthly visits. The cash-flow was coming in less and less, too, and it had been over three months since he'd shown up to throw another assignment at me. The usual storm of guilt in my head that swirls after I complete a kill is no longer a barrier, and I'm grateful for the break, but hateful for the severe cash drought it brought the family. Shay was gone every single night now that The Commander wasn't bringing in more money to provide for us, too, and I'd been forced to resort to asking Dawn to steal medical supplies just to keep Miss Pat stocked.

This cash drought was affecting us all, in different ways, considering it was a huge chunk of my Project Granny's income since her government checks barely covered her livable expenses. I put her on a monthly retainer, a healthy chunk of change to keep me patched up and avoid legal detection, but now? The only contracts that kept me from starving were the ones I'd begun taking on for the Kobayashi's.

Takeo, or "Si" for short, had grown from this dude I could use to get me out of a jam, to a main character in my street success. We'd developed a name for ourselves in the streets as the Ruthless Duo: The Violence and The Silence. I'd only ever heard about the criminal underground drug ring ran by the Kobayashi's, and even then, did my best to avoid their side of Pollock where they owned the drug game amidst the immigrants and impoverished populations that occupied that side of town. Whenever they'd need a wet job done, I'd become their guy, but I never gained their full trust enough to carry those contracts out alone. After we'd completed the kills in half the time I'd ever done solo, we'd made some good money and a name for ourselves. The Violence, I'd been called, since I took most of the kill shots with my main girl, Luci, and never missed. Takeo,

The Silence, usually snatched our targets like a thief in the night, quick and without a sound or witness, to be hauled to their final place of life and lying-in wait for Luci.

I smirk as I respond to the coded message from the second half of our ruthless duo. 'Bring the mop,' meant there'd be wet work and that he needed me there since, between us both, I'd been the best shot.

> **ME**: *Alright, bet. Drop the address.*

I walked the few blocks from Cooper to Jefferson Heights apartments. It had been a while since I had the chance to see my Project Granny or restock her med supplies she'd used to patch both Si and me during our last assignments. A tight feeling twists my chest from the guilt of not checking in on her or visiting as often, knowing the severity of her empty nest syndrome and her tough exterior she'd used to deny it. But I knew, like me, she'd missed the visits and dinners we had whenever I got the chance to come see her in between deployments.

I nearly reached the parking lot that lined the large two towers of apartments and stopped dead in my tracks at the sight.

Instead of the two huge buildings I'd been partially raised in, there's only one singular tower and a large construction crew cleaning the debris from where the previous building stood. The strength it took to stand drained from my body as I looked on with astonishment at the left building my family's old home was situated inside. Now it was rubble. Ashes and rubble getting swept away by large machines and little people I'd had to resist the urge not to pull out Luci and shoot.

I bit down hard as I climbed the steps to the remaining building where Miss Pat's apartment was located, my trigger finger itching the entire way.

"What the fuck..." I breathed as I read the pink slip on my Project Granny's front door.

As if sensing me, the door opens to reveal her plump frame and frown lines. "Shamel! Baby, come in. What's that you got behind your back?"

"Supplies." I mumble absently as I enter the house, forgetting about the trash bag and reason for my visit that fast. "What's this I found on your door? They kicking you out?"

"What you talkin...?" Her voice trails off as she studies the pink slip. "Eviction Notice? Oh, *hell* no!"

"Right." I bark, anger boiling every ounce of my blood as I pace the floor. "They knocked down Building B? When did this happen? And now they kicking you out?"

She sighs a dejected breath before sinking onto the couch. "Apparently, the landlord sold the property to some big real estate group from New York. They talkin about turning the building into high end condos next year."

I walk over to her. "They just decided to knock the buildings down and kick the residents to the curb out of nowhere? This don't even sound legit."

She bit her lip nervously. "It don't. That's why I'm fighting for my home. They been threatening us residents for months about this new development. Said if we decided to stay, the new rent would triple. Not double. *Triple!* How I'm supposed to afford that?"

An eerie thought comes to my mind that has me rearing back a bit. "Hold up. You mean to tell me, you knew about this demolition shit all along and didn't call me?"

She shrugged, a scowl still on her face. "For what? Why would I worry you, a child, about a problem as serious as this? You got no place in my living situation or expenses."

"A child?" I sneer. "Well, this *child* has been keeping them stacks coming in real regular since you agreed to help with this under-the-table nurse business. With all due respect, you should have told me."

"Like hell." She snapped, standing to her feet. "Again, a child stays in a child's place."

"I ain't no regular child, Miss Pat!" Though I just turned sixteen, my six-foot stature towers over the older woman I cherished, but desperately wanted to strangle. Always with her headstrong ways, I grumble inwardly as my mind racks with solutions to this new mess. I don't realize I'm yelling until a hand nuzzles into my thick dreads and yanks. "Ouch– fuck!"

The person I can't see punches my back causing me to lose my breath and sink to the floor in pure agony. My fight or flight existed along the lines of 'cut or shoot,' and whenever triggered it was an ugly sight. A bloody one.

I'm not afforded a second to comprehend the situation before my gun is aimed at the attacker, whose chubby brown face and short frame made my heart stop.

"Angie?" I panted, still winded.

The nineteen-year-old girl flashes an apologetic half smile that turns my insides into mashed potatoes like always before whispering, "Sorry, Mel. But Mama isn't feeling so good today, and the last thing she needs is some angsty teen screaming at her in her own house."

"Angie." I cough before sheathing the gun and the color returns to my face. "When did you get back in town?"

Silly question, I know, considering the barely five-foot girl planted a juggernaut punch to my spine that sent waves of pain through my body, but the sight of her...made me stupid. And even though I'm no average teen, no simple child with homework to worry about like the others, the mere picture she creates in front of me makes me dumb. Even though she'd left for college in New York, she didn't look much different:

her typical shoulder length curls gathered in a high bun and accentuated her sensuous jawline and juicy lips. Dick-sucking lips, Milio would have called them, but no. They were just perfect enough for me to press against mine, part a little with my tongue and—

"I'm back for Fall Break, for only a week." She started, interrupting my lecherous thoughts. "But I already saw Shay and we kicked it for a bit. I tried waiting for you to get back home to tell you I was back, but you never showed. So, I came back here. Didn't think you'd pop up at Mom's, though. Mel? You good?" She asked on a laugh, and I just now notice I'm staring stupidly at the girl who'd given me wet dreams for years.

"Um, yeah. I'm good. And I apologize for yelling at your Moms."

She chuckled before opening her arms. "Well good. Now come give me a hug! I haven't seen you in ages and now you want to act all shy."

Shy, she called it, and I wanted to laugh all of a sudden, but the steel in my boxers makes me cough and leap out of the way of her arms. She smelled too good. Looked too good. Seeing her stand there all smiley after delivering a jab so vicious had me dying to take her.

"I, uh, should get going actually. Just came to drop some stuff off with Miss Pat." I stuttered as I began towards the door.

"Wait!" She interjects while laying a gentle hand to my arm. I'm facing the door so as not to scare the women in the room with the surprise wood in my pants. "Please, stay a while? For dinner at least?"

I shrug from her clasp on my arm. "Nah, I got some shit to do. But trust and believe I'll get this eviction notice shit sorted out, all right?"

"Eviction notice?" Angie asked worriedly as she glanced between me and her mother on the couch. "What's this about an eviction notice, Mama?"

"Shamel!" Miss Pat growls, ignoring Angie. "Don't you get involved in this. I told you; I got it under control."

I heaved a small sigh before adding, "I'll stay in touch," and exiting the cramped apartment.

The anxiety generated from Angie's presence and the pink slip had me coughing for air when I make it to the parking lot. I hated losing control of my emotions, since that's what always got me into trouble I'd had to shoot my way out of. Seeing Angie Pierce, my sister's longtime friend who'd made up a third of their bestie-trio consisting of Shay, Angie, and a biracial chick named Eliza Gresham, always made me lose sight of reality. She'd often come over after school ended and help Shay with her Language Arts classes, since Shay suffered from a learning disorder that caused her to see words real funny. While Liz would often talk excitedly about who's-crushing-on-who, it was Angie that had the smarts and focus to study hard and make it out the hood. The trio disbanded after Angie left, however. She'd finished high school early and went off to NYU to study Special Ed, and the summer before last had been the last time I'd seen her in the flesh. Until now.

I had to steady my breathing before stepping into the light of day. I had to steady myself to focus on the true mission at hand. Since I had a few hours to burn before my meet up with Takeo, I started the two blocks walk to greet the motherfucker I'd potentially need to put a bullet in.

Before I get the chance to cross the street out of Jefferson Heights, a white blur speeds towards me from around the corner. The small body tackles me before I get the chance to make sense of it.

"Shame!" the child's voice beckons with high pitched glee as he wraps arm around my waist. "I've missed you, dude!"

The blaring heat exhausts the little patience left after that weird encounter with Angie, and I find myself pulling him off me while saying, "Jeremy, hey little dude. I'm actually in a rush—"

"Please, please, please come hang out with me?"

"Lil dude, nah—"

"But puh-lease!" He beseeches while sinking to his knees.

His orange-red makes him look like something from the Lollipop Guild, which I frequently teased him about when I lived at Jefferson Heights. He also had these seriously glittery green eyes that made him look like a tragic movie star. Eyes so shiny I'd know them anywhere, I figure, while glaring at him under the hot sun. Jeremy was one of those annoying neighborhood kids who didn't live in the Heights, but so close to it that all his friends lived there. He thought I was the coolest thing since ice water, worshiping the ground I walked on which had me feeling all kinds of strange. Aside from my little cousins, his reception of me was always warm when I ran into him while making drops to Miss Pat's.

"These boys keep saying that you'd never hang out with a dork like me, and I say, 'no way! Me and Shame are besties!'"

Laughter rumbles my chest at the phrase. "Nah, man. We homies. Besties is for girls. Remember that."

"Yeah!" He beams, pulling at my arm. "Come on! You come and tell them we're homies."

"Nah, lil dude." I protest, not budging from the spot he's pulling. "I got some things I need to handle."

His red cheeks sag in defeat as though my words were verbal bullets. "Aww man..."

Fishing around in my pocket, I pull out my last cash wad. Judging from the tattered holes in his striped t-shirt and too-small pants, it seems as though his family was just as poor as we'd been at the Heights.

"Take this." I say, handing him the crinkled Benjamin. "Tell anybody who got a problem with you, or want to talk some shit, to come to Shame. All right?"

He snatches the bill and beams up at me. "I'll tell them my homie will shoot them with his gun if they don't show me respect!"

"Why not." I uttered wryly, but chuckling as I pat him on the head and continue my descent into the hood.

Once I reach the rundown building, I pound on the rickety door with a sign on it reading "Shay Property Management."

Heath Shay, the tall blond slumlord, opens the door, a bored expression on his face. "What?"

Without warning, I wrap my hand around his scrawny neck and force him back into the tight room filled with papers. He's sputtering pleas for his life when I finally release him to gag on the floor.

"Stand the fuck up." I demand while studying his neck turn lobster red. However, he remains on the ground choking and hacking like a bitch. With an irritated flex of my jaw, I reach around and whip out my Colt Action to aim it directly at his forehead. "Did I *fucking* stutter?!"

"No, no!" He breathes, panicked, as he hobbles to his feet. His blond hair is tousled into his eyes as I press the gun into his neck. "Please don't kill me, I'll give you anything you want, sir!"

"Forget the 'sirs.'" I grouse. "Look at me. And remember this face."

He swipes a sweaty hand over his mane to soothe it back. Ocean blue eyes jump around the room for a moment before pinning into me. "Shame? Is that you?

What did I do? You want money? I'll give you money. Just please don't hurt me!"

A sinister half smile lifts the right side of my face as I cock the gun. "I gotta admit. I am in a bad mood. Bad enough to blow your tiny brains through this office if you don't stop that demolition."

He frowns through teary eyes. "What?"

Infuriated, I strike him in the nose with the butt of my favorite girl. Blood spews from the wound and I wipe the splatter from my face, training cold eyes on him. Needing him to feel the promise of my wrath.

"Don't be stupid." I growl. "The demolition on the Heights."

"Oh!" He breathes, and an actual smile crests his bloody face. "I can't stop that. We're already in the middle of closing on it. There's no way I can back out the deal now."

"Wrong answer." Is all the warning he gets before I hit him with the gun again— this time in his left nostril.

"Fuck, Shame!" He groans, spewing more blood and apologies. "Please, man! Understand my predicament! Those Manhattan developers offered me a deal I couldn't resist on that dump. They have plans to make all of South Camden a beauty."

"And hike the rent up triple fold, in the making? Y'all are forcing honest, hardworking people out of their homes of twenty-plus years!"

He sinks to his knees, his blue eyes searching and pleading. "I know, I know man. But I'm about to get married and we need that money to put down on a good house somewheres."

I glared at him, so mad I could spit fire. "So, fuck everybody else then, huh? As long as you and yours got all your finances straight, then that makes it okay to take from good people?"

The buzz from my phone reminds me that I have a call incoming, but I ignore it as I glower at the bloody dickhead groveling on the floor. This sort of filth, entitled pieces of garbage like this, makes my trigger finger ache with murderous need to destroy. I want to unleash all the pent-up shame and emotions swirling in from the confrontation with Dawn, Angie, and the pink slip on Miss Pat's door. Then a dark thought assails my psyche as I aim the silencer at his forehead.

"Shame, come on, don't kill me man!"

Right before I pull the trigger, my phone rings again, snapping me back to the rational world. The logical world I disappeared from momentarily to numb up enough to end this guy.

"What!" I growl into the phone, not bothering to check the caller ID.

"Daddy?" The frail voice questions feebly into the phone. "Daddy, I don't feel good."

"Daddy?" I demand, a sick feeling rising in me as I listen on. "Mike? Is that you?"

He coughs before whispering, "I'm at home with Mommy. When are you coming home? Devin left with Vonnie, so it's just me here."

"Mike, where you at?" I ask, trying to lace some love with the livid in my voice as I walk out the building. "I can come get you, little man. It's cousin Mel."

"Mel?" He asks curiously. A bout of silence passed before he coughed again, "Where is Daddy?"

I frowned, anger roiling through me at the thought of my Uncle Rando, The Commander's brother, leaving his son in the house all alone. "I'll be okay till Devin and Vonnie get back from their errand. Sorry to bother you, Daddy."

"Devin?" Who the fuck was this Devin guy he kept going on about? I almost demand he tell me where he is before the line goes dead.

I want to kick myself for not ever having the presence of mind to ask Quincy for Uncle Rando's address. All I remembered was overhearing him say that his family was based out of D.C.. I never even met that side of the family outside of my twin cousins, and an intense, raw, fear penetrates my rational thought as I attempt to redial the unknown number Mike called from.

No answer.

"Shit!" I bellow out before dialing the only guy I knew as the best tracker for shit like this.

"Shame?" Takeo, The Silence, answered on the first ring as I expected. "What's the situation?"

"How much time we got before this assignment?"

"What do you need done?" He asked, cold and flat as usual.

"It's something I need to do in D.C. real quick, but I need you to get some information for me."

A beat, then. "Done. Just text me everything you know about the target and I'll see what I can dig up. Meet me in a half hour at the shop."

I don't respond, only end the call before catching the next taxi back to East Camden.

Six

MALICE

It was all a fucking lie. All of it. Pure hatred circulates in my blood as the taste for vengeance perfumes my dry mouth. In fact, I'm still reeling from the news Si delivered to me on our way to the D.C. assignment.

"Dear God, by all that is Holy! Don't shoot me!" The bloodied man manages to whine around the sock gag in his mouth.

A cool gust of air breezes by and seems to bounce off the empty, abandoned warehouse walls and straight through my trench. Though only August, the wintry winds reached the tiny state of D.C., which only served to add to my wariness, since it was hard to focus on shooting with frozen fingers. The drive to the arguably southern state was a long one, filled with a tense silence due to the weight of my anxiety to reach the address my co-killer was able to produce for me after Mike's call. Was he in danger? Or sick? The idea of my little cousins I'd regarded more like siblings in any sort of danger made me, well, want to kill. But not in the usual way I did to fulfill a contractual obligation. Nah. But in the same way an escaped convict exacted their revenge on the guy who puts them in the clink.

Whatever the case, I intuit The Commander's involvement and all sorts of torture scenarios plague my mind as I observe Si punch the living Jesus out of the fat exec in the chair.

"I told you!" Fat Exec hollers after spewing another river of blood. "I don't know where he is!"

Si grins, which mirrors more of an evil twist of the cheeks than any kind of joy-gesture, as he places his weight on both arms of the rotted wooden chair. Staring the target dead in his eyes, he says, "You made an agreement with the Kobayashi's. Now you're afraid to honor it?"

"I know, I know!" He cries. A fresh wave of panic overcomes the tubby dude who's sitting there awash in blood, sweat, and who-knows-what other secretions his body leaked from the hour-long beating Si enacted on him. "But I'm telling you– I ain't seen Monty in weeks!"

Si's eyes linger on him before alternating to the dead body on the floor.

Sighing my frustration and utter lack of interest in the man's lies, I approach the scene from the darkness.

Fat Exec's bloodshot eyes bulge as he watches me walk toward him. "Wait, hold on, who's this guy?"

"I'm getting tired of this shit!" I roar, aiming my silencer at his right temple. "Don't you get it? You fucked up. And *this* crazy motherfucker" I jab a finger at Si, who's still staring into the man's eyes, "don't talk. It's dipshits like you, who make him waste energy on words, that don't live that long."

Si rips the gag from his mouth. "You should heed his warnings, Eugene."

His face reddens more as the tears flow. "But I really have zero clue where he is. He hasn't responded to my calls in—"

"Five." I growl, cocking the gun.

"Wait, what?"

"Four."

"Please, okay, don't do a countdown. I want to tell you, but—"

"Three." I say, sweat gathering on my back in anticipation of the blood show I secretly hated witnessing.

Fat Exec, or Eugene, howls "Help!" into the vacant house, provoking the knuckle sandwich doled out by his kidnapper/punisher.

"Are you trying to end up like your partner here?" Si asks in an emotionless tone while nodding to the corpse I had to put a bullet in to silence his similar cries for help. Erecting to his full six-foot height, he steps back from the scene and speaks to him while pacing. "I'm sure you've never encountered my colleague, Shame, here. But, unlike me, he has an insatiable desire to kill. An unquenchable thirst for spilling the blood of dishonorable men like yourself. You'll tell me where your son is, or it's the end for you."

"No." He mumbles, his dirty blond hair spilling into his eyes as he hangs his head dejectedly. "Monty, tricky bastard that he is, is still my son. And, I know he made this deal with your family and used me as collateral, but I can't give him away. Can't send him to a death by the hands of you if I have the chance at preventing it."

Si nods, a glint of admiration I recognize coloring his face. "Your loyalty to your family is something to be respected, Eugene."

He chuffs, a hopelessly deflated sound. "Yeah, well, look where that's gotten me."

"I must agree." Si acquiesces in the dark, bowing a head to me to signal my next words to the man.

"1099 S. Fourth Street." I say, repositioning the gun at his head.

Eugene's eyes widened in abject horror at me. "You knew this whole time? Knew where my son lived in Jersey?"

"Of course." Si supplied wistfully, stepping out from the shadows. "I'm the Collector for the Kobayashi Clan. That information was a mere phone call away to my contacts in the Census office."

Another terrified look passes Eugene's face before he lurches over. "You son of a bitch! I ought to kill you for kidnapping my partner and me to get tortured in this hellhole. Release me now!"

"Like I said," He started, stalking closer. "Your loyalty is admirable."

"Two." I say, resuming my countdown on his life.

"But your honor is in dire repair, Mr. Praxel."

"Fuck yo—"

Wordlessly, I pump a silent slug into his temple, effectively silencing the pissy/sweaty/bloody exec. While I was accustomed to Si's mode of operations by now, I didn't realize till now how irritated the bloody blowback had been. The Silence used frontal interrogations for his attacks, relishing in the gory display of stabbing his targets in the guts, or cutting off fingers. He'd usually rattle on about honor before completing the kill, but his kills were always messy. Not evidence-wise, since we'd both been in the game a while and were aware of what not to touch to avoid forensic identification, but I can't help but glare at the blood splatters all over my trench and shirt.

"Yo, Si." I uttered, forcing the impatient irritation in my deep voice. "You got to do this shit in a cleaner way. This is the third polo all the bleach in the world probably won't make virgin-white again."

A faint, ghost of a chuckle escapes him before he regards his own clothes. "Stop your wailing and change your clothes. Spare clothes are in the trunk, remember?"

"Man, there ain't no clothes in there!" I lament when I return to the house empty handed.

I found him picking up shell casings when I re-entered what I supposed was the living room. "No? Check again. Yume wouldn't have forgotten those details in my spare clothes bag."

I grunt, recalling the tiny Japanese teen sister he'd referred to. "Si. There. Ain't. No. Clothes!"

He stood up, annoyance clear on his face. "New plan. Let's go to City Center and find some commoner clothes to change into before we go to that address."

I bit my tongue to tamp down on the fury roiling through me. "How we supposed to walk into a crowded mall looking like Cary after the prom? We'd get arrested on spot."

"Hmm." He hums in thought. "True."

"Wait a minute." I say, an idea turning in my mind that I nearly forgot. The Commander owned several wash houses and laundromats in D.C.. He'd never allowed me to accompany him on out of state runs, despite my pleas, but I remembered following him after one of my deployments to a swanky hole in a wall building that read "Q's Wash N' Go," on the front. He'd established one "Wash N' Go," in south Camden near the Heights, and that's where the residents often went to do laundry.

"Come on, I know where to go." I say, resolving myself as we made the drive to the laundromat I discovered in secret a couple years back. I hadn't been able to reach The Commander for the past few days, which wasn't abnormal considering he answered the phone whenever he felt like it, but his moves in the streets that diminished the household money flow made my trust in him decrease. Little by little, I'd been making a name for myself in the hood my father owned, and the Kobayashi's were a monumental part of that success with the high-paying assignments they'd hired me for.

The Commander existed as the information hub in Camden, since nothing got around without him knowing about or orchestrating it. But now, the usual blind trust in him was replaced with a go-getter: the streets existing less as a place of torture and more of an opportunity. Si was one of those opportunities I appreciated and developed a life-trusting partnership with. Whenever I'd needed something done, it was done. I'd asked him to pull some information on where Mike's phone call originated, and bam. Just like that, and a few strings pulled from his contacts in the police department, The Silence was able to gather the address and registered owner of that phone line.

The phone had been registered to a woman named Helen.

"Helen?" I queried as we got off the turnpike to leave Jersey.

"Yes." Si answered in that flat way of his. "My contact pulled her address on file, and it seems she's a stay-at-home mother with three children. And..." He hesitates, and the hesitation draws a new wave of fear and trepidation through me as I gawked at him driving.

"And...what?"

"Uh...I ordered my contact to reconfirm these details, of course. But, uh, Helen Cooper has an active marriage record on file."

I sigh a breath of relief. "Yeah, man. Probably my Uncle Rando. That's probably his wife, the twins' mom. No sweat."

"No, Shame." He corrects, and the next words that leave his mouth make me laugh, initially, by their absurdity. That couldn't be true. The so-called "record" he found couldn't be real since The Commander had been the best of the best. The best drug kingpin in the tristate area, running shit thorough while holding down his wife and kids.

Except, we weren't his wife and kids. Not really. Not in the reality that son of a bitch sold to us since my nearly fatal entrance into this world.

"Will Quincy be in there?" Si asked, yanking me from the hatred haze I'd been submerged in as we walked toward the small laundromat on the corner.

The sky loomed with ominous looking clouds overhead as we strode towards the back entrance of the place. I recalled watching The Commander disappear into this place when I followed him that day.

"I hope so." I answered. "Got a bone to pick with him."

After several yanks, the door still doesn't give under my weight. I blow out an exasperated breath before pulling out my favorite girl and aiming it at the steel knob.

One shot. Two shots. Three shots.

"I don't think that's going to open, my friend." Si adds warily while placing a hand on my arm.

"Back up off me right now." I grit out, the mere prospect of finding the old man inside turning me murderous. I wasn't sure if he'd been inside, but we did also need clothes.

"Where is Quincy?" I demand bitterly to the older Asian woman at the front desk.

She eyes me down with disdainfully bored eyes before returning to her magazine. As if the blood all over us was something she'd witnessed every day. "He no here. Back tomorrow."

"He what?"

"I said!" Asian lady over enunciates her broken English words with in tune claps of her hands. "Mr. Quincy. No. Here! Come back later."

"When is later?"

"Next week."

"Bit—" I start, unknowingly advancing on her then pausing by Si's hand on my shoulder. Accustomed to his nonverbal communication warnings, I took that slight moment of pause to calm my breathing. The wild rush of my heart and blood rushing to my face drove me from hovering to falling over the edge of reason.

My nerves are on edge also from the need to hunt this dude and shoot him for all the lies. Sighing in deep, I readied myself to break our code, one of The Commander's most valued rules: never reveal the true nature of our relationship to strangers.

"Ma'am." I say, splaying out my hands to reveal my sincerity. "He's my dad. I need to reach him, and I know you know where he is. For the sake of our family, just please..."

Seemingly fed up, Asian lady slams her magazine to the floor before shooting to her feet. "You *lie!* You no his son! Mr. Quincy's son small boy. Not big boy like you. Get out right now or I call police!"

My jaw ached from clenching my teeth so hard in restraint, but fuck this, I figured as I reached a hand in my back pocket. If this was how she wanted it, then I'd make it my mission to dole it out the hard way. It was clear The Commander was hiding from us—or me—and I just couldn't handle the disgust enough to use reason.

Before I felt myself ramping up too much, Si places a gloved hand on the counter. He says something in Japanese to her with the warmest smile on his face. Now, I'm not easily shocked nor do I scare easy, but that innocent smile he flashed the elder Asian woman does some kind of mysterious magic.

I watch with inward disbelief at how The Silence was able to get her to action: A faint blush colors her face as she stands and leads us to the backroom, and I open my mouth to ask my co-killer just what he said to that old lady but stop abruptly when I get a look at the backroom.

Si bows his head slightly to the blushing old woman as he turns. "Our sincerest gratitudes, Li Mei."

"Please, take your time." Li Mei whispers, demure and bashful before glaring at me and taking her leave.

"Old bitch." I grumbled. "What did you just say to her?"

"Told her to take me to Mr. Masters' office. Li Mei is an old friend of my late brother's. She'll be no more trouble to us."

"Using that old 'Kobayashi Charm' again, huh." I chuffed, unamused but still curious as I studied the small room that appeared to be more of a security nook.

"Worked better than shooting her in a heavily sur-veillanced laundromat." He retorts, studying the small television screens lining the walls same as I am.

"Well then she shouldn't have made me beg." I say absently while examining the images on the screen. "Just what the fuck is this room?"

"It would appear Quincy has this place under 24/7 watch."

"No shit." I whisper in awe as I occupy the single chair situated before the small oak desk.

The desk is clear of any personal belongings: no papers, figurines, nor even a shred of office supplies were in sight. It was like whoever occupied this seat emptied the desk under clear instruction to rid it of personality. Or prints. I didn't know. But I studied the wall of cameras from my low vantage point, noticing there was a camera concentrated at a three-sixty angle of the laundromat. I understood the line of business The Commander was involved in, but the Fort Knox level security over this location baffled me. Was he hiding some of his product here? I'd only ever saw him when he visited us for bimonthly visits and to accompany him to Remy's, the bar he'd may as well referred to as his second home.

But it wasn't. The bar was just a bar, in the grand scheme of things, since his second home was in this very city I was determined to get some answers within.

"How much more information was you able to dig up, man?" I asked.

Si bristled as he stood, his grimace conveying loads of uncertainty. "My contact could only pull an active marriage record and an address."

"He couldn't find out more? I need to find out where Quincy is and dig up some more info on somebody named Devin."

"Hmm." He hummed, rocking on his heels a bit before continuing. "I can get you information. Easily."

A wave of relief and camaraderie gushed through me, and I fought to resist the urge to hug the silent bastard. "Thanks, man."

"At a price." He said, cold and direct.

I reared back, his words dumping a bucket of ice water over the warm fuzzies I felt mere seconds prior. "You serious?"

"Completely."

"Stop fucking with me." I said before laughing and retraining my gaze on the wall monitors. "How fast can you get that info?"

A tight smile tugged at his lips, and the act looked way more maniacal from the dried blood on his left cheek.

"Shame. You understand my duty, right? As the Kobayashi Clan's Collector, these services are offered at an exorbitant expense. An expense, I'm sure, you do not have the means to afford."

"Say what?" I barked; his words were only adding to the welled-up futility I felt beside the shame of being my father's oopsie family. I kept picturing those lifeless brown eyes staring into mine as my father doled out an order. Or explained to me in blunt detail of how precious an asset I was to the family business. I started putting in work at ten years old, and the small boy in me knew those contracts I killed over was to get a little closer to his graces. To just soak up a little of the pride he'd never expressed having for me or Shay. The pride I was sure he reserved for his on-record wife Helen and their three kids.

"Lower your gun, Shame." Si adds cautiously, and I'm barely registering that I'd aimed Luci at his forehead in the midst of my inner wallowing. "Killing me would only worsen your problems. Trust me, as a friend, those who become indebted to the Kobayashi's are burdened for life. Killing me would be one of those forever debts I won't be around to relieve you from."

I'm fighting the battle for sanity as I wrestle with the itch to tug the trigger. These bursts of rage were nothing like my true character. Nothing like the laid back Shamel I'd been working on becoming while holding down a crazy babymoms and a bloody night job.

My arms slinks to my side as if another bullet pierced through the gunshot wound I'd gotten two years ago.

"Sorry, my guy." I breathe, raking a hand through my short locs as I sink back into the chair. "I appreciate your help with all this. Word up."

Si, calm as water, inches towards me, and when I look up at him, there's no pity there. Even though he has every reason to feel sorry for a fucked-up kid like me, he doesn't.

"I won't lie to you by saying I understand your plight, because I don't. But allow me to tell you this."

I roll my eyes. "Nigga, cool it on the Jedi talk. I ain't in the mood to hear no sainthood poetry from you today."

Unsmiling, he says, "Go with that feeling. Take all those emotions you're feeling and eat them. I tell you this because you are a few years my junior, and are as charismatic as I was at your age. Don't let the shame of your parentage make you weak. Instead, swallow it. Channel it into muscle, and take no prisoners."

I nodded, not exactly sure how to respond to the advice that made his dark eyes glow with a level of intimate understanding I wondered about.

He took a step back to study the screens, and I almost allowed my mind to wander a bit before I heard him ask, "Who's that?"

"Hello, Devin!" The familiar voice of the Asian receptionist sounded through the center screens. This particular camera was concentrated on the main room where the machines, tables, and entry door were.

"Devin?" I hissed, more out of curiosity as I studied the small screen with fervent purpose to the old lady smile at a boy with a large black bag in his hand.

The picture appeared slightly grainy as I examined the black teen. I could make out the white tee and dark pants he was wearing, but not the expression on his face. I'm guessing it's a troubled one, considering his head sliding left and right as if he's being chased.

Or watched.

Which, in a way, he was.

"Hi, Li Mei," the boy I assumed to be Devin said. "Here's the drop for this week. You got the rest?"

Li Mei's face contorts in the cheesiest ass-kissiest grin before she ducks low behind the counter. "All for you, Devin. And right on time as usual. Be sure to tell Saint to have all the money this time, okay?"

I watch in abject confusion as they exchanged black bags. Devin threw one of his long braids over his shoulder before mumbling something to her I was not able to comprehend from the cheap security system speaker.

"You don't think this is..." Si uttered in a confounded whisper.

"Shh!" I demand while squinting my eyes at the screen. Surely I wasn't seeing what I thought I was seeing. Wasn't witnessing the small figure beside this mysterious Devin character reach up and grab his hand.

Her large puffballs give her identity away immediately.

"Devin!" She whines, and the fear in her voice twists my insides as I rise to watch it. "I wanna go home! Mikey's not feeling too good and he's all by himself."

Devin does another perimeter scan before kneeling before her. Again, I can't see his face, but can hear the tenderness in his voice as he responds. "Vonnie, I know. But Mommy's home with him, he's not totally alone. Remember, we got to run one more errand before heading back. Okay?"

She squeals a little in disappointment while yanking his hand. "Devin...I'm scared."

A wall of panic and fear and fury erects around my brain. I'm growling and vibrating with renewed rage as I grab hold of Luci and exit the security nook. Why was my little cousin here, in the middle of the night, on a school night of all places? And just who was this Devin kid, dragging my cousin around the most dangerous corners of the hood anyways?

Whoever he was, I prayed for the sanity I lost en route to this laundromat as I entered the main wash room.

"Yo, Devin!" I called to the little prick with long, nappy braids. When he snapped his focus to me, I noted the fat bags under his eyes and bruises on his face.

He stood up, terror written all over his face as he pulled Yvonne close to him. "Who-Who are you—"

"Run!" Li Mei hollered at them, and in an instant I'm not too present in, Devin bolts out the front door with my cousin and the huge black bag he traded from the elder receptionist.

"I'll deal with you later, bitch!" I growled that promise to her as I took off after the mysterious boy in the night.

"Fuck!" I screeched while watching them climb hastily inside a large black pickup truck and speed off. My head was spinning off the tracks as I considered my next move.

"Shame!" I heard a voice yell from the street.

Unthinkingly, I sprinted towards it to see Si in his Audi with the engine humming.

"I still see them!" He assured me, urgent and clear cut as his sleek ride eased through the night traffic. My mind and heart are racing as fast as the black pickup we're tailing as it exits the highway. The trucker takes us on a wild goose hunt, probably noticing that he's being followed, and after another few minutes pass and the truck slows at a steady pace, I realize we're in the clear. Si maintains about two cars worth of distance between them, and before long we end up in a decent sized neighborhood. There are several colored houses packed tight on the streets, and I study the black truck park outside a dark blue house with an eerie intent.

"Canal street." I say in a hushed tone. "This is it. The address."

Si nods, his breathing heavy. "Correct. How should we proceed?"

I answer that question by tightening my hold on the gun and exiting the car. From my stance, I'm able to make out Devin rushing Yvonne inside the house and shutting the door. I'm channeling all my serial killer energy as I walk with predatory focus towards the black truck.

I'm anxious to get to the bottom of who was driving the getaway vehicle that stowed my young cousin. So many questions and rage and frustration gathered all at once in my head and hand as I reached the truck.

In a flash, the truck speeds off into the distance before I'm able to glimpse the identity of the mysterious night driver. I shout my rage into the night sky, uncaring as I note the many indoor lights shine on at my loud bellow.

"Shame, let's go." It's Si, like always, sneaking up from the shadows. "Before we get spotted in a residential area in what we're wearing."

I clock that we're still robed in our bloody attire, but I don't fucking care. I'd been so close to answers and justice all night. It felt like it was a pinch away from unlocking some undercover shit The Commander's been up to. I'd come all this way to find out what's been going on with my cousins, to get a sense of their welfare all the way up in this area I'd been too idiotic to visit.

"Fuck that." I sneer, turning to the front of the blue house full of secrets. There's a black bag sitting on the front step, as if inviting me to come close and inspect. A few seconds tick by before realization dawns.

It's the bag Devin had been holding. The one he traded with the bitch receptionist I'd have to deal with later on.

"Take that to the car." I instructed a nervous looking Si.

He follows my gaze before asking, "Shame, this isn't a good idea. We'll get caught if–"

"I'll grab it, then! Fuck!" I roar as I reach for the bag. It's heavy as hell, as though seven bricks lined its insides. I'm wondering how such a small teen kid was able to lug that more than five feet before I toss it to Si. "Take it."

He catches it before leaving me with a lingering look. He looks as though he wants to say something, to warn me again about being stupid and too emotional like in the security room, but decides against it.

Without another word, he runs back to the Audi.

I take a step to follow him, but...

The call to kill was too great. My senses were too primed and I craved to know the welfare of my cousins with a raw intensity. I couldn't turn back now. Couldn't turn back for fear of losing myself completely to the darkness of doubt. I had to see this through.

Taking a deep breath, I lifted my fist to knock on the door. It didn't take long before someone opened it and my mouth dropped at who I saw.

"What the fuck you want?" The light skinned woman with long curls demanded.

She's gorgeous with a banging body, I can't deny, but it isn't her beauty, nor needle marks in her arms, that distracts me. It's her face. I recognized the face of the woman I found in The Commander's pocket. It had been during one of his visits that I saw a 4x4 picture of the pretty lady with shiny white teeth and long hair fall out of dad's pocket one day. When I found it, I approached my mom's bedroom door where they'd been making love noises. The noises stopped when I knocked, and Mom swung open the door to yell at me before I presented her the picture.

A sad smile crested her face before she knelt down, kissed my forehead, and told me, "This is daddy's picture. It isn't polite to steal things from him. I'll replace it before he notices it missing, yeah? Go on back to sleep, Shamel."

I'm sputtering as the woman's dark eyes give me a harsh onceover. "Oh, you one of them? Well, my husband ain't back yet."

"Your husband?" I ask.

She glares at me, and for a second, I can't explain, I'm overcome with a need to flinch. The aura of this pretty lady from the picture I found was dark. Intense. "You tryna cop, right? Well, we all gotta wait till my man comes home."

I force an arm through the threshold of the door she nearly slams in my face. "Hold on. Where is your husband? I need to talk to him."

She rolls her eyes in that same distasteful way Li Mei did when I threatened her. "He. Ain't. Here. What the fuck, you stupid or something?"

"Nah." I bit out, barely able to contain the anger. "He owes me something. And I know he in there."

This was hard, to say the least, since people knew not to cross me in the streets. They knew my word was law and attached in some way to Quincy's name. I was the extension of his wrath, the shame of his existence, and a force to be fucking reckoned with.

Helen did all sorts of reckoning as she worked her jaw before yelling, "Come back later or cop somewhere else."

"Hell nah!" I grunt and soon as I know it we're wrestling for control of the door: her attempting to shut me out and me forcing my way in. It's no use though, and sirens blaring in the distance let me know I fucked up. My mind numbed at the neighbors Si warned me about alerting as I kicked my old Jordans through the front door. There's a huge hole in the old wood that makes Helen stop fighting.

"Did you just kick a hole in my damn door?!" She screeched in rage-filled bewilderment. "You paying for that shit."

"Quincy!" I hollered inside the house, my voice breaking with the unshed tears and fury from the buttload of info I'd gotten this evening. "I know you in there, you fucking pussy! You tell your wife about your son? Your real son with the other woman you knocked up?"

The sirens were getting closer, and I supposed I should have given a damn, but I had to know. I couldn't leave here empty handed and always wondering.

Helen did something I'd thought the pretty woman from the picture incapable of: threw her head back and laughed. But not in a supermodel coy type of way, no, it's a sinister cackle that makes my insides burn with a desire to strangle her silent.

"Oh, so this is his first son, huh?" She said between gales of laughter. She clenched her sides as if I'd been the opening act on Def Comedy Jam and not the shameful bastard of her beloved husband's. "Boy that shit ain't no secret. You think I gave a damn about Quincy's little side ho and her ashy-black babies? That bitch could never be me. And y'all ain't nothing but some mistakes your mama should've swallowed."

My hand. It's typically trembling over my gun at this point when I'm this riled up, but...

Her words stab me through the chest like one of those poisoned tipped swords in that Shakespeare play. I recall the poisoned-laced weapon the dude used to deal Hamlet the final blow and resonate with it. It's as if all the shame and guilt I'd harbored for existing, Helen shaped into a blunt knife that stabbed at all my sore parts. My chest...it's really aching. The air is swirling around my jaw dropped state as I stare stupidly at the woman.

Helen turns slightly inside the house to address an unseen person. "Baby, come get this boy. I know you said to tell him you ain't home, but I can't listen to his little questions anymore without punching his ass. Can I get my allowance tonight, like you promised?"

A squeal sounds throughout the room as if someone's disturbed the furniture before that familiar baritone that haunts my dreams says to her, "Woman, get your ass upstairs before I punch you. I'll handle this since you obviously ain't used to handling."

A petulant frown mars her beautiful face before she shrugs and obeys. Just like that. She's gone, and in her place stands my brooding father, The Commander and spinner of his own tales.

Like that English play, I realized we all lived to play a role in his world. The one he so carefully carved out from our ignorance and blind trust.

"Now, what you crying for boy?" He demands with a disgusted look on his face.

I shook my head and wiped at my eyes. "Who are you? Who was she?"

He looks toward the direction of the sirens. "Why you up here? And how you know about this place?"

"Goddamn it!" I screech my anguish as I raise the gun to his face. Those dark eyes glittered, not only disapproval, but an eerie level of evil I'd never saw till now. "You answer my questions or you get a bullet through your fucking skull, *dad!*"

"Shamel." He chuckled. "Put that gun down, boy. You forgettin your place. Who bought you that gun. Now answer my question. How you find this place?"

"You think I won't shoot? Is that it?"

"Nigga, you a punk. Always been a little sissy. Too emotional for your own good. Why you think I stop coming around, huh? Think I ain't know about that contract you fucked up with that LC?"

"Nah…"

"Found themselves wiseass enough to send a goon my way to slit my throat while I'm in bed. Shot that fucker before he got the chance to turn my bedside light on. Don't you get it, boy?"

"You lying." I mutter, fear and panic in my being as I recall the botched kill from two years ago. That same contract that solidified my and Si's partnership was the same one that– apparently– almost killed my father.

That Latin Crip saw me. And the comebacks were brought against The Commander. *Fuck.*

I swipe angrily at the tear in my eye before blurting, "Pops, that's my bad. All my fault. Why ain't you tell me about the comeback?"

He sighed, long and droll. "Because, Shamel. I decided then that you wasn't worth it. That wasn't the first time you fucked up an easy-peasy contract. That ain't the first gangsta that tried my life because of some stupid shit you did in the street."

"I could've handled it." I breathed, unsure if this was his way of bluffing but feeling horrified all the same.

"You wanna know where I been at? I been here. At *my* home. *My* house. With *my* wife and kids. Kids that's gonna be something in this world and nothing like the stubborn trick I got for a daughter or sappy mistake I used to call my best shooter and son. Nah. I got Devin for that now, my new son. He might not be mine by blood, but he's valuable. He's been who I'm training in your place to run this shit the way you never could. The boss I know you'll never be. My pride and joy."

"Y-You...you lying. Take that shit back." I growl as several screws go loose in my head. I cock my gun again. "Now."

He continues his harmful onslaught, but I'm blocking it out as I glare at him. Glare past him actually, to see the little boy wrapped in a yellow blanket at the staircase. His little nose is red as if he'd been sniffling or sick or crying, I wasn't sure, but the cold cave in my chest warms as I stare at him. Alive and well and staring at me with an expression I don't recognize. Futility. That's the emotion that meets me as I hold tight to the gun and block out the sirens getting closer.

"Mike!" I hiss, not sure how my voice is coming out but needing to reach him. "It's me, Mel-Mel."

"Mel-Mel?" He hedges as he stands and takes a step towards us.

"No!" Quincy barks at both him and me. "Don't you come close to him. Go to your brother's room and I'll be in soon to tuck you and Vonnie in, okay?"

There's an emotion in The Commander's tone that I'm not familiar with as he coaxed the small child away from our porch standoff. A warm sound that makes me do a double take at the cold Commander spouting off terrible truths to me seconds ago.

"Brother?" I asked, my brain in a haze. "You mean brother as in that Devin kid? In what way are they brothers? What does this shit mean?"

Once Mike disappears upstairs, the dark glint returns to Quincy's eyes, alerting me of The Commander in his stead.

"Put two-and-two together, numb nuts! There ain't no Uncle Rando." He bites the words with a penetrating emphasis. "Helen is my wife. And the twins ain't your cousins."

"You dirty son of a–" I raised Luci and slammed it into his forehead. Relishing the usual protective powers she filled in the gaps of my wounded soul.

He laughed as he wiped the blood from his face before looking down the street. "You might want to run home before them cops arrest another nigga in the hood with a gun."

"This the burbs, Quincy." I spit. "Nothing like the trap house you got us in."

He shrugged. "Y'all want better conditions, find them. Sick of y'all wasting my good dime just to lay around and be nothing. Sommer got good pussy and she's a survivor, so y'all won't go hungry if she decides to sell it for a lil sum sum. Like I been encouraging her to do."

Before the maniacal laughter comes and the blaring sirens approach our street, I do it.

I do the thing that sets me apart from the other characters in his play of lies. Just as Hamlet does the fake king, I create my own tragic ending to this tale.

I pull the trigger.

SEVEN

NEBRASKA

Keeping with all the wondrous luck I'd been having, the gun fires only empty air instead of the curtain-closing bullet. I soon find myself squeezing the trigger several times while Quincy laughs at my frantic fumbling with my favorite firearm.

This couldn't be possible, I thought in haste as I slapped the barrel and checked the clip. True to form, the magazine is hollow where bullets are usually stocked on the inside.

"Fuck!" I cry, delivering another kick to The Commander's second front door as I recall using my very last bullet on the back of the laundromat door.

Cops are crawling around the block as I make a split decision and sprint down the opposite end of the street. I hear The Commander mumbling something as I run away, and most of it is incoherent as I make my escape, but I do understand his final few words.

"Bye, son." His words are deep grumbles that I only half believe.

I don't give myself the emotional space to make room for that strange farewell. Not even sure if the bereaved tone with which he uttered them were even reserved for me or his younger son at the stairwell as we fired bittered words at each other.

His other son. Or sons, I gathered, were his pride and joy. His new beginning that fills me with traitorous envy and soul shattering bitterness.

The stark reality of the lies this man fed us over the years brings on only more questions, too. I remember Mom's reaction to the pretty woman in the picture as well as Helen's nasty familiarity of her husband's second family. As in the words of the Shakespeare play I'd read twice over, there was something rotten in the state of my father's affairs. And I would get to the bottom of it by any means.

Michael and Yvonne, my long cherished and intensely loved cousins weren't my cousins at all. They were the brother and sister I never really got the chance to know. Sure, they visited when The Commander made his bimonthly visits every so often, but that had been the extent he'd allowed us in their lives. It was silly, I know, but that silly was our normal for as long as I could remember. It had almost been a year since I glimpsed a peek at my cous– no, siblings.

Mike had gotten taller and scrawnier, and now I knew the truth, looked a whole lot like me at that age.

Yvonne, my precious sister with the same feistiness all the Masters women inherited, looked a reticent shell of herself. Clinging on to Devin's skinny hand as if she'd be swallowed by a madness I didn't see surrounding her. And maybe there is a madness there, I intuit, and fight to control the bout of fire welling in me to annihilate the unseen foe. The Commander, I could live without, but them? My brother and sister? I made a vow to myself as I whipped out my phone to do right by them. To be there for them. Though I wasn't sure how.

Si had long since disappeared from his parked position down the street, and I had to bite my lip hard to keep the frustrated tears at bay. While The Commander was no father of mine from this point on, his rules still hovered in my consciousness like a thread in my being: bosses never cry.

Ducking into an abandoned alley and out of the range of the sirens, I sucked in a deep breath and dialed the only number I knew would pick up. The main person I knew would come through in a time where I needed her most even with blood I couldn't explain on my clothes.

"Hi Daddy!" the toddler screamed as I got into the raggedy red SUV of my babymoms. I twisted in the passenger seat to smile weakly at her.

"Hey, beautiful." I told Lexus, the rose color that filled her cheeks I anticipated whenever I gave her a compliment.

Dawn is eerily silent as she weaves through traffic on the highway on the way back to Camden.

I open my mouth to give her an explanation, to apologize, to say anything that might relay the level of futility and sorry I was to drag her out this time of night. I want to fill her in on the details behind the blood on my clothes and the mystery around my location, but...

Nothing. Only sputters of nothingness emit from my mouth as I stare at her huge belly pressed against the steering wheel and the tears cascade down her face.

"Dawn–"

"Don't!" She snaps, her voice low and full of an anguish I'm too used to putting there. "Not here. Not in front of my baby. I won't let her hear me call the only guy she knows as a father the complete disappointment you bring to my life. Just, not right now. Okay?"

Her words are so low they sound calm, but the emotion behind them let me know they're anything but that as I nod and avert my gaze out the window.

Lexus's happy songs filled the car during the almost three-hour drive back home. And right as we exit the turnpike and the toddler's snores replace her nursery rhymes, I turn to the girl I'd disappointed one too many times.

"Baby, let me stay at your crib tonight." I say.

She rears back but doesn't meet my eyes. "Looking like that? Shame, you know I can't let that happen. Besides, that ain't my crib– it's my mom's. She already don't like you. She got so pissed I took her car in the middle of the night to bail you out of whatever trouble got that blood on your clothes. Fuck that."

Desperation, an emotion I'd gotten familiar with these last few weeks since the decrease in our household money flow, washes through me as I stare at her.

"Dawn, baby, please. I promise I'll be better. I want us to get back to the way we used to be. Let me be there for y'all. Let me stay the night."

She shook her head. "Hell no, Shame. You gotta figure this

out on your own."

"But why? You my girl, ain't you?"

She averted her eyes before mumbling, "I don't know about that. But what I do know is that I'm supposed to be on bed rest till Luxury gets here in a few weeks. Shame, I'm tired."

"You don't know?" I spit, deciding to harp on her initial indecision about our secret relationship. "You supposed to hold me down no matter what. Ride or die. What happened to that?"

"First of all, you better lower your voice around my baby! Wake her up and I'll slap the shit outta you."

Sick of begging and sick of the joyride this emotional rollercoaster of a day put me through, I lean in real close to her. "Do it. Hit me. I promise you ain't gonna like the outcome."

"Oh, yeah?"

"I don't bluff, girl. And I'm sick of your fucking mouth. Always got some smart shit to say. Go ahead. Do your worst."

Fury lights in her brown eyes, and she finally looks at me for the first time. Her right fist is raised while her eyes alternate between the road and me. She rears back to deliver the blow I'd asked for, the one I figured I needed to get my head straight, before she just stops.

Suddenly, the car stops, and I see she's pulled up to the curb of Jefferson Heights. She didn't have my real address, so it's only logical she'd drop me where my Project Granny resided.

"Just get out my car." She whispered, her voice warbling from the tears resuming down her face. "I don't want this no more."

"Dawn." I grit out, the fury subsiding with the desperation coming back. I reached out for her, but she dodged my outstretched hand and screamed at me.

"I got another man, okay!" She hollered, waking Lexus and rocking her swollen belly back and forth. "And don't you see? This ain't gonna work. It ain't been right since I showed you that pregnancy test. You changed. *We* changed. Now, get out of my car before I call the cops."

"Who is he?" I demand.

She shakes her head again. "Nobody."

"Who?!" I howl, hot tears pricking my eyes as I study the terror in hers. That almost makes me back down. I can't handle the fear I placed in her eyes as I pull away from her.

"He's nobody, all right?" She says, in a meek and afraid voice I'd never heard coming from her.

In an unthinking moment of loathing— the self kind — I open my mouth to breathe fire at her.

"How I know that's even my baby you got inside of you anyways? Since you apparently been fucking this other nobody-ass nigga right after you finish fucking me."

It isn't quite fire that I'm breathing as I hurl the grimy insults at the girl I promised to love. Nah. They're more like bullets, judging from her shocked face and physical recoil.

"How the fuck could you even say some shit like that to me?" Though she hollered, her eyes were wet. Her spirit, completely broken. "Get out."

"Bet you hate me now, huh?" I say, more accusatory than questioning.

She sucked her teeth. "I gotta get my baby home. Just go. I ain't getting into it with you. It's useless."

The pain in my gut was unexpected, same as the desperation that manifested beside it. It suddenly feels like I'm at that front door again. On Canal Street. In DC and on the receiving end of Quincy's words that felt more like gunshots despite the fact that it was me holding the gun.

"Dawn, listen—"

"You're not worth it!" She screams, broken and weary as Lexus's cries louden and intensify. "Please, just get out of my car. Please!"

I could only stare at her. Even though Lexus was wailing like crazy in the back as a result of our arguing, all I could do was stare. I fought to keep the barrier around my heart a solid fortress against the shame of my existence. The fact that I carried it everywhere I went.

I exited the car, and she peeled off the curb like hell was after her. Except, that hell was me, and she'd been absolutely right in putting as much distance between us as fast as possible.

My brain in scrambles and pieces, I staggered over to the stairwell leading to Miss Pat's. I could barely see through the unshed tears and welled up emotions. If someone saw me, saw the respected Shame of the ruthless duo that made up half of The Violence and The Silence, then they wouldn't recognize me. Wouldn't recognize the man with glazed eyes, bloody clothes, and an empty heart in dire need of repair after the night I'd had.

"Shamel, that you?" A raspy voice called out to me before I set foot on the first stair.

I didn't need to turn to identify the drugged-out woman approaching me from across the street. She's no more than eighteen or nineteen, but the bags under her eyes age the gorgeous third of Shay's bestie trio.

Liz, the once pretty biracial best friend of my big sis, looks scraggly now. Only a large green army jacket covers her skinny body and her chestnut-colored curls are matted to her sweaty forehead. Drugs took her, however, and I'd only been selling to her for a couple of months now, but she'd return more frequently since. Begging for higher quantities of a product we fittingly labeled as that 'hardcore shit.'

"Wassup, Shamel?" She says, scanning the perimeter in that drugged out way that most addicts did to avoid police detection. Her rancid breath and huge pregnant belly are hard to ignore. "Let me get a bag from you. I'll pay you next week."

"Fuck nah." I snarl, climbing the steps and determined to ignore her for the most part. I was afraid of my actions if she were to press on, egg on, or follow.

Like clockwork, she trails behind me up the stairs. "Come on, kiddo. Spot me till next week. I'm good for it."

"Nah."

"Mel!"

I whip out my empty gun and aim it at her, anticipating her eyes to saucer and her legs to propel in the direction from which she came. I ain't have the time to deal, with drugs or people, and though the missed opportunity is a hit financially, I don't care.

I muster the remaining strength and hardness left in me to knock on Miss Pat's door.

Instead of the heavyset old lady, an angel answers with an initial bright smile that flattens at the sight of me.

"Mel?" Angie gasps, her eyes working overtime to study my depleted face and sullied attire. I never made messy moves like this, and always made sure to keep my bloody underworld where it needed to be.

But my mind is sort of floating as I try to make words at her. I try. I do. But similar to Dawn, I'm speechless as I stare at her and fall to my knees.

"Mel!" She gasps again, her face horrified as she swallows the distance between us to wrap her arms around me. Her plush body would usually wooden my dick in my jeans at this point, but not today. Not right now.

Right now, the hardest thing between us is my heart that needs repair.

"My chest..." I start, my words dying on my lips. "It's burning."

"Shamel..." She says, like a chant or maybe a prayer as she rocks my body against hers without fear of sullying her robe or having some of my shame rub off on her. "Shamel."

I sniffled into her hair, my arms hanging limp and lifeless at my sides. "Why don't he want me?"

"I'm sorry." She whines, and I feel her tears in my hair as she mews and cries with me. In this moment, this one singular moment, we're totally infinite as time and space blur around our joined bodies.

EIGHT

NOBODY

I wake up naked, and to the feel of a soft body wrapped around mine. A warm smile crested my face at the realization of where I was, and I squeezed my hold around the sleeping woman in my arms.

"Good morning, Shamel." She mutters contentedly, as if it's the rightest place she'd ever been as she reaches up to kiss my lips. "Want a ride to school?"

"Yeah, thank you, baby..." I answer her absently, accustomed to our routine by now to pay it any notice.

Except, the snappy retort I expect from Dawn doesn't come like it usually does. And there were only a few people who knew me by Shamel, as I enforced my street nickname of 'Shame' towards everyone else.

Dawn lived in the 'everyone else' category.

In fact, there's much more curves in her thighs, belly and ass than I recognize before an eerie realization hits me like a sack of coke. I peel my eyes open fully to examine the modest room lined with books and painting on the walls. I'd been in here before, but where was this?

I turn to the woman on my right and everything falls back into place:

"Angie?" I croak in a sleepy whisper.

She reaches up and places a gentle kiss on my forehead. "Morning. Thought you'd never wake up in time for school."

I eyed the room usually off limits to Miss Pat's general house guests in suspicion. How did I end up in here?

"Angie," I start. "What happened last night?"

"Come on, get dressed." She roused while climbing out of the twin sized bed. I noticed how she artfully dodged my question and glimpsed her naked ass cheeks as she bent over to retrieve her strewn clothes from the floor.

Instinctively with her, I shut my eyes. "Whoa, Angie. What the hell? Why you walking around all naked and shit?"

She giggled while shimmying into a pair of blue jeans. "Mel, come on now. You really want to act shy after last night?"

"Uh, yeah? You're not exactly filling in the gaps for me here. So, yeah. I ain't trying to get cut by Miss Pat for being around you naked."

"Boy, whatever."

"Girl, chill." I countered; my lids still cinched closed as I sat up in bed. "What's going on?"

"Okay, okay. I'll stop messin with you." She said before sitting at the foot of the bed. "It's safe to open your eyes now. All dressed."

"All right." I blew out a relieved sigh and sank into the bed.

I peeled my eyes open with deliberate sluggishness, my big head wrestling with the one below the waist at the desire to pull her close. She looked every bit as delectable as the smell of cherries and amber in her small room. Her usually perfect hair was mussed and formed a black cloud around her chubby face. I bit back the need to touch her, pull her close and do what I think we did when I arrived last night.

The memory rushes back to me as I think of last night and the tears. I cried more than I did in years the day before, and I cough as I try to come up with something to say to her now. Something to say to wash away the memory of my weakness.

I showed my hand, and in gambling, that's what separated the winners from the losers.

"Hey–" we began together, our words jumbling and nervous laughs matching that follows.

"You first." I offer.

She grins. "Okay. Well, I just wanted to say that I think you're strong. And that I'm sorry I couldn't be there for you yesterday. I don't know what you went through to bring you to my door so...so..."

"So, what?"

"Broken. You came here yesterday and was so broken by whatever happened. You looked and smelled like something died."

"I don't know if I want to talk about it, for real for real." I grouse, shifting in my seat. "But I don't know why I can barely remember anything after that."

"Ah." She said, her amusement returning as she jabbed a polished nail towards the clear trash can. A large bottle of cheap booze lined its insides and I winced. "Blame your old friend, Irish Rose."

I groan as the memory of the cheap liquor burn returns. That cheap corner store shit tasted like vinegar and rotten asshole, and I normally made it a point to never buy liquor under fifty bucks. But that cheap shit right there...set your brain on fire and leave you naked and clueless.

Like now.

I shook my head again. "Where you even get that dollar store liquor from anyway? I didn't even know you drank."

"College girl's gotta have her secrets, you know?" She winked at me, and I grit my teeth to keep from hardening again at that beautiful smile.

"Angie the bad girl, huh?" I say appreciatively.

"Don't tell Mama." She chuckled, though I noted the sad tinge to her voice.

"Did we...do anything? Like, you know, that involved me...*in* you?"

"What a weird way to ask. But, to answer your question, no. We did not have sex."

I breathed a sigh of relief I'd been unaware of holding until after confirmation of the worst.

"You got sloshed and asked for me to hold you. So, I did. But you were shivering, and no matter what I did, you wouldn't warm up. So…"

I sighed. "So, you just figured 'hey, let me strip and rub my naked titties on Mel's chest.' I don't understand you, girl."

"What you mean?"

"I mean," I say, edging closer to her. "I been tryna see wassup with you since forever and now you want to give me some play? When I'm sappy and drunk out my damn mind?"

"We did not have sex, Mel!"

"Right. Sure."

"We didn't!" She huffed angrily, her voice raising in pitch.

"Besides, we used to be half naked all the time when we were little and you never made anything of it before. What's the big deal now?"

I only shook my head and laughed. This woman…

"Who said I never made it a big deal? Girl, if only you knew what really went down after I saw you looking like that when we were kids. Innocent Angie couldn't handle the truth."

"Boy, whatever." She says while standing. "I know you ain't talking! You been a daddy's boy since forever. Always following him around whenever I came over to y'all house as kids. Should be calling you 'Innocent Mel.'"

Everything...and I mean all of it, crashes into me at once. The mere mention of my father sends awful memories of yesterday flooding my mind just as horror and futility leave me empty. I collapse onto the bed as my chest heaves from the visions of Quincy grinning evilly at me. Mike's red nose and terrified eyes as he watched me with the gun aimed at his dad. At *our* dad. And then there were the vicious words of acknowledgement from his bitter legal wife and the memory of Yvonne's eyes as she gawked at me in that laundromat...I felt just like the thing the kids saw me as now. The same thing I suspected haunting Yvonne's eyes as she clung to Devin for dear life.

A monster.

"Hey, hey." Angie's voice cuts through the thick fog of futility, and I blink several times at the feel of her shaking me. "Stop chewing those nails up!"

"I'm good, I'm good." I dismissed the panic in her eyes, knowing if I acknowledged the emotion there that it'd trigger all the shame in me. Would deactivate my normal state of numbness required for me to make dirty deals in my underworld. After all, I was just like Lucifer. In a hell all alone and deserving of it. There's no way I can disrupt the twins' lives now, since I'd only make it worse.

I don't even notice that I'm munching hangrily on my nail buds.

"You don't sound good. Or even look it. What's up? You know you can talk to me, right?"

I shake my head again, but not only as a refusal to reveal, but also to rid it of the visions. Of their eyes on me. The monster.

"I'mma go before Miss Pat finds me here, all right?"

"Wait! I can drive you to school. Just let me get the rest of my clothes on and–"

Hating the panic rising in my chest, I lean over and press my lips to hers. I needed her to stop. Needed the rapid-fire inquiry about my mental state and the going-ons in my underworld to silence, so as not to invite her to my world of pain. Since Luci was nowhere in sight, my beloved gun that anchored me to this world whenever we touched, kissing Angie had been the next best thing.

As if remembering herself or some control, she rips away from our kiss and breathes, "Grab your clothes so I can take you to Marlton."

A lopsided grin spreads across my face before I can stop it. Her rosy red cheeks and frenzied eyes are turning me the fuck on.

"All right," I agree playfully. "Let me get up and get dressed."

"Um, okay." She mumbles, still disoriented from the kiss as she rises carefully from the bed. "I'll be in the bathroom."

"I'll be here." I answer, still smiling but grateful for the mood change as I remove the covers and stand up.

My breath catches in my throat, forcing me to choke on the convivial vibes that lingered temporarily in the air after that kiss as I stare at the clothes in the corner.

It's obvious they'd been washed, judging from the fresh smell of fresh linen and faint pink spots on the white shirt I wore to shoot that exec. She washed my clothes, I thought in disbelief. The gesture was un-believably sweet, and a pang of guilt split my chest as I thought of my bloody presence disrupting her straight-laced life. I don't want to be the point of reason for a downfall she didn't deserve. A dark descent into my underworld I'd been too submerged in to lift up and see light.

The familiar buzz from my cell sounds all my inner alarms as I retrieve it from the nightstand.

There are four messages that make me sigh.

T: *Calc homework is done and submitted. Just FYI*

SILENCE: *Meet at the Shop later today.*

SHAY: *What's this I hear about you missing school? You better get to school TODAY before I whip your ass!*

Perhaps the message that's most appealing/annoying is the one I peep from Milio.

> **MILIO**: *Need a job done.*

"Shit," I breathe while scrubbing both hands over my face.

Milio had been asking me constantly about doing some contracts for him since I joined the Kobayashi's. After the Comm—no, Quincy, abandoned our household to leave us in a financial rot, I let the streets get to know me. Not really me, but The Violence, or the ruthless cold killer that burned the streets with the wrath of my fury and moral depletion. While Italian, Milio was part of the LC's, and though I made it a point not to abide by Quincy's old rules anymore, that was the one I couldn't resist abiding for safety: don't deal with gangs.

That gang shit was messy moves, and an affiliation that could potentially end my street freedom and land me in a box. There was too many politics involved, and I enjoyed the steady blood cash afforded to me from the meager dope deals and contracts from the Kobayashi's. That work kept the lights on and mouths fed.

I tap the readily made response back to him with irritated fervor. Maybe he sees me typing my response, I don't know, but his next message brings me pause and makes my fingers hover over the send button in mute shock.

> **MILIO**: *10k upfront.*

Resolving myself, I hastily pull on my bloody clothes and slip easily out of her bedroom. I hate to leave her and bail on my word to wait, but I had to get out of there. It was like the haze of her room full of perfume and perfection was clouding my brain with pussythoughts again, and I needed my head to be clear for this next task.

NINE

INTENT

"Thank you, *mamacita*." I tell Tierra as she hands me the booklet of papers that made up my History project.

We're sitting in our final period, U.S. History, which was taught by Mr. Wiggins (a goofy-looking white dude who had it out for me), and I'm smiling at the loyal girl sitting next to me.

She turns a little in her seat to pin the sweetest grin on me. "I got you, Mel."

She's fine as hell, no doubt, in her ruby red picnic dress and white chucks. Not skinny by any means, and I lick my lips as I study her cross her thick caramel skinned thighs. Her short curly hair makes her look like the sexier, curvier version of Betty Boop, and I had to curse myself for neglecting to cuff the kind, nerdy, baddie who'd had my back since elementary school when I had to ditch out from class to complete contracts.

It got to a point where I stopped showing altogether from sixth grade, and T's loyalty shone bright through all that. She'd often encourage me to return and complete my missing assignments without me having to ask.

She'd been the smartest girl in our grade year and obsessed with a nobody like me.

I smile at her. "I know you got me, mamacita. And you know I'm in a spot right now with the cash, but you know I got you, too, when my money start coming in a little more regular. Bet."

She chuckles, the rose blush coloring her cheeks like I expect, before responding, "Just take care of yourself. That's all I ask. I know you bout that life, so just keep doing you. Keep showing up, and making an effort."

I snort at that. "I try, you know I do. This school shit be irritating. I could be out here making money, nah mean?"

"Shut up." She hisses, swatting my leg. "It's important. How else we supposed to get out the projects if not for this?"

"I don't give a fuck about all that." I say. "Just want the money. Cash rules everything around me, for real. That's it."

She makes a face before retorting, "That's it? You know it ain't that simple. Trappin ain't the only way out."

"How you figure?"

"People work hard. Have dreams. Aspirations. Work hard to be something and make it happen. Like me: I'm serious about my art. So, I'm gonna study hard and get into a good art school far away from Camden."

I nod, considering her words and the utter emptiness inside of me. Dreams, hopes, and aspirations died at The Commander's house. At least his first one. All I'd ever been meant to do was follow his footsteps and shoot my way through the days until the very end of this wild ride called life.

"And I know you can make that happen, T. You sexy, artsy, and smart as hell. Keep it pushing, you got it. But this is the only way for me."

"Not true, Shamel." She whispers, pity in her voice that makes me uneasy. "You got options."

"Yeah?" I say dryly. "And I got a baby due to be here in a few weeks. Try that for options."

She sighed and stole a glimpse at the front where Mr. Wiggins was lecturing about historical trade and tariffs before saying sullenly, "Well, you the one that went and knocked up my big sister, Mel."

The very mention of her older sister Dawn had me thinking about our last interaction. The one where she stared at me with fear and proclaimed herself cuffed by some other nameless nigga.

"It takes two to make a baby, you know." I grit out. "Shit ain't all on me."

"Well, it's not all on Dawn either. You broke her heart you know? This has been the worst pregnancy by far. She stay in the hospital from high blood pressure and stress. You need to go easy on her."

I frowned at that. "I try to be there. All she do is holler at me, call me a deadbeat, and push me away. That shit gets tiring after hearing it every day."

A sad expression mars her pretty brown face that looks identical to her older sister's, save for the chubbier cheeks.

"Keep trying then. Don't be a pussy."

I rear back, an undeniable smile cresting my face as I watched her cheeks redden some more. "*Mamacita*, you cussing now? I must've really pissed you off."

"Shut up!" She growled playfully while hitting me again. "I mean it. Treat my sister right, or I'll beat your ass."

"Oh," I say, studying her body appreciatively. "You can beat me anytime you want to, girl…"

"Stop it!" She hissed, blushing and squirming in her seat.

"For real, girl." I say, leaning close to her ear. "Make me believe I chose the wrong sister."

Her smile faded gradually as she froze in her seat. It looked as if she was studying my face for any lingering playfulness that usually displayed there, and when she detected none, her head tilted to the side.

"Why do you do that?" She asked.

"Do what?"

"Cover up serious conversations with playboy humor." She shook her head. "It may work to distract everyone else, but not me."

My mouth opened to answer her, but no words came. I hated that she saw right through me– saw what was real and the topics I avoided.

I adjust in my seat, uncomfortable, but trying to hide that too as I answer her. "I'm good. Ain't nothing to cover up."

"Hmm." She grunts disbelievingly.

"What?" I demand.

"You know I've always liked you, right? Like I don't do all I do for you to be nice. I've been in love with you since fifth grade, and always want you to be safe. Your best self, and safe."

"T, come on man..." I whisper as I watch the loyal girl's eyes mist with unshed tears. "I like you, too."

"Never mind, Mel. Just be good to my sister, and we won't have any problems."

Did she know the status of our relationship? I wondered as I studied her crestfallen face some more. If she didn't know, then it wouldn't be me to break the news of my and Dawn's official breakup to her.

Rule Ninety: say no more than necessary. I'm reminded of The Commander in that moment, and just how his rules truly programmed my brain to trust no one. While I naturally skirted on the side of cautious, his incessant rules only heightened it to paranoia and left me totally protected, but also isolated.

Working in tandem with Si had been a major milestone for me, since I trusted no one. While that partnership was formed out of desperation, it morphed into something else. I consider my next moves as I enter the Caddy Quincy discarded into my care.

I was to meet Si at his family's meat shop in a few hours, but had to make a quick stop at the place I hadn't been in days, or so it felt.

I wanted to call the shack home, but it was so much more and less that.

I find my mother on the living room floor, her legs crossed in a pretzel style and hands touching in prayer.

Her eyes are closed when I enter, and before I get the chance to say anything she says calmly, "Quincy, babe, I've missed you."

"Wrong guy." I corrected her, and the sound of my voice must have spooked her good since she yelps when she hears me.

"Shamel, sorry son!" Her hand is holding her heart now as she rises. "I thought...I thought...never mind. How was school, darling?"

That familiar tightness forms in my chest whenever I have to interact with mom. Our tepid conversations often just left me empty, and I know it was The Commander who trained us to never reveal more than necessary, but I wished in that single moment that we were more than that. More than puppets or characters in his play to act out his will.

I cross my arms before continuing. "It's all good. You were expecting Pops to be here?"

"Yes. Well, no. I haven't seen him in weeks. I worry something happened to him." Her usual calm depletes as she goes on. "What if he's hurt?"

I flex my jaw, trying to tape down the anger before responding to her. "He's all right."

Her eyes rounded in hope. "Yeah?"

"Yep. Alive and well."

She takes my arm to guide me to the living room couch. Once we're seated, I do my best to meet the joy and hope in her eyes I'd only seen reserved for The Commander's presence.

"Go on then." She prompts.

I sigh. "Mom, this ain't what you want to hear. I barely had time to come to grips with the shit yet."

"If you know something, then I need to know it, too. Don't chat to me about knowing where he is if you don't intend on telling me."

I shook my head. "I ain't chattin nothing. I'm telling you this ain't what you want."

"He's my husband, darling!" She hissed, exasperated and desperate while shaking my arm. "I'm bare worried about him! I haven't slept in days. Even my Night Potion isn't enough to bring me rest."

"I got homework." I lie, already enlisting T's aid to complete my assignment for the next few weeks again. "We'll talk later."

I stand and walk to the staircase leading to my bedroom.

"Xavier!" She calls my middle name out in that knowing way. I hated the fucking name: it sounded like she hand-picked it from a vagina factory it's so soft and straightlaced. Nothing like Quincy groomed me to be. "Please! I'll do anything to know he's safe. Anything…"

Taking a deep breath, I turn to face her. "Mom, stop it. All right? Your tears ain't gonna make me tell it."

I lift my foot to start on the stairs when something stops me. It's Mom, her arms wrapped around my legs preventing me from moving.

"Get the fuck up, Mom. For real." I bark.

She sniffles. "I'm tired, Shamel. I can't be kept in the dark anymore. He's been gone for days."

"Mom…"

"He's my husband, son!" She cried, her little body quaking. "I need him to be safe. Need him to be with me."

"And what about us, huh?" I holler, my hand cradling the bulge in my pocket where Luci was. I needed her calm right now, more than ever, to keep from hurting my mother. Not with my hands, but with the knowledge I know she can't handle.

"Us?" She queries.

"The two kids your beloved husband left you with, I mean! Did you even care to know where I been at these past few days? Or Shay?"

"What about Shayne?" She asks quietly.

"Exactly!" I scoff, glaring down at her. "You don't even know what she been doing. Shay is never home. Never. And neither am I, but you never dig deep. All you care about is the man who left you in this abandoned shack to die. You know he said you were no better than a ho with good pussy to sell. That's what your loving husband said."

She shook her head. "You're chatting shit."

I scoffed in disgust. "The only one doing that is you, apparently. He ain't coming back."

"Don't say that!" She screamed.

"He's not!" I countered, attempting to shake her off me to no avail. "Get off me."

"I love you guys, Shamel. I love your father, too. That's how I know he wouldn't say that. He loves us, we're family."

"Nah." I say. "He loves his real wife. His second family. We just his sloppy firsts he needed to get rid of." She stays quiet, and I take that as ammo to keep firing at her. "Why ain't you tell me Uncle Rando was fake? That the twins were our brother and sister, and not our cousins?"

She remains silent, her clutch on my leg weakening and her eyes casted to the floor.

"You don't gotta look at me. You never do, and that's why we're in this mess."

"Darling..." she whispers sullenly.

"Helen is her name. That's his real wife. Legal and all. I don't know what he told you, but whatever y'all got is nowhere near legit. He lied to us."

"No..."

"Yes." I say. "Tell me. You gotta stop fooling yourself that he's all yours. That he's all about this family. Tell me her name. What's his wife's name?"

Silence.

I shook her a little with my leg she half hung on to. "Say it!"

"I'm his girl." She whispers.

I drop to my knees to shake her. Shake the sense into her I know she needed. "Say it!"

"No!" She cried.

"Stop lying like you don't know! Tell me her name!"

"Stop!"

"Tell me!"

"Please!" She screams, her face red from tears and frustration. Her voice drops a few emotional notches as she mumbles, "Helen."

"I ain't hear you." I rasp.

She gulps before repeating, "His w-wife's name is Helen."

"And you knew about the twins, didn't you? You knew all along that they were Quincy's kids and our siblings, right?"

She does a weak up and down with her head.

"What did you just say?" A voice from behind me asks slowly, and I swear under my breath.

I turn to face my big sister at the top of the steps. She's watching us with open mouth shock, much like Mike did when I confronted Quincy with the gun.

"Shay..." I gasp, not knowing what to say but knowing she heard all of it. All of the truth I'd intended on telling her in private. To break our father's lies gently to her as opposed to the fucked-up way I found out. "Did you hear any of that?"

"Mommy," Shay mumbled to our mother who's still looking at the floor. "Is...is that true?"

Mom nods again.

"Shay, wait!" I call to her retreating form. She's already disappeared by the time I race to our bedroom, escaping out the window like she usually did in the middle of the night into her own darkness.

TEN

TOMORROW

Two weeks of stealth and staking out flew by and still I'd been too much of a pussy to hone in on my target. I sank into the driver seat of the rundown caddy of Quincy's as I scanned the perimeter in the broad daylight. I had to make sure no one saw me as I squinted from my parked position across the street of the building teeming with children. Both kids and parents alike swarmed the front entrance of Forest Park Elementary

My heart did that frenzied thing in my chest as I watched and waited for my target to exit the building. It was a little past time for them to leave the building with huge grins on their faces as they met the preteen they knew as their only brother.

Instead of squeezing the trigger to my favorite girl and sniping out the target clean like usual, I chose to wait. To exercise some patience, since the twins usually came out no longer than fifteen minutes after to meet the boy waiting to escort them home.

Another three minutes ticked by with my heart palpitating, and I see them. I breathed a sigh of relief as I observed both kids burst from the front entrance to jet to the kid they adoringly greeted as, "Devin!"

He kneels with open arms to receive the antsy kids while saying, "Hey y'all. How was school today?"

"So cool!" Mike chirped, and I could see the open gap in his mouth from where his tooth fell out. "Ms. Diane let us make our own glue! Vonnie got scared because Nala rubbed some in her hair!"

"No, I didn't!" Yvonne whines as she rubs at the back of her head.

Devin smirks as he looks at her. "Really? Where did she end up getting you?"

Yvonne stayed silent, fuming as she regarded both boys.

Devin leaned over and studied the back of her head I couldn't see. "You're okay. There's not much in there that we can't wash out."

She nods, muttering something like a petulant acquiesce before Devin extends his hand to them. "Y'all know what time it is?"

Their faces glowed with excitement as they took his hands. "Ice cream time!"

Pride accompanied the misery in my heart at the new reality of things. That I'd been too cowardly to

approach them and demand a spot into the twins lives
as their rightful older bro. All these milestones I missed
out on that I could never reclaim. I also deemed this
Devin kid decent, considering the joyous glows on their
faces whenever they met their big brother during the
routine after school pick up. An unfamiliar emotion
wells up inside of me as I watch my twin targets embrace Devin with cheesy grins. An emotion I'd hadn't
a use for with my placement in the social order of my
underworld and school: jealousy. That's it. I was fucking
jealous of a thirteen-year-old kid. My fingers ache as
I squeeze the gun tight in my pocket, considering the
underworld that disallowed me from opening up and
letting in. Even if I were to approach them, there's
no guarantee they'd remember me. Or welcome me.
And hell, I didn't have much, but would give anything
to see them greet me with that same joy. However, I
was a realist amongst other things. I faced facts that in
the darkness, watching from afar, was the best place to
be if it meant I could have some place in their lives.
Experiencing life as their silent adjacent older brother.
The darkness had me, but from within these shadows
I'd do my best to keep them in the light.

So, I got familiar with their routine.

Every morning, the school bus took them to the in-
ner-city elementary school. I followed the yellow vehicle's route as it picked the twins up and dropped them
off. I'd kill time during their school hours either selling

some product or hanging out at a bar before returning to the same spot across the street to watch Devin pick them up to walk them home. He'd often walk them home or to a big blue house in the burbs that made me curious about who lived in it.

They'd be greeted by a scrawny little white dude and spend several hours inside. I went with my gut and with vibes, and even though I'd never even been inside a house that nice, I didn't suspect weird shit from the visits. Probably was just one of Devin's little friends from school, I surmised as I watched every movement and moment from the street.

As the third week passed, there was no place the twins went that I didn't know about.

Sometimes a skinny tomboy of a kid I'd only been half sure wasn't an actual boy would accompany Devin to pick the twins up from school. Her smile was always big and genuine, and I got a real good vibe from the crew as they made their descent home.

Home. The word reverberates in my head and leaves me growling my frustration at Quincy's lies. This man had two whole homes, two "wives," and two hosts of children that called him "dad." While I was nowhere near sainthood, I knew what a thing or two about honor. Honor would have made him tell us in the beginning what the truth was, instead of feed the lie to us like hungry, stupid hippos, needy for his time and care in the shadows.

Satisfied with the twins' safety, I revved the engine to begin my trip back to home. Back to Trenton and reality. After nearly putting the caddy in Drive, I stopped when I caught a look of a lean white dude walking inside the big blue house in the burbs. Devin took the twins here after school, like he occasionally did before stopping at Ma Rose's for ice creams, but this time I clock the odd-looking white guy enter the house.

I couldn't explain the cold rush that iced my veins as I observed the strange man with eyes so blue gleamed like sparkly oceans from across the street, making his devious nature crystal clear from where I sat parked on the street.

Maybe he wasn't devious, he could be an honest working man just getting in from work to relax like everyone else. But the vibes with him.... seemed off.

After he adjusts what looks to be a lab coat, he locks his car doors and heads for the back of the house. His eyes cut from side to side, as if he's breaking and entering the house instead of kicking off his shoes like he owned it.

My fingers twitch with the need to pull a trigger. I don't know this man with snake eyes, but I want to get to know him. In all the three weeks I'd followed the kids around, this man never made an appearance.

Ditching reason, I get out the car and jet across the lawn with immaculate flowers. I'm no gardener, but they look like roses and lilies, like romance and innocence swirled in one, and a pang of guilt slices me for a second for what I'm about to do: wet the flowers with his blood.

The sky was darkening at six in the evening, providing me with just enough light to creep up on this sneaky motherfucker and end him. I notice he's in the backyard messing with something. There are three large jugs in the corner labeled kerosene that he's rearranging under black tarp when I creep up behind him. I didn't know this guy, but I knew my gut, and my gut and trigger finger were a dangerous pair when on one accord. I couldn't afford to take the risk when my brother and sister were inside, and I didn't like uneasy. Anger, pride, and joy I could do. Those were straight up emotions.

Uneasiness only made me reach for Luci.

"Scream and you die." I snarled in his ear as I jabbed the gun in his neck.

His breaths came quick as he raised his hands in the air. "I'll give you money if that's what ye want. Don't kill me, my children are inside."

I frown. "Nigga, are you Scottish or something?"

"Dublin born and bred." He answers with a quavering voice. "Don't pull that trigger. I don't want my son to find me like this."

"I don't want money, and I don't give a fuck if you're Irish, Polish, or half alien." I say before wrapping a hand around his neck.

"I can get you drugs! How much you want?" He chokes out.

"No drugs." I say, my hand tightening on his neck. "Don't need that shit."

"What do ye want, then?" He gargles.

"Nothing, man. Just don't like the way you look. Why you sneaking around all creepy and shit?" I spit.

"I can't...breathe!" He cries, and I clock his face turning lobster red before releasing him.

"You know what." I say, cocking my gun and pressing it to his head. "I can't afford to risk it."

"Wait, no!"

Before I pull the trigger to my favorite girl and watch his body drop, I hear a voice from the backdoor.

"Pa!" A kid's voice calls, and I hear the light footsteps approach us then. "Pa, Michael is asking about some experiment you promised to show him. He's whining real bad about it and interrupting the video game."

A second's worth of pause passed before he whispered, "That's me son. My Kale. Please don't ruin his childhood by finding me like this."

"Shit!" I hissed, my nerves unwinding as the tension thickened in the air. The kid was getting closer, and I'd be spotted if I didn't act quick.

Without a moment's thought, I sprint through the yard and back to my car. I'm peeling out of there same as when that LC used me for target practice after I sniped his homie. I know what it looks like. Trust me.

I'm fully aware of how monstrous I seemed to murder a man in cold blood in his own garden with his kid steps away, but I made it a habit to trust my gut. My gut was telling me to get rid of the guy, and that's something I'd come back to do. He was an unfinished contract; one I'd keep an eye on for the here and now until I could dig up some more dirt on him.

For now, he's safe.

The two-and-a-half-hour drive is consumed by my incessant thoughts on Shay. I hated delivering that news to her in the same way I got it– hard and fast instead of in private like I planned. I'd been texting her for days since then to no success: she wanted nothing to do with me. I left home that same day. Si was cool enough to let me kick it at his place, a luxury apartment in Trenton I tried to sneak in and out of during the early morning and late nights to avoid the hustle-bustle of the streets.

It's been three weeks, and between stalking the twins and finishing contracts, there was little else that filled my days.

I took out my phone to tap the quick message I knew would heed no response from my sister.

> **ME**: *Hey Shay. Home safe. Homework is done. Text me when you get the chance.*

Three dancing bubbles appeared in the corner to indicate her typing her response, and I fought to conceal the excitement filling me and lost.

After another minute of dancing bubbles, they disappear altogether. No response, like usual. *Fuck.*

I take a minute to study the history of one-sided messages I sent her over the past few weeks. I can hear The Commander's words at the desperation poured through the status updates I sent to her. Since she now knew the twins' real existence to us, I tried to keep her in the loop with a few things.

> **ME**: *They go to Forest Park Elementary in D.C.. It's a couple blocks from their house.*

> **ME**: *Mike just aced his science quiz. He sounds real excited about it.*

> **ME**: *If you ever want to meet up and go see the twins together, just call me. I'm there pretty much every day to see them off.*

The last one makes me squint hard to keep the tears back.

> **ME**: *Forgive me, sis.*

Dread and pure stress eats me as I turn the key to Si's front door. An Asian girl about the same height as Yvonne sprints towards the door I'm shutting as if there's someone after her.

"*Sumi-masen*, Shame-san!" the fifteen-year-old breathed in a hurry before bowing to me. "I'm in a rush. Brother asked me to take care of his dry-cleaning long time ago, and I got lost in my personal entertainments and forgot the time."

"Yume," I said to his baby sister who'd always seemed incredibly overworked and stressed out wherever our paths crossed. "Just slow down. You'll get that taken care of in no time. You're running all through here and cleaning, cooking, and doing god-knows what else Takeo tells you to do. Do you ever sleep?"

She nods, one tight swift motion. "*Hai*. I owe Oni-sama everything. Please forgive me for running into you. I must leave you now. Are you finding your stay to your satisfaction?"

I breathed out hard, knowing I'll never get through to deprogramming his overworked sister/maid/cook/secretary. I sympathize with the girl who, just like me, was born to be somebody else's worker-bee. I never expressed this to Si, but it was an aspect of his life that I didn't like or respect.

"It's great, Yume. Thank you."

She bows again. "*Hai*. Don't hesitate to text me should you need anything at all. Good night."

"Night." I respond shortly before she bows again and leaves the apartment. Exhausted, I collapse onto the modern leather couch in the living room before raising my phone.

There's no chime to signify any unread messages, but I unlock the phone to Shay's text thread again anyway. Still nothing. Only my one-sided status updates with desperation bleeding through.

I nearly close out the screen to get ready for bed when I steal a glimpse at another text thread. I snorted when I read the message I didn't bother responding to in Angie's room. From Milio.

> **MILIO:** *10k upfront.*

The money sounded fucking phenomenal, no doubt, but solid logic and Rule Twenty-Three warns me against it. Milio was still good peoples, but I didn't hesitate to tap my clearcut response.

> **ME:** *Nah man.*

His response is quick, like usual, and despite the three-week gap in my reply.

> **MILIO:** *All good. I knew you wouldn't do it. Going another direction with this guy anyways.*

I debated pressing him for details, since I resolved myself against getting involved, but curiosity drove my fingers across the screen as I typed back.

> **ME**: *Who was the target?*

Certain there was no way in hell my ganged-up homeboy would tell me, I locked and sat the phone down. But, to my surprise, it hums instantly with his uncharacteristically quick response.

> **MILIO**: *Dude named Juan Cruz. You don't know him, and it would have been too messy a job for an inside guy like me to do. But it's all good.*

Inside guy? I queried internally as I studied the text thread. The LC's were a whole unit out in these streets, and treason was a rare sight within the ranks. I'd been gang adjacent enough to sniff out the social order of the cold killers I warned Milio against joining a few years ago, and even I knew them to be best kept as allies rather than enemies. Despite the Latin Crip I gunned down a couple years back, my standing with them was always as good as it was with Milio.

I moved to type a follow up question on the matter to see if he'd reveal a little more, but the abrupt subject change of his next text threw me off. Well, it throws me off and makes me nearly piss my pants in laughter.

I roll my eyes at the inevitable stanzas he shoots off next.

> **MILIO**: *Yo, man. Tell me what you think of this. I just cooked this up an hour ago:*
>
> *Secrets have a way*
>
> *Of ruining reality*
>
> *Secrets aren't too difficult*
>
> *Yet, not so easy*
>
> *Look into my eyes*
>
> *And find some truth there*
>
> *Because words mean little*
>
> *And compare nothing to the stare*

I threw my head back and laughed at my predictable friend and homeboy who I often pegged way too artistic to make it as a thug.

> **ME**: *Stupendous, dog. Tell that secret lover of yours I said wassup.*

MILIO: *Dickhead.*

"Good evening, Shame." Si's voice cuts in from the darkness, making me cry and jump from my seat.

"Shit, man! Make some noise or some shit when you enter a room."

He chuckled and lifted a dark brow after turning the light on. "They don't call me The Silence without reason, man."

Instead of the predictable black long johns and long-sleeved shirt he goes to bed in, I notice him in full assassin garb: a black jacket, black beater, completed with black skinny jeans and black tote bag. All of it looks typical for a contract, but I frown at him in blanket confusion.

"We got work to do?" I ask.

He shakes his head. "I do. This is Collector business. No need for your services this go round."

Though I asked, I knew exactly where he was going. I'd been able to charm the information out of his overworked teen sister, who spilled the beans on his routine flights to South Carolina. What was in the south, of all places, that demanded him to divide his time between there and Jersey was beyond me. But I ain't ask him a bunch of questions about it, just relished in the alone time his mysterious trips afforded me.

"Cool…" I agreed, nodding a bit awkwardly as he continued to stand there and stare. "You need something?"

"Sort of." He says as he adjusts the tote bag in his arms. Then he throws it at me.

"The fuck is in here?" I ask. The sack hit my stomach and knocked the wind out of me.

"Payment." He answers as I comb through the stacks of cash in the bag. Except, it's way lighter than usual.

"Where's the rest of it? Supposed to be 15k in here."

"A portion was taken out for your lodging and food. Plus, the access to Yume."

I blew out an exasperated sigh. "Access to Yume?"

He nodded. "Yes. Her services come at a fee. I outlined all this information in our temporary lease agreement, Shame. You did read it, right?"

"Oh, yeah. Of course." I lied, admittedly hating to read anything that didn't deal with underworld demon literature or dead kings.

He eyed me curiously. "Everything all right?"

"I'm good. I appreciate you for having my back through this tight spot I'm in."

He shrugs as he walks to the door. "I told you, Shame. I see me in you. A man with eyes like a dragon and the integrity to match."

"Thanks, man." I repeat.

"You're welcome to anything in the kitchen, as always. Oh, and remember to stay out of the third bedroom. No one goes in there."

"Not even Yume?"

He only glares at me, a dark and ominous energy charging the room as he clips his words out. "No one."

Grinning and mildly intrigued, I raised my hands in mock surrender. "Yes, sir."

"Takeo is fine." He says cucumber-cool.

I lean back in the chair to idly count the stacks before saying, "Nah. I'll stick with Si. I'll be here when you get back."

Two or so hours flew by with me remaining on the couch fully clothed and web surfing on my phone. That botched contract with the Irish dude had me uneasy. Still, I didn't like that gray-area feeling, so I did the thing most psychos like me did: found him on the socials.

I barely used social media, seeing as I had no use for it in the undercover work I did.

And he wasn't an easy find, but through some intuitive digging, I was able to find a picture the bony white kid tagged Devin in, which showed up on his page and enabled me to link the McAllen family together.

Clifford McAllen was a chemist and appeared to be an upstanding citizen. He was linked to volunteer groups for group homes and had a passion for children in need, at least that's what his blog said. Even though he looked every bit square and humble as apple pie, I'm reminded of the guy with honesty for a name The Commander had me put a cap in. Well, Si technically

got him, but the point was obvious: even the most innocent looking motherfuckers had bones in their closets.

His beady little eyes as he hugged the crowd of teens
for a fundraiser made me want to find him and take
him out. Now. And I'm partially sorry for taking this
guy away from his wife and son, who'd been plastered
all over his social media wall, but the twins meant
everything. Always would mean everything to a nobody
like me with shame in his name, so if these types of
preventative measures had to be taken to ensure their
safety, then—

A picture popped up as I idly scrolled down my feed
to show the worst. The thing that actually would make
me spill blood tonight on somebody's flowers if I met
it in person instead of on-screen.

The image of the girl I'd confessed to loving in
the shadows sucking face with the enemy. The
dark-skinned man with sagging clothes and purple
du-rags tied around his head and upper arm served as
identifiers for the betrayal and let me know what I'd had
to do.

Dawn. It was her pregnant belly the thug was rubbing
in the picture captioned: "And Baby Makes 4."

Her vicious words from a few weeks ago float to my
brain as I rush to put the pieces together. She said she
had a new guy, but kept him nameless. I didn't want to
believe the picture vividly painted in front of me, but
had to.

Dawn, my girl. The girl pregnant with my first child due to be here soon, was fucking with the one nigga ranked highest on my Shit List: TuFace.

Eleven

HOUSE

The vibration from my cell stunned me awake, in all honesty, but I played it off sitting upright on the couch like I hadn't been asleep. The morning light stabbed through the large square windows and dead into my eyes that felt cinched closed with grog and crust. I must have passed out after my social media dive, I figured. That was some of the best sleep I got in, hell, years. After making that resolution to kill that Irish dad tonight, it gave me the courage I needed to step out of the shadows. I meant it. Maybe it was finally time I approached my secret siblings and carve a spot into their world.

In fact, pride and confidence is buzzing in my heart as I check the text thread that had long been one-sided. I'm grinning like an idiot when I read her message:

SHAY: *Good morning.*

SHAY: *Let's meet up at Forest Park tomorrow to see the twins. Text me the address and I'll meet you there.*

"Fuck, yeah!" I growl happily before responding with the address to Forest Park Elementary School.

Perhaps God was shining down on me to afford me this tiny pleasure, this minuscule minute of forgetting to believe I wasn't the shame of my family's existence. Mommy and The Commander were no longer a part of my purpose, but maybe me, Shay, and the twins could carve our own happily ever after. Starting today. We'll approach the twins before Devin comes to pick them up and introduce ourselves. This simple task was one I'd been avoiding for weeks because it wasn't that simple. Not simple to potentially introduce a man from the underworld into the iridescent lives of angels.

I prided myself on not having that many fears, seeing as my favorite girl helped me shoot through those kinds of feelings, but this? I was scared shitless at the thought of ruining their lives.

"Shit!" I howled when I looked at the time.

It was two hours until their school dismissed, and I almost spit my disgust when I realized I overslept. No way I slept four hours over the time I usually woke up to stake out at the school. I liked to see them safely get on the school bus and into the building in the mornings, but a quick check at the time on my phone let me know I'd already fucked that up.

Why did I sleep so hard? I recalled the social media dive into the McAllen family accounts, which strengthened my resolve to kill the man with beady eyes I didn't trust, which didn't stress me out. I crashed into that pillow hard and did not awaken until midday– the worst time to be alive.

I scramble into the kitchen to grab a freshly baked muffin Yume stocked the fridge with every morning and froze as I reached to pull the fridge open.

A dried, cruddy substance caked into my fingernails. In fact, there's several splatters of the stuff on my white beater as I look down to study my front.

Dark, expired blood was all over me, I examined as I stared into the bathroom mirror after abandoning the baked good in the kitchen. It covered spots around my mouth and arms, but most noticeably were my hands. The long digits were drenched in the stuff, and I recalled that Shakespeare play I found on Si's living room bookshelf that kept me company after returning home from assignments. The one where the lady's hands are covered in blood. She's freaking out about it, but instead of crying, I frown to put the puzzle together. I'd intentionally worn a white shirt yesterday to force me to keep my hands clean, to not shoot anyone and make a mess, but...

Then it all comes back. All of it.

The gory scene that took place after finding Dawn on the socials all hugged up with that 8Road motherfucker. My mind is racing as I speed down the highway to D.C. to make sure I'm not late for my rendezvous with Shay or approach to the twins. This was supposed to be the day that gave me pride. The first step our new family would take in becoming whole. I make the drive in nearly half the time since I stomped the gas and hiked it up to nearly a hundred on the freeway and off the turnpike.

Forest Park Elementary was just down the street, and I cut off a few families as I waded through the line of parked cars to find my usually empty one spot across the street.

It was nearly time for the twins to come out, and I waited anxiously as I checked my face in the rearview mirror to make sure I'd scrubbed all the blood off from the shower I took previously that existed more as a birdbath. I needed this to go perfect, I thought, I needed this to be right. I scour the row of parked cars in search of Shay's tall frame. There's no one, and I'm panicking a bit as the minutes tick by and kids start piling out the school.

My mind drifts again to the bloodbath of last night, and I have to resist the urge to punch myself at expending unnecessary energy. I overslept because of all that rage that led me to 8Road territory last night. I wouldn't usually be foolish enough to cruise into gang territory to take out the dude who'd I heard become co-leader, but he'd dissed me too many times to let this go by unpunished. First he stole from my father, crept around with my big sis, and now this? Fucking around with babymoms wasn't exactly a crime, but fucking with mine? The dude with enough shame in his name and hell in his soul to put a slug in you without blinking? Bad business on his part.

By fucking around with Dawn, my girl, he made it personal. Combine that rage with the missed opportunity of shooting that Irish fucker from earlier proved motive enough to cruise over into 8Road territory in search of TuFace.

Seeing no sign of him last night, I drove to the only place I knew he'd be in the middle of night, since I was no stranger to sneaking into her room around those hours myself: Dawn's house.

It takes about an hour or so before I catch the tall banger exit the house. Before he's fully out, he turns and bends low to place a kiss on the waiting girl's mouth. *My* girl.

Red and black coats my vision as I sneak out the car and tiptoe to the front porch.

I don't look as I reach around the side and unload the silent clip into the dude from behind. From the screams and groans of pain accompanying the blood on my arms, I know Luci hit her mark.

I blacked out shortly after that, and found myself waking up much too late on Si's couch.

And now I was here.

Nervous I'd fucked this interaction up because I'd been too dumb to set an alarm.

Where the fuck was Shay? I couldn't help the question as I got out of the car. I stayed in the shadows until I was sure Shay would show, but as I hear the jubilant voice from Mike across the street, I know I'll have to do this solo or not at all.

I sent off two text messages to her asking where she'd been and if she was fucking kidding me, before taking a deep breath. I had to do this, now or never, or be forever in the dark of their lives.

"Mommy!" Mike chirped before I had the chance to place my foot on the street.

I frowned at his greeting, and squinted from my placement to see the same pretty lady in the picture, or Helen, waiting impatiently for the twins outside the school. Her hair was wrapped in a bonnet and her clothes looked more like pajamas, judging from the worn Care Bare top and bottoms and bedroom slippers. Her ratchet attire wasn't what brought me alarm; however, it was the look on the kids' faces as they walked up to the woman who didn't normally come to collect them.

"Where's Devin?" Mike asked the question I'd wondered inwardly. Yvonne looked terrified, but stayed silent.

"Y'all ready to go?" She asked, ignoring him and turning to set off down the street.

"But Mommy!" Mike complains as he follows her. "Devin usually picks us up. Why are you—"

"Shut the fuck up!" She snaps, and my hand immediately flies to my gun as I watch her disrespect my little brother some more. "No fucking questions. Now, let's go."

My phone vibrates in my hand as I take my gun out. I'm torn between approaching the trio, putting a slug in the bitch's leg, and taking the kids with me, or just tailing them. The traumatized look in Mike's eyes as I held our father at gunpoint floats back, bringing me pause. Deciding to tail them, I reenter my car. I didn't like this bitch, nor did I trust this bitch, so keeping an eye on them to make sure she stayed homeward bound seemed the best action to prevent that terror in the kids' eyes. I don't want to hurt or confuse them more than they were, but seeing that look in their eyes as they trudged behind their mother gave me chills as I started the engine.

My phone vibrates again, and I curse impatiently as I study the screen. Two text messages from Si, and in the middle of the evening. I knew what this meant. An assignment I'd been too broke to turn down.

SILENCE: *I found Monty. Bring the mop.*

Monty was the fat exec's son. Eugene was his name, and I also remembered Si telling me how high a contract he'd been out for since being on the Kobayashi's Most Wanted list. If Si found Monty, then it meant a whole lotta cash for me to get the job done. Long story long, I had to be there. But...

Hating the idea of turning this huge sum of money down, I text him back.

ME: *Can't. Busy.*

Instead of the typed response I expect, Si ends up calling me.

"Shame," he says, his tone flat, "Listen, come meet me at the Dirty Kitten Club in Atlantic City. I found Monty."

I grunted. "You told me, I know. But, listen man, I can't this time. I know this is worth a lot of bread, but you gonna have to do this without–"

"You need to be here. Trust me. This is urgent. Meet me as soon as you can and bring as many weapons as you can carry. He may have a crew with him." Si didn't usually ask twice, and I'd never heard that small amount of panic laced into anything he'd ever said, so, hating every shred of myself, I replied with the inevitable.

"All right. GPS says I'll be there in three hours."

"Three hours? Where are you?"

"I'll explain when I get there."

A pause, then. "Shame, are you in D.C.?"

Pissed, I spit, "Nigga, I'll tell you when I get—"

The round of gun shots popping into my car makes me drop the phone and duck under the seat. I hear people outside screaming and teachers beckoning their kids back inside the building for fear of getting hit with the shots that were clearly intended for me.

The shots pause for a minute, that gives me the time to sit up and look around for their origin.

And then I see him. *Him.* But maybe he's a ghost, since I clearly recalled shooting him to death the night before. His distinct limp makes him obvious as he runs towards my car with the AK in his hands.

"You mad because I'm fucking your girl, Shame?!" TuFace hollers as he limp-runs towards me. "So, you came for a war? I'll give you a war son of a bitch!"

More shots.

"You shot at me and my girl– pussy! I'm coming for your ass once and for all."

More shots.

"Be careful who you texting all your business to. You never know who's watching, pathetic mother–"

Deranged laughter follows the next shots and my blood chills at those last words.

Before he can blast off another round of shots, I peel out of there, my mind respawning a grim history as I feel the burn of another gunshot wound in my shoulder this time.

Fuck, fuck, fuck! I scream inwardly and drive like a speed demon down the highway from which I came.

***

After a quick stop by Remy's to load up on a few choice heavy machinery, I'm soon making the short drive from South Camden to the city of lights, where our apparent target was living in secret under the identity of Charles Monticello. I'm not familiar with all the semantics on the deal gone bad between him and the Kobayashi's, but it must be something serious enough to go to war. This was more than a deployment, I thought as I entered Atlantic City and the sun disappeared in the sky. I had to pay Remy double the usual price to rent the ten guns, since it was a last-minute rush order, he emphasized, but it isn't the jacked-up prices that make my heart beat wildly in my chest as I stop into the parking lot of the Dirty Kitten Club.

It's TuFace. Or, rather, how he knew I'd be at that specific spot across the street from the school. My mind churns over and over on the details, of the only few possibilities that allowed him to be privy to this information that make me physically sick. All of them involve one person at the center I'd need to shake some sense into: Shay.

It could have only been her at the center, and the reason behind the new gunshot wound on my shoulder I was an expert at cleaning and bandaging now to make sure the blood didn't spill out too bad. Miss Pat taught me that, and I'm grateful to her for the skills, but seething at the prospect of Shay's betrayal.

She was still seeing TuFace after I warned her to stay away. After The Commander threatened both their lives if he ever saw the two in the same vicinity again, but she wouldn't listen.

In my world, there was only one way we dealt with traitors, and suddenly the bullet hole in me feels more like a mosquito bite compared to the ache in my chest at Shay's betrayal. How could she? How *fucking* could she?

"Whoa, little man." The meaty bouncer three times my size cautions me as I walk up to the front door of the strip club. "Need to see ID if you wanna get in."

"I'm old enough." I grumble, pushing past him to no avail and running into his chest. "Out the way, man. You tryna dance or something?"

He huffed and scanned the perimeter before saying, "No ID, no entry."

"Yo," I start, "I'm looking for somebody. I'll be real quick."

Out of nowhere, he places his burly hands into my chest and shoves me backwards into the street. Thank fuck there were no cars whizzing by or that would have been the end of me.

I'm losing the battle for sanity, I feel it, see it slip past me in whisps into the darkening sky as I adjust myself and stalk back to the entrance. This fucker wanted to dance, it seemed, so maybe the Salsa was best. Luci was a great orchestrator, and I looked forward to the shakes and jerks coming from the big guy as I pumped a few bullets into him.

Reaching for my gun, I prepare to make him Salsa before a voice comes through from inside the club.

"Coffee, he's cool." Si says to the bouncer when he comes into view from within the dark club. "He's with me."

"This kid?" Punk ass Coffee asks The Silence.

Si nods once, and that's all it takes before Coffee moves aside to allow me in. We're glowering at each other as I walk in and Si claps my shoulder as he guides me through the dark club. The trap music inside vibrates the walls and my teeth chatter as we walk by one of the large speakers in the room. The only light in the joint is spotlighted on the dance floor, where a thin athletic girl with a highlighter yellow wig is swinging on the pole. She doesn't have the large ass or tits expected of a dancer at these clubs, but she's straight up mesmer-izing, to say the least. Her body twisted like a work of art around the steel pole, and my jaw fell slack as she did a move that mimicked a walk on water thing. To put it simply, she was the closest to Wonder Woman, seeing as she straight up did magic flying around the pole.

Her body hit the ground in a finishing split that brought a standing ovation from the crowd.

"Can't nobody tell a lie with the serum Ms. Truth be doling out!" The announcer jeered through the speak-ers.

Men everywhere shot to their feet and threw cash at the woman smiling bright at the pole. "Give it up for The Truth, y'all!"

"The Truth?" I asked unintentionally out loud.

Si led us to a vacant table in an empty corner of the club. From this vantage point, we disappeared in the dark room filled with smoke and high ballers spending it all on the women working the room.

"What?" Si asked as he followed my line of sight to the dance floor. "Ah, yes. That's one of the resident dancers here. She's called The Truth. Very popular with the regulars."

I frowned at him. "Why you know all the particulars about her identity? You come here often?"

He shrugs. "Not really. It's just my job to know all the players in the business I'm in. Regardless if they know me back, or not."

I nodded, unable to disagree with that, but still curious about the yellow-haired baddie on the floor. Even though I'm riled up from the events of the day, her athletic twists and spins that display flashes of her nipples and pussy make me hard instantly.

"Why are we here man?" I asked, desperate to get my mind and eyes off the fine ass girl leaving the floor.

He bit his lip before starting. "I wanted to warn you before I took you to the back. Monty is in what they refer to as the Champagne Room, a room that allows for a high-end experience for men willing to spend large amounts of money. It's about a thousand every half hour to take the dancer of their choice back there for a private dance."

I blink a few times, wondering if there was a point he'd get to before blurting, "I know how a Champagne Room works. I've been to dozens of them. Should be an easy kill then, right?"

He pursed his lips, silent in his usual way.

"Si," I yell over the music, "let's go. Let's get this money. Why we over here waiting?"

"Follow me." He says, a sour look on his face before standing.

A pit forms in my gut as I follow him through the crowds of men to the back. I clock the identical bartenders, one with gold-ish hair and the other with purple, as we make it past the drunk and rowdy crowd. They're gorgeous, I note, as we make it to the door of the Champaign Room, but nowhere near as majestic as The Truth. I'd resolved myself in obtaining her number after this assignment ended.

"He's in there." Si said, avoiding my eyes. "You did bring the guns, right?"

I patted the duffel on my back loaded to the gills with the heavy artillery that set me back a few paychecks. "Yep. What's the strategy?"

His eyes do that avoidant thing again before he says, "This will not be a pretty sight, my friend. I need you to look through the curtain before we make our move."

"Why?" I demanded. "Let's just cap this dude and be done with it. I got shit to do."

He nods before pulling the curtain open, "Just take a look. We can't strategize until you see this."

I tsk before peering through the door curtain that provided a clear view of the Champagne Room. From inside, the tall dancer with even brown skin and curls falling down her back can be seen riding the white guy on the sofa. In all honesty, it's pretty hot, and I watch with avid curiosity as the woman gyrates her hips on top of the thin guy with the tailored suit on.

The purple lights don't detract from the view either, and her big round ass claps on top of his naked lap that exposes his tiny pink dick.

The dancer's moans are so loud they make me feel a bit dirty as I watch the semi-public scene, and it takes me a minute to realize the pair are engaging in actual intercourse. In other words, he was fucking the shit outta the stripper with the huge ass and tits, and she sounded like she was enjoying it.

"What's the point of–" I begin to ask Si about the significance of watching this scene ripped right out of a cheesy porno, but pause when the woman turns around on the man's lap. Her face is on full view just as her ass previously was and my entire body heats with a fury I'm afraid will actually melt my insides.

"Is that–"

"Yes." Si answers. "I didn't know a better way to tell you. So, now you see Monty in there for yourself, we can strategize how to best do this without harming your—"

"Shay!" I bellow while kicking the door. It opens without much give, allowing me to force my way through and aim my gun at the skinny white idiot beneath her lap.

Si remains at the door, keeping watch.

"Mel?" She screams in horror while scrambling off Monty and covering herself with his discarded suit jacket. "What the *fuck* are you doing here? And with a gun?"

I alternate the gun between our intended target and my sister, my brain mushing into nothingness at the horrifying sight of Shay in the nude.

"Are you stupid or something?" She screeches again. "Get that gun off me! And get out!"

"Shay," I sputter stupidly as I numbly follow her demand to lower the gun.

"Who the fuck are you?" Monty, in all his elusive glory, shouts, but he's not exactly panicked by the sight of my gun at his face. He just looks annoyed at my barging in. "You trying to get a turn with the whore? Well, wait your fuckin turn. This dance is on my dime."

I flex my jaw in raw aggravation before re-aiming the gun at his face. "Ten."

"What's he doing?" Monty asks Shay, who's cowering in the corner with the thin piece of material covering her body.

"Nine." I add, sweating and glaring at the naked fuck who had the nerve to touch my sister.

"Get that thing away from me, kid. You won't like what my security will do to you if I have to call them in here."

As if on cue, the loud *fwop* of a weight dropping to the floor sounded from behind me. I don't need to turn around to gather the details, since Si was on door duty and damn good at it.

"You mean, this security?" Si asks plainly, stepping over the muscled white dude dressed in a lethal black suit as he enters the room. "He went quickly."

Blood pools around the body and I step a few feet left to avoid the blood stains on my new Nikes.

"Kobayashi?" Monty's cool demeanor fades instantly at the sight of my lethal co-killer. I can literally see the sweat gather on his forehead and mix in with the tears falling in fat drops down his face. "What the hell are you doing here?"

"You're wondering how I found you, correct?" He asks, sucking up all the power in the room from the teeth-chattering fugitive.

"I told You People I had nothing to do with the disappearance of that last shipment. If you want answers, find my dad."

Si's face was immovable ice as he ran a hand through his curls. "Eugene was an honorable man. His loyalties were merely in the wrong place."

"Was?" Monty asks in a weak whisper with his hands in the air. "What did you do, you monster!"

Si shrugged. "Your father went quickly as well. After the three hours of torture to get him to cough up the information to locate you. He fought to the very end. I want you to know that."

"No!" He whined, and I clocked his hand slowly gravitating to his right pocket.

"Sorry, Shay." I grumble before blasting a silent bullet through his right hand.

"Stop this!" Shay screamed alongside Monty's strangled groans of pain. "Mel...why?"

She stood to take tentative, cautious, steps towards me and my aimed position at the white dude who'd been fucking her earlier. Flashes of memory assailed me then, my mind conjuring up TuFace firing his AK at my car, in the same vicinity of the twins' school, and that ugly anger rears back up.

"Yo, sit down." I snarled.

She took another step. "Mel, just listen to me okay? Put the gun—"

I aimed the Colt Action at her forehead and trembled with the indecision to pull the trigger.

"I said sit the fuck down! And that ain't my name, you back-stabbin ass bitch!" I hurl the words at her from somewhere deep and dark in me, a reservoir I'm not used to tapping into when regarding her.

"I stabbed *you* in the back?!" She asks.

"Hell yeah you did."

"Says the guy who kept the truth from me after all this time about Quincy and the twins? Or the guy who busted up in here pointing a gun at my head?"

Fed up, I fired a round into the wall beside her. The bullet barely missed her and I lowkey relished in her terrified squeal and jerk.

"Okay, okay." She cries before resuming her seat on the couch. "I'm sorry, Shame."

"Your name...is Shame?" Monty asks skeptically as he watches my and Shay's exchange.

I leap over to the man to close the distance between us, shoving the barrel of my gun down his throat.

"I go by all kinds of names. Shame is one of them. I also go by Violence...want to see why? Huh? You wanna try a little of Shame or a little Violence? Take your pick!"

He grumbles and chokes around the metal in his mouth.

"That's what I thought. Butt the fuck out before this end up being your last conversation."

"Shame." Si says. "Not yet. I got a few questions for him."

I glare all the hatred surging though me into the man's blue eyes before pulling back and spitting on him. "Yeah, all right. Call my sister a whore again and lose your other hand."

"I'm sorry!" He whimpers in agony and fear on the couch before Si approaches him.

"This will all end quickly if you just tell me where you sold it. My family entrusted you with a large shipment of narcotics. The sooner you tell me who the buyer was, the better."

"I can't, man." He cries, wiping his tears with shaky, bloody fingers. "They'll kill my entire family if they knew I told you."

"Is that so?" Si asked matter-of-fact.

"Yes!" Monty bleated in desperation. "You under-stand, right?"

Si leaned real close to him, close enough their lips nearly touched and said, "If you don't tell me, then I'll be sure your wife and daughters go as quickly as your dear father. That's not a threat, Monty. It's a promise."

"Okay, okay." Monty blubbered, snot oozing down his face just as profusely as the blood pouring from his hand.

"LSD?" A female's voice carried from the hall as a pair of footsteps neared the room.

"Jerica, don't come in here!" Shay pleaded in a strangled voice, leaping to her feet.

I aimed Luci right back at her.

"Sit." I growled.

Her tortured, betrayed eyes bounced between me and the door as she obeyed and flopped to the chair.

"Girl, time is up!" the voice added in amusement before she stood at the threshold. "Calico, been flashed the Red Light to signal your time was done in here—oh."

Her words dropped when she glimpsed the room filled with a crying Monty, scared Shay, and well, violent us. Si and me were technically the odd ones out with the all-black attire and guns in our hands.

"You got my girl in here, sir." The woman who I haven't fully turned to look at says to me. "I'mma need y'all to pay Coffee at the door and leave." Nobody moves. If anything, the room gets even more tense before she crosses her arms and re-emphasizes, "Now!"

"Bitch, get in here." I bark at her before turning and finally seeing her.

My entire body freezes as I study the majestic, yellow-haired woman from the pole. She's dressed only in a black sequined bra and thongs with tall heels to match. Her eyes are round, yet squinted in fury as she regards me.

"Who you calling a bitch?" She demands indignantly.

"Do I need to shoot this ho to send a message?" I asked my sister. "Does she not understand I'm holding a gun?"

"All due respect, sir." She says, walking up to me until her forehead touches the end of the barrel. "This toy piece doesn't scare me."

"Oh, yeah?" I breathe, the entire interaction on the verge of hardening my dick to steel in my pants.

Her eyes hooded as she nodded against the nozzle. "Gets me wet, though."

I winced in complete confusion. "Say what?"

"I said." She said, gripping the shaft of the weapon and stroking it, simulating the action I'd been daydreaming about between her and my dick the second I saw her. "Guns get me wet. I like my orgasms with a side of violence, for max pleasure. Now, why don't you let my girl go and allow me to give you what you need."

"What's that?" I croak, like an idiot as my eyes pinned into hers while she rubbed her titties against my chest. The action shot dizzying sensations through my body that nearly had me vibrating to bend her over.

She leans up on the tip of her toes before placing a quick kiss on my lips. "The Truth."

"Jerica!" Shay hisses, reviving the people in the room who momentarily died to me a couple minutes ago.

"Get away from him. He got a gun. Just get out of here while you can."

She snapped out of the trance that previously ensured me when I looked into her eyes to turn to Shay. "Girl, I'm trying to save your ass!"

"Can somebody get a medic?" Monty begged.

Si punched Monty in the face. "Tell me where it is!"

Before I knew it, raucous chatter filled the room between Shay and Jerica's back-and-forth, Monty's cries, and Si's threats getting louder, which was way out of character for the lethal Collector dubbed The Silence.

All of it added to the pandemonium cycling inside my head. I wanted it all to stop. Everyone to shut the fuck up so I can go home and curl into a ball. My head pounded as I aimed the gun at the ceiling and fired.

"Everybody shut the fuck up!" I threatened before an eerie quiet befell the dark room. "All of y'all, come with me."

"What?" Someone asked, I wasn't sure who since it was a collective question I didn't care to answer as I sheathed my gun and exited the room.

I lead the group to my car and usher them inside.

Right before Jerica gets in, she stops to stare into my eyes.

"You got something to say?" I say.

She shook her head. "You're Shay's brother, huh?"

"Nunya business. Now get in the car before I put a bullet in you."

A knowing, arrogant, smile crooks her lips before she does it again. Before I can act, she reaches up and plasters another warm kiss to my lips that sends me back to that trance-like state. I wrapped my arms around her to deepen the kiss, wanting more of the comfort it filled me with amidst the storm cloud of my mental. I wanted more. Needed more. Had to have the yellow-haired Wonder Woman flying through the air just as she flew into my mind and left her truth serum behind.

"I won't tell your secret, okay?" She whispers as we parted.

"All right." I agreed in a daze.

She begins her walk back to the club and I'm left to ogle her juicy ass and hips as she walks away.

"What's your name?" She asks, pausing midway and staring at me.

"Shame." I grunt, uncomfortable and antsy with the groaning captive in my ride.

"Nah," she refutes. "Your real name."

"That's one truth you ain't getting out of me." I answered gruffly.

"Okay." She replies, resuming her walk to the club. "Well, don't hurt my friend, Shay's Brother, and we won't have any problems. And don't worry– I'll tell Calico some random thugs fucked up her Champaign Room."

Despite the rage in my heart, I chuckle wryly. "Sound a whole lot like us."

"Good night, Shay's Brother." She calls with an amused finality, sending a lingering look into the passenger seat where my sister sat before reentering the club.

"Where you want me to drop Monty off to finish the job?" I asked while we ate up the highway in my caddy.

Monty still whimpered in the backseat, where Si sat beside him with a beretta pressed to his temple.

"Let's go to the shop. I've already texted Yume to leave the back gates unlocked." He said.

"Word up." I respond, my hands gripping the shot-up caddy that's taken one too many bullets.

The forty-minute drive is made in near silence as we enter Pollock Town where the Kobayashi's meat shop was.

Shay's eyes slide over to me before she utters, "What did I ever do to deserve this, Mel?"

I allow the answering silence to stretch between us for a moment before saying anything.

"You see these holes in my whip?" I gesture toward the shot-up windshield, where she directs her gaze.

"I thought you didn't want to talk about them?"

"Nah, I don't. But those are new holes. New shots in my already shot-up ride. From your mans."

She frowned. "My mans?"

"Come on, now." I chuckled darkly. "Don't do this."

"Do what?"

"Play me like I'm an idiot, Shay. I'm not stupid."

"What are you talking about?"

"Still playing dumb, huh?"

"I literally don't know what—"

"Forest Park Elementary." I spit, ramping up again and trying in earnest to focus on the road. "I texted you to meet me at the twins' school today. And you know who showed up instead? With an AK fully loaded and firing off at me, spouting some shit about me being careful who I text my business to."

Shay is deathly silent. A level of quiet the normally sing-songy girl just never is, but I keep going despite the tears threatening to fall from her evident admission of betrayal.

"I never wanted to shoot somebody as bad as I want to do right now." I grit out.

"Mel…" She whispers, futile and small and reaching for my arm.

"Shut it." I growl, shrugging her off. "I don't trust what I'd do with this gun or this car if you try to calm me down. I told you to stay away from TuFace. You knew he wanted me dead, and you…and you…"

I couldn't even utter the words my heart still didn't believe.

I didn't want to believe the girl who kissed all my boo-boos and mothered me best when our own mother chased after a commander who made her second place. Until now, she'd been the one of the few people I lived and would die for to protect.

"I didn't know." Shay breathed, ugly crying and shaking all over in her skimpy two piece. "Please believe me. I didn't know he would do that to you. I swear this on my life."

"Your life, huh?" I croak around the lump of emotion in my throat. "Good to know."

"What does that mean?" She whimpers in the same pathetic tone as Monty before I park the car at the loading gates behind the meat shop.

I don't answer as I usher Si and Monty out of the car.

"Stay here." I tell Shay before grabbing the opposite side of our target.

Si and I drag him into the open gates where there's already a chair in the middle of the room. The only other thing inside the empty loading bay is a tiny, ancient, fat back television sitting on a cooler. The TV was used for the loaders whenever they had large shipments that demanded them to work extra hours unloading freights of meat and narcotics. The picture was grainy, but from my position I could see the evening news was playing.

"I'm so tired." Monty breathed as we threw him into the chair. "Let me go home, guys."

"You know the deal." Si says before brandishing his Beretta. "Tell us about the buyers or we resume the countdown."

"So tired." He slurs his eyes rolling to the back of his head a bit.

"Hey, man!" I say, shaking him a bit. "Spill it. Don't you die on us."

"Tired…" He slurs again, his head lolling to the side before he goes eerily still. Blood poured from his hand that lay limp at his side now.

"Fuck, no, no, no!" Si spits frantically while shaking the guy. But it's no use. He's as dead as I felt inside and soon to push up daisies after Si's cleanup crew got to him.

"No!" Si hollers his frustration. "Why did you shoot him, Shame?"

I rear back, flabbergasted and pissed at the accusatory tone he was taking. "Say what? Nigga, I was helping you out in there."

"No, you didn't!" He grunted. "You got emotional after he called your sister a whore. You lost your mind, like always, and got trigger happy before I gave the sign to shoot."

I wiped the sweat from my forehead before squaring off with the arrogant dickhead. "I did my job, man. Nothing more, nothing less. Give me some credit."

"Credit?" He says with a smile that creeps me out before pulling out his gun. "Here's some credit for you."

I aimed my gun right back at him as we circled each other. "Now, you're thinking what I'm thinking. Ain't nothing emotional about this shit man. It's business. And you better pay what you owe me after this contract. I did my part."

"But not at the right time! The timing was piss-poor and now I'll be paying for this. We'll both pay for this. The Kobayashi's are a relentless clan to return to empty handed."

"I know that!" I bark.

"Then what do you suggest I do, Shame? Tell me. Tell me. Tell me!" He screams, his entire face reddening as he inches closer with the gun.

Several things happen that make my heart completely stop and my mind numb. It's not the threat of danger as Si holds the gun to my face that makes me nearly faint.

It's the newscaster's voice on the ancient TV.

Rain strikes through the clouds and falls in buckets as I listen to the horror of my actions that make me want to die.

"Deadly scene today as investigators work to understand the senseless shooting of a teen mother at 22 E. Windsor St. The shooting appeared to have taken place in the early morning hours between three and four a.m., where neighbors said to have seen an African American male flee the scene in a brown Cadillac. If you have any information in connection to this shooting, then contact Camden City Police at..."

Her words trailed off as the reality of what I'd done weighs on me.

It's Dawn's address.

My brown Cadillac.

My misaimed bullets fired in the dark.

Her blood on my hands.

I sink to my knees as I watch the EMT haul Dawn's motionless body onto a stretcher, her swollen belly protruding through the white sheet covering her body as several cops line the streets.

Before my mind shuts down and pure darkness clouds my vision, the sound of an engine revving in the distance rings in my ears as I succumb to the shame.

Twelve

DESSERT

I wrapped trembling lips around the barrel of my most coveted possession and favorite girl as the tears fell in waves down my face. Closing my eyes tight and praying to however many sky authorities in charge of fate and justice to let the next shot be the real one. The final one meant to sever all ties and fling me to the fiery realm I deserved. Despite Si and Quincy's jaded accusations on my mental state, I wasn't an emotional motherfucker by any means. I knew logic. I knew reason. But I also know those two values meant shit if they weren't exercised when needed. I lost my mind, truly, and I can barely find an excuse to prevent my next actions. The ones that would completely cleanse the streets from a breathing piece of patheticness like me.

I took a long swig of the cheap brown liquor I found in The Commander's stash, eying the chunk of metal that usually brought me joy. There's no joy right now and there hasn't been the past week I've been holed up in my old bedroom.

I committed the one act deserving of a man meant for hell. And not the metaphorical underworld I rightfully named as the gritty streets that bred me.

My eyes cinched closed as I allowed the images to flash like a major motion picture in my mind. I had to dig through the numbness to recall her screams as I fired blindly at her front door.

I intentionally placed one bullet in the chamber, shooting a silent prayer with my loud cries to eject the fatal shot through my skull.

I hear her screams again and recall the dried crust in my nails the following morning. It's not TuFace's blood, like I artfully intended that night when I drove to her place, but it's hers. *Her* blood in my nails, on my hands, and in my dreams.

I pull the trigger, and...nothing.

"Fuck!" I howl, a muffled sound due to the gun in my mouth. Biting down on the barrel, I roar my anguish at my own failures.

Deep down I knew I was the reason Quincy dropped us like yesterday's news. I was the shame of his existence. Of my mother's dreams, and the thing that kept the horror etched on the faces of my three siblings. I knew how to load a gun, but had no clue how to atone for what I did. It was always an eye-for-an-eye in this underworld where betrayal got you eighty-sixed, so I closed my eyes again as I put the naked gun in my throat. Hit the mark, god dammit, I prayed before pulling the trigger a third time.

"Shamel!" My mother's angry voice penetrated the dark room I hadn't left in days since the botched contract at the Dirty Kitten Club.

"Get out!" I slurred before throwing the nearly empty bourbon bottle at her.

She dodged it and charged towards me.

"Give...me...*this!*" She said as we wrestled for the gun in my hand.

I had the advantage of height over her, but barely, seeing as she stood only an inch or two shorter than my six-foot two stature. Her other advantage was weight and sobriety, considering the little effort it took to snatch the gun away and toss me to the bed.

"Just get out!" I'm still slurring as more red clouds my vision. I keep hearing the screams of my dead baby-moms. Kept hearing her mother's cries on the news the day it happened.

"Shamel, you've been in here for days." My mom spoke from...somewhere, I wasn't sure. My eyes are trained on the ceiling as I lay in a dejected heap on the unmade bed. "Come on, it's time to get up."

"No." I grunt and yank free from her clasp on my arm.

"Darling, please." She begged, pulling again.

I resisted. "Where's my drink?"

"Your drink?"

"It'sssoverthere." I slurred while pointing to the half empty bottle on the floor. "Hand it over."

She reared back, her arms crossed over her chest in disgust. "No! You shouldn't be drinking. Please get up and have a shower, love. This isn't good for you. Ever since you returned home you've been worse than ever. And now Shay won't answer any of my calls or messages..."

"I don't care." I didn't realize my mouth had been moving to allow the words past, but that was truth.

She sits beside me on the disheveled bed. "I know, darling. And it's all right. I've been doing a lot of thinking since you were away. I deserve whatever animosity you feel towards me. It's been me that's been failing you both so terribly."

"I don't care."

She continues, a sad smile on her face. "It's all right, love. I promise to do better by you. Just please let me try. Okay?"

"I don't...care."

"Shamel," Her voice breaks. "Where did you get that weapon?"

I retrain my eyes towards the crusty ceiling of my bedroom. I was home. Back at the shack my small family shared and my mother was talking to me. I had to remind myself of reality every so often since my mind had been playing tricks on me with time. I keep hearing her. Her screams. Feeling her blood splash on me. It's still on me. All over my face, hands, and arms and I can't breathe.

"Look at me, darling." She grabs me and pulls me upright into her arms. She's warm. "Calm down! Slow your breathing and meditate with me."

I shook my head as my body continued to thrash from the visions of her blood on me. And the screams. Her mother's screams. And the baby I'll never get the chance to—

"Hmm." She hums, a soothing noise I recognize before she whispers. "Tell mummy what happened. I'll fix it. Just tell me, my love."

"I..." I say, my words dying in my throat as I thrash in her arms.

"Whatever it is you done, it's all right. It's all right! Mummy's here..." She crooned as she rocked my body into a calm state.

"Don't care." I choke out.

"Hmmm." She hums again in that sad sing-song way that Shay does when she thinks no one's watching. "I know."

I feel the tears fall as the rain begins to pound my window. The vibration from the thunder rocks my chest and I clench my fists. I needed to end this. Now, before any more of these useless tears could betray my resolve to end it all and atone.

"Gun." I say.

She shakes her head, still rocking me. "No, gun, darling. When you're ready, tell mummy what's ailing you."

"I don't care!" I fume, resuming my thrash and jerk in her arms.

She doesn't budge. "No! I won't let you harm yourself. I won't lose you again, just please—"

"Dawn!" I shout for her. I reach for her. But it isn't her. Not the girl who looked at me with so much trust in her eyes and love in her soul. All that love was for me, but I fucked it up. I kept her in the dark when I should have forced her into the light. I didn't know what life in the light looked like, but I would've tried it all for her.

I hear her screams again. All around me. Just like the blood that starts on my hands then crawls up my arms.

"Dawn?" Mom asks.

"She's gone!" I wail. "All my fault. Need to..."

"Need to what?"

"I need..."

"What, dearest?"

"To die. Take her place...and my baby."

"Your baby?"

"Yeah." I mutter, stilling and fighting to quiet the screams in my head. "I killed her. With that gun. So...I gotta take her place, Ma. Don't you get it?"

More tears fall down her face, but she nods. "Okay, love. I see. Her name was Dawn?"

I nodded.

"All right. And you...killed her? The cops been 'round here asking about that young girl who was shot last week...and you did this? I thought them mad for coming 'round here, but..."

She does some mental math, piecing together the puzzle from the bits of the story she'd probably heard from the news and my admission.

"I...shot her. But I ain't mean to. I swear to God I ain't mean to."

Her face stiffens and jaw flexes with an unknown emotion. She places a kiss on my forehead before heading to the door.

"Ma?"

Her back to me, she says, "I'll get this sorted. All right?"

"How you gonna get—"

"Just stay upstairs, no matter what, all right?"

She bends to collect the strewn gun and remaining bottles of liquor before exiting the room and leaving me in confusion.

A few hours pass, and I know that because I'm waking up with the worst headache of my life. The room is even darker since it's nighttime, and I scan the small room in search of Shay. But like usual, she's gone. All that's left in her wake is her neatly made bed and a few clothes in her hamper. It's a stark difference from the state of my side of the room with empty food plates and liquor bottles, but I don't harp on it due to the pounding in my head.

It's as if the world didn't exist before a couple of minutes ago, and I'm fighting hard to remember the events from before I fell asleep.

Then I remember.

The gun. The Russian Roulette. The screams. My mom and her promise to take care of things after I spilled my deadly secret to her.

"You are the lowest piece of rubbish that's ever existed, you burly weasel of a man, you!" I hear a woman's voice yell, and it takes me a minute to gather that those words came from my mother.

I frown as I lean forward to listen to the tongue lashing she's doling out to...I have zero clue who she's talking to. But in a split second that's difficult to rationalize with the tension headache, I open the door and slink out of the room.

The conversation becomes clearer as I inch lower down the steps to hide near the wall before the kitchen. She's arguing in there with an unidentified person who's much taller than her, judging from the shadows they casted.

"My Rose, I'm sorry." The voice soothes. "You know I love you. I've always loved you. Don't do this to us."

"So, I'm to blame for all of this?"

"Nah, but—"

"But what, yeah? Quincy, you've dragged this family for far too long, and I should've stepped in when I saw it. Should have fought when I saw that picture in your wallet. But I stayed for the love I had for you. It's you who broke us, not me!"

It's him, Quincy, the former Commander whose mere presence made me choke and numb up, begging my mother for forgiveness. Which is weird, since I've never seen him beg for anything.

"You talking about Helen? You know she good with what we got. I thought we had an understanding that I was no one-woman man, baby. Come on, you know me."

"*You* had the understanding. I just took it because I was afraid you'd leave me if I ever questioned you about it. Mighty daft, I was. But not anymore! You sullied this family with your lies and scandal, and now look at us!"

"I can fix it!"

"You can't!" She screeches. "How can you fix what's already done? You're married to her. Married! I thought I was your wife. I let you handle all of the paperwork for our wedding and this is where it got me. A fake fucking marriage license? How dare you?!"

"I was young and dumb, baby. I ain't want to commit to a whole marriage at that age. Then you got pregnant and tied me down with those kids..."

"You act like I got myself knocked up. You were a more than willing participant if my memory serves me correctly. I left my home. For you. Let you saddle us in this shanty house. For you. Never asked you questions about your job and now look where that's got me. Look at what you did to our children!"

"Stop it with that. They fine. They grown. They'll be all right."

"I hate you. I hate what you've done to us. My dear boy, my Shamel, is in a state upstairs over what you put him through. But that's on me. As his mother, I should have done something when I saw the bruises, the bandages, and bags under his eyes after he come home in the middle of the night with so much fear in his eyes. And Shayne has resented you from the beginning, and all of our fights were always me defending you. Now I know why she didn't come home. This house is not a home! Especially when there's never been love here."

A brief silence befalls the room, and my chest tightens from her words. She'd never done this before, I realized. She never stood up to him or protected us from this bastard who took so much away from us. I'm too transfixed on the argument to intervene.

"I guess you ain't seen your precious children for who they really are, huh?" He said.

"What do you mean?"

"What? I mean the Dirty Kitten Club is where your daughter been shaking her ass for the past two years, maybe more. And it's your son who's got more bodies than most veterans I know for his age. They're wild, both of them, and it's not because of me, or you. Baby, we got to be strong for each other through this. Can't let them drag us down."

Another pause before she says, "If all that is true, then they were misguided because of you. And me. We're to blame for our children's scars, Quince. I want to do right by them. They're all that matter to us."

"To you." He corrects, quick and clipped like he fired it at her from his gun. "All I need is you. I need you to hold me down for a little while, baby. I got a few people I owe money to in the streets, and I need some cash before I go."

"Your audacity is unmatched, Quincy Masters."

"And so is your loyalty, my rose. I promise I'll pay you back when I get to where I'm going."

Another pause before she answers. "Of course, I'll help you, babe."

My heart sinks at her typical acquiescence just as Quincy howls with delight. There's shuffling that I can only judge as the sound of him scooping her in his arms.

"That's my girl! Let me hold a grand till I get outta here."

"Sure." She said. "But only if you tell me if it was you."

"If what was me?"

Her next words send my soul and mind into the galaxy. I mean it when I say my knees gave out completely when I hear what she says that I needed to be false.

"The twins." She starts, her voice quavering. "Were you behind it? Did you have something to do with the kidnapping?"

"Hell no!" He hisses. "I ain't have nothing to do with that, Rose. I swear to God, I'd never hurt my kids."

"But you've only hurt your kids since they've known you. At least the ones you share with me."

"I...I..."

"I know you had something to do with my son coming home and nearly blowing a bullet through his skull today. I know you had something to do with my daughter's spotty appearance at home. But I know also, and with full certainty, you had everything to do with Yvonne and Michael's kidnapping by that horrid man!"

"I swear to god I ain't!" He sputters.

"Get off of me!" She spits. "You're the reason that child was killed. It's been on the news all week, and it smells like something you had a hand in."

"Mikey is dead because of *her!*" He yells, his voice loud and unhinged as it rattles the old door to the kitchen. "It's *that* bitch who led him to that Irish joker. She's the reason my twins were taken and why my son is dead!"

My feet move on autopilot as I'm propelled forward from the news. I'd been nothing but pissy drunk and zoned out all this week to check the news or the socials. I hadn't heard anything about the awful truth I needed to be a lie.

No. No. No. No!

"Dead?!" I roar as I enter the kitchen. The usual numbness that washed over me whenever I got in his presence didn't come, oh no, I felt every shred of power and anger like a shot of heroin to my system. "The fuck is you talking about, old man? You disappear for weeks and show up lying? I'll kill you!"

"Do it!" He spits in my face, and we're shoving each other and squaring off in the kitchen.

"Shamel!" Mom yells, getting between us as we circle each other. "I'm sorting this! Go back to bed."

"No!" I scream, seething as I stare into his depthless eyes. "You can't just let him walk up in here lying on some shit. I'll kill you for lying like this."

His eyes are round with an unmatched insanity, seeing as they're bloodshot and his forehead beaded with sweat.

"I'm sick of your long talk, boy! Where's the gun now, huh? You were talking all that shit the other day but ain't want to act on it like a man. We gonna do this or what?"

"Quince, don't encourage this!" My mother pleaded from somewhere, since he's the only thing in my sights that needs to be discarded. "He's your son!"

"He ain't no daddy of mine." I growl.

"Ditto." He agrees. "You know what? I got something for your ass."

He turns around and grabs the butcher knife from mom's prized knife holder set she'd begged him to buy for her. He slashes it quickly through the air, and I lean back just in time as it nearly slices across my throat.

Mom punches him ineffectually in the gut. "Stop it!"

I smiled. "Aw, you gotta do better than that, dear dad. That's all you got?"

"I already lost a son yesterday." He growls, swinging the knife again and missing. "I ain't afraid to lose another one."

"Please!" Mom yells, still between us and dodging the knife just like I am. "Quincy, I've called the cops. They'll be here any moment."

He chuckles as he stabs at me again and misses. "You lying. You ain't called nobody."

"I did!" She snarls, punching him in the stomach one more time to get his attention. "Told them you were responsible for that girl that got shot last week. Told them I thought it was you who shot her and that you're in my home right now, armed, and dangerous."

He stops to glare down at her. "You said what?"

"That's right." She said, smug and embittered as she faced the much taller man. "It's all on you, and they're on the way any minute."

"I ain't do that shit!" He barks, advancing on her now.

Mom's eyes are still squinted and taunting him as she backs into me. "You're going down for this. Not my child."

This was what she meant, I summed, when she said she'd fix it. To blame my crimes on him? This monster who tortured everyone in our town and family would potentially go down for Dawn's death?

I'm in total shock by her words but alarmed when I see those insane eyes turn on my mother. If at all possible, he looks crazier as he glowers at her.

I had to get his focus off her, I think in a panic. *Think, think, think, Mel!*

"That's right, you sick fuck." I say, breathless and menacing to him. "You're going down for that shit. All of it."

He cuts bloodshot eyes to me before roaring, "fuck you!" while charging at me. I'm backed into a corner with nowhere to run, and I close my eyes after I clock him running towards me like a spartan, slashing the knife through the air as he nears.

"Oh, fuck!" He cries as the sounds of sirens wail from the distance. "Baby, I'm sorry!"

My eyes are still closed when I notice the lack of pain anywhere on me. If he'd stabbed me, I sure as hell didn't feel the finishing slice of flesh I anticipated to spare my mom. This wasn't exactly how I planned my last moments alive, but it'd suffice, I figured.

However, Mom's groans of pain were what met me in the dark behind my lids.

"Quincy, how dare you..." She whispered, and I opened my eyes to another life-ending blow. There's blood pouring from her stomach where the knife is jabbed, and it takes me all of a few seconds to gather what happened.

"Mom!" I screamed, catching her before she fell to her knees. "Why did you do that? You shouldn't have jumped in front of a nigga with a knife! Are you crazy?"

She smiled at me, but her eyes got distant and unfocused. "No way in hell I'd let him hurt my child. I told you...I needed to be better for you. Please don't cry, my love..."

Like the ending of that tragic Shakespearean play, Quincy bolted out the back door at the sounds of the nearing sirens, leaving me in the shack kitchen to hold my dying mother. The curtains are closing on her real fast and I'm left there, saturated in more blood. More screams. And more shame than I can reconcile as I cradle my mother to her final sleep.

PART TWO

SHAME

Thirteen

Out

"If it isn't Shame in the blood and flesh! Wassup my brother-cousin?"

All Bad called as he exited through the thick columned gates that secured the front of Camden County Correctional Facility. His heavily tatted face and shoulder-length plaits could be seen from space; it's so distinct. He wore a baggy white shirt and denim pants that looked way too big on his skinny muscular frame. I clocked the guards watching him as he crossed the street over to my parked rental on the street.

"Wassup, cousin." I greeted, pulling him in for a proper dap-and-hug as I clapped his back with my free hand.

He steps back to slide appreciative eyes over the cobalt Mustang while wearing that familiar hyena grin of his.

"Peep your ride," he says.

I shrugged. "Something slight, nah mean?"

"Nah, bro." He responds once we're in the car. "This shit look luxury to me after eight years in the pen. Man, the closest to a car I been was in my dreams."

"Word up." I agree, nodding and considering his words. Shaheim "All Bad" Dabney, while technically Quincy's youngest half brother, had existed more as a cousin to me growing up at the Heights. He'd bounced around from one foster home to the other before coming to live with us at the cramped two-bedroom apartment. He'd been one of first best friends, real talk, and I can only smile as I remembered all the crazy schemes he'd concocted to get candy, coke, or cash back then. He was a little over four years older than me, but we'd been thick as thieves as we stole more often than bought items from the corner stores. He'd earned the nickname All Bad from his general lack of good choices and moral constitution: he was the dude running the drug game before me for The Commander, but it was his temper that always got him in situations he couldn't skate off.

He'd only stayed with us for about six or seven months before getting pinned on aggravated assault and drug charges.

He'd been locked down for eight whole years. Eight years he's spent away from the only family he's known and most of his childhood. Even though he'd been one of the only relatives Quincy allowed us to get close to, he'd still existed as one of my favorites. Long story long,

All Bad was the dude you turn to for a good fucking time.

It was a no-brainer when he called home last week to ask if he could stay at our crib.

"It's good to see you, man." He said as we cruised down the road. "Looking all grown and shit."

I chuckled at that. "Whatever, man. I'm grown enough."

"Grown enough to get some bud for the night?"

"Ain't been out an hour yet and already you looking to get blazed."

"Hell yeah."

"No sweat, dog. I set you up real nice for your Homecoming," I said after digging in my glove compartment. After fishing out the large ball of bud wrapped in plastic wrap, I waved it in the air. "This the good shit."

His eyes were entranced by the sway of my hand with the bulbous bag of weed, and I laughed when I glimpsed his head moving from left to right.

All Bad snatched the bag and brought it to his dark lips. *"I love her just the same..."*

I laughed as I got off the exit. "Nigga, what?"

"Mary Janeee!" He sang, his voice uncharacteristically high and discordant as he damn near shoved the bag into his nostrils. "You know how long it's been since I even touched some weed?"

"About eight years?"

"Nah," he sniffed the bag again. "About a week."

"You wild." I guffawed. "The hood missed you, man. For real, for real."

"You ain't got to lie, Shame." He said. "I know you missed me."

"Yeah, right." I snorted.

"Always gotta be so tough, huh? Come here!" He chuffed before pulling my head under his arm.

"Yo!" I hollered, struggling to keep my eyes on the road and take control of the swerving car. "Is you crazy?"

He waved me away after I punched him in the gut with my semi free hand, forcing him to release me.

"Just bustin' your chops, man. Damn. Got to be all serious and shit."

I reared back. "Nigga, I'm driving a whole car! You tryna die?"

A grim look befell his dark face in that moment. "There's shit in this world worse than that."

I opened my mouth to demand what the hell was worse than death, the forever silence, but held back. Flashes of last year flooding my mind and making my breaths come in uneven. Shooting Dawn. Attending her funeral in the same way I attended all her track meets, from far behind the crowd within the shadows. A small shred of light stabbed through the darkness, though, considering Luxury. Since Dawn was full term, the doc was able to save the baby. Our baby. Luxury Ladawna Sales, the name her mother chose for her before her death, came into the world and melted the cold stone in my chest. Robyn, Dawn's mom, didn't let me in the hospital to sign her birth certificate, though I showed up sweaty, confused, and without a plan. Told the doc to keep me out. She had sole custody of my baby girl, and I fought the arrangement at first, but slowly retreated. I was the reason the family had to plan a birthday and funeral all in a week. It was all my fault, and even though the cops were able to link enough forensics to connect the crime to Quincy, who'd still been on the run, I knew in my heart of darkness that I had no place in my beautiful girl's life.

Every time I thought of that grand week of losses I couldn't breathe. The ability to breathe turned into an elusive bodily function that wasn't so natural when I thought of Dawn's death. Then Mike's murder.

I squeeze the steering wheel as we enter South Camden until my knuckles blanche. I should have capped that Irish motherfucker that night, like I almost did, but his kid's appearance stopped me. In that moment, I exercised the compassion the McAllen prick didn't give a fuck to use towards my little brother and sister in that basement.

One week.

They'd been kidnapped and tortured for a full five days before the same kid I nearly met that night caught him butchering the little bodies under the house. I don't remember all the particulars, just remember the

story was in the news for a few days and blacking out
when I went to search for Yvonne. I checked everywhere, too. Every spot I recalled tailing them in those
few weeks after I became aware of their true relationship to me. Mike was dead, but Yvonne made it out
before disappearing again. Quincy was still on the run,
considered armed, dangerous, and with two kids he
didn't technically have the authority to take. Devin and
Yvonne never returned to school or went on playdates.
I lost everything that week, and between the drugs, alcohol, and rock n' roll lifestyle there was little room for
anything else I used to value. I was seventeen now, and
a professional partier and flunky in school, considering
T stopped doing my assignments. I didn't press her,
since she had her own assignments, deadlines, and now
my baby to raise with her mother.

Another wary feeling rocketed through me at the state
of Si and my relationship. Or, rather, our former relationship. The Violence and The Silence were officially
a thing of the past after that botched contract with
Monty. While he excused me from owing him the large
amount of cash I apparently cost him, the email from
Yume that contained fancy words like "lease violation"
and "immediate eviction" were clear enough. I left that
same night, and we hadn't spoken since.

My jaw flexes in tight irritation as I remember the
night Quincy fled town with my little sister. What a
pussy. He'd been lucky enough to escape me or that

Luci wasn't within reach that night. If not for that, then it would've been my face plastered on the news for murder. The gun in my mouth after Mom caught me and saved my life and the fact that I couldn't do the same for her that night only added to my shame.

My mom's limp body in my arms nearly made my heart stop completely, and I prayed more than I ever was accustomed to for her to stay with me. I promised her I'd make an effort to stay living, stay thriving, like she wanted, if she didn't leave.

"What's the moves, man?" All Bad asked, jolting me from my absent recollection as we sat parked in front of my house.

"Home sweet home." I tell him, returning to reality and watching as he scrunches his face distastefully at the South Camden shack that blended into the abandoned houses on the street.

"Y'all not at the Heights no more?" He asked.

"Nah," I answered. "Remember I told you we moved a couple years back?"

He nodded, as if the memory of the conversation returned to him. "Right, right. This place look like shit."

I shrugged before getting out of the car. "Take it or leave it, bro."

"I mean, this looks worse than prison, man."

"Yeah, I hear you," I say, twisting the key in the front door before kicking it open.

"It's nice in here though, nah mean?" He commented as we walked into the dimly lit living space. The space I usually found Mom meditating or mixing some herbs while smoking a blunt.

"Where everybody at?" He asked as we ascended the ratty steps to the second floor.

"Man, we ain't gonna be here forever. Just stopping to pick up some supplies before we head out." I told him while searching my room. It had to be somewhere, I thought as I flipped my twin bed over to reveal more dirty clothes instead of the item I needed for tonight.

As I'm rummaging through the second pile of worn clothes in the corner of the room, something silver catches my eye. Since the windows are pulled apart to allow some light in for once, some shards of light bounce off the few reflective surfaces on Shay's side: her hand-held mirror specifically gleams under the pene-trative sunlight, but that isn't what rips my attention to the rotten floorboards. There's a board slightly fitting out of its usual place, revealing a dark hole under it and another blinding beam of light.

"What the…" I whisper, reaching under the boards and totally entranced by the secret cubby filled with junk.

At least, it looks like junk, I judge as I sort through the cardboard box of expensive pieces of jewelry, sev-eral boxes of condoms, and photos. The photos are old family portraits of several people I recognize: of our mother holding two finicky toddlers in her lap and there's also one of Yvonne with a huge gummy grin after she received her gift of a Wonder Woman figurine she'd been begging for for her birthday. She couldn't have been more than four or five in that pic, I ruminate with misty eyes and a heavy heart. However, the third pic is a polaroid of a skinny dark-skinned boy holding two toddlers on his lap. The infants are identical, save for the curly fro on the girl with the cheese mush on her face. A warmth spreads through me as I recall the light of the times, the stark contrast to my dark and stormy current existence where love died, and hung my head. Mike and Yvonne, my Big Mike and VonVon I affectionately called my siblings, were gone forever. I had to accept that, but these pictures in this strange cubby hole was like a portal to the past. Something unraveled in my chest, an emotion I'd been an expert in numbing from all the dope-smoking in the days that followed Quincy's escape. Were all these mementos belongings of Shay's? I wondered as I stuffed the personal items back into the brown box. As I moved to rearrange the items as if I'd never disturbed them, a bit of green paper peaked from the bottom of the box. Paper I'd been too familiar with chasing these past few years.

Wads of crumpled bills filled a black trash bag at the bottom, and I mean an insane amount that had me doing some quick calculations. There had to have been at least eight or nine stacks present, and my eyes saucer at the crumpled, liquor smelling bills that could have gotten us out of this shithole for real and for good. If this was Shay's, then how could she have collected this much? I grimaced at the image of her bouncing on that white dude's dick at the Dirty Kitten last year, and a stark realization hits me at just how she got all that cash.

"Look like a tornado been through here, man. What happened?" All Bad commented again, snapping me back to reality. "What you looking for anyways, man? I can help you find it if you want?"

"Nah!" I grunt, forcing the bag deeper into the hole with shaky hands.

"Why you acting all goofy? Let me help you—"

"I'm good." I reemphasize with more grit and conviction, tossing a glare at him over my shoulder.

I don't see him but intuit his hands raising in mock surrender as he backs up. "All right, cool. Just tryna help a brother out. You acting worse than them fairy ass guards in the pen."

It was a snide comment I'd probably deserved but intended on ignoring. However, I froze in place when I heard the melodic song float through the halls.

"Shay, wassup baby girl?" I heard All Bad say behind me.

"I'm good, All Bad." Shay responded hesitantly as she entered the room we technically shared but never occupied at the same time. We were careful to avoid each other. "I didn't know you was getting out today."

I made a show at scrambling to my feet and jabbing sweaty hands in my pockets, attempting to look cool despite the horse race my heart rate set on. I was careful to keep my back to her, though. Shay was like a truth hawk in that way, seeing through all my shenanigans and bullshit since we were young.

"Yeah, it was about time." He answered wistfully, "I got transferred to Camden County after aging out of juvie. Caught a few extra charges they made me serve in the grown-up prison. Them guards were some weak bitches."

She giggled. "I bet. Try to stay out of trouble, AB, okay?"

"Can't promise you that, baby girl. I'm All Bad, ain't been good a day in my twenty-two years of living."

"You are something else." She said, and I could hear the smile in her voice.

"You know who else is something else? You. And them pipes you got. You ought to get paid for that shit, nah mean?"

Her voice trembled. "I don't know about that."

"Well, you keep at it, beautiful. You got talent for real." He complimented her, and I didn't need to turn around to sense Shay's discomfort at it. She always got embarrassed whenever someone commented on her songs.

"Where them twins at, by the way?" He asked, his voice rising a few notches. "They were small when I got locked down."

A tense silence filled the air, an immediate switch from the former good vibes in the room.

"You ain't tell him?" Shay asks, low and cold.

After a few minutes of trying to relax my breathing, I turn to face them.

"Nah." I answered. "Uh, they not here no more."

"What you mean, 'they ain't here?'" All Bad countered suspiciously.

"You ain't seen the news or nothing while you was locked down?" I asked him, incredulous and dazed from broaching the topic we never spoke about in this house.

His face falls, "I was in the hole for the last year for shanking a guard. So, I ain't seen much of anything but a dark room for the past four hundred days, if my math serves me right."

I take a deep breath before taking the plunge. I could do this, I thought, encouraging myself from the thing I feared more than death itself. Talking about all the loss directly resulted from the shame of my actions.

"Mike and Von are—"

"Mommy wanted to talk to you for a second," Shay interjected in a rush. I frown at the woman I'm only just now noticing is holding a brown plastic bag in her hands.

"What?" I retorted in confusion.

"Yeah, um, she wanted to talk to you real quick. She's still in bed. Go see her."

My jaw falls slack momentarily as I regard her quick thinking. She expertly read the tension in the room, and in that moment I'm grateful for the save.

I flash a small smile at her in gratitude as I walk to the door, only to get an eye roll in return.

"We'll be here when you get back, Shame." She said, seeming to overemphasize the street name she'd previously refused to call me.

She'd always said that name was an inaccurate representation of my soul, and that she refused to refer to me by a word steeped in pity. I felt weird about it back then, her fixed judgment of my character, but now...shame tenfold blooms in my heart as I leave the room. She wanted nothing to do with me, and somewhere in my mind there was a smaller side of myself unable to handle that.

"Yeah, Ma?" I ask Sommer Masters, catching her lying in bed flipping through a magazine.

She closes the editorial to stare at me standing at her door. "Hello, son. You doing all right?"

"I'm good." I say, shrugging.

She nods. "Good. Just wanted to make sure you made the drive in one piece. Is Shaheim with you?"

"Yeah."

"All right." She states, her eyes searching beyond me to no avail. "Well, where is he?"

A slap at my upper back alerts me of his presence.

"I'm right here, Miss Sommer—oh damn!" All Bad sings before cutting his sentence short upon entering Mom's room.

Mom frowned at him, sitting up a little in bed. "What's wrong?"

"Not a damn thing, apparently..." His eyes squint appreciatively as he studies her. "You got thick as hell, Miss Sommer. You've been frying more of that chicken like Miss Pat taught you at the Heights?"

My Mom's cheeks burn at the compliment. "Oh, Shaheim, you're a sweetheart. But you're right– I did learn from the best! I only use Miss Patrice's recipe till this day."

"All right, all right." I lament, stepping in front of All Bad to block his path to my mother. "We got to go if we're ain't trying to be late to this party."

"What party?" My mother asked in that familiar upward inflection that conveys her curiosity and concern.

I sucked my teeth, hating to admit the truth of our destination to my innocent mother. Since Si and me no longer hung out, I wound up doing the thing that violated one of The Commander's most cardinal rules: Milio and I often chilled at his crib where most of the LC parties occurred. I can't say we were as thick as thieves, like Si and me became during our brutal but profitable partnership, but Milio helped keep the bills paid. I sold product any chance I got, and the payout was nowhere near as much as a headhunt on a high-profile exec or the unlucky motherfucker on the Kobayashi's Most Wanted list. The work was steady and relatively secure and not unfamiliar since it had been an aspect of my previous employment for The Commander.

It had been a while since I completed a lethal contract, and I made my peace with ending that lifestyle forever after the tragedy of Dawn and Mike's cut-short futures. I vowed to keep my hands clean, and made it a habit to not so much as kill a fly. I mean it, considering the occasional roach infestations in our hood house and the anxiety that rocketed through me after harming one of them. I just swept them outside and kept it moving, and I was fully aware of the dangers involved with me associating with gangs, but it was unavoidable, really. How else were we supposed to keep the lights on if not for the drug deals in the dark? It hadn't been a road I'd wanted to venture down, but the household bills along with my mother's medical expenses racked up after another contract drought.

After Quincy stabbed a hole right through her in the kitchen that night, I was barely cognizant as I hollered for an EMT into the phone. Was somewhat floating through subspace as I watched the men wheel her into the emergency services truck and her eyes glaze over before focusing on nothing.

"It's always you." Shay whispered lifelessly as we awaited news on mom's condition in the waiting room. She occupied the blue chair several seats down, and I had to strain to hear her hatefully uttered words.

"I know," I muttered brokenly before hanging my head low.

"It's always *you!*" She fumed as tears trickled from her face. "In the center of everything! Why can't you just be a *normal* guy? A *normal* son and brother? Instead of putting everybody you come into contact with in complete danger."

"Shay..."

"Quincy was right." She spat, her face and eyes reddened by the flames of her fury but voice stone cold.

"What?" I catch myself saying, breathless and strangled from shock.

She swipes at her face before nodding slow. "He always said you were his greatest failure. That one day you'd make a mistake that'd cost us the heart of this family. I never believed in what he said. Not until today. Not until I stared down the barrel of that fucking gun you put to my face! There's no hope for you. None. Whatever goodness I ever saw in you was just an illusion. Quincy was right, and this family was never real."

Those words, I thought as that tight feeling twisted my chest again, were the end of me. The end of any goodness in me as I allowed the hot tears to fall. I stood up and rushed to be with the outside after hearing those words I feared and screamed my anguish into the wind. I scared off a couple of people, but I didn't care. Even after the doc came from Mom's operating room and expressed his deep regrets I barely heard him past the words that seemed to scream through my mind.

While the wound wasn't fatal, the knife lacerated part of her right kidney that gave the doctors cause enough for a total removal and very unexpected news.

"That stab wound may have very well saved your mother's life, miss." I overheard the kind Black doc say to Shay from several chairs over after I returned to the waiting room.

"Saved her life?" She asked, bewildered.

He cleared his throat before continuing. "Polycystic kidney disease, or PKD, is a hereditary illness your mother suffers from."

"What is that? Will she be okay? You just said the surgery was successful so why would you come in here and lie—"

"Whoa, whoa." The man I thought introduced himself as Dr. Paige cautioned in a gentle tone. "My apologies for wording that so clinically. Let me rephrase; PKD is a condition in which cysts form on the kidneys over time. This condition usually chronically worsens as the patient enters into their late fifties or sixties; however, your mother's kidneys were riddled with fluid filled sacs after we examined her."

"Can you cut to the part where this stab wound ended up being a good thing? Because that all sounds pretty fucking horrible to me."

"Of course," he mumbled. "In your mother's case, the kidney that was stabbed ended up needing to be removed since it was in advanced stages of renal failure. She has one kidney remaining, but it does also contain several cysts that'll require careful monitoring over the course of her lifetime."

"Cysts, as in, tumors, right?" She asked in a shaky voice, and I'm caught completely off guard on how she'd know that information the doctor confirmed with a tight head nod.

"Correct. Cysts are soft tumors, in a sense. But your mother's cysts are not life threatening on her remaining kidney. In other words, she'll be able to live a normal life with minimal treatment if the cysts enlarge. But that leads me to another question, Ms. Masters."

"Rose," she corrected swiftly. "My name is Shayne Rose."

"Of course, Ms. Rose. But I'll need to perform a records request from your mother's current healthcare physician so that we'll be able to treat her condition appropriately. What practice does your mother belong to?"

A tense silence fills the air before Shay says, "Um, my family doesn't exactly do doctors and hospitals."

"Ever?"

"Not really," she responds slowly. "Mom's an herbalist and doesn't believe in Western Meds."

He nods with a considering look that reveals the judgment probably scuttling through his mind. I knew how it looked. How it sounded, too, that we didn't do doctors. Docs were often associated with the cops, and neither of those had any place in our family's underworld.

Shay and I left the hospital separately that night and made it a point to never engage in real conversation since then. Well, that was a year ago, and the tension in the air as well as the lingering accusation she tossed at me that night in the hospital still chewed up my insides.

Quincy was right. And I couldn't agree more with those forbidden words that made my heart hurt as I watched my mother struggle to stand from bed.

I nearly lose it as I catch sight of her stumbling over an obstacle I couldn't see beside her bed.

"Watch it," I scold her, but there's no menace in my tone like usual, only fear and shame as I zip across the tiny room to catch her in my arms.

She smiles up at me for a brief moment. "Oh, it was just a silly slip of the ankles, darling. These dreadful meds put my mind in a tizzy."

I fight the tight mask on my face to return the smile I don't feel and lose. Instead, I sit her upright and keep a guiding hand on her upper arm. "Just be more careful, Ma. All right?"

"I thought I was supposed to be doting on you more, you know?" Her words followed a whimsical chuckle. "I'm all right. You two have fun at your party and don't be home too late."

I stare at her for a long moment, blinking away the tears that liked to torment me from time to time whenever in my mother's feeble presence. "You sure?"

A weak smile crossed her face before she placed a feather light kiss on my cheek. "I'll be all right. As long as you and Shayne are okay then I'm okay. Okay?"

I smiled at the aggravating woman who finally saw me after all these years of sneaking around with bruises I couldn't explain.

I return the kiss on her cheek before gently depositing her on the bed. "Get some rest, Ma. And call me if you need anything at all."

Even though she'd apparently just awakened from a seven hour stretch of sleep, it was difficult to not notice the droopiness of her eyes as she laid back against the bed.

"I'm all right, love. I'll just have a little rest before my afternoon yoga," she sighed before yawning.

I didn't dare voice the fact that the afternoon had long been replaced by the evening dusk as I met All Bad at the door.

"Take care of yourself, Miss Sommer," All Bad said, all traces of humor vanished from watching the state of my mother on the bed. We hit the road shortly after

I found the item I'd been in search of, and the grim silence that followed during the drive did nothing to quell the chaotic three words that hummed in my head like one of Shay's sad melodies.

Quincy was right.

FOURTEEN

RULE 23

"I swear y'all bout to make me fucking cry in this bitch." All Bad whimpered sarcastically as the front door to Milio's crib swung open to reveal the crowd of hustlers hooting and hollering rounds of "Welcome Home All Bad!"

The usually pristine clean that Ms. Ricotti took pride in was a thing of the past as I gazed my eyes over the empty beer bottles, red solo cups, and takeout containers on the floor, lining the stairs, and, well...everywhere. There was also an upbeat bachata tune blaring from the rundown speakers, and I noticed the half-naked Spanish women gyrating in tune on what looked to be the living room floor. You'd think this level of mess would bring Ms. Ricotti to a stroke or something, but she saw all of Milio's "gangster" friends as family, and opened her home and heart to their wild ways. Milio's house was also the designated meetup spot for the crew for this reason.

"Yo where the ho's at?" All Bad whined from the couch as we passed the blunt around. A full hour had passed and ended with the four of us, Milio, All Bad, an LC named Ricky, and myself sitting on the worn sofa in the center of the living room as the music changed from up to downbeat.

"*Mira,*" Ricky, a tall Hispanic dude I remembered as Milio's tightest gang brother said to my cousin. "You don't see those girls on the floor? They're for you tonight, man."

All Bad sucked his teeth before waving a dismissive hand at them. "They all right, but not all that. Nah mean?"

"Nah," Milio answered after hitting the blunt. "I asked my girl to hook you up with some of the baddest bitches she knew. They fine as hell."

"I appreciate that, dog," All Bad started, straightening himself. "But that warm vanilla ain't exactly my taste."

"Warm vanilla?" I say, choking on laughter as I eventually understand his meaning.

"I like my women chocolate, nah mean?"

"Bro, you just did an eight-year stint and come out turning down pussy?" I asked, barely containing the laughter and dizziness. Was like a tornado twisting my brain.

"Not any pussy," he grunts. "White ones."

"But they ain't white," Milio emphasizes with a tilt of his head towards the group of Hispanic women dancing for him.

"Well, they ain't black, either."

"Dale," Ricky chuckled and waved a dismissive hand at him. "You're doing too much."

"Y'all ain't doing enough," he retorted, matter-of-fact and sort of snide.

Milio's cough and laugh mirrored Ricky's when he asked, "Well, All Bad, we don't want to disappoint a legend. You was always out there gettin that money with us, and never complained about having to Put in Work. For all you did for Hector, too, back in the day..."

"Yeah," All Bad answers, his voice tight with the restraint of something tense unsaid. "No need to rehash that."

His face sets in a hard frown as I further observe him caving in on himself at the mention.

Another tense silence befalls the four of us as I inwardly wonder about this thing with Hector that got my usually boisterous cousin so quiet.

Ricky slams his beer that he's only half polished off into the wooden floor. "I'll kill those blood rat fuckers myself for what they did to Hector, man."

I knew that name, I thought, and the increased tempo of the rise and fall of my breaths let me know my subconscious figured it out first. Hector. Hector. Why was this name ringing such a damn bell?

Suddenly the chatter in the room falls into a demonic hodgepodge of noise. I notice the room spin and the world darken for a few unrecognizable moments. That strange dizziness returned, but this time increased the tempo of my heart and shrunk the room.

"Yo, Shame," Milio asks in concern while holding my body steady. "You good, dog?"

"I'm good," I say, attempting and failing at sitting still. It felt like my skin was crawling and ants were gnawing at the backs of my eyes.

"Really, dude, if you need to lay down just let me know."

I swat at his outstretched hand that tried to steady me, feeling everyone's eyes on me in the room. Seeing all the laughter. I hear the noises– the laughs. The sweat on my forehead leaks into my eyes as the room closes in.

"You're too emotional," Quincy groused from the opposite end of the couch with a laugh. Or maybe it was All Bad? I'm not quite so sure as I raise to confront the fucker.

"The fuck you say?" I demanded the cold asshole who'd haunted me for years. *Not here*, I think. Not anymore.

"Huh?"

"Call me emotional again and see what happens!"

"Bro," Quincy warned. "Chill out. I'm not sure if you took some shit or what, but I'll knock your little ass down if you don't back out of my personal space."

"Do it then!" I holler.

"Shame, bro," Quincy says again, the anger melting into concern. "What you take?"

The temp in the room heats to a boiling degree that sizzles my common sense and insides. There's more ants and gnawing, and the saliva spilling down my jaw leaves me feeling suddenly dry.

I shove the person in front of me. "Just fucking kill me already!"

It's the shirt, I realize. The white tee is the source of my itchiness and boiling skin and I almost rip it off when a rough hand stops me.

"Enough of this," he grumbles while shaking me. "It was only a little Dust in the joint bro. Chill out, you tweekin.'"

"Get off me!" I scream at the Hispanic man I thought I'd buried. It's him who's back to haunt me too. What's he and Quincy doing here, anyways? "You 'sposed to be dead, Hector!"

Somewhere in the background, I hear someone call for Kenny, the leader of the LC's, to ask what was in the blunt we'd finished. Then there's a sweet voice guiding me into a small room with yellowish lighting.

"Quincy was right," the soft voice said to me before a cool sensation met my forehead.

I blink my eyes several times to get the image right, to make sense of the woman staring into my eyes with blazing malice and cold hatred mixed with disappointment. It's Shay, I realize in a split second before reaching out and wrapping arms around her. She's smaller than usual, but that's okay. As long as she sees the truth, that Quincy wasn't right.

"Shay," I choke, whimpering into her hair. "I ain't mean to get Mommy hurt. I tried to protect her. For real."

"Shay?" She asked, soft and probing, but not infuriated like I expected. "Sweetie, calm down."

I shook my head and held on tight. "How am I supposed to do that? I got Mommy hurt. And now Vonnie's gone and I don't have a dime to find a way to her."

"Shamel," she stated firmly. "You're having a bad trip. Just breathe through it."

"What you mean, Shay?" I felt myself slurring and slightly in awe by her use of my government name.

"I mean, your boys out there clowning you mad hard. Come on, breathe and chill out for a second. Then we'll go back out there."

"Breathe," I choke out, unintentionally obeying her command as I rock back and forth in a seat I had no recollection of occupying. "Breathe."

"That's it," she encouraged me, and I had to keep my eyes closed to level myself and the swirling images in my head. When the room quieted and stilled and the chaos lessened to a degree, I let my breathing return to normal and paused. The suave Prince Royce tune blasting through the house reminded me of reality, of where I was and what just happened.

"You okay?" She breathed, and I coached myself before opening my eyes and facing the sister who hated me.

"I'm—" I start, but the sumptuous curves, honey brown skin, and Betty Boop curls make me sputter in silent surprise. "Tierra?"

FIFTEEN

WORK

I'm still sputtering nonsense as I gawk at the gorgeous girl with dark circles lining her wide brown eyes. The usual blatant affection in them on reserve for me is no longer there, like there's a light that's been snuffed out of the previously nerdy, cheery girl who'd admittedly been crushing on me for years. In fact, everything about her is wrong, I gather while assessing the skimpy attire revealing a little too much of her big tits and sumptuous ass. I shake my head to clear it, sure I was seeing her bolder older sister instead of the historically conservative art nerd I picked on for wearing too many layers in P.E. class. She looks nothing like herself, and I struggle to come up with a word to describe the barely-there girl who'd always been there for me.

Weary. She looks totally worn from something as she looks up at me with soulless eyes.

"T?" I ask again, mostly of myself to make sure this wasn't a dream. Or nightmare.

She rolls her eyes as she stares up at me. "There something wrong?"

Though high on some hallucinogenic shit I couldn't identify, I made sure to force all the indignation in my expression at that question.

"What?" She squawks indignantly. "Don't give me that look, Shamel. Don't even."

"Why are you here?"

"Why are *you* here?"

"Don't be stupid," I grunt, reaching for her. "What you doing at an LC kickback?"

She jumps away from my hands as if there's poison on them before wrapping trembling arms around her body.

"I'm grown. I hang with who I want to. You don't get to judge me for this."

"I ain't judging," I say, standing up slowly despite the spinning of the room. "Who do you even know here, huh?"

Her eyes dart away from mine before answering. "A few homegirls, that's it."

"You barely had friends in Camden, and now all of a sudden you hanging tight with some LC girls way up in Queens?" I laid it on thick, I knew, but I had to get through to her.

"Guess so," she shrugs noncommittally.

Sighing and exhausted, I grab her arm. "You need to go home. Now."

"Excuse me?" She fires back, fighting my hold on her arm.

"Nah, excuse you. You need to get out of here. Get home before you worry mom."

I blame it on the drugs for my poor balance. Yeah, that's what it was that slowed my movements enough to face a direct punch to the gut from the former mousey girl.

"Get off me!" She growled, pulling back to adjust her thin skin tight dress. "Like I said. I ain't going. I just came to check on you. That's it. Didn't come for a whole lecture and escort back to Robyn's house."

I frowned, not only from the pain in my stomach, but from her cold use of her mother's first name. "Everything all right?"

"You being serious?" She sucked in an irritated breath while flailing hands in the air. "Yes. Everything's great. All dandy, really. Especially if you count the drunk bitch I gotta go home to every day after school. Especially if you count the orphaned toddler I get to take care of, practically full time by myself, since the so-called "mother" of mines got so damned depressed after her favorite daughter's murder she decided to empty the entire medicine cabinet in her gut every night. Don't even mention the one night I get to sneak away from the shitty diapers because her shit-faced grandma is being babysat by one of her sympathetic neighbors."

"Hey, hey," I choke out, pulling her into my arms. "Don't cry, T. I'm sorry."

Her shoulders wrack with the sobs as she collapses in my arms. "I'm fine, Shamel. Just leave me alone."

"T, forgive me. Okay?" I say, more guilt and self-hatred reviving my hazed brain. I tighten around her. "I don't know what to say right now."

"Say nothing," she blubbered, pulling away enough to glare at me. "Just *do* something."

"Do what?"

A tense silence befalls the room for a moment as we stare into each other. It's like our eyes are conversing outside of our bodies as the bachata in the living room fades into a low pulse.

"Help me." She whispers before grabbing the back of my neck and crashing her lips into mine.

The kiss isn't like I expect from the nerdy girl from school, since it's demanding and upfront. Our tongues are the only things dancing to the calm Spanish music from the speakers.

T abruptly steps back and that's when I notice her brandishing a small black tube from her dress, and without a second's worth of hesitation or thought, brings it to her nose to inhale deep, alternating the powder between both nostrils. She shakes and jolts for a minute before extending the hardcore shit to me with a devilish grin.

"Nah," I slur a little from the exhaustion and head-spinning.

"Wanna help me?" She hums silkily, taking a slow step towards me as I back into the wall.

"Mmhmm."

"Then breathe in," she says with another smile, before forcing the tube into my right nostril.

"Wait..." I say, bobbing and leaning before inhaling deep. Every cell awakened at that moment, causing my eyes to fly open like quick appearing window blinds. "Fuck..."

She shoves the packed tube into my other nostril, quick and efficient, and my mouth is back on hers in a minute I can't keep track of. Our ragged breathing matches as we ride the tide of high desire, and the usual inhibition I had melted away as I ripped the top half of her dress away with a satisfying tear.

"Should've chose me," she pulled away briefly to hiss.

My head is still in the Atlantic Ocean, in other words, it's nowhere near the real world or connected to sense enough to unpack her words. There are only two things in front of me that need attention. And conquering.

"You're mine..." She moans with her eyes closed, almost as if she's reading from some unseen diary I shouldn't be witnessing, "...she took everything from me. Even you."

"Shut up," I growl while my hands explore her body.

My dick twitches to life in my jeans as my gaze shifts to the two large reasons behind my sudden surge of desire. Her titties are nearly on display, her nipples, hard pebbles that call me to taste. This was really wrong, but I couldn't give two fucks as I wrap my larger hand around her neck.

"I'm nobody," I say. "Nothing at all."

"We're the same," she breathes and writhes some more as my hands continue choking and exploring.

I feel a pressure on my jean front, leading me to believe it's T's shaky hands fumbling to free my wood.

Time slows and speeds at the same time, making me believe I'd imagined the angry voice behind me.

"Get off my girl, *puta!*"

I turned around after the third time I heard him demand it, sort of in a slow-motion spin.

"Milio you better get your homeboy." The infuriated LC growls as he stalks towards us.

The entire house is silent, I note, as I watch the crowd of LC's and their naked women eye us from the living room. Milio appeared out of nowhere, too, since I watch him shoot across the room to bar the angry LC from getting to me.

"*Cálmate.*" Milio hisses, anger and caution mixing into his words. "Come on, Kenny. It's Shame. He's cool, remember?"

"He's *your* boy, man. Not ours." The LC leader spits furiously as he studies both me and T's naked upper half. "Get over here, baby."

T's face falls at the command, but she only obeys after shooting me a long regretful stare that nearly sobers me. Nearly.

"Look," I start, attempting to reconcile with one of the three Kenny's doubling, then tripling, before me. "My bad for stepping on your toes. I'm faded."

"Shut the fuck up, Shame!" Milio spits in a hushed tone belaying every ounce of his rage for me ruining the party. It's probably coming from him always trying to have my back to his crew, too, since I'd lived with the suspicion that they'd been trying to end our lifelong friendship since joining the Latin street gang.

Milio raised his hands as if about to bow and pray to the god of the LC's. "Don't mind this asshole, all right? He probably didn't know T was LC. He's harmless, man. You have my word on that."

I have the urge to sit and stand at the same time, if that was even possible on the high tide both T and I were riding before everyone else's intrusion. The Violence wouldn't let Milio snap at me that way, I think wistfully on the dead title and reputation from before. Shamel would've probably sent him a menacing look before separating him from the crowd to have an actual discussion, one where he explained himself and I apologized for my actions. Apologies didn't really exist in Shame's realm, however, since my life was about survival now. I vowed to keep living since what happened to my mom, so I couldn't take the shameful way out like last time. I got comfortable with the numbness, though, even as I slink back into the seat in the room I'm just realizing is the kitchen.

"Party ain't over y'all," Milio says, resuming his social playboy demeanor as he approaches Kenny. "All Bad wants to see some real action tonight. Ricky and I know just the place."

Kenny's fiery brown eyes blazed into mine as he answered, "Where we moving this party?"

"What's the one place a man can get all the cheeks, liquor, and pussy he wants for a good price?"

SIXTEEN

SILENCE

TAKEO

I should have called Shame.

Those words traipsed through my mind more often than not during the months following the severance of our ruthless partnership. While a few years my junior, Shame was the most adept marksman, never encountering complications when it came to hitting a target with one efficient shot. Never too bloody. Never a mess. Always calm and steady as if his sole existence was inextricably linked to the dealing end of a weapon. I resonated with his conviction and integrity, considering the reasons I allowed him into the delicate social order of the Kobayashi's. So calm and poised he was, existing as a stark contrast to my brutal rashness I tried to keep hidden. That same rashness would be the death of me, and when I noticed Shame's aim slipping and his hands losing their usual steadiness while securing a target during our assignments, I did my best to call him out. My best was mostly brutal criticism, a tactic adopted from the brutal tiger parents I referred to by first name.

"Dishonorable boy," Tensei Kobayashi, my father and head of our Clan, spat at me when I returned home with an A Minus on an exam. Those same words I grew accustomed to, even comfortable with, during our weekly interactions or whenever there was a new assignment he'd needed taking care of.

"Dishonorable boy," he snarled again when I returned home after accidentally murdering the man Father hired as his underworld accountant. "Stanley True stole from the Kobayashi's. Took something precious we'll never be able to get back. You were sent to teach him a lesson, and now I hear from the news that he is dead. I don't need to ask if it was you who did it. I know it was you."

I waited patiently outside the white ranch style house paid for by Kobayashi dollars. I didn't wait long before the statuesque Japanese woman answered the door wearing her characteristic mild grin. She's no taller than five foot two, which requires me to stare down at her.

"Welcome, Takeo-sama." She greeted, bowing her head so as not to make direct eye contact per Japanese custom when greeting superiors. "I'm humbled by your presence."

I sigh, readjusting my leather jacket. "No need for formalities, Sayuri. This is just a routine house call, same as usual."

"Yes," she says, still bowing despite my command but stepping aside for me to enter the immaculate home. "I appreciate you. We both appreciate what the family has done for us since his passing."

His passing. I consider the mild euphemism and cringe inside at the memory of Kenji's funeral. All the blood. So much death that happened in the wake of my return from Japan.

"Your gratitudes are not accepted," I say as I sip the tea she made for my return. We're sitting at the kitchen table and chatting face-to-face, per our routine interactions upon my visits to South Carolina. "Kobayashi's look after their own. Where is Koichi?"

"Koichi will be returning from school shortly, maybe ten or fifteen minutes from now. He'll be so delighted to see you."

I kept my face stony and voice flat as I regarded her with a nod. "I only have a few minutes, unfortunately. There is business I must attend to back up north. I am merely here to ensure your wellbeing is tended to."

"Oh," Sayuri's face fell, the expression aging her older than her thirty years. "Of course. He'll understand. I'll be sure to tell him you will, as he says, 'catch him next time.'"

I almost give way to a grin at her use of the American colloquialism. Almost.

My phone rings and it's exactly the person I'd been anticipating hearing from with good news. Pertinent news on my deals with the gangs further south.

"Shindo," I say instead of a hello.

"Good and bad news." Kenji's former best friend responds in a tone mirroring my flat affect. "Negotiations with the 590's are becoming more difficult than usual. They're demanding an eighty-twenty split of the profits to deal in the D.C. area."

"Eighty-twenty?" I nearly choked on the absurd percentage as I paced the kitchen. "Did you offer them our terms?"

"Yes. I outlined them just as you instructed: to mobilize our suppliers into the D.C. markets, the Kobayashi's were prepared to offer the 590's twenty-five percent of the profits earned on their territory. Saint Millard rejected."

I swore in my mother tongue before answering. "This is not good. We'll require their piece of territory if the Kobayashi's have any chance to expand into the southern markets."

And this was true, since the 590's controlled large portions of the drug scene in the DMV area. There wasn't a drug sold in D.C. outside of Saint Millard, the 590 head, knowledge or orchestration. Our families were in negotiations for nearly a year now, and I got the sense that Saint prolonged these talks to maintain his silly semblance of power. Saint was lucky; however, he received the kind side of Tensei Kobayashi, considering his usual methods for torture and blatant annihilation of his enemies. While tempting, there was no way we could go in guns a blazing and claim 590 territory without a blood bath. In other words, this negotiation was vital for our narcotic expansion.

"How do you want to go about it?" Shindo's usual calm seemed a thing of yesterday, as his Jersey accent emphasized his irritation. "It's been nearly a year, Takeo. Kenji wouldn't let this shit drag on this long."

"I'm not Kenji, now am I?"

"Calm down," he says. "All I'm saying is they making us look mad weak out here. An eleven-month negotiation is unheard of."

"I am aware of this, Shindo."

"So, what you gonna do, Collector?" He asked, in a tone that would have been insolent had it not been for our tight relationship since Kenji's demise.

I offered a solemn nod to Sayuri, who'd been patiently awaiting my return to our conversation, before leaving the immaculate ranch house.

"I'll meet with you today to discuss our next moves. Father will be displeased if we do not get these talks underway. I'm going to the airport now."

"Cool," he says before adding. "And, uh, that isn't exactly why I called."

"Go on."

"I mean...what's the name of that guy who went on the run after shooting that pregnant teen in Jersey?"

I frown slightly as I regard his words, then realization strikes. "Ah, yes. Quincy Masters. What about him?"

A brief silence before he continues, "I overheard a couple of 590 goons talking about how he took off with a huge bag of cash and drugs before skipping town. Saint wants their heads."

"Their?"

"Yeah. Apparently he's planning on taking out the kids he's got with him, too. You know, the tall black kid with braids and the little girl with all the hair?"

"Of course, I know who they are." I say, speeding through the streets to get to the airport in my rental Audi. "Saint wants them handled?"

"Yep. Streets are real sore about this guy and his thieving kid."

I shook my head at this news, considering. While the Kobayashi's were a clan to be trifled with, we had a strict moral code of never harming children and women. It seemed no matter how much old age and hatred embittered Tensei Kobayashi, some of his conservative Japanese ways were left intact. He violated many of his own rules, but never that one.

A thought strikes me as soon as a possible solution does. "Wait a minute. Shindo, how do you know what they look like?"

"You mean Saint?" He probes.

"No!" I bark, my impatience heightening to new lengths. "Quincy and the children. You just described all of their attributes to the T."

"Oh, that," he snorts. "Because they're standing right in front of me."

The thought circulates through my mind again at his words, but not from shock. Shindo, much like myself, was great at hunting as the former Co-Collector for the Kobayashi's. He and Kenji were an unmatched team when given any target, more notorious than the newer formed The Violence and The Silence.

"Well done, Shindo." I commend him, barely focusing on the road from my chaotic thoughts. "We can leverage this to our advantage."

"Exactly my point, man," I can hear his grin on the opposite end. "I'm thinking I can take Quincy out right now, clean and smooth. Then the 590's will owe us."

"No," I fumed. "You are right. Negotiations have gone on far too long. New plan."

"I'm all ears."

As I explained the new deadly strategy to Shindo, my mind turned ten times over with the recurring thoughts never uttered out loud. These words would be the key piece in this plan succeeding if the Kobayashi's were to gain total control of southern territory. A heaviness set in as I stared at the gold band on my finger. The Kanji inscription on the inside reverberates in my mind as I consider the words I didn't want. Honor. Move forward with honor, and crush those who disrupt it.

This victory required pure violence.

And Shame.

Seventeen

EXCHANGE

Dirty Kitten Club

Time moved in a series of frames, jumping from one scene to the next at a pace I could barely keep up with. One frame containing a fumbled apology to All Bad for our almost fight back at Milio's. Another containing the party piling into someone's vehicle to hit the highway. Another frame consisted of a pitstop at my crib to grab cash, and the final one being me slumped over and sweaty in the VIP lounge where the LC's were welcomed with open arms by a burly woman named Madam Calico.

"This here is my club," Madam Calico said, grinning with a twinkle in her eye at Kenny when he sought her out. "But when you're here, I'll share the spotlight. Y'all are some high ballers huh?"

"What you think?" Kenny's voice oozed seduction and mischief as he stared at her.

Madam Calico giggled and wordlessly led us to the VIP lounge. "I think I'm sending in only my baddest bitches for y'all tonight."

"*Muchas gracias,*" Kenny whispered devilishly before the crew piled into the large section with circular seats.

We sat slightly above the room full of chain-smoking regulars in the pulpit, and I had to admit I was barely there when I clocked the four women entering the lounge section.

"Gimme some of that chocolate, girl." All Bad called to the woman in a red bedazzled two piece and red hair.

From the corner of my eye, I see T observing Kenny's lap dance hungrily. A loud trap song filled the air, and I noticed the stripper grind her hips to the beat on his lap while she watched T sitting beside him. I couldn't hear what they were saying, but ground my teeth as I saw the mocha skinned dancer kiss T's waiting mouth. Damn, I thought, whistling low as I watched the soon-to-be *ménage à trois* share kisses and body rubs. My dick hardened to a painful degree and I swore under my breath from the sight. I needed some of that, and soon, considering the ramping up effects from all the white I snorted a couple of minutes ago.

My brain felt like it was spitting in two as I shook my head to the music. I didn't realize my eyes were cinched closed until I felt my pants being fucked with. Not just fucked with, though, I consider as I peel my eyes open slowly to the sight of one of the chocolate strippers Madame Calico sent in. She's thick with hips and thighs to match her devastatingly juicy plump lips. Her large brown eyes have a devilish glint to them and I can't contain the groan when I see her lack of panties. She's completely naked, save for the sequin black bra that reveals her pebbled nipples budding through the sequin and fishnet.

"Wassup with you?" I growl at her.

"That's what I'm tryna figure out with you, High Baller." Her voice was like liquid silk, sultry and delicate at the same time. "You scared of spiders?"

I emitted another grunt as I considered her with a large grin. "Not much. Why, you tryna teach me something?"

"They say the Black Widow is the deadliest. You want Black Widow to take you on a ride like never before, or what?"

"Hell yeah," I say, grabbing onto her hips as she grinded slowly into my lap. "You scared of snakes?"

She chuckles as she continues her slow grind. "Snakes, huh?"

"Fuck yeah. Cuz this anaconda needs some attention. Don't play with it, girl."

"Tryna get caught in Black Widow's web, hmm?" She bit her lip as she casted excited eyes where I wanted: right at my dick that struggled to get free from my pants. "How much you willing to spend for a tangle in Black Widow's web, baby?"

Before I could respond, a familiar male's voice cuts in from beside me on the lounge couch.

"Treat my boy nice, now." Milio said, tucking a wad of bills in Black Widow's bra.

"I got it," I grunted to Milio as Black Widow peeled my jeans off. My dick stood proud and free in the dark club, begging for a taste of whatever the sexy stripper was willing to give.

Milio shrugged as he watched Black Widow drop to her knees in front of me. "No sweat, brother. I'm feeling generous tonight."

I nodded once at that, stifling the sharp moan from slipping past my throat as Black Widow did magic with her lips sucking hungrily at my dick.

"She's the best," Milio smiled as he watched her take me in deep and rise to repeat the throat dance again.

"Hell yeah," I whisper as the world falls away momentarily.

"But I need you to take care of somebody for me." Milio's words were casual, as if there wasn't a half-naked seductress slurping me down in the dark room.

"All right," I say, my mind in wonderland as he continues on.

"Good. Need this dude dead by next week. That's when prom is, and I think that'll be the best time to catch this Rasta motherfucker alone. I'll get some numbers together and work out payment tomorrow. Capiche?"

"Capiche, capiche, capiche..." I groaned in sheer ec-stasy as I neared my climax. "Damn, Black Widow. You got good mouth girl..."

"Don't let this young face confuse you, High Baller." She said after removing my flesh from her mouth with a wet *fwop*. "Black Widow is all woman. And all about her paper. You gonna slide me something extra before these lips make you cum, or what?"

"What?" I breathed, a mix between pain, panic and pleasure as I regarded her and my steel dick she's cir-cling around her mouth.

"If you want to cum, then Black Widow need a lil sum sum extra. Come on, don't you want me to finish you off...let Black Widow take that anaconda to heaven for a minute."

I dig around the wads of sweaty cash in my pocket and throw it at her. Fuck gentle, I needed to cum more than I needed my next breath in that moment.

"Heaven, coming right up." She breathes, before slurping down my dick to the very back of her throat. Her tongue lapped rhythmically at the tip as her head rose and fell and that's all I can take before exploding into her mouth with a tortured moan.

The music soon becomes a buzz in my ears as I lay against the chair. Somewhere in the background I see Kenny plowing his dick into the fire-haired stripper, whose mouth is buried between T's thighs. There are several other LC's getting sucked, fucked or overall get-

ting high and watching as they pass the women back
and forth. After blinking a few times to control the
racing of my heart and mind, I see Black Widow already
riding Milio, her bare pussy juices gleaming under the
few strobe lights occasionally flashing into the dark corner of the room as she glided her sheath on Milio's dick.
The sight makes me hard again, but I resolve myself to
find the bathroom as the urge to piss hits me.

I'm sure I look like a wounded dog as I limp myself
into the room labeled Restroom in dark, scrubbed off
letters.

My breaths were coming in more ragged than usual
after a fuck, and my heart skipped a few paces as used
the rest of my strength to kick the stall door open.

"Fuck!" The woman screams as the door swings open.
She's sitting on the toilet and covering her half-naked
body as I watch her with wide eyes. "Get the fuck out of
here! Are you crazy? Kicking my door open like you the
damn police!"

"Yo, my bad, Shawty." I slur, the harsh lights in the
pink room killing my high and splitting my brain.
"Need to pee."

"This is the women's restroom, you…" Her voice
trailed off as she took in my appearance. "Wait a
minute. You're Shay's brother?"

I reared back, squinting to study the girl who obviously knew more about me than I did her. "What's it to
you?"

She laughed as she wiped, flushed, and stood. "Makes sense why you wouldn't remember me. You look higher than a race horse. What you take?"

I shrugged, leaning my head against the wall as my eyes drifted closed "I'm high on life."

She leaned in close to sniff me. "Yeah, okay. Life smells a whole lot like gin. You better slow down on that shit, Shay's brother."

"Why you keep calling me that?" I asked the woman who appeared more of a blur to me.

"You wouldn't tell me your real name before. And you don't look like a Shame to me."

"Oh yeah?"

"Yeah," she snorted. "So, until you give me something real, Shay's brother will be who you are to me."

I laughed, attempting to steady the swirling in my head as I sank to my knees. The weight of my body was just too heavy, and there was no way I could make words and small talk at the same time.

"Whoa, be careful," she says, catching me and hoisting me up. "You look like you need to lay down."

"Nah," I groaned. "Need to pee. Excuse me."

"Excuse *me*," she retorted, tightening her hold on my larger body. "Sit down for a second. Try to breathe."

The last thing I heard her soft voice say before the darkness took over was a thing I thought I'd imagined. "I kept your secret safe, don't worry. I got you."

EIGHTEEN

COLOR

"I kept your secret safe, don't worry. I got you."

The soft words floated on a cloud in my head from an angel, I figured, as I slowly opened my eyes.

The room is dark, and from where I'm lying, I'm able to make out the worn chairs and fat back TV from a few feet away. The smell of coffee rouses me to sit up slightly, yet a sliver of sunlight pierces my vision that sends me backwards.

Where was this place? I queried inwardly as I studied more of the small, but tastefully decorated living room. Yeah, that's what this place was, someone's home that I didn't recognize, and a fit of panic surges through me at that. Last I remembered was Black Widow's mouth webbed around my dick before blacking out. Did Milio drag me home, or to someone else's crib? Maybe this was one of the LC's cribs. Yeah, that made sense. Because if it wasn't, then I was almost certain that I'd been straight up kidnapped.

"You ugly," a small voice chirped from my bedside. Or, rather, couch side since it was the sofa I woke up on.

"Say what?" I groused, my throat dry and groggy from sleep.

"I said you ugly as hell," the voice repeated. I don't have the mental capacity to get angry, so in curiosity, I turn to face my potential next target.

A skinny kid, no older than eight or nine, is standing there with a head full of ponytails with purple barrettes dangling off them. Her eyes are big and she's frowning disapprovingly at my strewn form on the couch.

"Who the fuck are you?" I ask.

"How did your ugly ass get in my house anyways?" She demands just as bitterly as Dawn would've.

"Yo, kid," I grunt, struggling to sit upright. "Where your moms at?"

"Jolie!" A woman hollers as she enters the living space. Without warning, the skinny woman forces the blinds open to allow a whole bunch of sunlight into the room. "Leave our guest alone and go get dressed for school."

Jolie pouted and stomped her foot, "I was just asking him a question! You ain't got to get an attitude."

The skinny woman is rocking a bonnet and pink satin robe. She spreads her arms akimbo as she glares at the tinnier version of herself. "Don't make me whip your ass. Go do as I said."

"You ain't my momma!"

She looked around before thundering, "Find me somebody that gives a damn. When Mommy ain't here, I'm in charge. Now go get dressed for school before I give you something to whine about!"

"Ugh!" She screeched before running down the hall.

"Where am I?" I asked once the kid disappeared with an answering slam of the door.

The skinny woman rolled her eyes before sitting down next to me on the couch. "How are you feeling? You had me kind of scared back at the club the other night."

"The club…" I mutter, piecing together the happenings of yesterday.

"Yeah. You totally passed out right after barging into my bathroom stall. You pervert." She laughed good naturedly and I allowed myself to study her. Really look at her to identify who she was and where all the time went. Her words made a little sense, but it was still foggy. "Let me guess. You don't remember any of it?"

I shook my head.

She rolled her eyes. "Well, you look fine enough to me to go home. You really don't remember busting into the women's restroom with your dick swinging through the air?"

"Nah. Sorry."

"I'd say 'it's all good,' but it ain't." She said. "It's me, though. Jerica. Shay's friend? You're her brother who came in that night and killed that bodyguard? You came with that Asian guy."

It all rushed back to me then. The memory of the night my big sister died to me, in a sense, considering I didn't trust her any further than I could throw her these days. Though a contract executioner, there was so much death that permeated that day between the ending of my and Shay's bond, Si and my partnership, and...

The image of Dawn's smile flashed like a collage in my mind, and I shook it away before I could become slave to the shame.

"What time is it and where am I?" I ask her.

"About ten in the morning. And you're at my place in Maple Shade. If you're not in a hurry, then I made some coffee."

"How did I end up here? Did you carry me or something?"

"Hell nah," she chuckled. "Coffee helped you to my car. You passed out in the bathroom."

"Oh...okay," I say, considering the same loser bouncer I referred to as Punk Ass Coffee. "I do need to get going."

Her bubbly smile crumbled, making my chest sink a little for putting the look there. "Oh, all good. I figured you'd be busy."

"Yeah," I grumble. "You got a bathroom?"

"No."

"What?"

She threw her head back as a fit of laughter took over. "This ain't a third world country, of course there's a bathroom."

I couldn't resist staring at her exposed collar bone. She was a tiny thing, petite, and no taller than five feet or so. The only identifiable feature on her that indicated any kind of maturity was her neck tats: two Kanji characters were inked just below her jawbone, and I couldn't resist the urge to feel them under my fingers.

Her skin is as soft as velvet under my hands, and I don't even fight to resist the readily hardened dick that's manifested at her appearance.

Her laughter ceases, and she keeps her neck craned to allow me to explore her skin, much to my surprise.

"What do these characters mean?" I ask.

"*Shinjitsu,*" she says in fluent Japanese and in a dialect that conveys her mastery of the language. "It roughly translates to 'The Truth.'"

I roam calloused fingers across more surface area, attempting to ignore how her body and voice trembled.

"That's..."

"...weird." She finished for me, a weak chuckle escaping her, "I know."

"And *not* what I was going to say."

"O-Oh."

"This is straight up beautiful."

A warm color flushes her cheeks red. "Stop it. It's stupid, I know. To get my stage name inked on me is so basic beyond belief. No need to sugarcoat on behalf of my feelings."

I licked my lips and grabbed her jaw, bringing her eyes to meet mine. I could see how she got along with my sis, considering they did the same thing. Deflected compliments like bullets flying at them.

"Are you fluent?"

Her eyes search the room before she realizes what I'm asking and nods. "Mostly. My brother was stationed in Okinawa where I spent the first chunk of my life. Got bullied like you wouldn't believe."

"Beauty and brains." I tell her, my voice falling to an intrigued husk as I retract my fingers from her trembling body. That magnetism is still there, same as when she wrapped her lips around my gun, but there is something different about her. The confident, yellow-haired vixen I compared to Wonder Woman is gone. Standing before me was someone I felt like I was meeting for the first time.

She snorted, and wrapped arms around herself. "I don't know about that."

"Why do they call you The Truth?" I couldn't resist asking.

"It's sort of a play on my real name."

"Jerica, right? It suits you."

"Thanks." Another faint blush before she adds, "that's me. Jerica True."

A strange feeling swarms my senses, like a distant alarm is ringing that I need to pay attention to, but I block it out. We're now just standing there, staring into each other's eyes as words seemed to escape us and float through the air unsaid.

"Why are you called Shame?" She whispered.

"Just because," I answered, turning to find the bathroom. Panic ignites as the grim reality stretches before me. She wants to talk. Get to know me. Everyone I allowed in, allowed into my underworld ended up suffering. All because of me. All because of Shame. "Is the bathroom down this hall?"

"Hey!" She called as I power walked it to the bathroom door. "Don't walk away from me. What's so top secret about your name, Shay's brother? Even Shay wouldn't clue me in. She just says to call you Shame, or The Commander. Whatever that means."

I stop at the mention of that name. That same nickname we penned our father as an epitome of our disapproval and unexpressed hostility where he was concerned.

"Shay said that?"

"Ouch!" Jerica slams into my back, sputtering from my sudden pause. "And yeah. Said that's who you turned into these days. Again, I don't know what that means. Some strange inside joke, I assume?"

"No," I answer, my voice straining from emotion. "My name is Shamel."

"Shamel..." she breathed my name like a song, testing it on her lips behind me. "Beautiful."

"Nothing beautiful about me, girl."

"In the eye of the beholder, right?"

"Then you don't need me to remind you how good you look. Got me hard as fuck." I growled, doing the thing T accused me of to derail the serious direction of the conversation. Using playboy humor.

To my relief, Jerica doesn't press the issue further.

"Shit," she breathes sharply again, stepping back. "That's a lot of honesty for ten in the morning. I'll let you handle your business. Coffee is ready if you want it."

"Thank you, Jerica."

"You're welcome, *Shamel.*"

"Don't wear it out, now," I tease before shutting the bathroom door.

The casual playboy grin disappears as I choke on the tears that threatened to fall at Jerica's words. Shay thought of me as The Commander? The fucking Commander?! I had my faults, and hell, I was sure there was a pretty place carved out for me in Hell, but I was nothing like that dude. He did evil for evil's sake, whereas I was born into the darkness. What choice did I have other than to make him proud?

I'm hyperventilating by the time I finish my bath-room business, and it takes all the strength I have post-high to get my shit together enough to rejoin the unexpectantly bashful girl in the living room.

Si's words from the laundromat came back to me then and filled me with a resolve I needed to move forward:

"Don't let the shame of your parentage make you weak. Instead, swallow it. Channel it into muscle, and take no pris-oners."

He was right, like usual, and I had to get my shit together. Had to champion up and make this money, even if it meant pushing chronic for the LC's for the foreseeable future.

"Shamel, I made toast, too!" Jerica called from the kitchen like a dutiful wife. I kill that daydream before it had time to fester into misplaced desire. There was no place in my future for anything as normal as that. Nothing as pleasant as that.

"Appreciate you!" I call, opening the door. "But I think I'll take off—"

The hallway is lined with family portraits I hadn't noticed upon my hasty beeline to the restroom. The photos are magnificent, really, and Hallmark quality that displays a large African American family sitting and facing a camera. There's a plump matriarch in the middle with dark skin like cocoa. She's holding an irate infant in her lap with a nest of curls on his head. Three identically-faced children are sitting around her on their knees. I recognize the smart mouthed girl Jerica called Jolie sitting beside two similarly aged boys in royal blue uniforms and slacks. Two people are standing in the back, and it's hard to conceal my smile as I study the scrawny, nerdy looking girl with large rimmed glasses, braces, and short curly hair. She looks so kind and nerdy at the same time. It's Jerica, the yellow-haired vixen from the club and bashful bonnet-wearing woman from a few moments prior I'd been trying to figure out. My mind turns with several wisecracks I'd readily prepared for our discussion when I rejoin her in the living room, but all thought dies when I study the man beside her in the family portrait.

He's outfitted in a royal blue military uniform that denotes his Air Force status. And while his unsmiling face resembles the other five family members, I can't help but notice the man whose death birthed the ruthless duo, The Violence and The Silence. The man I had a hard time reconciling the way his entire death went down, how torn up I'd been over that botched contract that Si and I had to cover up to save both our asses.

The same man who was so straight-laced he'd had honesty for a name.

Stanley True.

"Yo, Jerica!" I call.

She appears beside me in an instant wearing a worried frown. "What's wrong?"

I gulped. "Who this?"

"Oh." She said following my gaze to the portrait. A warm smile crested her gorgeous face. "That's my family. That's my mom and the Trips."

"The Trips?"

"Yeah," she smiled. "My brothers and sisters. We nicknamed them the Trips because they're triplets and equally always up to no good. Jolie, Jaylor and Jayden. They're literally a trip."

"And the baby?"

She chews her lip before answering, "That's my son, Hakeem. He was so little then."

Something unravels at the thought of Jerica happily cuffed or married to some other dude. I don't fucking like it. Not at all.

"You got a man?" I ask, unable to tamp down the rage sprouting in me.

"No." She answers quickly. "His sperm donor's out of the picture. It's just us and the troublesome Trips. The True Crew."

I almost join her in laughing before I point to the guy in the portrait who's smiling at me in a way I can't bear. "And him?"

Her previous joy dissipates at the sight of him. "That's my big brother, Stan. He, um...he's not with us anymore."

I'm choking on the ready-made sentiment I had a couple minutes ago but decided against it. It's condescending as fuck to do that. She didn't need that from me. Already, my shame was rubbing off on her, and like Shay implied, disaster followed me everywhere.

Wordlessly, I walked to the living room to collect my things. My things, in actuality, were just a belt and a phone with way too many missed calls on it. I do a quick study of the screen and notice several numbers attempting to reach me: school, my mother, and Miss Pat. It had been a little while since I saw Miss Pat, considering the steady supply of cash I try to give her. Even though I didn't do contracts anymore, I attempted to help out where I could to combat her constantly rising rent payments. My heart sank at the reality of things, that I had not sent her a check in over three weeks. I made a vow to return her call once I left the small house I noticed was an apartment complex upon opening the front door.

"Wait!" Jerica calls, rushing behind me. "Where are you going? You okay to walk out of here?"

I turned to her, and her large brown eyes on me shined hope and possibility, same as Dawn's did when she looked at me at one point. Unable to stand it, I pull her into my arms.

"Shamel?" She asks, breathless and confused. "Everything okay?"

I placed a kiss into her bonnet clad head, knowing this would have to be our final goodbye. To keep her heart and safety intact, I had to cut out the cancer. Which was me.

"Take care of yourself, Jerica. I left my number on the coffee table, so you can call me if you ever need me. Okay?"

She snorts. "That sounds super final, Shamel."

"Shame," I correct, my voice hard.

She wraps her arms around me. "So, we're back to Shame again. Was it something I did or said?"

I kiss her again, savoring her smell before letting go and starting down the street.

"Whatever it is you're trying to protect me from, then forget that. And don't be stupid."

I pause and turn to face her. "Go back in the house, Jerica. It's nothing you need to worry about."

"I told you I got you." She said, winded, as she raced to stand before me down the street. "And I ain't no punk bitch."

I scrunched my face at that. "Where was the girl from the living room with all that red in her cheeks from my hand on her neck? You was grinning like a girl Jolie's age through our whole conversation back there."

"I got a few sides to me." She says, taking another step to swallow the distance between us. Our chests are touching now. "Most days I'm Truth. The bitch who takes no shit when it comes to her family, funds, or peace. Other days…I'm Jerica. The girl who snorts when she laughs. The girl who might be a little obsessed with watching Anime and reading cheesy romance novels."

"Who am I talking to now, then? Huh?"

"Well," she husks, wrapping her arms around my neck. "That depends on how much time you got. Let me help you, Shamel."

"Nah," I grunt as I peel her arms off me. I had to put some distance between us before I ended up doing something I sure as hell shouldn't. Like dragging her back to her crib and tasting her pussy like I'd been wanting to do since meeting her.

"You can't just leave me here. I don't know what trouble you got yourself in with that Asian dude again, but I'm good at solving problems. I solved yours that night after the bloodbath y'all left Calico's Champagne Room. *I* did that. Know why?"

I stared at her, my eyes full of questions for her and myself. I often wondered why I let her go back into the club that night instead of dragging her with me. Instead of dragging her back to the loading dock and discarding her same as Monty, I let her leave. Empowered her with the lethal knowledge of my underworld at the risk of everything. But her words...her misplaced devotion...warms something ice cold in my chest.

She re-wraps her arms around my body, but it isn't sensual like before. No. It's as if she's afraid I'll disappear in thin air if she doesn't hold me tight.

"I like you. Let me in, okay?" Her voice is tender, meek, and searching. Nothing like the bold tone of the side she called Truth.

"Jerica..." I choke out. "Why?"

She spoke after I returned my arms around her, pulling her close and just as tight. If not tighter.

"I don't need a reason to be me. I just am. I was just like you a time ago. I want you to learn to trust. Trust me like you did that night to have your back."

A long moment passes with us holding each other and saying nothing. She's right, I realize, I don't trust easy. I don't trust at all. Trust was too costly a virtue in my underworld. She had a way of pushing through the jock humor and evasiveness, sort of like Shay, she'd been trying to get me to value myself. To be real and bring Shamel from the dark.

But I couldn't. Not now. Maybe not ever, because it's *her* brother's blood on *my* hands. Mine.

"Thank you," I mumble into her bonnet, inhaling deep before letting her go and resuming my dark descent.

"Don't..." She whimpers, as Jerica or Truth, I wasn't sure.

I don't bother to respond to her, despite the fierce beating of my heart to turn back, sink to my knees, and grovel for forgiveness. With a heavy heart, I leave.

NINETEEN

OUTPLAYED

The twenty-five-minute taxi ride from Maple Shade gave me the emotional space to sort some shit out. Stanley fucking True was her big brother. Of course, of all the women I couldn't keep my hands off of, it'd be the one whose brother my former co-killer and I eighty-sixed and covered up. Our deal back then consisted of me taking credit for that contract, taking the payment I received from The Commander and splitting it with Si since he dealt the actual lethal blow. I paid Stanley's remaining debt owed to the Kobayashi's in exchange for Si's gun. When the dude's death gained media attention, like it was meant to, the outlets listed the exact gun that finished him, and it was convenient to produce that same weapon as proof to The Commander. Something to show him it was me who killed the man with truth for a name, instead of Si, who'd lost his cool.

I knew this shit would come back to haunt me, and in the worst way. It didn't take a rocket scientist to decipher the raw attraction crackling between us. When she entered the room, my brain turned to mush, as did the lethal side of me.

My mushy mind and heart battled with each other with how to go about dealing with Jerica when I climbed out of the cab. I notice my rental parked on the street of the shack, and have to take a few breaths to keep my cool at the realization. All Bad drove my ride back to my house. Without me. What the fuck was his problem? I'm fantasizing about all the torture scenarios I'd enact on him when I saw him, but froze when I noticed the person sitting at the front porch step.

He's rocking his signature black leather jacket and jeans, assassin garb I'd called it, but I knew this was just his style. I'd been the psycho who couldn't resist the white wife beaters with my signature FILA joggers to complete contracts.

"Shame," Si greets me as he stands up. "How is everything?"

"The fuck you doing here, man?"

"Skipping the pleasantries as usual, I see."

I only stare at him, wrestling with the notion of knocking his ass out since I no longer carried Luci on me. Bullets got too expensive these days, between keeping the lights on, paying Mom's medical bills, and helping Miss Pat.

He sighs. "How is business going? Keeping steady work?"

"Something like that." I grunted, walking past him. "Think you in the wrong part of town, pretty boy."

"What do you mean?"

"I mean, this is East Camden. As gritty as it gets. Not a penthouse in downtown Trenton."

"Are you implying that I can't handle the hood? My work takes me to all sorts of neighborhoods."

"Congratulations." I sneer. "You want a medal or something? Now tell me what the fuck it is you want before your pretty boy face ain't so pretty anymore. I'm tired as hell."

He stares probingly into my eyes, assessing something before saying, "You've been getting high."

I'm fumbling with the key to the door before I feel his hand on my arm.

"Shame." His voice is deadpan, low. "What are you taking?"

"Same shit as always." I couldn't resist answering with the truth. My head throbbed too damn bad to lie this afternoon.

"What shit? Marijuana?"

"Nah," I cackled mirthlessly.

"Crack?"

"I ain't no Head. What you tryna say?"

"I'm not trying anything. I'm just guessing, since you aren't being exactly forthcoming with that information. Come on, Shame. We're partners."

"*Were* partners." I emphasized.

"Either way," he says. "I still care. Now what are you taking?"

A long silence before I said into the quiet, "Like I said. Same as always. My Pops paid me very well those days. And not just in cash."

"That so?"

"Yep." I sneer. "Payment came in the form of green bills and little blue pills."

There's that look, I think, that pity expression that I'm accustomed to when I tell even the smallest portion of my story to anyone who'd listen.

He rears back before continuing. "How long have you been taking these... little blue pills?"

"About seven or eight years now."

His shark eyes bug at this information I shared with no one. "You're only seventeen years old. You mean to tell me that you've been micro-dosing with prescription meds since ten years old? Am I understanding that correctly?"

"Why are you even here, my dude?" I ask, pivoting the conversation to a much more digestible material that didn't make me hyperventilate. "You came all the way over here after an entire year of radio silence just to shrink my head?"

"I...came over here to offer you a contract."

"No!" I bark, resuming my fight with the doorknob. "I don't do that shit no more."

"You experienced a lot of loss last year, Shame. I want to respect your space and healing. But I know you've probably been having a hard go at it since the end of our partnership."

"I do just fine."

"Are you willing to come out of retirement for thirty-k?"

Damn that number was enough to swear under my breath. I hadn't made money like that since...well, I had contracts.

My fingers itch with the desire to grab my gun. Luci isn't there, but damn it if I didn't need her healing powers bad right now. After the night with the LC's and the morning with Jerica True, it's impossible to dredge up the energy to fight this conversation. Simply put, I needed a shower and a recharge from all of that, and the idea of executing another contract...of taking out another target...all the blood...I just can't handle it. Not again. Not anymore.

"I've found Quincy Masters," Si says coolly in that way of his, so cool and casual it takes me a minute to put two and two together.

"Si," I whisper, my voice a depthless hiss. "Is that the truth, or are you just tryna pull me back into the business?"

His hard dark eyes bore into mine as I do a slow twist to meet him face-to-face. Funny, I'd been so emotionally depleted before this conversation, yet from the weight of his words, I'd been suddenly revitalized instead of weighed down.

"Both," he responded with the same cool. "I wouldn't be here if I didn't need you. You're the best man for the job. The Kobayashi's aren't executioners, we deal with drugs and debt collection, not...the kind of contracts Quincy facilitated. I need your expertise on this."

"What you need me to do?"

"What you do best."

"I'll kill him myself!" I snarl, hot anger burning my insides suddenly. "Where is that bastard?"

"New York. He's been hiding out in Queens, of all places. But we will not be killing him."

"Why the fuck not?" I demand, my eyes crazy and scanning his face for any trace of deception.

"No. I have other plans for him."

"Then why are you here if you ain't tryna talk business? You know what I want. I want this nigga dead with my own hands. What kind of deal would possibly make me turn a blind eye on deading that son of a bitch?"

"He's wanted by a rival gang in D.C., the 590's, headed by Saint Millard. The Kobayashi's have been trying to expand our territory into parts of the south, and they are proving to be a complication."

"So?"

"So." He hesitates. "We've found evidence linking Saint Millard to Quincy Masters's escape. After combing through the books of the Wash N' Go, it can be surmised that Quincy has been funneling money from the 590's and keeping it for himself."

"First of all, who is 'we?' And why should I care if that pussy stole from some D.C. gang? I want him dead yesterday. That's all I care about. And you're gonna tell me where he at!"

"Calm down, Shame," he says, stepping away from me. "I'm getting to that. My associate Yamada Shindo and I have been working to get the negotiations settled with the 590's for almost a year now unsuccessfully. Long story short, they're too dirty to make further deals with. They'll need to be taken care of if we're to expand into the southern markets at all."

"So y'all want me to take him out? Saint?"

"No."

"Then who?"

"We're hatching a plan to lure the 590's to Quincy, since they're looking for him. They'll have no clue that they're showing up to a bloodbath. We'll be disposing of the entire gang."

I blink slowly. Deliberately, before responding. "Y'all want me to take out a whole gang?"

"Yes."

"Let me get this straight," I snarl. "Y'all want to use Quincy as bait to lure an entire fucking armed gang to his location, where I'll be waiting for them. Then kill them all. Am I getting this right?"

A pause, then a look, before he nods.

My fists clench in restraint, but I warn myself to calm down. This was the emotion that Si and Quincy talked about was my Achilles heel. There's no way in hell I'd lose it again after those merciless accusations. Inhaling deep, I compose and stare into his eyes.

"All I want is Quincy, man. I don't do that shit no more."

"Really? So, you're comfortable pushing menial drug deals for the rest of your life? Comfortable with the hundreds, instead of thousands, you're making to support two households? Your mother's not insured, Shame. Tell me you have a way to pay for that surgery she needs. Tell me."

"How you know..." I nearly asked, before realizing my question. Realizing who I was speaking to. He was The Silence, but most notably known as the Collector for this reason alone. Had a talent at digging up people, info, and your biggest fucking bones buried deep in the closet.

I stagger back to sit on the porch steps. My head was spinning now, from the all the sense he made. He was right. Mom was getting worse, and I even noted the pink in her urine after she'd forgotten to flush the toilet one time. The doc wanted to take a deeper look at whatever was going on, to see if there was something causing her only kidney from functioning right. But that cost serious green. Serious green the LC's drug deals only made a tiny dent in. That's why my blood boiled as hot as it did when I found Shay's hidden stash of cash.

"I don't know, man..." I whispered weakly. "I'm not sure if I'm cut out for that type of work no more."

Si took a tentative seat beside me. "You are. Don't forget who you are."

"A fucking shame." I said in a hollow voice.

"Not *a* shame. But *the* Shame. The Violence. You're an expert at sniping crowds of men in seconds. It's why I came to you. You have a gift that I was not born with. A talent and integrity of tigers that's brought us riches and status. We can reclaim our name, but I also want to set you up nice."

"Set me up nice?" I inquired disbelievingly. "What you talking about?"

"I want you to lead our operations in the south. Once we succeed in annihilating the 590's, their influence will no longer prevent our operations into the southern markets. I've thought long about it, and you're who I can trust to run our ops down there. You'll be in charge, and money will be a worry of the past for the foreseeable future. You'll be surrounded by more money and means than you can imagine. How does that sound?"

"Fuck." I swore, considering his words. The deal sounded larger than life and reality, one too sweet to come true. I remember the blood in my nails after that night, and hear her screams all over again. I couldn't do it, thought. Not again.

I shook my head. "Yo, I don't think I can. The last bit of blood I'm carrying on my hands is my father's. He's who my final bullet belongs to. Not some gang."

He nods. "Well, okay. If I can't convince you of your greatness, then I hope the gift I left will be enough to change your mind. Your mother has it in her possession. Think about it. If you want your retribution, give me a call at my usual number. We'll both be able to get our vengeance this way."

I'm shaking my head, attempting to wrap my mind around the larger-than-life deal as I enter the house. I could buy my way out of all my problems, and escape this hellhole that was Camden, once and for good. A change of scene could be just the thing to bring my mother back to health, and put me back in Shay's good graces. Also, if he found Quincy, that meant Yvonne was alive. That meant she was safe and existing in some place without me. I had to get to her, and even though I'm no good for her, I had to try. I made a decision, then and there, to devote my next few years to getting it right. My new mission, I told myself, would be to see her smiling and safe with me. I had to do what I had to do.

"Shamel, darling, shouldn't you be in school?" Mom asked as I trudged into the house in mild daze from my conversation with Si. He'd found Quincy, and invariably, that meant Yvonne was found, too. Found alive. Found safe. It was too late for Mike, but I had to make a plan to get to her. To be better for her.

"Shamel?" She repeated, snapping my focus to her and All Bad occupying the wobbly dining room table we barely used. "Is school over with?"

An energetic fur ball bounded towards my ankles as I'm walking towards the living room couch.

"Uh, nah. Didn't go today." I said, keeping it real for lack of room for dishonesty right now, but also mildly distracted by the animal yipping at my heels as I sit down. "Whose dog is this?"

"Oh, okay." She says, her face falling slightly as she lifted a teacup in the air. "Shaheim brought the family a puppy! Isn't he just the cutest?"

"A puppy?" I questioned; my voice already ripe from the frustration of him driving my car. "All Bad, what the hell possessed you to get us a dog? We don't need that right now."

"Well, that's good then, because I bought Ozymandias for Miss Sommer, anyway." He said, his tone snide as my fingers twitched with the desire to fuck him up.

"Ozymandias?" I countered, attempting to calm the hyper Australian Shepherd with my hands. Ozymandias took a large bite out of pinky finger, making me leap back from the sting. "Ouch, you little shit!"

"Oz, for short," All Bad chuckled as he watched my losing battle with the ankle biting pup. "Got the name from that book you sent me while I was locked down. You know, the one filled with old farty ass poetry and shit?"

I needed a minute to remember that, and when the memory of me stealing the book of sonnets from that hateful ass Mr. Wiggins a year ago floated back, much of the irritation in me simmered down. I sent it to him as a joke at the time, knowing he'd probably never read it, much less recall names from it.

"You read it?" I couldn't conceal the shock.

He only nodded, returning his gaze to my mother. "That's right. Kenny's dog had puppies and this little dude was the last one left. So, I thought, Miss Sommer might bring some light into his world just like she does for everybody else."

"And who's going to feed it, huh?" I sneered at the irrational man whose irrational ways landed him in a pen for the last eight years.

An angry tic set in his jaw before he turned to me. "I got it. I'll make sure Oz and Miss Sommer stay straight. On God."

"Join us for tea!" Mom said nervously, gauging the tension crackling in the room between us. "Shaheim made a dessert of some sort. I'm sorry, what is it called again, love?"

All Bad's cheeks reddened at the endearment, diffusing the blatant anger from before as he spoke. "I made a prison staple: State Cake."

"Ah, yes!" Mom sang before taking a bite out of the strange substance on her plate. "It's quite nice."

"Come get you some lil cuz." All Bad ushered me over with his insistent hands towards the available dining chair.

"I ain't eating that shit. Ma, you better spit that out if you don't wanna punish that toilet later."

"Shamel!" She reprimanded while chewing. "Our guest made a sweet treat and I'd like you to have some with us."

"Yeah, come on, Mel." All Bad added, scarfing down the prison cake like it was out of style.

"I'm good on that." I respond, grimacing at the mysterious dessert. "But was there a package left for me? Or like a bag?"

Mom frowns consideringly as she nibbles on the prison food that looked more like strange science. "Oh, yes! There was actually a black bag left at the front door this morning with 'Shame' written atop. I assumed they were addressing you, by that horrid name, at that."

"Yeah," I grunt. "Thank you."

"No problem. I set it in your bedroom on your bed. It's waiting for you when you get the chance."

"You so damn considerate, Miss Sommer." Al Bad said dreamily, drawing a cringe from me and a blush from Mom.

"Shaheim, you're a gem"

"Fuck all that." He says with a wave of his hand. "I want to be your man. You could be my gem, though."

"You're too kind." She whispers, avoiding his intense stare and my obvious distaste from across the room.

"Kind ain't me." He says, grabbing her hand. "Ain't never been me. But I like this. Kicking it with you and eating State Cakes. You been the only one who ain't treat me different since I been out."

"Of course not. You've always treated my Shamel as the best big brother back then."

"But I ain't that either. I'm not a little boy stealing from the candy store no more. I'm all man. A real man. Just like you need."

Mom's blush darkens as she shoots to her feet in one quick motion. "I'll be in my room if you boys need me, all right? Come on, Oz."

"Miss Sommer, hold up—"

"Let her go." I caution him while glaring at the exchange.

I didn't know what was going on neither did I understand the embarrassed panicky way Mom shot from her seat, grabbed the finicky puppy, and all but bolted up the stairs. But I sure as hell was going to find out.

"What's all that about?" I ask before walking over and occupying the previous chair he offered me.

All Bad casts a forlorn stare at the staircase, as if he's torn with himself on whether to follow her or not.

"Eyes over here, man," I tell him.

Heat blazes in his eyes at my warning. "And who the fuck are you? Can't you see that was an A and B conversation? We was in the middle of some real shit."

"You ain't fucking my mom, All Bad. Dead that idea."

"It ain't about fucking. We was just...vibing. Nah mean?"

I sigh while casting him a wary look. In all honesty, I was bone and soul tired, and had very little energy or patience for this convo that should have been a no-brainer.

"Yeah, and I know my dumb ass brother did a number on her heart and shit. And I'm sorry about that. Especially after hearing what he did and where he is...on the run with some kids? She ain't feeling her best right now, and I want to be the man to show her what love look like. The genuine kind you feel for somebody and not the kind you get stabbed over."

"She good. Just leave her be, man. Can't you see she healing from the shit? I ain't gonna let you stick it and leave with her. She damn near raised you, so show some respect. Where is all this coming from anyways? You only been out for like forty-eight hours at this point."

"Yeah, but I know what I want. Prison teaches you that time ain't nothing to waste. It waits for nobody, so I want to shoot my shot."

I stare at him, studying him for even the slightest detection of humor or game, but I sense none. In fact, he looked just as sure as I felt about my new mission to protect long lost sister, and a piece of the hard stone in my chest crumbles a little at it. I wasn't the typical son to bulldog my mom's love interests. If she wanted to get back out there, then I'd encourage her to. I wanted to be the fountain for her. Solid and nurturing, sure, but also a fountain of support to her just like she'd been to me these past few months. She finally looked at me, dug deeper, asked me questions and nagged me. Sommer Rose Masters, the previously willfully ignorant trap wife, finally made an effort to see and be there for her children. So, if this was what she wanted...

"Don't expect for me to call you daddy, nigga." I grumble, loosening my fists and smiling a little.

All Bad's smile was young and spread from ear-to-ear. "Nigga only in your wildest dreams would I be your Pops. Chill on that."

We laugh good naturedly, and I reveled in the restored calm in the air.

"For real though, man." I say after thirty or so minutes of aimless chatting. "You don't even have a job. How you gonna take care of her? Her med bills?"

He averted his eyes for a minute before mumbling something I couldn't hear.

"Speak up, nigga."

"I said, Milio got me some work. Said if I did him this favor he'll slide me a couple of G's."

My heart freezes at his words, as well as the vague ones I recall him shouting at me over the loud music in the Dirty Kitten.

"What exactly did he offer you?" I asked.

He frowned. "That's between him and me, bro."

"All Bad, for real man." I all but growl. "Tell me what he said."

He sighs. "All right, all right Don't wet your panties over it. He asked me to take care of some high school kid. Said it's all lined up and it'll be easy-peasy since he'll be at a dance or something."

"Fuck," I swore under my breath, furious that he'd go and ask All Bad to do this job. All Bad had no prospects, no money, and was an easy target for jobs like this. Though I'd been violating Rule 23 for the past year by dealing with LC's, enough was enough. It was clear that Milio was willing to take down whoever and by whatever means, even at the expense of my semi-desperate cousin.

This meant war.

And a war I'd have a chance at winning or escaping from new mission and offer from Si. He offered me the deal of a lifetime. It just meant that I had to shed some more blood, and a lot of it, but at this point, it was one I couldn't refuse. Especially after Milio pulled that snake ass move, asking me while I was high and then going to my cousin as backup for when I eventually came to and re-refused. He was on some mad despicable shit since his girl got pregnant by one of his homies.

"I need your help with something, man."

"Anything, cuz." All Bad said in earnest, folding his arms. "Shoot."

I take a deep breath before taking the plunge with the ask. If was a big one, one I had to be sure he was prepared to take with me since it meant betraying the LC's.

"My old partner came to me with a deal I want you to get in on."

"Hell yeah. All Bad loves himself a deal. How much money we gonna make?"

I open my mouth to tell him about the beaucoup bucks guaranteed to us if we went through with this deadly deal, but my phone rang and interrupted the flow.

Shit. It's Miss Pat, who I'd meant to call *way* earlier after I left Jerica True's apartment.

"Granny," I smile into the phone. "Wassup with you?"

Sniffling from the other side of the line could be heard before her gruff voice spoke. Firm and militant, and not at all like her when it came to me.

"I don't...I don't have the words." She said instead of a hello.

I frowned and looked at the phone to be sure I wasn't being pranked. "Miss Pat?"

"Don't you come back around here. You cost me my home! I'm gone...I'm gone..."

"You gone? Don't come around?" I demanded while standing. I was already throwing my coat on before she responded.

"My landlord is dead. A suicide the news called it. But I know it was you. I told you to leave it to me, but you...you...you cost me my home of thirty years! They forced me out and it's all because of you. I told you to stay out of it, Shamel!"

She was screeching a few other obscenities I couldn't comprehend from the mix of yelling and tears.

"Miss Pat!" I called frantically. "Calm down. What are you talking about your landlord committed suicide?"

"That's what the news said. But you did it! You took care of him just like you probably took care of your daddy. You killed my landlord! You evil fucking snake ass liar! Don't you ever come near me again. I'm homeless because of you. I hate you so much I'm seeing red."

"Miss Pat! Hold up!" I holler, but three beeps let me know she's already hung up.

TWENTY

IDOLS

"She does *not* want to speak with you!" Angie thunders from the opposite end of the phone.

I got desperate after the call disconnected so suddenly and wouldn't allow me to connect again. Was that person really Miss Pat? My Project Granny who looked out for me all these years? The same woman who'd bandaged me, mothered me, and kept all my blood secrets out of respect for me and fear of my father? She blocked my number, I realized, after another failed attempt of connecting with her line for the sixth time.

"Angie, please, let me know where she is. How was I supposed to know she got forcefully removed from her crib?"

She snorted. "Right, like I'm going to believe you had no idea how her landlord ended up with a bullet in his own head a couple days ago."

"What the fuck are you trying to say?"

"I'm not trying to say anything!" She spits. "What I'm actually saying is that you had no right meddling in her business. She told you that she would handle it, and we were working on getting some legal support until you went ahead and..."

"And what? Go ahead and say it, so I know exactly how to handle this conversation."

"You see?" She screamed. "See what you do? You bully and intimidate. How has that tactic worked for you before, huh? Did peace ever follow an interaction like that?"

"I'm not a bully." I grouse, pacing the floor of the living room now. "I've never treated none of y'all like that or even raised a hand to you."

"Abuse has many faces, Mel."

"Oh, shut it with that college-talk mumbo jumbo. Talk to me real. Have I ever bullied you? More so, have I ever treated Miss Pat with anything less than respect?"

A pause, then she whispered. "Sort of, yeah."

"How? When?"

"When you came over after finding that eviction notice on her door? Did she not tell you that she'd handle it?"

"I..." My words trail off into thought.

I recalled the terror on Heath Shay's face as I held him at gunpoint. Yeah, it wasn't exactly angelic means, but I figured I'd scared him off enough to pull the plug on the demolition. However, I admittedly didn't verify or confirm anything after receiving that call from Mikey. Everything, in all actuality, blurred into the abyss of unnecessary after that discovery.

I pinched the bridge of my nose, coaching myself on calm before speaking again. "I'm sorry for not always listening to her. I know I'm fucked up, all right? But that don't mean I stopped loving her. Loving both of y'all. If she was evicted from her crib, then I should have known about it. I could have helped."

"You're still not understanding it, Shamel." She breathed with just as much wariness as me. "It doesn't matter, either way. She doesn't want to see you."

"And she can feel how she wanna feel," I retort. "But that don't change the problem, do it? Tell me where y'all at so I can meet you."

"Absolutely not."

"Angie! Come on, now. Let me help. I might have a way to solve this shit."

"Not again, Mel. She can't take anymore disappointment."

"Angie, you can't keep at your place either. You stay in student apartments. They won't let her stay there, at least not forever."

More silence, silence that I interpret as agreement.

"See? Let me fix this. I'll take the blame, that's fine. I'll even apologize. Just please trust in me one last time, okay?"

She sighed, aggrieved and irritated. "I don't know."

"Well meet me at this address when you figure it out, all right?" I say as I tap the screen to enter the address into our text message thread. "I'll be there in about an hour. Make sure she's there around that time, too, okay?"

"Bye, Mel." Angie hissed before, yet again, the three beeps let me know I'd been hung up on. Again.

"What's up, cuz? What's the moves?" All Bad asked, a concerned frown on his caramel-colored face as he watched me pace. "You said Miss Pat got evicted?"

"Yeah," I grunt, still pacing the room and thinking of what to do next. "They forced her off her property and threw all her shit out."

"Word?" He barked, rising to his feet in just as much fury as me now. "Where them niggas at, huh? Let's go show them how we do shit in Camden, man. Fuck all that politically correct shit man, her landlord know better than to do some sneaky snake stuff like that in our hood. I thought you was keeping him paid and quiet?"

"I was." I said between clenched teeth. "But we got problems now."

"What problems?"

"Apparently, he got found with a bullet in his head the other day."

He frowned. "Bout time somebody iced his crooked ass. You know who done it?"

I didn't answer that, my head splitting too bad from the rage and futility of them thinking me capable of doing it. I was capable, sure, but I'd been trying to keep to the straight and narrow. Been trying to keep everybody alive and fed with all the bills paid. I paid Miss Pat's bills with money I ain't even have, but considered it a necessary evil in securing her happiness in the home she built for her blood and neighborhood kids like me.

"Oh…" He breathed incredulously. "They think you did him in?"

I nodded.

"Did you?"

"Hell nah!" I hollered, my fury knowing no bounds at this point. "Why would I do that, huh? Why does everybody seem to think the fucking worst of me? I ain't no damn monster."

But I was a shame, a small voice drifted on a cloud of anxiety in my head, repeating the words that resounded loudly in my heart. I took the minute I needed to steady my breathing, keeping Si's words in my mind so as to keep from floating off. I had to keep my eyes on the goal. Keep my mind on the mission, and while this was a mild setback, it wasn't a permanent hindrance in my overall plan.

I ran for the stairs towards my room.

"Jackpot," I breathed, fingering through the stacks of bills in the goodie bag Si left me as advance cash. I grabbed three stacks from it and returned to a confused All Bad in the living room. "Let's go."

"Where we going?" He demanded, but continued to put his shoes on.

"I'll tell you more about it when we get there. We just got to get there in an hour."

"All right, cuz." He muttered agreeably while heading for the door.

"Hold up." I said, extending my arm in front of him to block him from reaching the front door. "I'mma need you to get the dog."

"Who, Oz?" He asked, bewildered. "For what?"

***

"It ain't much, but with a little love and elbow grease, it could be something cozy for a little while. Right?" I said gently to the Project Granny who'd shouted about how she wanted nothing to do with me just two hours prior.

The four of us, me, All Bad, Angie, and Miss Pat were walking inside the ramshackle house in Harlem that I'd instructed them to meet us at. The one-bedroom house was in bad shape. And I meant it, as my eyes scanned the rotted floorboards and holes in the wood and windows. There's a foul stench coming from down the hall that make me believe that a rodent family had taken residence in what used to be Quincy's Harlem safehouse. This house was where he stored product for his New York deals, and I often checked this place for any sign of him after he fled town. But no dice, I thought sullenly, since this house had been empty for almost a year now.

"I don't know about this, Mama." Angie hedged as we passed by the singular bedroom with rotted furniture inside it. "This looks uninhabitable. Why don't you just stay with me?"

"No." She spat. "I won't be a bother to any of my children."

"Mama, Monica will let you stay with her if you just ask her."She snapped around with a devastating quickness I wasn't sure her capable of to face off with her concerned daughter.

"I don't want to hear that name come out your mouth, young lady. She's made it clear how much she values that man over her real family."

"But, Mama, Patrick isn't so bad—"

"Hush!" She snapped again, cornering her. "That jezebel chose to marry that man, that's her business. She's grown, and I can't tell her how to live. But she sure as hell won't have a say in how I operate either. Neither of y'all will."Her crazy eyes flashed over all of us at the proclamation, making me squirm like I was eight years old again.

"Mama, try to calm down." Angie gentled her tone so as to appease the old lady who I suspected was sitting on all that anger until now.

Until she exploded."I ought to kill you, Shamel. For losing me my home and ruining my daughter's innocence."

"What?" I choked on the word as my gaze snapped between the old lady and the former girl of my dreams. I casted a questioning but anticipatory stare her way, waiting for her to fill me in and correct the snide woman on what I thought she was thinking.

Angie chewed on her lip and dipped a nervous finger in her big curls. "Sorry, Mel. I, um…"

"You what?"

"I sort of told Mama the truth about what happened between us. You know…last year?"

"I don't…" I start, then gag on her meaning. As I finally grasped her words, a sinking feeling weighs down on my chest. "You're not talking about that time I stayed overnight…?"

"Yeah…" She breathes, face red with shame and eyes sliding everywhere in the room but at me.

Miss Pat tuts three times before saying, "Of course she told me. My daughter was pure and innocent before she got with you. Our relationship was strong before then."

"It still is!" She cries, fuming. "Mom it was just one time. Just sex."

"Angie, you told me we didn't…that I just got drunk and passed out. Why would you lie to me?"

She shrugged, her shoulders sagging. "We both woke up naked, Mel. Of course, we had sex. I just didn't want to make you feel worse than you already had when you showed up the day before. I know you would've beaten yourself up if I told you what actually happened. You have your faults, might be stubborn and militant like your dad, but you're a good guy. You respect my mother above all else, and always made sure she was taken care of even after both my sister and I left home. So...that's why we're here."

"Oh shit!" All Bad swore in amusement. "Y'all actually smashed? Damn, bro..."

"Chill, AB." I told my suddenly proud cousin who's holding a sleepy Oz in the cradle of his long arms. "I barely remember it."

"Ouch." He muttered as he took a few steps back. "I'll give y'all some privacy. Miss Pat! Let's take a walk around. Cool?"

"Jezebel." Miss Pat hisses. She's seething as she regards us, her foot tapping in impatient fury. "I can't even believe what I'm hearing. Y'all had all the privacy you needed to engage in that debauchery in my home. Guess it doesn't matter now."

"Mama, please calm down. What happened to our chat about being more open minded to uncomfortable conversations? You asked me to be more honest with you about my social life, and I did that."

"I regret that." She sniveled.

"So do I." Angie countered. "That was personal information. Wasn't meant to be broadcasted to an audience, especially not Mel. That was my business to share with him when I was ready. I'm not surprised you would air my dirty laundry, since that's all Monica and I are truly good at it, in your eyes. Pleasing you is tiring."

Miss Pat's jaw is still set in an aggravated tic when she chuffs, "Losing my home to children not knowing their place is also tiring. All of you are liabilities at this point."

Fed up, I clear my throat before cutting in. "Look, I don't care what you say about me, but show Angie some respect. She's sacrificing for you, too. She is supposed to be working on her degree right now, but she's here helping you. Like always. So, give her some credit, Miss Pat."

Miss Pat only rolls her eyes before storming off down the hall. Possibly to the origin of whatever strong fish smell was perfuming the small quarters. All Bad follows her after shooting me a look that conveys an apology for Miss Pat's actions.

Angie expels a long breath before scrubbing her hands over her face. She's young, same age as Shay, but the stress on her face ages her a bit. "She's just impossible to please." She breaths.

I shrug before stepping closer to her. "Take it from me when I say living your life to please anybody is a wasted effort. Live your life for you, and take no prisoners. Fuck all that people-pleasy shit for once."

She nodded. "You're right."

"I know." I chuckled humorlessly. "Had my fair share of making people proud in vain. It's all shit at the end of the day."

"Mama is frustrating beyond belief," she starts, "but I can't let her just live here. Not unless we fix this up or something. I need to make sure she's safe here, I mean, how did you find this place anyways?"

I shrug, deciding on a half truth to tell her. "It's family property, nah mean? And trust me, nobody will fuck with her here."

She stares at me for a long wondering minute. "How do I know I can trust you?"

I couldn't resist the scowl. "You talking to me about trust? Says the girl who fucked me and lied about it?"

"Oh." She blushes, full force, now. "I didn't fuck you. We both had consensual intercourse, Mel. Come on, don't make it sound all yucky."

"Yucky?" I laugh. "Yeah!" She says, her tone lighter and face brightening some. "I doubt a bottle of liquor was enough to erase your memory of what happened completely. Surely you remember the strip poker we played before that."

I hated the color in my cheeks at her words I faintly wrote off as a silly dream. More like, a wet dream concocted from my desperation and longing for my childhood crush. I slightly wonder, just for a millisecond if those little blue pills that existed as part of my daily regimen to get through a day or an assignment hampered my ability to remember it right. But I chase those thoughts away as soon as they come and pull her into my arms.

She hugs me back before muttering. "I'm sorry, Mel. Truly sorry for telling Mama before you, as well as her ambush on your character."

"Yeah," I mutter, not entirely sure how to respond to that apology. "No sweat."

"No, really." She twists in my arms to stare up at me with watery eyes. "You are golden. And I'm sorry for letting her get in my head about you. You'd never have done anything to jeopardize her safety or security."

"You really think that? About me?"

"Yes. You've always been sweet to us Pierce women, even when we didn't deserve it, like now. Like I said, that's why we're here now. I trust your decision to keep her safe here."

"Of course. I'll always have Miss Pat's back, even if she wants nothing to do with me." I say.

She nods. "Thank you."

"No 'thanks' necessary."

"Well, *thanks* anyway." She chuckles before burying her face into my shirt. "You know...I wouldn't be opposed to a repeat of that strip poker game..."

I laughed, full bellied and good natured, as I regarded the college girl gone bad in the best way. Only in my wildest dreams did I picture her offering to fuck, and I'm kind of miffed at the lack wood in my jeans at that idea. The only one I'd even wanted sitting on my dick was the tiny woman with honesty for a name and yellow hair some days. I'd even imagined bending her over in that tiny ass kitchen of hers as she's waiting for the coffee to cycle through and driving my dick deep in that pussy. I should have gone back, I thought warily. Should have gone back when she begged me to stay this morning and ate her for breakfast like I'd envisioned for the past year.

"Seems like your little friend is in full agreement of that." Angie whispered thickly as she palmed my hard flesh.

I don't dare tell her that boner was meant for the woman who pledged her loyalty to me for no apparent reason. Hell no would I tread on territory so delicate and fuck with her feelings more than her dear mom did mere seconds ago.

Instead, I place a kiss on her forehead. "Ain't nothing little about that friend, sweetheart."

"Ah, so that's how it's gonna be." She says before pursing her lips and stepping out of my arms.

"Yeah," I breathe apologetically. "Afraid so."

"Totally cool. Maybe a raincheck on that, then?" She probes with a tone full of hope that I hated shattering.

Instead of the 'no' I nearly spout, I nod my head. "Maybe."

We're laughing by the time Miss Pat and All Bad return. The old lady is muttering cuss words as she reaches us and holding Oz in her arms.

"This will work." She grumbled to me while staring at the puppy.

"What she means is, she's decided to live here." All Bad translated from behind her. "With some conditions."

I nod. "Cool. What's up?"

He sighed before continuing in her stead. "Said she'll take the place as reparations from you, considering you owe her and all."

"Fine."

He rubs the back of his neck in obvious distress before he says, "And she wants Oz. Said he's going to be her newest most trusted family member."

"You cool with that, AB?" I ask, already equipped to offer the dog as a potential bargaining chip to compel a yes out of the stubborn old lady. But I'm mindful enough to not let All Bad on to that plan. I just wait for him to respond.

"She told me she'll take care of him, so...yeah. It's cool." He laments as he casts a morose look to the donated pup. "Guess I'll get Sommer another gift. I just hate to disappoint her is all. But it's all good."

"We'll need to give you a strong name that fits you, too."

Miss Pat cooed to the squirmy Australian Shepard in her arms. "I'll call you Busta for now. Till I can think of another name."

"Busta is nice." Angie says, though Miss Pat ignores her as she crooned to the puppy.

I sighed and reached out to dap my favorite brother-cousin who was really my half uncle. "That's wassup, bro. You the MVP for that."

"It's all good." He repeats, but I'm sure it's more self-convincing than anything.

Since my energy was relatively returned from its previous depleted state after the interactions with Jerica and Si, I'd considered my new mission again. The mission to become whole for my little sis.

"Anybody got the time?" I ask the crowd.

"About two o' clock." Angie answers after checking her smartwatch. "Somewhere you need to be?"

"Yeah." I say. "All Bad, come on."

"All right. Where to?"

I smile wickedly as the mission and vision reappears in my mind. "Making good on that favor."

TWENTY-ONE

ENOUGH

"It really is a pity that you're dropping out of school, young man. Is there nothing else we can do to set you up for success?" Counselor Riviera asked cautiously between small bites of her fish bagel.

Well, it looked and smelled like fish, my nose auto-detecting the pink flesh poking out from the sides of it as something belonging to the sea. Fucking nasty is what it was, no doubt about it.

I shifted in the seat opposite of the fat Spanish lady, being careful to hold in my breath a few precious seconds before responding.

"Uh, yeah," I sighed. "The best way to move forward is letting me drop out. Peacefully. And without my parents too deep in the process."

"Peacefully? Any trouble at home? I'd be glad to follow up with your parents if—"

"Not necessary."

Flustered, she took another bite from her smelly fish bagel before lamenting, "Shamel, son, please understand this is a serious matter here. You've exuded nothing less than academic excellence since you began at Marlton High, and it's just my job to counsel you about this possibility."

I tried really fucking hard to keep the barf from coming up and hardened my face as I stared at her crumby one. "Like I said, Counselor Riviera, that's not necessary. There ain't no problems at home. In fact, my Old Man been nagging me to drop this school shit for a minute now."

"Surely, that isn't true?"

"Too bad it is. And I been fighting it, but now I think it's time I go. Just show me the paperwork necessary to start the process."

"Shamel," she extended her hand to me, her eyes sympathetic. "Can you not hear the problem in that statement?"

"What's the problem?"

"More like, *who's* the problem? Surely, your father is not encouraging you to withdraw from high school. That's unethical."

"Well, I ain't exactly his pride and joy." I respond, my tone flat and withholding. I was more like his shame and fury. And it was true, I thought, as I considered his permanent frown and shitty disposition when it came to me. "But if it's his approval you need, gimme a sec."

"Okay." She agrees as I slide the newest edition iPhone from my denim jean pocket. I dial one of the three numbers saved in the contacts and place the trilling phone on loudspeaker as we wait for it to connect.

"Fuck you want, man?" My old man demands in his usual setting of pissed off.

"Trying to drop out of school. Counselor's giving me a hard time, saying I need your permission, or some shit. You on loudspeaker and I'm in her office."

I anticipate the fury behind his next retort. "Tell that bitch I said you want out. Yesterday. And to send me any paperwork needed to make that happen. Understand?"

"Yep." I met her eyes, which were round with shock.

"I'm talking to your teacher, not you boy. Do you understand what I'm saying?"

"Y-Yes, Mr. Masters," she stammered in embarrassment while wiping the crumbs off her face. "Loud and clear."

"Good." he sneers. "Now don't call me again unless it's an emergency." He hangs up without a goodbye, Commander style, and an action I've long since stopped getting in my feelings about.

"So." I begin. "We good here?"

"Shamel, I really wish—"

"I'm trying to play this shit nice!" I stood up, pissed at her protests but also unable to be in the presence of that nasty fish sandwich she devoured minutes ago. "Gimme the papers, or I'll get them myself. I ain't come

to you for counseling. Or your pity talk. Or your disappointment. Fuck all that."

"Excuse me?!"

"Nah, excuse *me*. I gotta find somebody who actually
can do their job without all the fucking condescending
ass, gentle ass, third degree."

She's sputtering and hurling threats my way as I turn
to the door.

Somehow, her enraged scolding puts me in mind of
my old man whenever I returned home with the unsold
product he placed in my charge to move, and a dark
smile curves my lips as I exit the office. Waste of talent,
she calls it? A pity? Nah, I operated with ease in the
shadows and took pride in people's general lack of faith
in me. Maybe my ties to the real monsters on these
gritty Camden streets was my downfall, but if I went
down, at least the fall wouldn't be alone or in vain. I had
a mission, and I dedicated my next few years to seeing
that shit through for a change.

Was it a pity to be dropping out of this underfunded
dank ass school? Maybe.

Was it a waste to be leaving the only home and family
I ever knew to start this mission? Possibly.

Was it worth it? Hell fucking yeah.

Pity played a huge part in me dropping the "L" in
my government name so that I could live and profit
comfortably from the shadows.

Ain't that a shame? Yeah, that's me, and you'd best learn not to forget it, is what I wished I said to Riviera before aiming my favorite girl at her head and demanding she do her damn job without all the questions. But that wasn't my reality. Reality was finding another counselor who actually assisted me with the paperwork necessary to withdraw from high school. As luck would have it, I eventually do: She's one of those cold, detached office workers who looked way too unbothered to interfere with the deep line of questioning. Perhaps she'd had a bad day, or bad pay that didn't constitute enough of a reason to care as I filled out the papers and left.

"How'd I do?" All Bad asked as I reentered the Mustang's driver seat.

"You sold that shit, bro." I say to him before starting the engine. "Sure, you and Quincy ain't twins? 'Cause you sounded just like him. Had that counselor shaking in her heels she looked so scared."

"I need to be on Broadway, man. Told you I was the shit!" He guffawed at that, and I couldn't resist joining in on the laughter as I gunned it across town.

"I appreciate you for that." I say.

"No sweat, Cuz." He answers as we cruise down Marlton Pike. Home was a few minutes away. "What's the moves now?"

I frowned at him. "What you mean? Nigga I need a shower. And a nap."

"And I need some money." He snorts. "Ain't no rest for the wicked, nah mean?"

"Yeah, well, this wicked nigga need a hot shower after being in that dank ass house."

"Word." He agrees, nodding. "I do feel like I just got outta prison again. That type of dirt just ain't right."

"On God."

I pull the rental into the empty space in front of the house and turn an expectant look to my cousin. "All right, bro."

"You coming in?"

"Nah." I say. "Gonna head somewheres else for my shower."

"Let me find out you holding out on some pussy out there." He smiles devilishly at me while eying me up and down.

"And I thought you was all about my moms."

His face turns serious as stone. "Fuck yeah, I am. Ain't shit changed about that. I'm gonna make her see reason soon. Bet. She still tryna play innocent stepmom on me, but I'll get her."

I nod, one tight motion I hope doesn't convey the awkwardness in me. "Give her time, man. She been through a lot."

"I know." He agrees with a conciliatory nod. "I got you, bro. I ain't in the business of loving her that way. Word is bond."

"Solid." I extended him my hand, but the dap doesn't come. Instead, he stares at my outstretched gesture with a strange look on his face.

"Something I been meaning to ask you about since the party." He said.

I rescinded my hand, glaring at him on high alert for his weird temperament. "Wassup?"

He shrugged. "I'mma keep the shit one hundred and just say it: did you off Hector?"

There it is, I think, that chill that crept its way up my spine at the mention of the LC I'd been contracted to deal with on the Kobayashi's request.

I shifted a little in my seat, averting my eyes to my lap and unsure how to proceed. Fuck yeah, I was going to lie, but an eerie understanding makes me suspicious.

"Why the fuck you think I done that?" I demand.

A slight smile curves his tatted face. "I knew you did it."

"Yo, bro." I start. "I ain't did that shit. I ain't admit to that shit."

"Ain't have to." He chuffed, scratching his beard. "You didn't say no. All I'm wondering now is, why?"

I fight to control the sweat trickling down my back at the glacial tone that replaced his usual easy-going demeanor. He sounded exactly like the contract shooter Quincy originally groomed him to be before me and before his prison stint.

I gulped. "Man, you buggin."

"Is that right?"

"Fuck yeah." I bark. "Why would I even do something like that? Shoot a Latin Crip? My boy is LC. What makes you even ask me that?"

He shook his head, and his thin plaits move to the sway of it. "I never said anything about him getting shot."

More panic shot through my body as I watched him tilt his head from one side to the other, as if in restraint from committing something violent with his hands. I didn't like what his body language was saying. Nah. The line of questioning had me tripping, but I covered it up with anger.

"I heard from his boys that he got shot." I bite out, staring at him full on now. "Chill on that shit, AB."

A long silence stretched out before us before he spoke again.

"Fuck Quincy. Hector was my brother if there ever was one," He began in a low growl almost. "He held me down way before I caught our Mom dead with a needle in her arm. Even caught a couple charges protecting me from some dumb shit I pulled in the streets. So, it was a no-brainer taking the fall on those aggravated burglary charges that landed me in Juvie. He always looked out for me, and he was on his second strike. So, I did what I had to do. Nah mean?"

I nodded, realizing this was the tense explanation left unsaid back at the party that Milio brought up.

"That's wassup." I say.

"That's what brothers do. Back each other when it counts." He responds to my weak affirmation. "And you know I see you as way more than a nephew or a cousin. You my bro, on some real shit."

"Swear to God, man." I chime in. "You my nigga, too."

He meets my eyes, a hard glint shining in them before he says, "I always got your back, just know that."

"Word up."

"But I won't even hesitate to ice you if I find out you been acting sideways to my peoples. Feel me?"

I freeze at that threat, at how easy he rattled it off as if he'd been ordering a five-dollar footlong. Confusion, panic, and...straight up fear clouds my brain as I work to rearrange logic and composure in my head. No way in hell my favorite brother-cousin but really an uncle would say some grimy shit like that to me. His true family.

Steeling myself, I look up to meet his eyes.

Suddenly, he leans back and howls in laughter as he meets my hard gaze.

"Yo, bro!" He chuckled. "I'm just fucking with you. Calm down it's all love. All right?"

He pulls the door open and exits the car. I almost think he's completely disappeared, but then he leans over to motion me to roll down the window.

Unsure how to react to the icy threat then subsequent laughter, I do as he instructs and gawk at him as he continues.

"Take care of yourself out there, bro. Streets *mad* grimy. Nah mean?"

***

My mind races just as fast as the sports car zipping through the streets during the drive to my destination. What the fuck did All Bad even mean by that? And how did he find out about Hector? Maybe he was just assuming. Yeah, that's it. He knew about the line of work our family had been in and assumed I took him out. But that shit didn't sit right with me, considering all the bullshit with Miss Pat seeing the worst in me. Had to keep my mind on the mission, I thought in spite of the trembling fingers that gripped the steering wheel. So much success rode on all aspects of my plan coming into fruition. It was a no-brainer after showing Miss Pat her new living quarters that I'd take that deal from Si. After sending off the text confirming my participation in his bloody plan to out wolf the D.C. gang, he texted back immediately.

> **SILENCE**: *Prepare to build your legacy, Shame. Your future awaits. I'll stay in touch.*

My legacy, he called it. So much about my life involved survival, living in the day-to-day and trying not to let my next contract be my last. But for the first time I smile at the prospect I'd not previously entertained for fear of disappointment or pain.

The future.

Wishing, hoping, and dreaming weren't ever a part of my underworld, but I can barely refrain from balling as my heart pitter patters from joy for a change. And excitement from the apartment complex I rolled up on for the second time.

Despite that dangerous encounter with my brother-cousin, I'm shaking from hope and excitement as I wait for her to answer the door.

"Shame?" She asks in a tone belaying her supreme confusion as she eyes me as if I'd been revived from the dead. "What are you doing here?"

Maybe I am revived, I think, as a surge of electricity ignites my insides and powers my next moves.

There's no yellow wig or pink bonnet like from before, but her natural curls are on full display and sitting just above her shoulders. She's dressed in a black Rutgers sweatshirt and gym shorts that show off her smooth blemish free legs. Despite the wintry October winds, my blood heats to a stimulating degree as I pull her close and claim her lips with mine.

Her impending protest dies in her throat as we maneuver ourselves into the quiet apartment with our joined bodies.

"We have maybe an hour until everyone comes home." She whispered after breaking the kiss.

"More than enough time for me to taste that pussy like I been wanting to do for months."

"Months?" She asks with breathy incredulousness. "Really?"

"Hell yeah. You gonna feed me?" I growl, my dick hardening to a painful degree as she rubs her belly into it. "You bout to make me ruin jeans, girl."

"Don't cum yet, Shame." She purred while guiding me down the hall to a modest bedroom.

A funny feeling stabs my chest at her words, and instead of reaching for my gun like I'm used to whenever this feeling hit me, I reach for her neck, pinning her back to the wall as my body blanketed her.

"You don't ever call me by that name."

Her eyes widened in evident shock, and shit, I'm just as surprised at this violent streak that compelled me to choke her against the wall. I nearly give in and release her for fear of scaring or hurting her, but her pretty smile stops me.

"What you gonna do about it, huh?" She strangles out.

"My little Hellcat." My tone was gravel in her ears as I tightened my hold on her neck. "You disobeying me?"

"Told you," she rasps, her eyes hungry and needy as we stared at each other. "Violence gets me wet."

"Fuck yeah, I do." I say.

"Then what you waiting for, Shame?"

I smile too, my dick straining against the seams of my jeans at this point. I needed to end this. Needed to be inside her with an urgency I never knew before, but I also want to savor her.

"What's my name?" I husked, placing slow trailblazing kisses on her ear and continuing my descent down her neck. "Tell me."

"Shame!" She whispered, stalling my heart again from the incorrect name but filling me with excitement at the prospect of punishing her.

"Wrong answer." I growled, replacing my kisses with nibbles as I tasted my way down her body. My hand remained around her neck and I enjoyed the smell of her arousal filling my nose as I tore her shorts off.

No panties.

"Fuck, you got ready for me, baby?"

She chewed on her lip and shut her eyes. "I knew you'd come back for this pussy. Knew you wouldn't stay away for long."

"Oh yeah?"

She does her best attempt at a nod with my hand wrapped loosely around her neck. After releasing her, she swallows huge gulps of air as she stares hungrily at my concrete cock.

"Strip." I say.

She wordlessly obeys by slowly lifting her sweatshirt over her arms. And when I say slowly, I mean it. She's moving at a snail's pace to remove the fluffy barrier my arousal is demanding I rip off her.

"Like this?" She asks coyly and teasing as she slowly glides the shirt off her arms.

Fed up, I snatch it from her. "On the bed. Now."

Again, her steps are slow and deliberate towards the simply made queen bed. My jaw aches from clenching my teeth together from restraint. It takes serious effort to keep from blowing my jeans, especially when she's doing a slow grind dance toward the bed. Her back twists as fluid as water as she places her palms on the covers and bends over to flash her sopping wet pussy in brief shakes of her hips. I notice her eyes flutter closed as she dances to an unheard rhythm, almost as if she's back at the club, but not really. The proud smile she wore during her Wonder Woman performance isn't here, since her eyes are closed and a focused mask of desire overcomes her face. There's only one word that drifts to the forefront of my mind as I stalk over to her naked body.

Truth. This beautifully complicated woman who pledged her loyalty to me for a reason I'm still unclear on can be compared to nothing less than the real article. She's the heaven to my underworld, the light to my dark, and I needed her. Needed inside her with an achingly painful intensity like you wouldn't fucking believe.

My clothes are a thing of the past, and I relish the cool AC splashing against the heat building in my groin and chest as I grabbed her hips.

"Jerica..." My voice is little above a gruff whisper as I line my thick meat into the moist flood of her leaking pussy. "Who's fucking you?"

She goes rigid at the feel of my swollen length dripping and dipping slightly in and out of her tight channel. She's so wet, so fucking tight I can barely keep the stars from exploding behind my lids as I toy with her shaky body.

"Shame." She hisses.

"You sure about that?" I say, taunting her with languid strokes of her slick heat. Her hot tunnel is sucking me in, almost as if it needed my hard dick just as much as I needed her. "That pussy wants me in. Let me in, baby."

"Shame!" She cries, one part frustration, one part desire as she grounds her hips into me. "Just fuck me already..."

I withdrew. "Nah."

"Shame!"

I reach up, grabbing her neck again and tightening my hold. "That ain't who's fucking you. Tell me you want this dick, and I'll feed that pretty pussy with what it wants. Tell me, sweetheart."

She shook her head, causing her curls to bounce. "You made it clear what we are. I gave up on that! So, *Shame*, put me out of my misery and fuck me!"

I stroked my dick into the moisture within her slick desire again. "Feel how hard you got me?"

"Mmm." She whines, undulating on my lap, her hungry snatch in search of my wood. "Yes..."

Even though my dick throbbed to a terrifying level of hard, I lifted her tiny body with ease. She yelped as her back hit the bed.

"Shit!" She swore. But I didn't allow her time to question my moves since I sank to my knees, hoisted her legs apart and tasted the sweet nectar I'd been drooling over for months.

"Oh...*oh!*" She cries as I lap at her delicious juices like a starving man at a buffet.

She needed to be taught a lesson, I surmised with a wicked grin as her moisture dribbled down my mouth. Not one drop slipped past my lips, though. I devoured her hot sheath like she devoured the dark parts of my soul. I felt her light pour into me as I drank my fill of her sumptuous waters. The more I sucked her forbidden button of desire, the more she gushed into my waiting mouth like a love river. This feeling in my chest. She made me feel...

"Shame!" She hollered in praise. Her body thrashed violently from side to side as her orgasm took control.

Though she came, I didn't stop my ruthless onslaught on her pussy. Even her whimpers weren't enough to deter or slow me down. Nah. I kept licking until her body rocketed off the bed a second time. Then a third.

By the fourth, the fog of desire and need cleared enough for me to hear her breathless protests.

"Please..." She whispers, in a tone that's nearing broken as her chest heaves. "Play fair. I can't...cum anymore. You broke me. You...you..."

I licked the length of her slick folds, relishing in the minor tremble she emitted. "What baby?"

"Win." She breathes.

"I ain't hear you." Another lick, then vibration.

She rears up like a bat out of hell to sneer, "I said you fucking win, okay?! Want me to say it louder? Shamel!"

Rule Ten hums inside my mind at her words as soon as the shame did: Win, by any means. There were some of The Commander's rules I couldn't avoid embedding into everything I did, including that one.

"You got a dirty mouth, baby." I say in a low voice, licking my lips while rising. "Think you need to get that cleaned up."

"Fuck you." She growls before collapsing back onto the bed.

"Exactly my plan." I say, and lift her into my arms. I teach her another lesson in the shower, and then three more after we towel off and run to the bed.

"Shamel," she breathes, her voice satiated but ragged from the exhaustion of cumming several times in the last forty minutes. "Why did you come back?"

We're laying in a crumpled, tangled heap in the bed I realize is situated beside a smaller toddler bed on the floor. The room is moderately decorated, I note, observing the military regalia on the walls and a single picture of a gorgeous black woman with shoulder length box braids. Her smile is wide and bright, as if she adored the taker of that pic as the sun bounced off her just right. I wondered who she was, and nearly ask the woman I banged for almost an hour until she asks me that.

I sigh. "I don't really know, to be honest. Was just having a good day."

"That's it?"

"Yeah." I shrug. "If you knew what my days looked like, you'd realize how rare it is. Never had many of those, much less somebody to share them with. So..."

"I'm glad I'm who you thought of to spend the evening with. I've been thinking about you, too."

The grin that spread across her face was so large and true that it made me flinch a little from its thousand-watt intensity.

There it was, I thought, that warm sensation blooming in my chest again. She made me feel...

Safe.

TWENTY-TWO

SUMMER

I pretended he wasn't there.

Had to, because every time I looked him in the eyes it was like I was falling into them. Though it was brown pupils he possessed, I still found myself magically sucked into the endless whirlpools of them. His scent is everything; a natural aroma mixed in with the essence of man. How I loved it. Could sit there and nibble on inedible prison pastries if it meant a few extra minutes of soaking in that smell. He was...he was...

"Sommer." A dark voice husks in the wind. Except, we aren't outside, but in the scant bedroom I shared previously with his brother. My back is to him, but my soul feels his slow entrance.

"Shah—"

"Not here." He grunts in a tone thick with desire. "In here, when it's just the two of us, you call me All Bad."

That dreadful name, I curse inwardly, as I stare at the worn floorboards I'm sure are suffering from a mild insect infestation. These street monikers the boys adopted would be the death of their self-esteem and energy. Did Shaheim know that adopting a name like 'All Bad' allowed in the negative flow of chi in his world? Or even worse, my dear son whose name I fought his ex-military father for. Aceon, he'd wanted to call the giggly presence in my arms I birthed in a hospital room alone. Thousands of miles away from my only family in Leeds and alone, since Quince had "work" to do that demanded his attention away from the birth of our boy. Instead of Aceon Leigh like I'd been instructed to etch onto his birth certificate, I'd fought for another route. Even suffered the painful consequences after it was done by naming him after a more honorable war hero I looked up to as a girl.

Shameel Haynes Rose was the name of my grandfather who'd died in battle so that our family could stay together. How could I not name my precious boy after a man who embodied all the pride of us Rose's? Quince demanded we call him Shamel instead of the intended Shameel, which I was forced to concede with to maintain the peace, especially since he gave me creative freedom in naming our first, Shayne Dorothy. Her name was a mixture of my mother's Dorothy Fae and a slight rearrangement of grandfather Shameel's middle name of Haynes. A name brought with it a powerful energy in how one views themself in relationship with the world.

My beautiful children. They shined so bright in the dark days of my and Quincy's time together. Even as I cast my gaze up at the boy who'd once been so tough, I see darkness there. A darkness in his aura not even my strongest herbs could cure.

"Hey," he grunts as he rounds the bed to stand before me. "I ain't that same boy from before."

It's as if he read the doubt and concern in my mind. But I keep my eyes averted, afraid of falling into them.

"I won't call you that." I whisper.

"Fine." He says, quick and smooth, unlike Quincy's brutal persistence. "Call me what you want. But understand I ain't no little kid whose boo-boo's need kissing. Nah...I need those lips elsewheres."

"Else..." I nearly voice the question that soon dies on my lips as Shaheim does it. Performs the reprehensible action that led to our lovemaking the first time.

He kisses me.

But I pull away, trembling a little in his arms that wound themselves around me at some point. "This isn't right!"

"Right." He growls. "And wrong are two pills from the same bottle. Exactly the same energy and power to influence the guy who eats too much of them."

"All right?" I whisper, sorting through his euphemism to get the meaning.

A calloused hand caresses my cheek. "My point? None of that shit matters at the end of the day. Was it right for me to stab that guard I caught raping one of the newbies at Juvie? Was it wrong for them to throw me in the Hole for over a year to keep me quiet?"

My lip trembles from the horror of his admission, and I can't resist reaching out for him. "Shaheim...is that true? What you went through?"

He shrugged, as if eight years of systemic torture were just an annoying afterthought. "Peas to a giant. It's my reality. And I want you start facing some of that, too."

"Wait," I reared back, looking up into his eyes now. "You're here to lecture me on what it is to be real? You, a young man whose had no prior knowledge on my hardships, want to help me face reality? Reality's always been here. Always on my heels no matter how far I run."

"Exactly." He says, grabbing my chin. "Look at me."

"I-I am..."

"Nah. Look at me for real. You been avoiding me since this morning. After I made you cum real hard before breakfast."

I hate how my cheeks redden at the memory of his words; of the sheer pleasure he insisted my body need-ed after being exposed to nothing but pain these past few years. I also hate how right he is. But I don't let on, instead, I look into his eyes for real and fall in.

Just like I feared.

"I'm here." I breathe.

"I know. I see that. And I want you to stay rooted. Stay in reality with me. We could be something real if you let us."

"I won't call you that."

"Call me what?"

"You know...All Bad."

He chuckles, the action revealing bright white teeth and a hyena grin. "Why's that, baby?"

"I wish you could see how skewed misnaming yourselves can be. Both you and Shamel. You're not all bad just like my son is nowhere near a shame."

"I know that." He says, but there's something in his tone I don't recognize.

"So, why allow in the all-bad energy that your name summons?"

A pause, then he says in a whisper. "Like I said. Wrong and right. Bad and good. Same bottle."

"Well then...All Bad. I'm sorry."

"Don't apologize. You think I made it on the inside for eight years by apologizing after every fight? That's why I'm here. To help you build up that muscle you keep buried inside you. It's like you're a summer flower in the dark. Beautiful, but not letting anybody see it past the shit you've been through. I know darkness. I been there."

"So, what do you want from me?" I seethe, tears falling down my cheeks from hearing so much truth in one conversation.

Without warning, he kisses my forehead.

"All Bad…" I moan, unable to help myself as he blankets my body down flat onto the bed. "What…do you want?"

"Fuck all that. What I need is some light. Give me some of that darkness so you can shine bright, Sommer. Come on…give it to me."

"I…" my voice catches on another moan as he trails kisses down my throat. "I…"

"Give it to me." He growls. "It's okay to feel. Be real with me. Give it to me…"

"God!" I swear on another tide of desire as he positions his hips into the warm seat of my lower triangle. There's so much pressure building in me that I can almost burst and disappear, I think, but his firm arms wrapped around my writhing body weigh me down. More like, anchor me to the current plane our souls are intertwined on.

"*Be* with me…" Are the final words I hear before my mind and body transcend the universe.

TWENTY-THREE

SYSTEM

Her favorite color is red.

The week flies by and I find myself spending every free second with Jerica True. I understood how wrong my actions were at this point, hanging with the woman I vowed to avoid for fear of rubbing off my shame on her. I knew it clearly. But I couldn't resist her. I found more than comfort from her company and heaven buried between her legs, because when we were together I felt invincible. Supercharged like Superman to her Wonder Woman and home all at the same time. Simply put, she'd become my addiction. I committed everything I learned from her to memory like her favorite color and foods she "couldn't live without!" California rolls and her mother's Cajun fried chicken were her two guilty pleasures. I learned about how she struggled with her weight since childhood, but not in the conventional way like I thought. She'd been diagnosed at seven with some metabolic disease that made it really hard for her to pack on the pounds. In the right lighting and without makeup, she'd easily pass for eleven or twelve years old."That's when Truth was born." She insisted one day after I taught her another lesson. "Nobody would call me Skinny Minnie or String Bean again. Sure, I'm petite, but all fucking woman. Get me?"Fuck yeah, I did. I got her several times that night before sneaking out before her moms and siblings got home.I learned about her son, too. She'd given birth to him at seventeen to some street head who caught a life charge. Hakeem was the best out of a toxic situation, she'd said about the two-year old who stayed with her homegirl during her shifts at the Dirty Kitten."Cool if..." I begin to tell her one evening as we finish one of our many fast-food dates in her bedroom. "Never mind.""What's up, Shamel?" She asked, her voice lowering from the concern in it as she turned to me in bed."It's nothing. I guess."With a brazenness only she could have when it came to me, she grabs my chin and makes our eyes meet. "No, clamming up. Remember? I'm only interested in the real. If you don't want to discuss it, then I won't ask you again."I take a deep breath before fusing our lips together in a gentle kiss. Though brief, it fills me with the strength I need to voice my dark desire."Sorry." I mutter, and try again. "Was wondering if it was cool with you...if you could meet my moms.""No, thank you." Her answer came a little too fast for my liking, and I made my displeasure known by glaring."Why not?""I mean...I'm sure she's a nice lady and all, but...I don't think it's a good idea.""I thought you wanted to be closer.""Shame I..." she begins on a strained breath. "I appreciate you for spending all this time with me these past few days.""Ah, hell." I mutter, waving dismissive hands in the air. "Why it feel like you breaking up with me?"She smiled. "I'm not. I promise.""Good." I growl while pulling her into my arms and tickling. I knew all her most sensitive spots at this point. "Because you're mine.""Shamel." She whimpered post-tickle attack. "I told you I ain't with all the lying and shit."I only stare at her.She sighs again before readjusting in my arms. "I want to be with you. I won't lie about that. I want to be the only one you fucking in the shower and calling yours.""You are." I say, my voice more deadpan than intended. But I needed her to see how serious I was. Ever since meeting the beautiful vixen flying through the air I was ruined for anybody else."Look at me." I demand and grab her chin to meet my eyes. "You the only one."She nods. "All right. If I am, then before we even think about taking that step I'll need all of you. Show me everything."Now it's my turn to look away. But she chases my eyes with hers until I grumble, "All of me?""Yes!" She breathes, caressing my cheek. "Yes, baby. I won't be with a lie. Show me everything. Even the Shame side."I gulp. "I...I don't want you to get hurt because of me.""I told you I'm with the violence, remember?" She cuts off in boisterous laughter that I don't join."Ain't shit funny about violence. Or my work. That shit is the real deal.""That's all I want." She says, sobering. "Then we can play nice and meet the parents."Taking a deep, steadying breath, I nod. "Okay. I got you.""I know you do. I believe in you, Shamel." She places a feather light kiss on my lips that turns my dick to concrete in seconds. This fucking woman..."But I am curious." She says between kisses. "Why?""Why what? Why are you mine?"Her laugh literally lights up the room and my insides, and I smile at her."No! I mean, why do you suddenly want me to meet your moms?""Oh." I utter, not sure how to answer. How would I go about telling her that I wanted her a part of the plan? A part of the new mission afforded to me by Si's sweet deal for a new life down south? There was so little I still didn't know about her, including the reason behind her obsession with truth, but I'm certain I needed her. I needed her to make this plan work, and this was just a necessary first step."I, uh...got a lot of regret for the shit I done in the past." I start. "There was a girl.""What girl?"

"Dawn, I called her. She was my girl. My entire world at one point. She was like the Ying to my yang at one point in time."

The red in her cheeks signals me to continue before The Truth came out, and so I did.

"She didn't deserve what happened to her. She didn't deserve how I treated her. I kept her in the dark and never introduced her to anybody. Not even me." A wry chuckle escapes my chest. "Wouldn't even let her call me Shamel. The only thing I ever introduced her to was the shame of me."

"It's okay, baby..."

"It ain't." I snarl. "It's never been okay. She begged me to just treat her decent. Take her out to movies. Go to her track meets. Hold my hand in public...and I couldn't even do that. Then she told me she was pregnant, and...all I could think was how I'm supposed to get rid of it before my Pops knew."

"Where is she? And where's the baby?"

"Fuck!" I exhaled deep, hating the tears that fell. "She's dead. And I don't deserve a place in my little girl's life even if I wanted it. I don't deserve her, but more so, she deserves a better man for a dad. I ain't no role model."

She wraps her arms around my larger shoulders, saying nothing as I release the sobs into her neck. She's my lifeline, this woman, who sought to scrub clean the dark parts of my soul.

"I won't treat you like that, Jerica." I say in a strangled whisper in the dark. It's a little past midnight and the slight tremble in the room from the trains whizzing by is the only noise around us. "I'm telling you this because I want to do everything I can to give you what you want. The truth...the real...the shame of me. I mean it when I say you're mine, and I'm a selfish motherfucker. No way in hell I'm letting you go."

"So, it's settled then." She whispers in my arms after several minutes of silence.

"What is?"

"We're gonna go see her."

***

I somehow let the woman who'd slowly been saving my soul persuade me to greet my demons. I find out the meaning of her cryptic vow to "go see her," as we exit the train the following day. We'd just left Eden Cemetery in Philly where my babymoms' was buried.

"She was gorgeous." Jerica breathes as she takes my hand in her smaller one. "She looked like an old friend of mine from when I lived on base in Okinawa. Can't believe something so awful could happen to a pretty girl like that."

"Yeah," I say, barely choking the word past the lump in my throat. We're walking hand-in-hand through the Transportation Center and I can't help the trembling feeling in my body as she pulls me through the thick crowds of people.

"Hey." She says worriedly, and I only notice it because she came to a full stop just before the transparent exit doors. "Where are you right now?"

"I'm here." I grunt, shrugging to steady the shakiness in me. "All good."

"You don't seem like it."

"I'm good." I retort, struggling to maintain some control.

"Don't fucking lie." She crosses her arms indignantly and shoots me a glare so icy it only makes me tremble more.

"All right—you're right—it was sad what happened to her. There. Can we go now?"

"Shamel," She whispers, her tone more tender as she stares with pity in her eyes. "It's okay to be vulnerable, babe. We just did a really difficult thing just now, and I understand if it's too much. But you gotta talk about it at some point if you want to move past it."

"I'm good." I grunt again, but this time instead of another accompanying lie, I shirk out of her hold and burst through the Transportation Center doors. I elicit several astonished reactions as I kick my way out of there, and I don't care. I just needed to get far away.

"Shamel, hold up!" She screams behind me. "Don't walk away."

"I ain't weak." I bark after spinning around and confronting her. My unexpected turn makes her slam into my front. "I told you I was good, Jerica. Why can't you leave it alone?"

"Because," she starts, "I care about you getting better. Especially since you told me about your daughter and how much loss you went through the past year. You literally lost an entire chunk of your family in a matter of months and you expect me to believe you're 'good?'"

My eyes meet the filthy ground as I listen on, unable to respond.

She cups my cheek in her warm hand, and I melt a little inside but in the best way. A way that calms the shakiness in me.

Hot tears threaten to fall but I force them back. Hell no was I crying in public the same as I did back at Dawn's burial site. No way would I turn to mush again at her soothing words to 'heal and be real.' I couldn't afford that, and in the back of my mind I hear Quincy's cynical laughter as he scolds me for more of my pussythoughts.

"Baby, you don't believe that. Do you?" Her words seem to question my inward dread.

I flex my jaw. "That a man ain't supposed to be all unglued and sappy like this? Nah. I should have never let you talk me into going to Philly. How I'm supposed to work with my head like this? You got me twisted."

"If there's anybody else on this earth who understands what you're feeling, then it's me. Losing Stan was the absolute hardest thing I'd had to face. All the drugs in the world couldn't pull me out of that slump. But you know what? I did it. I'm not healed by any means, but I make the choice every day to show up for Hakeem and the Trips and everyone I care about. Because that's what you do. You show the fuck up. Period."

The mere mention of his name sends me reeling from the torture of who I really was: a monster. One who definitely didn't deserve her or the truths she'd been dropping on me.

"It ain't as simple as showing up. Not everybody can just be real all the damn time. The truth ain't something I want to be all up close and personal with most days. The truth makes me mush. Makes me weak. And I can't afford to be caught slippin."

Out of nowhere, she slaps the daylights out of me, making me see stars for a second before blinking at her in awe.

"Stop it, all right!" She hollers, and I groan as passer-byers take out their phones and record our argument. "You're not weak because you bared yourself, Shamel! That's honest. That's what *you* need to heal and what *I* need to see the real you."

"What I need..." I breathe brokenly as I massage the heated flesh she slapped.

"Yes!" She hisses, shaking my shoulders. "Kill the excuses and talk to me, baby. Ain't no pills or drug that's gonna get you through this, so quit those. Tell me how you feel about all of this. About what we saw today."

I gulp as I take in her words. She was right, and I felt it just as much as I felt the slap she delivered to wake me up. Taking a deep breath, I do it. Try honesty for a change to see if that helped the shakiness and pain in my gut.

"She was beautiful." I mumbled.

"That's right." She says behind a mask of tears and a smile. "What else?"

"The flowers," I choke out. "Roses were her favorite."

She holds me tight, and I clock her body trembling a little too as she whispers, "You got this baby."

I hang limply in her arms as she cradles me on the sidewalk. To the untrained eye, we're dancing. But for real, if she were to let me go or walk away like I pegged her to, then I'd be nothing. Floating away into the nothingness that consumes everything I do.

I take another steadying breath. "It was nice to...see her grave taken care of after all these months. All the stuffed animals and pictures were...sweet."

"It's obvious she comes from a loving family." Jerica says in a broken whisper near my ear.

Her family. The memory of T at Milio's, hanging with the LC's and snorting powder paints itself into my mind. And I shake my head to clear it of the image, but it lingers. The knowledge that her mom turned to pills, like me, to numb the pain of losing her daughter. The fact that both Lexus and Luxury would never see the way their mom worked extra hard to keep them fed and happy nearly killed me. Then the screams that pierced the air after I unloaded the clip into Dawn's front door. Killing her. And all the blood that followed and caked my nails after the fact. I'd popped an extra two blue pills that night before going to her place in search of TuFace.

In fact, I'd cherished those blues I ate in secret to get me through the contracts and the kills. Waking up with the evidence of her blood in my cuticles was no biggie to process, since I didn't really have to. Came with the territory, I thought, secretly appreciating the blackouts that afforded me the cash I liked.

No amount of cash would bring her back. No amount of pills would cure what was really eating me. And the woman that usually brought me comfort in my arms only conjures up the images of a man with her same eyes begging for his life. The man whose death I claimed and covered up like it was nothing, and hating myself now because he meant everything to her.

The world blurs as I unlink her arms from me to step away. Her eyes are still shining, but there's a different emotion there now.

"Where are you going?"

"It's for the best." I mutter before turning and trudging down the street.

"But what about—"

"Follow me and I'll make sure you never make it home to that son of yours. That enough honesty for you?"

It was harsh. It was cold. It was everything that I'd been groomed to be since my nearly lethal arrival into this world. But I had to be sure she understood to stay away.

The idea of seeing Jerica in the same way, six feet under and surrounded by pretty flowers and mementos made me crazy.

"If you leave this time, don't come back." She barked.

And I fought to ignore the watery statement she shot through the wind with just as much force as a bullet from Luci.

Twenty-Four

ZENITH

Today was the last day I got to hang on to my cobalt Mustang. The thought entered my head as I gunned it from Maple Shade to South Camden on fumes. Though the fumes weren't a result from a damn-near empty gas tank, but from the instant depletion of energy left in me after that confrontation with Jerica.

Her words drift through my mind on a truth bomb I tried to deflect at the time: "You show the fuck up. Period."

Despite the tight pain twisting in my chest against the action, I find myself making the trip to the small government housing block where I used to stay all the time. More like, when I snuck in and out during the nights to get some nookie from the former girl of my dreams. Before...shit happened. Before I broke her heart and ended her life.

I groaned from the pain that came from how tightly ground my jaw was. That pain didn't compare to the fear though. As I cruised down the street marked by jagged sidewalks and potholes large enough to sink a man's tires, I fight to stop the trembling in my hands again. I'm no fucking good for her, I know this, but...

I parked the car on the curb and note a slim, elder man peeking through the door blinds of Dawn's home.

I'm out the car before I get a chance to read the situation.

"Wassup, bro?" I asked the old black man with dry skin.

My sudden approach takes him by surprise as I note him jump and clutch his chest.

"Oh, wassup Shame? It's me, Wendell. Robyn's neighbor from next door."

I study him behind squinted distrusting eyes before recognition hits me. I did remember the old head I caught more than a time or two hanging with Dawn's mom. Though I only visited during the nights, I saw him creeping from the back door a few times after I left. My guard dropped slightly with that knowledge as I climbed the porch steps.

"I remember you." I say as I peak through one of the blinds, too. "How's that wife of yours doing?"

His cheeks heat at that mention. "Um, she doing all right. Been in the hospital for her sugar."

"That's too bad. Hope she gets better soon."

"Thanks, young blood." He adds, his eyes averting to Dawn's front door again. "Been trying to get a hold of Robyn, but she ain't answering her phone."

"That why you peakin through her blinds?"

He nodded, scowling. "Yeah. It's like her to play a little hard to get from time to time, nah mean? But I ain't heard from her since Thursday night."

"Maybe she's busy. She does have a full time at the hospital."

"I know, I know." He muttered, unconvinced. "But...I been looking after her since her daughter died. Robyn's been having a hard time with it, so I stop by and help her with cleaning and cooking when she's up for it. Been appreciating her company while Bonnie's been in the hospital."

So, he'd been the neighbor babysitting Robyn, I think as I recollect T's furious words from the party over a week ago now.

"Something ain't right." He chants. "Something ain't right with this. This ain't like Robyn to not answer the door around this time. She don't work today, but no answer."

I could almost laugh at the absurdity of it all, at this old head feeling concern for his next-door side piece while his own wife was ill, but I don't. None of his sins compared to mine, and the sight of dried blood on one of the concrete steps draw my eyes shut in grief.

Coming here was a bad idea, I think in a flurry of panic thoughts.

"You...uh, try calling her?" I ask in order to distract myself from the wild beating in my chest.

"Didn't you hear me? Yes of course. No answer. I tried her cell, her home phone, and her other daughter's phone. Nobody been around. Nobody been answering."

I freeze at the mention of T. That wasn't at all like her to not answer her phone. She hadn't been glued to it like Dawn to scour the socials, but she'd been responsible. Too responsible to let her phone go unanswered if she knew somebody needed her. That was T, always looking out for people and listening to them, even going as far as entertaining telemarketers.

That thumping in my chest returns and I wrestle with the notion of running. Again. Same as when I unloaded the clip onto her front porch and ended it all.

"You show the fuck up. Period." Jerica's soft voice gone militant reverberates in my head again, and I take a few steadying breaths like she taught me. Stay in the present. Stay real. And deal with it. I chant this to myself before peering through the blinds again.

But, like before, there's nothing. Only darkness in the living room in the middle of the day. It was Saturday. A non-school or work day for both Robyn and T, so there should have at least been someone present inside.

"How long you been out here?" I questioned the old man at my side. He was looking through the blinds again, too.

"About twenty minutes, I guess. Why?"

"No reason," I retort gruffly as I scan the rest of porch. There's nothing to marvel at on the outside of the hood house, and the doorknob doesn't give when I twist it. I whip my phone out to call the one person who'd hadn't let me go to voicemail since I'd known her.

"You've reached Tierra..." Her voice sings through as an automated message seconds after I hit the call button.

"What the fuck..." I hiss after calling for a third time with the same failed result.

"See?" Wendell said, his voice a mixture of snide and concerned as he backed up from the door. "Been trying all day. Nobody is picking up. This ain't right."

Nah, it wasn't, but I don't voice my concerns as I consider some things. Maybe the family was out of town for the weekend. Or at some family's house or an event that demanded them be out of reach for a couple of days. Even as I come up with the possibilities, they sound more mismatched with reality. Robyn, from Dawn's account, was a fun-loving parent who loved to travel, but on a Janitorial salary the opportunities were few and far between. She could barely afford to leave the city much less an impromptu faraway trip. As scared as I was to admit it, Wendell's words rang true as the seconds ticked by.

Something wasn't right.

"Should we try to call Robyn's cousin cross town? I met him one time and got his number, maybe he might know something. Or maybe I can call my brother Cyril who know how to pick locks. How much money you got? He'll come down here and bust them locks for the cheap if—"

"Chill, old man." I growl. "Let me think on it."

He opened his mouth to protest but knew better. My reputation preceded me in this city, and he knew I didn't repeat myself. While Luci was retired, I wasn't. At least my fists wouldn't be when they found their way to his old crunchy ass face if he questioned me more.

"All right." I say, folding my arms. "Here's what we gonna do."

"All ears, young blood." He chirps, hunching to hone in on my words.

"I'mma call—" I begin, before a faint noise stops me. Like a dying bird or kitten trapped under a storm drain. The sound is weak and barely there, but present nonetheless.

"Call who?"

I glare at him in silent warning as I train my ears on the sound to hear if it happens again. Did they get a pet or something? If so, did they really just leave it in there while they took this so-called trip?

"You hear that?" I ask Wendell, whose head is cocked to the side to listen just as mine is. "Sound like a dog or something. Coming from the house."

He scowls. "That's odd. Robyn ain't have no pets. Everybody in that house allergic to animal hair. Robyn stay on me about washing my clothes before visiting. She knows my dogs sheds a lot."

I train my ears on the sound again, waiting for it. I almost relegate the noise to my imagination and anxiety until the faint squeak sounds again. But it's something more than just a squeak. Like a whine or a...

A cry.

"Stand back." Is all the warning I toss the old head before kicking my timberlands through the partially glass door.

"God damn it, boy!" He hollers as he staggers back. "You crazy or what?"

"Shut up!" I snarl before reaching in and unlocking the knob from inside. Once the door is open, a foul stench hits me full frontal as I walk in. It's so strong I have to bend over and heave into the foyer. The ham sandwich and Fruit Loops I had for breakfast are now all over the hallway floor.

"Smell like death in there!" Wendell chokes and coughs from behind me. He doesn't follow me inside, and I don't pay him any mind as I go in search of the smell. What the fuck was going on? T was responsible and so clean, even cleaning up after me after we ate lunch sometimes. Robyn got paid to clean hospital rooms, and I could always identify the smell of Pine Sol whenever I snuck over to hang with Dawn.

Now this? A foul-smelling abandoned house? My heart pounded and I shielded my nose with my shirt as I continued to search the tiny house. All looks clear, including T's room, which is spotless, and Dawn's old room that is littered with her old belongings and baby items. There's two playpens inside, but thankfully no Luxury or Lexus in sight.

The only room I hadn't checked was Robyn's, and it's unfamiliar territory I'd not been used to approaching, so the usual nerves that reared as I snuck in and out in the past come back full force at this taboo action. Moving towards her mom's door instead of avoiding it like the plague.

The only plague present now was the stench that resembled the smell of rotting flesh, and I hit the jackpot as I enter Robyn's modestly designed room.

The smell is coming from her room.

I take a deep breath I regret, inhaling the awful smell in preparedness to see the unthinkable.

In a matter of seconds, I uncover the reason behind the odor.

It's Robyn.

She's stiff and straight on her back and is lying surrounded by several pill bottles surrounding her body with the whites of her eyes on full display. I can't ignore

the school portraits of Dawn near her body that's surrounded by a sea of empty liquor bottles.

There's no mistaking it, not for one second, that she's
dead. But from the smell, she had to have been lying
there for at least a couple of days. The house is warm,
leading me to believe the automatic heat accelerated
the state of her decomposed flesh.

"Aw shit!" I swear, nearly vomiting a second time as I
fall to my knees. As a contract executioner, I'd seen my
fair share of corpses, but this?

This was pure sadness and shame mixed in together.
It had to be, to lead the normally strong-willed matriarch to OD'ing in her own home.

The kitten noises return, and I look over behind the
bed to see a little body weakly crawling over to me. Her
hair is a mangled mess of curls and there's brown stains
in her onesie that looked to be white at one point in
time. She's babbling and crying, and the rings around
her eyes let me know she'd been crying for some time.

"Baby girl..." I whisper, unconsciously lifting the toddler into my arms.

"Na na na..." She sobs and babbles. She's so tiny, I
think, and for a second the rotting flesh odor dissipates
as I stare into her deep brown eyes that look like mine.

A hot, frustrated tear slips down my cheek as I hug
the weak toddler to my chest. All I can manage past the
lump in my throat is a weak, "Baby girl," again as I take
a minute to get myself together.

My baby girl was in here...for hours...trapped with her dead grandmother's body and unable to be cared for. There was no one here for her, and so many emotions mixed in with the shame in me at that moment. Fury, sadness, hatred, but the most encompassing is the guilt. If I had only been here sooner to be here for her. Maybe she'd be smiling, I think, smiling in my hood house with my whacky mother who'd been trying her best at parental redemption.

Why couldn't I just fucking been here sooner....?

Those words play on repeat in my head until a scream emanates from the bedroom doorway.

"Robyn, no!" Wendell screeches as he bursts into the room. "Baby, why? Come on, stay with me—wake up!"

He's shaking her stiff body and sobbing, same as me, as he pleads with her to do the impossible and respond to him. To wake up.

"She's gone, man." I say on a shaky breath before standing up with my baby in my arms.

Her cries have stopped, and her head lays weakly on my chest. How long had she been crying like that? Begging for someone to care for her and help? Her tiny body heaves, but no sound comes out, and my heart breaks at every jerk from her trembling body, too frail to even utter an extra cry. I don't linger or stay behind as Wendell whips out his phone to beg the operator to send help. All I can think of is taking my baby girl out of there, and with a heavy heart, that's exactly what I do.

Twenty-Five

TODAY

I should have been there.

My mind is tortured with the futile thoughts as I reflect on my absent parenting. My baby girl had been trapped in a rotten house of horrors and just a few feet away from her dead granny's corpse. The sight of the heavyset matriarch, always so strong and present, lying in a dead heap surrounded by pictures of Dawn, pills, and liquor bottles, makes me wince. I needed somebody to get angry with, someone I could punch or hurt just as bad as my baby girl had been hurting all alone since Dawn's death. I don't know Luxury's day-to-day, but judging from T's mix-up with the LC's and the state of Robyn, I imagined there hadn't been much room to care for her. Not in the right way, at least. T should have at least been there to watch her, is what I want to spit, but regret makes me hesitate.

Luxury was my baby. My responsibility I've been forcing onto everyone else for far too long since Dawn's death. I think back to my accusations to Dawn over the doubt surrounding Luxury's paternity. Staring at the large brown eyes and chubby cheeks that were distinctly Masters genes, wrong was all I'd been. A shameful motherfucker who let his wrongs explode because he'd been either too jaded or too high to take charge of his life. Yeah, that sounded more like me.

A hate bomb explodes in me at the thought, that I'd willfully left Luxury out of my new mission because I thought my name attached to her would ruin her life in the long run. Was sure she'd grow up and see her father for who he really was, a shameful, violent dude deserving of hell. I'd gotten used to living in my underworld all alone and allowing no one else in. But something stone cracks in my chest as I steal a glance at the baby fast asleep in the backseat of my ride. Though dirty, she looks to be breathing evenly and resting up good. I made another decision, then and there, to show up for my baby girl and kiss her boo-boos like Quincy never did me. I'd be the reason she'd eat and sleep peacefully tonight, and every night after that. I vowed to be the cause of her smiles instead of her heartbreak in the years to come. From now on, I determine as I pull onto the curb of my family's shack, I'd do my best to be her pride. Even if only to see her smile again.

But she needed some food first, I thought as I gently lift her from the back seat and adjust her into my arms. A wave of panic crushes me as I twist the knob to the front door. In all my manic thoughts during the aimless drive home the one important one didn't strike me until just then.

Just what did babies eat?

Maybe some cereal and milk? I remembered milk was good for bones and babies...right? My mind is still reeling over the nuances as I enter what used to be my living room. The tattered sofa in the room is voided of its threadbare cushions, which I see tossed in various places on the floor. The dining table that's usually clean and put-together is destroyed. There are holes in the walls and everything...and I mean everything is scattered into large messy piles onto the floors. This was a warzone; I surmise as I enter the house further with Luxury still asleep in my arms.

"Shit!" I hiss at the realization. Somebody was in here, had to be, if the house was torn through like this. It looked like somebody was searching for something, and that single observation makes me jet to my room in search of Luci. I didn't have any bullets, but people tended to obey whenever I aimed her empty or full at their heads.

But nothing could prepare me for what I see as I make it to the top of the stairs.

From where I'm standing, I see a person, a woman, standing over someone on the floor in my room. Her back is to me. She's breathing hard and half dressed in a skimpy black top and booty shorts that say LSD on the cheeks.

"Shay?" I bark, mostly out of curiosity and disbelief at the woman panting. "You good?"

She turns to me, her eyes not even registering the baby in my arms. There's so much hatred in her eyes that I almost cringe from its intensity. But I hold my ground as I choke back the fear and confusion.

"This bitch stole from me." Shay bit out, low and in that deathly way Quincy used to.

I almost ask who but see the terrified woman on the floor. There are tears in her eyes and her body's trembling in fear as she looks at me.

"Ma?" I say, my mind doing backflips to piece together the situation. Shay is holding something in her hands, something she uses to gesture towards our weepy feeble mother on our bedroom floor.

"Shamel, just stay back!" Mom pleads with me as I get closer. "This is between the two of us. We'll sort it out. Everything's okay."

"Yo, why the fuck is she on the floor, Shay?" I howl at my older sister, whose body is shaking just as bad as Mom's. As I near her, I notice the object in her hand.

Shay's holding a hammer.

I finally figure out the reason behind those holes in the wall downstairs. She did this. But why?'

"Stay back!" Shay screams and raises the hammer. Her eyes are crazy, 'unhinged' Si would call it, but batshit is on my short list of descriptors for the woman with wild hair and eyes shining fury. "Unless you want some, too."

I move to immobilize the crazy bitch when Luxury stirs in my arms. I almost forgot about the feeble baby in my arms who I couldn't risk hurting anymore. She's awake now and staring with half hooded eyes at Shay.

But Shay ignores her as she spits, "I don't know what goes on in this wicked house of horrors, since I don't be here. But I do know one thing."

"Shayne," Mom hollers from the floor, clutching her leg. "It wasn't me! Please believe me when I tell you—"

"Who else could have done it?" Shay roars, crouching down to her face. "That money was all I had to my name, and you let that junkie uncle of ours take it, didn't you?"

"No..." Mom sobbed. "I didn't. He didn't, either. Don't blame this on Shaheim either."

"Where he at, then? Huh?"

Mom hung her head low. "Not here."

"I should hit you with this. I should fucking kill you like you killed my future for stealing my money. Four years. Four whole fucking years I worked for those stacks and now it's magically missing from my stash?"

My heart sinks at her words, and it takes me a minute to pick through the mental cloudiness as I watch the scene. Shay was threatening our mother with a hammer. Mom was obviously hurt. All Bad was nowhere in sight, and that money...

I recall the money I stole from the floorboard stash I knew was Shay's the night we went to the Dirty Kitten with the LC's. Everybody was pissed at me for the extra half hour pitstop at my crib, but after finding those pictures from our past mixed in with all the money that could've saved us a long time ago...I just didn't give a fuck. I wanted to hurt her, I thought, and could not blame those little blue pills I originally went in search for after getting All Bad from prison on my actions. I knew stealing from her would get her attention, but that was a week ago. Surely, if someone nabbed that much cash from my stash I would've noticed sooner. There had to have been at least fifty stacks in those floorboards. Fifty G's I threw at every stripper that walked my way that night.

"That money was my ticket outta here." Shay said in an anguished whisper. "All the money I had in this world to make a future for myself. You got no clue what I did for that cash."

"Shayne," Mom said. "I'm sorry! I know I haven't been the best parent, but understand I'd never steal from you. Never. And neither would, Shah—"

Shay cuts her off by raising the hammer in the air. "If you say his name one more time, I swear to God I'll knock your lying ass out cold for real. Stop fucking lying!"

"Get your ass away from my mom!" I growl, unable to take the scene anymore as I jump between them. Shay and I are at eye level now, so it's easy to stare into her fiery eyes as I continue, "Mommy ain't have nothing to do with that."

She glowers. "You just covering up for her!"

"I ain't." I grunt. "You know me. If I had any suspicion somebody stole that amount of cash from me, they'd already be dealt with. No questions. No hammers. Just handled."

She studies my face curiously but says nothing.

"Mommy ain't take that money from your stash under the floor. Neither did All Bad."

"Don't protect her!" She starts, but blinks and sputters as realization dawns on her. "Wait. How you know my shit was under the..."

"Yeah." I add, watching her jaw fall slack. "I took it. Spent it all at the strip club about a week ago. A little surprised you ain't noticed it earlier."

A heated moment passes, and I swear I can see all the hair on her head rise from the rage coloring her face. Instead of raising the hammer and swinging at me, she drops it. It hits the wooden floor with a thunk and I'm in total shock as I watch her bottom lip tremble before the tears flowed. Not another word is spoken on either side as the only noise in the room is consumed by her soul and body jerking sobs. She cries so long I think she's run out of tears, same as my baby girl back in that house of death, but nah. She keeps crying and I just watch her with a heavy heart. Now guilty over my actions I originally committed to cause her pain. I wanted her to hurt like I did for leaving me all alone when our mother got stabbed. And when Quincy left town with Yvonne. I wanted to blame it all on her, I realized as I study the woman-turned girl who's now a crying mess in her skimpy clothes.

"I'm sorry." I said, knowing it too tepid a response to all the pain. "But I can fix this. All right?"

She shook her head. "You ruin everything."

"I know." I say, before leaning over and placing a kiss to her forehead. Instead of jerking away like I figured, she reaches over to take Luxury from my arms.

"That's my daughter." I tell her.

"Your what?" Mom asks from the floor. "Y-Your daughter?"

"Yeah." I say, my tone gravel as I walk over to my corner of the room and dig into the closet.

"Shamel." Shay says, still rocking the toddler in her arms just as if she hadn't been holding a hammer seconds prior. "I need that money. You don't understand what you did. None of y'all do."

Her voice is calm now, as if all the crying existed as the flood gates that allowed out all her anger. Her usage of my name makes my chest tighten, but I don't let on as I fish out the black bag that housed the advance money I got from Si.

"I got you." I say before tossing the bag on the bed. "I got hired recently for a gig that's gonna get us outta here. Trust me. This cash I got as an advance to do it, but if you need it then just take it. There should be about half of what I took. Should be enough for you to start over somewheres else with."

Shay eyes me cautiously, her red-rimmed eyes distrusting as she approaches the bag on the bed. "I'm tired, Shamel. Tired of fighting. It took too long to get here and...I love y'all. But I can't stay. Half won't be nearly enough to cover what I need, but it's enough for me to leave tonight."

I nodded. "Take it."

"Tonight?" Mom asked, attempting to stand up. I rushed to her side to assist. "You're leaving us?"

"I can't stick around for much longer, no." She says as she unzips the bag. "I took the rest of this money from somebody who'll kill me once he realizes it's missing. So, no. I can't stay. It's got to be tonight."

I think both mom and me are shocked by how much she's talking, considering how private my sis had been throughout her childhood. But I understand her, I think. I understand that she's on her own mission just like I was on mine. If this cash helped her in some way, then it was hers. It was all the money I had in the world right now, considering my deaded relationship with LC's, but as long as the 590 contract was still intact, then there'd be much more to come later. All in good time.

"I'll pay you the rest after next week, all right?" I say as I help mom to stand up.

"Thanks, love." Mom smiles up at me. "I tripped and fell on one of your shoes and hadn't been able to stand back up. You're a gem."

"That really what happened?" I couldn't refrain from asking the question.

She nodded. "Yes."

"And Shay didn't hit you with the hammer?"

She reared back, appalled. "Heavens, no! It was a total misunderstanding, what you saw."

"Okay…" I lament. "Then where your mans at?"

"My mans?"

"Don't pretend you and AB ain't been kicking it."

"Oh!" She says, her cheeks ripe with embarrassment. "He's out. Shaheim mentioned a job he had to do or something. That he was going to a dance of some sort to collect payment from someone. Those are all the details he'd tell me."

Shit, I swear inwardly. He went to take care of that high school kid Milio tried to get me to do. The guy was apparently another dude his girlfriend fucked when they were on a break, and I didn't like to involve myself in shit over love or gangs, but the rage boils my blood again at Milio using my cousin to take care of this problem me nor any other LC would.

"There's no money in here." Shay's words crash over me like a bucket of ice.

"What?" I demand as I stalk over to the bag supposedly filled with clean bills. But she's right. The only thing in the bag is rolled up clothes from the dirty laundry that's situated inside strategically to give it weight. Like somebody put it there knowing I'd find it.

"What the fuck?" I roar, my entire body trembling with cold hate and the knowledge of what happened. A small piece of notebook paper is all I find in the bottom of the bag, and I almost toss it to the floor if not for the chicken scratch written on one side of it. That writing wasn't mine, and I nearly explode from the hastily written words as I read them:

"What does it say?" Shay asked, adjusting Luxury in her arms and frowning at me.

I nearly choke on the words I'm forced to say out loud. Terrified and bewildered for a moment at how he got this information.

"Reparations. For Hector." I recite the words that mirrored the actions that's haunted me for years. That LC I killed was the co-lead of the LC's and somebody All Bad laid his freedom down for. Of course, he figured out it was me who killed him. He didn't mention it, but it was implied he took this cash as hush money.

"What does that mean?" Shay asked.

I'm clenching and unclenching my fists at this point in restraint. I was fucked. We were fucked. If I didn't get Shay this money to get outta here, then her goose was just as cooked as mine if word got back to the LC's that it was me responsible for killing their leader. The room was shrinking in on me as I realized the only option I had to get out of this. My mission was a golden dream slipping further away from me, and the thought was so sweet while it lasted. The mission, at this point, would soon become The Plan. The one that got us out of this shit alive, if we did this just right.

"Please go feed my baby girl." I tell Shay as I dial the number I knew would get us out of this. "I need to handle this real quick."

"What's going on?" She asked again, but I ignored her as the cool voice answered on the other end of the phone.

"Shame." Si says, like usual, instead of a hello. "What's the situation?"

It takes me a minute to gather the guts to ask. Do this, Mel. I chant to myself. The mission was a thing of yesterday, but in order for The Plan to work, then this deal had to be done.

"I need another advance. For that 590 contract." I bite out.

"We're set to meet tomorrow in Queens to take care of the 590's, Shame. It's all set up. All you need to do is show up and do what you do best. Okay?"

I shook my head, the idea of offing Quincy and life-long riches so sweet, but an unfortunate impossibility now. The dream was gone.

"Nah, man." I choke out. "I'mma need fifty stacks today. I'll explain later and pay you back after the contract is over. My sis is in real trouble that can't wait until tomorrow. I need that money by today. Can you make that happen?"

He sighs, and I feel his disappointment like a tangible thing through the phone. "Remember what I told you earlier, man? Being in debt to the Kobayashi's isn't a place you want to be. Once you owe us, that's it. I can get you this money, but that deal is off the table. Take your pick, Shame. But please, think on this wisely."

"I have." I retort, shaking inside from the missed opportunity. "And I need it today."

Silence.

"Si." I choke out, praying my desperation bled through that single word without me having to beg.

"That means you'll be in debt with us, instead of employed by us." Si says coolly. "I'll still require your expertise with this contract, but understand that any payment promised as a result of that will go directly to the Clan as part of your down payment on your debt. You understand?"

"I understand."

"Okay." Another deep soul weary sigh before he says, "Meet me at the shop in an hour to collect."

"You the truth, man," I release alongside a whoosh as I allow air back into my lungs.

Another pause, and I can almost see him tapping an irritated finger into his crossed arms. "Sorry it has to be this way, Shame."

"Shamel," I correct. "That ain't me no more, man. And, uh... I'm sorry, too."

I end the call and discuss the mission with Shay that morphed into our new plan. This new plan meant betrayal, of the worst kind, and leaving some people behind as a result, but it was necessary. Only a temporary evil until we made it to a safe space, but nonetheless a plan that marked the collective descent of us all into a darker world of uncertainty.

And running.

PART THREE

ZAY

Twenty-Six

Vonnie

Six years later

My sweaty hands shake in my denim pockets as I pace in panic outside the funeral home. I had to get this over with, I chant over and over to myself while wrestling with the notion of jetting back to the crib. It's been a long time since I held my favorite girl but I can't help needing her protective powers as more of what Quincy would've called "pussythoughts" infiltrate my senses. Since we left Camden all those years ago, I tried my best at keeping my promises. And I promised myself to stay away from death as much as possible. Logically, it wasn't me who killed Stevie, the old matriarch who accepted both Shay and me without question when we moved here without two pennies to rub together. Knew I wasn't responsible for the total heartache rocketing through the farm that followed her mysterious demise. But still, I can't chase the fear away. I couldn't stand death. Mamma Dean, her longtime best friend and doting neighbor, organized a beautiful ceremony that I promised to be a part of.

"She loved you like the son she never had, Xavier." Mamma Dean said to me numbly after getting word from Dan, Stevie's twin brother and resident farmhand, that he'd found her dead in bed just before dinner.

"I loved her, too." I responded, hanging my head low with shame. I checked on her every morning, and cherished our real talks during which she'd take her morning meds and sip her coffee. We talked about all kinds of stuff, and she always kept it real with me. No BS. No nonsense. She and Mamma Dean made an unstoppable team and meant everything to the farm community. Mamma Dean, the sweet, and Miss Stevie's unfiltered approach on life making them a literal dynamic duo. Being around them reminded me of the old times; the days where I had my Project Granny to answer to if I fucked up in the streets before we fell out of touch.

I reflect on The Mission-turned-The-Plan all those years ago as I continue to stalk the outside of the church like a coward. The Plan involved running, so to speak. After picking up those fifty stacks from Si at the Kobayashi's meat shop, we ducked out at Miss Pat's in Harlem for a couple days. It was good to see my Project Granny comfortable and settled in her new hood home, even if she wasn't thrilled to see me. She still welcomed us, Mom, Shay, my baby girl Luxury, and myself to stay in her small living room. We grew into a cozy routine each morning of waking and staying low: never staying outside too long or reaching out to people. I'd even deactivated my cell and the only credit card I had for legit emergencies.

While good for a little while, that routine couldn't last. It tore a deep hole in my chest at Shay and I's decision to split and leave our mother. I didn't want to put her through the consequences of our terrible decisions. She, and Luxury, deserved better.

So, we packed up in the middle of the night and went running. Again. Leaving Sommer and Luxury with Miss Pat, alongside a hefty chunk of the fifty stacks I stole from Si.

There was so much running that year. Both Shay and I couch-hopped in various friends' homes until after the tenth month Shay told me something that blew me away.

"I got accepted into a school down south." Shay told me, dressed in a gold two-piece lingerie set and six-inch heels.

She'd been talking in a rush, and after glancing at my phone, I realized her shift at the local strip joint would start in a few minutes.

"You mean college?" I asked in the dark, sitting up on the couch that doubled as my makeshift bed in one of her homegirl's tiny apartment in Philly. "I didn't know you were applying."

"Yep." She mumbled around a bobby pin in her mouth as she manipulated her long curls into a high ponytail. "There's no talking me out of it, either. I'm going."

"Well," I started, a little dazed by that info. "All right. You work out the cash for it?"

She rolled her eyes. "I ain't owing nobody a single cent."

A mirthless chuckle escapes me before I can even make sense of it. "Rule Thirty-Four."

"That man may have been the worst person and father in the history of man, but he had good business sense. So, yeah. I ain't trying to get a bunch of student loans and fuck up my credit. I figure with the stacks I saved up and got from you, I can skate by. Especially with a good job."

"Where is this school?"

"It's the University of Virginia. They got a good Nursing program I'm dying to get into."

"I'm, uh..." I say but trail off in thought.

She frowns and looks at me under the dim light. "You're what?

"Happy for you." I finish, fixing my gaze on the carpet. "And I want you to go for what makes you happy for a change."

She says nothing, only walks over to the chair to stare down at me. It's quiet for a few more seconds until she says, "Thanks, Mel."

"No sweat." I grumble. "Just don't forget about me when you become some big-time doctor in the Hills. All right?"

"Wait." She says after a fit of giggles. "You think I'm going by myself?"

"Well, ain't you?"

"No way in hell you're getting rid of me that easy." She chuckles in a way that beams light into me. In a way that I missed. "You're coming with."

So, that was that. We packed up and left the following month, boarding a bus in disguise to the south. My heart ached at how different things were, that I'd been sneaking incognito on a bus to escape to the south, instead of kicking it in first class with the fat wad of green I'd earned after executing my father. But that was only a dream, I think warily, as I continue the ridiculous pacing under the blazing sun.

"Would anyone near and dear to the departed like to share a few words?" I hear Pastor Jennings preside to the congregation of weepy funeral goers.

His words snap me back to the present and the current challenge in front of me. There was no contracted target I had to take out or even a high-profile Kobayashi assignment to take care of. Nah. Instead, the thing that haunted me most was the kind lady that lay dead just inside the building I'd wasted an hour stressing over entering or not.

Go in, Zay. I tell myself, the new self I had to become to live beside my little sis for the past five years incognito. I had to go in and be there for her, since today wasn't only Stevie's going-home ceremony, but Vonnie's birthday.

Taking a deep breath, I reach for the knob.

Only for a crowd of elder's I recognized as former friends of Stevie's walk through holding tissues. In fact, there are several people piling out dressed in black, creating a sea of dark clad individuals swarming the front door. *Ah, fuck.* I swear inwardly at the facts in front of me. This meant only one thing.

I missed the entire ceremony.

I scrambled past the crowds of people to at least say something to the sweet old lady who looked after us when she didn't have to when we first got to town. The same lady who allowed us to stay on her property for damn near free and encouraged Shay and I to do our best in making a way for ourselves down here. Even when she got the dementia diagnosis, she'd still been so strong. A kind of strong that drew people to her instead of stirred fright, like Quincy when he turned Commander on those who owed him.

I had to say...something to her. Though she's dead, and the sight of her laying there without any light to her normally red cheeks that matched her red hair fucks my head up beyond belief, I decided to do it.

But my heart pounds in my chest when I make it inside. The crowd thinned and it was just me and her, for the most part, as I stood a few feet from her casket. My hands shook and the sweat coated my back at an indecent rate, making me swear to shower later.

Do it. Do it. Just fucking go to her and say...what? See you later?

I gulp for strength, resolving myself to numb up and do it, same as I'd do when I had a contract to take care of. But the little blue pills helped back then. Though we didn't speak anymore after that transportation center confrontation, I held my vow to sobriety. The only substance I afforded myself these days was weed, and yeah, maybe I should dead the relationship between me and Mary Jane, but that would be pushing it.

A verse from "Let it Go," one of my favorite Clint Norway songs, slams through my brain as I just stand there: What the hell is wrong with me?

Taking a deep breath, I take a step towards the white casket with gold trim. But the sound of a grating Jersey accent that sounds vaguely familiar rings through the air. Not rings, but his gruff tone is deafening and hateful as he addresses the person in front of him a few feet from me.

"Are you some crazy bitch or something?" The orange-haired man spits at the girl in front of him. His back is to me as I stalk towards the couple engaged in a heated exchange that boils my blood as I draw nearer.

The fluffy fro alerts me of the girl's identity as I roll up behind his towering form looming over her.

"Watch your mouth there, bruh." I bite out, ensuring to lace all the malicious intent in my tone as I sought to defend my little sister Vonnie from this unfamiliar prick.

Vonnie's face, once red from the heat of her own anger and embarrassment, lights up immediately at the sight of me.

"Zay!" She squeals, and her purely joyous expression nearly splits me in half with relief and contentment. This was it. That look on her face was what I fought for when we discovered she moved to Richmond all those years ago. We deployed and stayed in this southern state for her. And my heart straight melted every time I'd been successful in putting a smile on her previously troubled face.

"Hey, Von." I greet her, studying every inch of the dude I'd been considering bringing Luci out of retirement for. "This guy giving you trouble?"

"No, Zay." She says, straightening her back with confidence. "I can handle this. Besides, my friend Jeremy here was just leaving. Right?"

Jeremy? I ask myself, the name ringing an eerie alarm in my head at the last time I'd heard it. I attempted to ignore the pounding in my chest and latent panic that threatened to overcome me. Maybe it was a coincidence, I think. Yeah, that was it. The last time I saw the kid who admired me like a street god was over six years ago.

"Right," Jeremy chuffs, and before I get the chance to ask him where he came from or who he was, he bolted out of there without a second thought.

After a few rounds of chatting and laughing it up, Vonnie sobers and straightens to gaze up at me. I knew her by now, and could read the large question mark on her face as I stopped laughing.

"All good?" I asked.

"Yeah," She nodded. "I was just wondering what made you like that."

"Like what?"

"Like..." She paused to consider something, almost as if she's in the middle of a conversation I can't hear. "Like me."

I did my best to not reveal the shock or panic that dropped inside my head like a bomb. What the hell could that mean?

"What the hell does that mean?" I asked, noting the gruffness in my tone.

"I don't like death either." She whispers, her voice hollow and ghostly in response to my previous declaration of how much I hated death.

Though the room is still full of people, it's like everyone dissolves as I stare at the same troubled expression she'd get all the time when I first moved here. I secretly prided myself on helping pull her out of that darkness that stalked her like a storm cloud from D.C. Made sure to visit with her and indulge in all the things that made her face light up. Even though I fucking hated those dorky ass video games, I made extra sure to keep my PS4 fired up in the living when she came over.

I couldn't get out of this with playboy humor, like T pegged I did as a habit in the middle of tense conversations like this. So, I stuck with the facts.

"Hey, you." I said, before pulling her into my arms like I made a habit to after Devin left the farm. "No talking about death on your birthday. Got it?"

Vonnie Carlson, always so stoic and tough, wraps her arms around me and sniffles a little into my chest.

"Got it."

"All right." I say as we pull apart. "I heard Mamma Dean's cooking up a whole post-funeral supper."

"Sure is." She said with a weak smile. "Stayed up all night fixing all of Aunt Stevie's favorites, too."

"I want in on that." I tell her. "You in, birthday girl?"

That familiar huge grin I'd prayed to one day be the cause of spreads across her face, nearly freezing my heart in its cage at the beautiful sight. She was no longer the same little girl, no longer VonVon. In her place bloomed Vonnie Carlson, the eighteen-year-old sister I'd promised to cherish from behind the facade of Xavier Rose.

"Let's go."

TWENTY-SEVEN

PLASTIC

"Where is that sister of yours, Zay?" I anticipated Mamma Dean's question long before I even looked at her.

We're all sitting at the large rectangular dining table that would have stretched between two or three rooms of a normal starter home. Well, in all honesty, it would have easily stretched the length of the entire cabin Shay and I lived near the edge of Carlson Farms.

I chewed carefully on Mamma Dean's signature fried chicken (the chicken that sent folks to heaven with just a bite) before meeting the old lady's gaze across the table. She's sitting surrounded by old heads and funeral-goers.

"Uh, she had to work late." I mumbled, suddenly hyper-aware of all the eyes on me from what had to be at least twenty people.

"She is always working." Mamma Dean grumbled, scooping another hefty serving of potato salad on the small child's plate beside her. "Here, baby. Don't let this good food go to waste."

"It's not personal, Mamma Dean." I tell her, a bit resigned from the emotional overkill and repercussions of seeing Miss Stevie in a box. "She had finals, too. She's been mad stressed."

Mamma Dean nodded, a considering look on her face as she wiped the crumbs off the maybe five- or six-year-old beside her. "All right, then. Then make sure you take our girl a plate of chicken back with you. Let me know if I need to fix her some more mashed potatoes, since it looks almost gone."

"It's all good," I say, wiping my face. "Appreciate you."

"Of course." Mamma Dean whinnied. "Can't let our Shay starve. She already skin and bone."

"For sure." I agree, but shake an internal head at her smothering.

She was the kindest soul on this farm now Miss Stevie was gone, but that just wasn't facts. Shay gained an easy twenty or thirty pounds since we moved down here. And the stress of her nursing program and day job as a CNA didn't leave much room for the balanced meals she insisted on cooking when we first moved into the cabin that resembled our Camden shack. Her baking skills were hella good, and I wondered how she got so good at it considering our own mother never baked anything. But seriously, she started baking small cakes when she overheard Vonnie say yellow cake with frosting was her favorite dessert. It went from a hobby to a means of hustle; I often sold her cakes, pies, and brownies to the farmhands and whenever the farm got visitors from the main city. Her desserts literally sold like hotcakes and kept us afloat until she started school. These days, if she wasn't at the small assisted living facility in town or class, then she was knocked out asleep.

Tonight was no different, and I suspect my sis took on the extra shift to avoid the funeral but kept it to myself.

"I wish Viv and the kids would join us for supper..." Mamma Dean grumbled again, referencing the strange new neighbors who occupied Stevie's house. "But I guess not."

The stocky redheaded lumberjack near the head of the table stirs in his seat. It's Dan, Miss Stevie's twin brother and full-time caretaker towards her final days. His teeth were checkered with black dots that reveal the advanced stages of decay due to his daily tobacco use. And he looks pissed.

"Fuck her." He growls around a mouthful of greens.

Mamma Dean reached over and swatted him. "Hush up that talk, now!"

"Sorry, ma'am." He blushed, averting his eyes to his plate. "But you know I'm right. Viv's been uppity all her life. She left her mama once, and this ain't no different."

Eddie Carlson, Mamma Dean's son and Devin's biological father who also worked over three decades as a resident farmhand, shoots to his feet.

"You got a real nasty mouth, Dan." His voice sizzles with threat and warning. "I won't hear you talk anymore shit about Vivian again. Understand?"

Dan sputters and stands to meet him, "That right? You wanna try me, boy?"

"Boy, huh?" Eddie parroted, and I'm completely stunned by the display of emotion from the normally stoic farmer who'd always been slow to act and living solo.

"Best stay outta business that don't belong to you." Dan warned with a dark glint in his moss-colored eyes.

In all the years I'd lived on the farm, I never saw nor knew this side of Stevie's twin. A feeling twists my gut as I watch the interaction I'd wanted no part in.

Eddie nodded his head slow, as if running Dan's words through a processor in his head before formulating a response.

"It don't matter what you think of me." He starts, jabbing a finger at himself. "But I refuse to listen to more of your hate-talk when it comes Vivian Gresham. That's your own niece you talking about."

A tense silence charges the room as the two stare off; Eddie is a towering six foot plus dude glaring daggers at the five-foot five man who's miniature in comparison.

"Niece, girlfriend, dogs." Dan spat, moving closer to Eddie. "All can be bitches at the end of the day. My niece is no different."

Mamma Dean stood suddenly to diffuse the situation. "No matter how wrong Viv done her family or this farm, she's kin." She says. "*Stevie's* kin. Don't you go badmouthing her in front of all these people like we ain't got no sense. You hear?"

Viv was Miss Stevie's estranged daughter who moved here from "up north," Mamma Dean says. Since she ran away from home with three babies in the night and never spoke to Miss Stevie again, it caused all kinds of tension between the Gresham family. Out of all seven of Miss Stevie's children, Viv was the only one that left a watery expression on the strong matriarch's face whenever anyone brought up her name.

It was a part of her story Miss Stevie never shared with me, and I recalled telling her all sorts of stories from my past I didn't realize until now played a big part of my healing. She'd let me come over and talk and talk, something I never was allowed to do under The Commander's rules, but in all that talking she never spoke of herself. Just listened.

A large commotion fuels the room as their bickering continues, and I try to signal to get Mamma Dean's attention. I finished my food and had meant to ask her to make Shay a plate. It was almost evening, and my blunt was waiting for me where I left it on my nightstand. Eager to return to light up and play my scratch-offs I'd been lowkey addicted to, I waved again. But after waving at her for another few seconds, I realize it's no use.

I realize something else, too, in the corner of my eye. It's Vonnie, my secret little sis, sneaking out of the room. Her face is weary as she takes another exploratory glance backwards and tiptoes up the stairs to her bedroom, I assumed.

Vonnie was real delicate like that. Sort of fragile when it came to people yelling or arguing. Was like the fiery girl I balled with on the weekends who got all kinds of scrapes and concrete burns from the court would disappear during a fight. She'd sort of shrink into herself and hide, like now, escaping into the closest small space to get away.

I noticed her do it after a b-ball game turned heated between me and Malik, who lost but tried to be a hero and sucker-punch me after I made the winning slam dunk.

Since leaving my old life, I didn't do violence. Couldn't afford to resort to the shameful ways that had both me and Shay on the run in the first place.

But not that day.

That day, I matched energy and fists as we went at it on the court in my driveway.

"Stop it! Stop it! Stop it!" Vonnie hollered while rolling into a ball on the court.

I'd been intent on blood, frustrated that Malik would try to cheat the bet we all made on that b-ball game.

Winner got fifty dollars and a blunt, two things I desperately needed since my unemployed status left me
little options to get the high I liked.

"Chill out, y'all." Bone Alvarez, my other homie who
played as my second admonished while pulling our
bodies apart. At six foot six, he'd been a tall scary looking motherfucker, but played mediator this day as we
went at it.

"Pay up, pussy!" I hollered at Malik, who was still
reaching for me as Bone separated us.

"Fuck you!" He spat. "Cheating ass."

"Y'all!" Bone roared, getting both our attention. "Look
at her. Y'all freaking her out!"

"What?" I demanded, panting and eyes crazy as I
looked for the person we'd been freaking out. Once I
seen the then thirteen-year-old huddled in a ball, frail
fetal position on the court of angry ballers, I crumbled.

"Move," I said to Bone, shirking off his hold on my
arm. I ran to her side and sank to the ground near her.
"Von, you okay?"

She shook all over, whispering something unintelligi-
ble I had to ask her to repeat.

"No favors. No favors. Can't do the favor. No favors...."

She's mumbling so fast and rocking, and I'm just sitting there not sure how to handle the situation. Every
time I tried to touch her, to sit her up and get her to her
feet, she screamed and fought me. Her eyes were sealed
shut as she trembled and fought me some more.

"What happened?" Shay demanded as she ran to meet us outside. Bone and Malik merely stood there, dumbfounded by her suddenly frantic actions. "Zay! What y'all do to her?"

"I-I didn't—" I started but get cut off by Shay's hand in my face, prompting me to shut up.

"Just stop." She hisses, bending low to caress Vonnie's signature fro. "You're okay, sweetheart. You hear me, right?"

Vonnie calmed instantly at Shay's soft touch. After a minute of tense observing, Vonnie nods her head.

"Good." Shay says, smiling and calm as water as she eventually talks the girl into sitting up. "See? It's just us."

Vonnie studied the four of us in abject horror. There are twigs and leaves in her hair, and I'm completely numb and wordless.

Just what the fuck was that? I asked myself inwardly, since my lips were permanently frozen at that point.

"Sorry, guys..." She says in a voice so small it takes me a minute to gather that she's thirteen instead of the weepy toddler who used to visit us in the hood. "Sorry."

"It's all good, sweet girl." Shay reassures her.

"We're sorry, Von." Malik apologized, rubbing the back of his head awkwardly. "We should have been more careful not to have upset you. That's our fault."

I'm still just staring at the girl who made me die a few deaths from her actions a few seconds ago. She and Shay eventually went inside the cabin, where Shay talked her down and baked her some yellow cake to put a smile on her face.

I learned since then that Vonnie didn't do tension. She didn't do arguing or violence, and I caught myself whenever I was ramping up to punch somebody, especially if it was in her presence. I wouldn't scare her, I told myself as I stood up from the table in the middle of the dinner chaos.

I ducked out easy and unnoticed as I trail upstairs. I needed to make sure she was okay. Even if it was just my paranoia pulling me up the wooden staircase and down the hall to the right, I had to make sure to prevent that meltdown from before. Our arguing destroyed the life in her eyes, same as the day her other big brother Devin, who we called DC, left that morning of his surprise deployment. Something broke in her after that, something I knew I could never repair no matter how many b-ball rounds and video games we played.

Fuck that, I thought as I reached her closed bedroom door. My gut told me different, that she wasn't okay in the slightest. And ever since what happened to Mikey, I vowed to never betray my gut again since it lost me him, too. It was her birthday, for fuck's sake, nobody deserved to be in their room crying on a day meant to be theirs. Instead, my poor sis was surrounded by shitty family arguments and a funeral. How shitty.

After knocking and no response, I wrestle with turning around and leaving. Maybe she was playing her video games with those goofy ass gamer headphones on. Maybe, I think, but my gut still didn't like it.

Trusting it instead of any notions of courtesy, I turn the knob. To my shock, it's unlocked, and I'm suddenly inside the small nerdy oasis filled with alien posters and Christmas lights.

Instead of fighting the game controller and yelling at her TV screen like usual, I find her on the floor. She's laying on her back and the controller is strewn to the corner of the room. It looked as if she'd been playing a round of *Weapons from Zeldar* when she'd just passed out or something. She's changed into a t-shirt and gym shorts and I clock her hair up in a ponytail.

"Yo!" I call as I race over to her on the carpeted floor. "Von, you okay?"

Her body is still and sort of cold as I continue to shake her. I'm reminded of Dawn's mom, Robyn, lifeless and stiff on her bedroom floor from eating too many pills. My eyes scan the room in search of the drugs responsible for her unconscious state on the floor, but her groans stop me.

"Vonnie, you hear me?"

"Mmm." She groans again, almost as if it takes great effort to make the noise. "Stay here."

"Huh?" I demand, shaking her a little. "What you mean? Did you take something?"

"Stay here." She repeats in a dreamy groan.

"Stay where?"

"Living...room."

"Fuck that." I growl, already lifting her in my arms to take her to Mamma Dean's ancient truck. I ain't have time with the back and forth, nope, she was going straight to the hospital. I still didn't do hospitals, and used my knowledge of safe herbs from the farm to use on my cuts like my mom taught me, but I couldn't risk it with her. I had to keep Vonnie safe, and not because of the promise I made to her big brother who was now my tightest homeboy, but for me. I couldn't stand her hurt.

We're almost to the door when she mumbles something that freezes me in place.

"Say that again?" I ask her in a shaky voice. She's snuggled into my arms now, a contented smile on her face as she speaks again.

"Stay with me. Mel-Mel..."

My legs go on autopilot as I cross the room again to deposit her in bed. There's a green journal on the floor near the controller in the corner and I notice a few more minor details about her room I overlooked before.

The Free Krimzon posters actually had two aliens on it instead of the dominant one in the forefront.

There's an empty fishbowl in her room, and I wonder if there ever were any fish in it at one point.

A Ravens t-shirt I recalled Devin wearing all the time was on display near the TV wall, and my heart stings a bit as I realize she's framed her big brother's t-shirt like a work of art.

I go on noticing more things in the room while I await my brain to come back online and register her whispered words. Her even breaths alert me that she's finally settled into a deep sleep from the bed.

"Von?" I hedge, standing over her. "Say that again. Do you...remember me?"

More snores.

I lick my lips in thought, completely confused on how to move forward.

"Do you remember me?" I ask again. "It's me. *I'm* Mel-Mel. Your big brother."

Instead of rising and responding to ask me what the fuck kind of craziness I was spewing, a big smile curls her face and red colors her cheeks in her sleep.

"Mel...Mel." She reiterates, and this time it's clear. I hear the name I thought would forever die in the past on her lips. And, perhaps the fact that makes me feel light inside, is the smile. Her face is radiant as she mumbles the words a few more times and sinks deeper into sleep. I wanted to gather her in my arms and reassure her big brother was here, that I'd always be here for as long as she needed, but I step back. I had to get it together and head home before blowing my cover. She couldn't know that her favorite homie was really her big bro, not yet at least. Shay and I had a plan on how to break the news to her. We'd wait until Shay finished school and that Vonnie was totally all right. That time wasn't here yet, so putting some distance between us was the smartest thing to do until I sorted through the rubble after the brain explosion her words triggered in my head.

I left her room with a heart so full of cheer and confliction. It was good to see she didn't need a hospital or had another breakdown, but her words...they softened something in me.

The chaotic funeral party is still loud, and I clock several people drinking and arguing, but Eddie nowhere to be found. Mamma Dean and Dan are dancing to Earth, Wind, and Fire on the stereo and it's total pandemonium when I rejoin them in the dining room.

"Zay, baby!" Mamma Dean calls me. "Did you see Vonnie anywhere? Tell her she needs to come do these dishes in a few."

Pure, unadulterated fury fills my head as I stalk over to a large stereo and rip out its wires. The room quiets as all eyes are on me again.

"For real, y'all?" I bark, ignoring the half-clothed kids running through the house. "I get we're all sad about Miss Stevie. I am, too. But damn! Did anybody care to check on Yvonne?"

"What's wrong with my granddaughter?" Mamma Dean demanded, her eyes round saucers of concern.

"She snuck out when y'all started fighting. Y'all should know all that yelling makes her uncomfortable and shit. She don't need that. Especially not on her birthday."

"Let me go check on—" Mamma Dean started, but I moved in front of her as she attempted to walk towards the stairs. "Move, Zay!"

"Nah." I growl, glaring at her. "Let her rest. She needs a little bit of peace. She got a lot on her mind right now, especially with the anniversary of DC leaving, too. Just give her some time, all right?"

Mamma Dean glares right back at me but stands down. She turns to walk back into the dining room to address the crowd with a wave of her meaty arm.

"All y'all need to go. Party's over."

There are several rounds of "aww, man!" and "fuck you, Zay," as the crowd scatters and disperses and the hour goes by. As the house empties, Mamma Dean approaches me with a plate of food. There's aluminum foil wrapped around it and the smell of chicken is undeniable from within, since my mouth drools like a conditioned dog at the smell.

"For Shay," she says. "And I'm sorry. You're right. As her grandmother, I should have paid more attention to her today. That's on me."

I nod, taking the plate. "Well, you tell her that."

"I will." She agreed. "And you get on home before it gets too dark."

"Yes, ma'am." I chuckled. "But I'm grown. I don't think there's any monsters out to get me if I make it home a little late."

She frowns at me. "You never know! Monsters come in all shapes and sizes. Be careful out there."

"Yes, ma'am." I repeat before kissing her forehead and exiting the large farmhouse.

My mind is sort of hollow and quiet as I make the twenty-minute walk back to the cabin Shay and I shared. I was mindful to keep the walk brisk, considering the wild animals that roamed the farm and the delicious fried meal in my hands. Her chicken was worth wrestling a bear or coyote over, I think and laugh to myself as the cabin comes into view in the distance. I'm about eight feet away, and relief floods me as I draw nearer and nearer my waiting blunt and scratch-off like I craved so desperately at that post-funeral dinner.

However, there's a shadow at the front of the porch that sends me to the past. That shadow becomes a full outline of a person the closer I get, and his pale skin and hair puts me on high alert.

I remember Si standing at my front porch that day I got back home from Jerica's house, and that deal he offered me that I threw away due to this new plan to run. His cold dead eyes zero in on me as I approach. I instantly regretted leaving Luci, who I kept fully loaded near my No-Touch stash in case of emergencies inside my safe, behind for this situation.

"Si?" I call as I approach with the plate full of food.

The dude turns around then, and I finally get a good look at his face and all black attire.

"What?" He asks in an accent that's distinctly Jersey.

But it's not the cold shark eyes of Si's that I expected. Nah. This guy's eyes are round, glittering, green balls under the disappearing sunlight that sort of stab into me as I close the gap between us.

He's the redheaded guy from the funeral, I notice, and his steps are deliberate when he descends the porch stairs to stand before me.

"How are you, dude?" He asks, calm and collected.

"What you want, man?" I demand, tired and weary from the interaction already. I could knock this dude out from how he treated Vonnie from earlier, but decide against it. I wasn't The Violence anymore, and I left all those gritty tactics in Camden.

"Straight to business, I see." He says. "I knew you were a professional. That shows."

"Quit the long talk and spit it out, bro. Who are you and what's your business with me?"

Mamma Dean's words, ironic as they are, float to the forefront of my mind as he says the dreaded words I'd thought I left behind in Camden.

"It's me, Shame. Jeremy. From Camden." Jeremy says in cold clipped words, crossing his arms.

I squint to get a better look at the dude who had me nearly beat a couple inches in the height department.

His orange-ish hair puts me in mind of someone who may have been a relative of the little boy from the projects who revered me as a legend back home. I almost dismiss the resemblance, however, but his eyes always gave him away. Those movie-star greens that pierced me when he'd beg me to show off my gun to his friends.

"Little dude." I whispered unconsciously. "That really you?"

"Ain't little no more." He smirks. "And I need a contract done."

Mamma Dean's warning was on point, I thought as the fried chicken plate slipped through my fingers and into the dirt: Monsters, sure as fuck, came in all shapes and sizes.

TWENTY-EIGHT

MORNING

I lay in bed, which was really a ratty couch sec-ond-handed from Miss Stevie, and stare at the ceiling. While I normally spent the days lazing on the couch, fixed in front of the TV and smoking a blunt, this evening was different. This time, instead of the quiet storm in my head or a Clint Norway song powering through the speakers, it's my thoughts that are on full blast in my head.

Fucking Jeremy was here. Of all places. Was this a setup of some kind? A Kobayashi plot to get me to reveal my location or run back to Camden? Logic rules those fears out, however, as the memory of the poor little boy etches itself into my mind's eye again. His drab, holly, clothes that looked several sizes too small. His distinct dark curls that hang like a dirty brown mop on his head. In fact, the current orange tint to his hair makes me wonder if that'd been that color under all the dirt this whole time. The only shiny thing about the kid were those glittery movie star eyes, except they blazed with fury instead of the previous excitement to see me. My eyes squeeze shut, forcing my thoughts to linger on something else, anything else, other than the events of an hour ago when I saw the dark figure from my past show up at my doorstep.

"Need a contract done." Jeremy grunted after pulling out a loosie and taking a long pull of nicotine. "What's your going rate these days?"

My jaw was still hanging wide open enough to welcome in all the farm flies the spilled plate of chicken attracted. My chest, it got that tight feeling again like it used to do when The Commander announced another contract for me to carry out. The only way that chest pain went away was under the numbing effect of those little blues I kept all to myself for several years.

But there are no more pills. No more Commander either, considering the butchering the Kobayashi's put him and Saint Millard through that night. It was never confirmed the family of my ruthless co-killer executed my father and the 590 head, but from the description the news anchor gave on their bloody remains in some warehouse in New York, it didn't take a rocket scientist to figure out who done him in. I recalled the way Si, typically so cool and chill during an assignment, often lost his head and taking joy out of torture tactics to inflict on his debtors. The tied-up and starved state of

Quincy and Saint in that warehouse had The Silence written all over it.

Something crumbles in my chest at the thought of Quincy being tortured for days before his execution. Hate followed the sadness manifesting as the images flashed in my head. How could that be? The man who graced all of my worst nightmares and best dreams and abused the family he swore to protect. I felt sorry for him. But even though I was Zay now, the small presence in me, the Shamel part, recognized that as game, too. What I felt...ran deeper than that at the thought of him gone. Forever.

Instead of sinking into the reminiscent visions Jeremy's presence dredged up, I cleared my throat, puffed my chest, and performed.

"I don't know who this Shame is you're talking about, man." I tell him.

"Really, now?"

"Word up."

"Figures," he says on dark chuckle. "Everyone back home said you'd died. Now I see you, here of all places, turn up at my grandma's funeral looking every bit the square as every other bumpkin on this farm does. Only thing ain't changed about you is the accent."

"Fuck outta here, bro." I spit, stomping past him and toward the house. "Never met you a day in my life."

"Never, huh?"

"That's right." I snarl, turning around just before yanking the front door open. "Now make yourself scarce."

"Or what?" He challenged; his tone so flat it surpasses boredom. "What you gonna do?"

I didn't answer, my fingers for the first time in a long-time trembling with the need to go grab my underused gun from my living room safe. But I remember the breaths Jerica taught me to take when I got like this during our short walk in the sun together.

His crazy laughter disrupts the silent tension crackling in the autumn air just then.

"You should see your face, dude!" He cackled, holding his belly. "Bet you're dying to off me with that famous gun of yours. Ain't ya? Go on, admit it."

I glare at him and can't help the next words that slip through my gritted teeth. "Ten."

"Say what?"

"Nine."

"What's the counting for?"

"Eight." I breathed, still shaking with the need to shoot so bad. "Seven."

"Wait a minute." He interjects amusedly. "You're doing a countdown?"

"Six."

"What are we, in elementary? Cut that bullshit and hear me out—"

"One." I sneer before cracking my fist across his smug face. There's no silenced Colt Action this time blasting through his skull like I truly wanted. Nah. There's only my knuckles splitting into delicate flesh as I rear back and watch the blood spill down his forehead after the fact.

Fuck, that felt good.

"Shit!" He howled in agony as he cradled his face. "The fuck was that for?"

It was my turn to laugh now. And laugh, I did. In fact, I barely fell to my knees from the hilarity of the sight he made.

"What's so goddamn funny, Shame?"

"You, nigga." I coughed between rounds of more gut laughs as he rubbed his swollen face. "Was talking all that goofy shit until you got snuck."

He remains silent as he watches me, a petulant frown twisting his thin face.

"Get off my porch before I change my mind about fucking you up some more, kid."

Out of nowhere, the largest, purest grin spreads across his face. It's so large and megawatt I'm stunned motionless. Where the hell was that coming from?

"What?" I bark, confused and creeped out.

"Thank you for that." He says.

I rear back, eyeing him down for any signs of obvious head trauma my blow might have caused.

"For sneaking the shit outta you?"

He giggles. "Yeah. Now I know it's you, Shame. I need that energy. Despite this pretty boy charade, you're putting on for the people here it's good to see you're still you. Exactly the same fire I need for when you kill my uncle for me."

A few bombs explode in my mind as I attempt to process his words.

He steps closer to me. "Just hear me out. I'll have the money ready for you after the job is done. I'd kill him myself, but I got no aim. Neither do I have the equipment. But I'm sure you do."

I only stare at him, afraid saying anything would reveal the terror in me. The fear isn't coming from Jeremy, but the prospect of having to pick up and run again. Of being found out. Of Shay's reaction after I'd told her we were ID'd despite our careful disguises and fake backstories we fed the farm family. And, perhaps the thing that scared me most was using my hands, the same ones that fiddled with the game controller when I battled Vonnie on an alien game, to take more life.

"I'll give you a few hours to think on it." He says, just before I used my hands to do the answering again for me instead. "But I'm serious. I need him dead, Shame. I won't doubt you'll do what you do best in the end."

He turns to walk down the trail, back to Stevie's house, but stops suddenly.

"Oh," He starts as he turns to face me. "And if your sister's looking, tell her to holler at me."

"The fuck you say?" I demand, my chest swelling again but with anger and protective pride for Shay's honor.

"Come over here and say that to my face."

"No, thanks." He says, turning his back to me again. "I'd rather do the cumming for your little sis. She's rude as fuck but I like my women spicy. Vonnie, right?"

"W-What?" I couldn't help but stutter. There was no mistaking it this time. Pure terror filled me at the knowledge kept sacred between Shay and me.

"I wonder if she knows about all the bodies her big bro got in his closet. Looking forward to your decision, Shame." Is all he says before disappearing down the trail.

My phone chirps, pulling me back to the present as I shudder and dig around my pocket for my cell. I'd forgotten the invitation I sent to Vonnie earlier. I blinked like a madman as I studied our recent text thread that replanted me to the here and now.

> **ME**: *That fried chicken Mamma Dean made was good as hell.*

> **VON**: *Heck yeah, as always.*

> **ME**: *Oh yeah. Stop by my crib later on. I forgot to give you your birthday present.*

> **VON**: *Lol I'm skeptic, but I'll be there.*

Before I get the chance to type my response to my secret sister, the phone lights and vibrates from an incoming call. The number is unsaved, which isn't unusual since I didn't store contacts in this phone for fear of being tracked. But the familiar area code I committed to memory makes me swear under my breath at forgetting to give the guy a call like I promised and at our usual time every week or so.

"Would you like to accept these charges?" The feminine operator asks like usual.

"I accept."

After another moment, my homie's gruff voice sounds through the phone. "Wassup, dude."

"Sup, Milio." I say to my incarcerated homie. "My bad, bro. Meant to give you a call earlier."

"All good, Shame." He says casually. "After all, I got all the time in the world. Right?"

I sigh at the morbid joke he often inserted into every conversation since his conviction. After unsuccessfully capping the teenage dude who'd been creeping around with Reina, his off-on girlfriend, he'd been caught and indicted on a laundry list of conspiracy, gun, and reckless endangerment charges that landed him on the inside. It went without saying that he wouldn't see the streets until he was somewhere in the old, gray, and on oxygen category. And even that was too optimistic of a prediction for his future.

"Chill on that shit, bro." I say, sitting up on the couch now.

"How that conversation go with the attorney?"

"Says we can appeal the court's decision, but to be honest, my chances ain't looking too good."

"Chin up, dude." I said, scrambling to my feet to set up the new video game I got on prerelease in my PlayStation. "The appeal might go through. Have some faith."

Vonnie had to be a couple minutes away now since she sent that text nearly twenty minutes ago. I liked to keep whatever video game she was really obsessed about fired up whenever she was coming over. The hot topic today was the newly released Space Mafia, and since she'd been on an alien kick, I figured her walking in on my "avid gaming sesh" would be an invitation for her to play and stay. Again, I didn't play those dorky ass games, but relished in watching her face light up whenever she grabbed the controller and did her thing. My little sis was badass, and more often than not I wondered if she would take her gaming skills professional or even if that was a thing people did for cash. If it was, Vonnie was a savant for sure.

"This still Shame I'm talking to?" He half asked half laughed.

"Yeah. What the hell's so funny?"

"Oh, man, nothing." He continued to laugh at me like I was the best butt of the joke. "Just never knew you'd be capable of saying that. Have faith?"

"Shut up, stupid." I growled then sucked my teeth. "Shouldn't have even taken the call."

"Really, bro." He sobers. "I appreciate you for it anyways. Especially after how everything went down all those years ago. You know, with me and All Bad getting caught up with the cops after what I did. Or tried to do. What an idiot I was."

"Hey, man." I interjected. "I wrote to both of y'all. You was the only one who thought I'd been worth talking to. How's he doing in there anyways?"

"Oh. You know how things go inside. He's with the blacks most of the time, but other times he's just to himself. I don't go near him, since the only reason a light bright motherfucker like me would approach him would be where fighting or fuckin was concerned. I got no qualms about either."

I nod, taking in his words and usual response whenever I asked about my brother-cousin but really an uncle on the inside with him. Shortly after settling on the farm, I began to pick up other books beside demon literature copped from the thrift stores in town, like The Bible. By no means was I a religious motherfucker, but I couldn't deny some of the action-packed similarities between Milton and the Good Book. I honed in on the later parts that dealt with forgiveness, and how an eye for an eye in my underworld only made people blind. Romans 12:17 kept me going, and I slowly grew to replace the rules I worshiped by The Commander with the lines that stood out to me from The Book I avoided growing up.

"Help me abandon my shameful ways; for Your regulations are good."

I muttered Psalms 119 like a manic repetition when old thoughts crept in. Tempting me from doing good.

"Fuck, maybe I am going soft." I sighed unconsciously out loud.

"You are," Milio agreed. "But don't lose that. At least you got a chance to make things right and think like that. I can't go soft in here, no matter how hard I want to hear her voice. No matter how much I want to tell her how sorry I am for ruining her life like that. Just want to right my wrongs, kiss my ma, and move on. For real and for good."

"I know man. Thank you, too. For being the same nigga I always knew from before." I say.

"No prob, softie." He says on a note of amusement. "I heard from one of the Cholos inside that she had another kid."

"Word?"

"Yep." He answers. "Couple years back. Apparently Rick has a kid, too. One of his cousins inside told me he and his girl came to visit a few times."

"I'm happy for him." I say in earnest to the LC I heard nothing else about after fleeing the state. "What his girl look like?"

He chuckled. "Bro, I don't know. I only know as much as his cousin Bean tells me. She's cute I heard. A pretty black chick named...I think it was Angela or something."

I froze in the same instant the knock came at the front door. It was Vonnie.

"Say what?"

"What?"

"Her name. You said it was Angela? She a real short girl, kinda thick, with big brown eyes?" I'm rattling the question so fast as I stand up.

Maybe it was a coincidence. Maybe the Angela he's talking about is someone else. That was a common name, so...

My gut told me different, however, as I listened.

"Dude, I said I don't know. Calm down before you bust an aneurysm or something."

"Find out for me, will you?" I asked, but it felt more like begging as I grabbed the blunt from the coffee table. I needed some bud to calm these nerves that seemed to be getting set off by...well, everything. Vonnie's sleep recognition of me, Jeremy's threat, and now this.

Angie, like Tierra, mixed up with an LC.

"All right, all right." He agreed reluctantly.

"Peace, bro." I replied, taking a hard drag from the blunt and relishing in the calming effects. "We'll chop it up later. All right?"

"Cool. Peace, bro."

Once the call ended, I chucked the phone on the table and raced to the door. Taking a deep breath, I open it.

"Vonnie, what's up?"

Twenty-Nine

COBRA

One month later

There are several things about Camden I chose to forget, but Jerica True seemed to be the most difficult. Even now, as I stare into the empty plate where Shay's homemade lasagna existed before I inhaled it after a strong bout of the munchies hit. I find myself sort of faded and missing her. I wonder what she was doing. How she was feeling and faring after all these years. Did she even remember a nobody like me? I had nothing to offer her then as a pill-addicted teen with a murderous chip on his shoulder against the world, but the little I had I wanted her to have.

Before everything blew up.

We had no contact with anybody from the past, per Shay's demand to lay low until she finished college. We hadn't even spoken with Mom, who we last left under Miss Pat's care. Was my baby girl all right? It would soon be her sixth birthday, if my math was right. And a sharp pain shot through me at the thought of not being there for her. Again.

But I had to be there for Vonnie, a whisper eases itself into my brain as soon as the doubt does. I could have left the farm ages ago, like I planned, but after Devin surprised us all by leaving for the military I saw Von break into thousands of little pieces. I couldn't abandon her, I told myself. Not after that. Not ever. The guilt from leaving her and Mike all those years ago still ate me, I admit that. If I'd only been there to tail the kids that day like I planned, I would've been able to shoot that Helen bitch in her head and rescue them. Preventing the incident that took away the most precious pieces of my fam.

"You okay, Zay?" Shay asked from across the table.

"Huh?"

"Earth to Xavier!" She repeated while waving her arms for dramatic affect. "You hear anything I said just now?"

"No." I grunted. "Didn't catch it."

"Typical." She sighed. "I asked if you thought, um, if Dev got lonely. You know, in the military or wherever he is."

"Why you calling me 'Zay,' when there's nobody around?"

"Are you even listening to me?"

"I hear you loud and clear." I say. "But call me Shamel in private, like usual. All right? That Zay shit is boloney."

She rolled her eyes. "Well, I had to say something to get your head out of whatever cloud you were on. How much weed you smoking?"

"My shit good." I answer, grinning. "Should hit the blunt sometime with me. Will calm you down."

"I'm a nurse." She said. "Studying to be a doctor some-day. Do you have any idea how stupid it would be for me to put that brain-cell-killing stick in my mouth? Thanks, but no thanks."

"Yeah, all right." I heaved an exhausted sigh, weary from the impending lecture I didn't need. "Suit your-self."

"I'll do that." She mumbled, casting a look down at her plate. "But, really...you think he really forgot about us?"

"If it's DC you're talking about." I start while staring at the woman through slit eyes. "Then stop worrying. You know him better than that."

"That's just the thing," she whispered. "I thought I did. But how can a guy just propose to a girl then just leave?"

"Easy. He just does."

"Just like that? As if his family were just an after-thought?"

"Remind you of anybody?" I ask, studying her face closely as it changed from searching to resolved. Then pissed.

"That *fucking* Quincy!" She blew out in a rage. "I knew it. I'm damned to repeat Mommy's mistakes. Am I her? Just some ignorant woman waiting for her emotionally unavailable man's return? My life forever spent in the shadows of waiting and wasting away? That...can't be."

Shay, always so strong, cradled her wet face into her hands as her shoulders shook with rinsed fury. All she looked now was a sad shell of a woman on the brink. And even though DC was one of my closest friends now, some of that old misdirected anger resurfaces as I watch her break in front of me.

I sit up, blinking to gain composure in the swirling room. I was fucking blowed.

"Yeah, that's how it looks." I said to her. "But remember who you are. You're Shay, the badass who got no time to waste her tears on some dickhead too sorry to even tell her goodbye. Come on now, muscle up."

"Period." She sniveled. "And I know that."

"Oh yeah?"

"Yep." She sniffled then beamed a weary grin at me. "Just wanted to hear it from you. Girl's gotta do what she gotta do for a compliment from your ass. Sheesh."

I chucked a crumpled napkin at her and laughed as she dodged it with a theatrical whip of her head.

"Hey!"

"Silly ass." I grumbled, and we broke into a comfortable laughter after that as the minutes pass.

I'm washing dishes, since it was my turn that night, when I felt a tap on my shoulder.

"Sup?"

"Would you mind taking Mr. Eddie a plate? I promised him some dinner since he fixed my car for next to nothing in return." Shay asked as she wiped down the counters.

"Man," I groan, slumping my shoulders in defeat. "Tonight? Can't you see I'm blowed right now?"

"Can't you see me not giving a damn? Especially after this huge spread of food I cooked for you tonight and a twelve-hour shift that tore up my feet."

"Chill out." I said, petulant and resistant. "I'm all over it."

"Thank you." She replied. "It's the container wrapped in foil in the fridge. Take him a beer, too."

"Oh, for real?" I asked, confused. "But you always gettin on him about his 'diabetes this' and 'diabetes that.' Ain't beer on the 'can't have' list?"

"Usually, yeah. But it's his birthday today, so...I wanted to do something nice for him. He's so sweet to us when he has no reason to be. Dev don't realize how many people were hurt by his decision to cut and run. Just take it to him this once."

"Cool." I say, shrugging as I take the plate and begin towards the door. "Oh. And Shay?"

"Hmm?" She sings her response as she continues her cleaning.

"Devin's a good guy. Remember that. He had his reasons."

She froze, taking in my words and giggling a little mirthlessly. "Thanks, Mel."

"I got you." I respond, shooting her a long look before walking out.

The sooner I got this random chore out the way, the better. Besides, I had some tilling to do for Mamma Dean tomorrow I needed to be somewhat fresh for.

Two dark figures in the night eat up the small front porch as well as my nerves that were on a higher alert when I got blowed.

"Sup, Zay." Bone greets me in the darkness before Malik chimes in.

"Hope we ain't scare you."

I gulped and removed the hand clasped over my chest. Thank fuck it was too dark outside for the guys to see the fear written all over my face.

"Nah, I'm delighted." I bite out. "Totally excited to see two goons waiting for me in the dead dark of night. Fuck y'all doing here?"

"Tryna smoke something." Bone drawls before giggling. "Bet you almost shit your pants, man."

"Shut it." I warn, but in typical Bone and Malik fashion, they egg on.

Malik is next. "Poor Xavier. Did we frighten the little boy scout?"

"Fuck y'all." I growl while continuing my descent down the trail that led further into Mamma Dean's neck of the woods. The guys are tailing me and continuing their onslaught of teasing.

"Zay ain't no boy scout." Bone said. "He too fucking scary looking for that shit."

"On God." Malik chimed in before they howled in more laughter.

These guys were really getting on my fucking nerves. They were lucky I didn't live life in the underworld anymore, considering their heads would be blown through clean by my favorite girl– no, my gun. I had to keep reminding myself to disassociate all positive emotions from that cold piece of metal. I relied on it too much for a warmth that could never be.

"Bet this scary scout could fuck your girl. Any time. Any place." I spit at Malik, whose girlfriend I remembered was crazy loyal to him.

An additional ten minutes pass as we walk through the dense forest trail leading up to DC's dad's house, and we're close enough now to see the lights on in his windows. Was he awake? As late as it was, Mr. Eddie wouldn't have been as irresponsible as that. He was the most reliable dude I ever knew, no cap. So, it was weird to see him staying up so late at the risk of missing or being late for work at six in the morning.

Instead of the retort from the short-fused guy like I expected, he and Bone share an exploratory look.

"What?" I asked, concerned a little as they came to a stop. I stopped, too, to look at them.

"How much?" Malik asks.

"Nigga...what?" I demand. "What you talking about?"

"How much you wanna bet on that?" Bone answered instead. "On Indira. You thinkin she'll fuck you?"

There were so many questions swirling around in my head as I just stood there. We just about arrived at Mr. Eddie's and the bowl of lasagna suddenly feels like a dumbbell in my hands as I stare stupidly at them. Did I hear them correctly?

"What y'all sayin?" I demand again. "Because I'm not about to believe Malik gonna suddenly be cool with me fucking his high school sweetheart."

"I ain't." Malik cut in while shrugging. "Not unless you think you can win her."

"Win, huh?" I inquired, or perhaps Shame did as one of The Commander's cardinal rules came back to me.

Win, by any means.

The weather man predicted some of the worst snow to come to Richmond in years, and my mind drifts to my little sis. She wagered on Kimmy, Miss Stevie's granddaughter and the girl I suspected Von was feeling in a major way, in a bet over that game with Jeremy. That fucking prick. I still hadn't responded to him about killing his uncle, but after that damn bet Von lost on the court with him I had to abide by it. Something snapped in me at the thought of wagering another chick like Von did with Kimmy on the courts the other day, and I found my resolve solidifying at that.

You could take him out, Shamel. Do him before he does you. Make your old man proud.

It was like I could hear Quincy whispering those thoughts in my ear. And my heart seized, as it usually did when a contract was rendered. Not because I was scared, but because he was right. It would be so easy to dust off Luci and take care of my Jeremy issue. But another thought chased my dad's words away as soon as the flirtation of murder came.

Help me abandon my shameful ways; for Your regulations are good.

It took a few minutes, but my heart stabilized as though reassured by the angels. Fuck, maybe I was getting soft, but no matter. I wanted a clean heart more than deading my enemies. That wasn't me anymore.

And, yet, Malik spoke amidst my inner turmoil, returning me to the present.

"I'll text her right now if you think she'll go for it." Malik said like a loan shark eager to make a deal in the dark.

"How much?" The shame in me can't resist asking.

"Eighty bucks." Malik offered. "That's all my shop tips for the week."

"I'll pitch in, too, if you think you can get her, Zay." Bone cut in all eager-like too. "I think she too loyal to fuck your ugly ass, but hey, miracles happen every day."

"Y'all mad goofy for that." I wave them both away and don't give them a chance to fill my head with anymore fantasies as I jet to the front porch.

"Eddie!" I called after two rounds of knocking didn't alert the old man enough to come to the door. Yet another unusual characteristic about him. "Shay made you dinner!"

Only more silence greets me as I stand there like a knob. Why the fuck was I here anyways? As cold as it was and as warm as that bed was back home, only an idiot would be out here begging a man to take a plate. If he didn't want the delicious meal my sis cooked from scratch, then more for me.

Resolved, I nearly turn to head back home when a sound stops me. I'm reliving Jersey all over again, I think, as the groans from inside resonate loud enough for my ears in spite of the wintry winds whipping around.

"What's wrong?" Bone drawled in his distinctly southern accent as he and Malik ran up to me. "You heard something?"

"Yeah." I said after sitting the food on the porch. "I think he in trouble."

"Shit, let's get this door open then." Malik volunteered, meaning business as he banged on the front door. "You think he having a heart attack or something? Sound like he in pain in there."

"Back door." I ground out while rushing around the house until I got to the back door of the cabin. I remembered he often forgot to lock his back door after needing to make a similar delivery to him after DC left. That really messed him up, Shay too, since it was her who made me deliver him a plate of whatever she was manically baking to distract herself from the pain of her tentative fiancé's absence.

Same as before, the door is unlocked and I'm rushing through the tiny house in search of a dead man.

Or so I thought...

"Holy fuck!" A woman with rosy red curls screams when she sees me standing at the entryway. Eddie's cabin is open concept, sort of like a studio styled apartment that left only the bathroom walled off near the entrance. His bed is the first thing you see when entering, since it's only that and a two-seater that occupies the little space with meager furnishings.

I study the red headed woman I recognize from Miss Stevie's funeral, her slim thick body and full pink hips straddling Eddie as he lies flat on the bed.

"What are you doing in here?" The woman screeches while wrapping herself in the family quilt he told me belonged to a long line of Carlson women. The family relic was now good for one thing this night, and that was covering up dirty little secrets like this from getting out.

"My bad y'all." I say without averting my eyes from the curvy woman whose tits made me salivate instantly at the brief sight of them.

"You're all right." Eddie mumbles, calm and casual in typical Eddie-fashion. He always kept shit cool and never had I seen him wear an ounce of shame on his face like I usually did. He sits up. "Want a cigarette?"

"I'm good." I reply, clocking him reaching over and lighting up the cig.

"Suit yourself." He says.

"Eddie!" The woman hollers in horror as she watches our exchange. "What the fuck are you doing?"

He frowns. "Smoking a cigarette."

"How can you do that right now?! With them watching?"

He shrugs, "Real easy. You nearly broke my dick you were riding me so hard, woman. Man needs a break here and then."

"That's wassup," A voice says beside me, and I'm only now registering Malik and Bone manifest at either side of me. It's Malik, gawking at the pair with a lewd lick of his lips. "What's your name, girl?"

"Girl?" She yells.

"Oh, yeah." Bone interjects as though he's solved some sort of puzzle. "You're, uh, Vivian right? Yeah, I think that's how you introduced yourself back at the funeral. Stevie's daughter?"

Her face reddens a deep shade of strawberry as she buries her face into the covers.

"Kill me." She whispers, and I observe Eddie bring his hand up to caress her back.

"She's real sensitive, y'all." Eddie answers slowly with a pleased grin. "And them noises y'all probably heard weren't me dying. Well, not from a heart attack at least."

A chain of chuckles erupts from the three of us that I can't hold back. I was still a little blazed as I watched the tenderness in his eyes. Realization hit me then, at why he got so riled up at Dan's shit-talk about her back at dinner that day after the funeral. Emotions weren't just high because people were sad about Stevie, but he'd been protecting his girl. No, not girl. She was all woman, I thought as I drooled over the skin revealed outside the covers that displayed her thickness. It got me hard, and I hadn't fucked a soul since a couple months ago. Some chick I met in town I forgot the name of.

"Guess y'all better get out of here, boys. Unless there was something pressing needing my attention?" Eddie said, snapping all our attention back to the present.

The fog cleared enough for me to remember my sole purpose of being here.

"Right," I chuffed. "Shay made you some lasagna. Told me to tell you thanks for all your help."

Eddie cracked a small lopsided smile. "She didn't need to go to the trouble."

"She insists."

"That's Shay." He says, somewhat wistfully as he exhales a cloud of smoke. "Always so tough, but makes the sweetest of gifts for an old bastard like me. I'm grateful."

The covers stir just as Vivian appears with a suspicious frown. "Who's Shay?"

Eddie continued stroking her back as he muttered his next words. "A dear friend of mine. No need to be jealous, Vivie."

"Eddie..." She whines through a mask of red before re-covering her face.

Eddie lingers on her disappeared form under the Carlson quilt. "Do me a favor and don't tell Mamma bout this. All right?"

"Word up." I agree after realizing he's addressing us. I'm straight up reluctant to tear my eyes away from her exposed flesh.

"Good deal." Eddie says as we're walking out. "Gossip spreads like a goddamn bushfire on this farm."

A few minutes pass as we make the silent trek back to my crib. I knew the guys would probably end up spending the night at ours since Shay didn't mind them.

"Want to roll one?" Bone asks as we nearly make it back to the house. They carry on talking as I fantasize. My dick is hard as stone as I consider the fine white woman Eddie was causally fucking in his cabin, and I make up my mind in a split second about what our next moves would be.

At least, I knew what I wanted mine to be. "Yo, Malik."

"Sup?" He answers.

"You ready to lose some money?"

"Huh?" He questions before freezing. A knowing grin crests his dark face before he whips out his phone. "Grimy son of a bitch. I'll text her now."

THIRTY

RIVER

My phone vibrates in my pocket three weeks later with the call I expect from Camden County Corrections. I accept the call and brace myself for the grating Jersey accent of my incarcerated homeboy.

"Milio?"

There's static before he starts talking. "I hope you're fucking satisfied with the pickle you put me in, Shame."

"What pickle?"

"Well, I got that information that you requested. But it cost me a grip in commissary from Bean to get it."

I roll my eyes and blow out an aggravated sigh at his theatrics. "You mean the favor I asked you for three weeks ago?"

"Yeah," he grunted. "That one."

"Heard you been on lockdown for the past few weeks. Everything all right in there?"

A beat, before he answers. "Uh, yeah."

"Milio, wassup for real? Don't sugarcoat shit from me."

"I ain't." He grunts. "But I got Ricky's girl's name and phone number if you want it."

Joy illuminated my heart at the prospect of speaking with Angie again, since I ditched all my contacts along with my old phone years ago after we ran. In fact, I'm still not sure if this is still the same Angela from my past, but my gut told me to trust this info.

"Thanks, bro." I said. "What is it?"

"About that...I'm gonna need something in return for that info."

"Say what?" I snapped.

"It's not personal, brother." He reasons. "It's business. That's how it works in here: give and get. Equivalent exchange and all that."

"I see what this is." I say as my brows furrow in suspicion. "You want me to pay you?"

"Hell yeah." He insists. "Got J-pay?"

"For a phone number and a description?"

"Yes!" He snaps. "What part of equivalent exchange ain't you gettin? I risked my neck to get you that info."

I nod, respecting his hustle before adding, "All right. I'll pay you. But tell me what happened in there that kept you from calling three weeks in a row?"

"Ah, fuck." He hisses. "Really, dude?"

"Yeah." I answered. "No info, no J-Pay."

"Coldhearted bastard. Guess I'll let you in on it." A long moment passes before he continues. "There was a riot."

My eyes bug at that plausible information I couldn't fathom Milio being involved in for some reason.

"Word?"

"Word." He affirms. "Cokehead broke into the infirmary and stabbed two nurses to death after eating two bottles of something. Entire prison got locked down for weeks after that. No visits. No calls."

"Fuck..." I breathed in abject horror at the mere imagery his description conjured up. I imagined what it must have been like to discover the dead nurses, both who probably had their entire lives ahead of them. Death was nothing more than an annoying afterthought in my Shame days, but now?

I fight to control the unsteadiness in my voice as I respond. "That's rough, man."

"Sweet girls, too." He whispers sullenly. "Those nurses."

"Sorry you're in there, bro."

"Nothing we can do to change it. At least not in this life. Until then, pay up."

Another fifteen minutes of chopping it up flies by before the operator warns us the call would be ending in thirty seconds. We hung up with promises to keep in touch next week for our regularly scheduled calls. Seconds later, I'm dialing the number he apparently risked life and limb for in hopes it isn't my Angie he saw visiting the prison.

The line trills exactly three times before a high-pitched voice I missed sings into the other end. "This is Angela."

"Angie...hey." I sputter in disbelief.

"Shamel?" She hisses in a combination of emotions I didn't have the mental capacity to identify. "Is that you? Please tell me I'm not dreaming!"

"It's really me."

"Oh my gosh, oh my gosh, oh my gosh!" She mumbles frantically, and I can almost hear her pacing. "Where are you? How are you? And is Shay okay?"

"Slow down," I say, my tone lighter than how I felt somehow. "We're fine, Shay and me. Just laying low for a bit."

"Laying low? Where at? I can come get you if you need me to."

"Nah, it's not like that. That ain't why I'm calling."

"Okay..." She says, her tone guarded. "Then why are you calling after all these years?"

"I..." I didn't know where to even begin. "I'm calling to say...hi."

"Hi?"

"Yeah. How are you?"

A long pause before she sighs. "I guess I'm all right. I'm a mother now. My daughter, Emma, will be five this year."

"That's real nice." I say, a small pain starting in my heart. "I'm happy for her. You and your husband must be real proud of her."

"We are." She says rapidly, without any doubt. "We're...happy."

"You deserve it all, Angie. I'm glad you could find a man to make you happy." I say as if there's gravel in my voice.

She sighs again. "His name is Enrique Reyes...you may know him. He used to be in a gang a while back."

"Heard of him." I say casually, lying to protect her from the truth of my old life.

"Oh, okay then. Maybe you can meet both Emma and Ricky in person one day."

"One day, Angie." I chuckle at her optimism I'd nearly forgotten after these years apart. "But I want to ask you something."

"Sure."

"Have you spoken to Miss Pat lately? Or my mom? Last I checked, she was staying with her and I wanted to make sure all was good."

There's another pause that I wasn't too comfortable with as I clear my throat. "Angie?"

"I'm here." She whispers. "Yeah, um, Mama moved in with Monica a little while ago."

"What?"

"Yeah. Last I checked, Miss Sommer wasn't living there."

Several bombs explode in my head as I listen to this information my heart didn't want to believe.

"You're telling me Miss Pat ain't living in Harlem anymore?"

"No, Shamel." She answered. "The house was a mess the last time I checked on her. So, Monica took her back to D.C. to stay with her family. Long story short, I don't know where your mom is. I'm sorry..."

"Fuck!" I roar as the frustration bleeds me dry. "Do you have any clue where she might be?"

"Sorry, Mel." She repeats in a small, futile, voice. "I don't. If it helps, I'll text you Monica's number and address so you can speak with Mama herself. That all right?"

"More than all right." I ground out, pinching the bridge of my nose. "You're still the best, Angie."

"I know." She says behind what I know is a sad smile on her chubby face. "And you let me know if you need me to come get you. Or to help in some way. You're family, Shamel."

"That address is more than enough. Thank you."

THIRTY-ONE

ERSATZ

"Are you sure you want to go to the wedding?" Shay's voice penetrated my aimless thoughts as I studied my fresh loc retwist into the bathroom mirror.

"No," I answer, sort of gruff and grieving, tortured by the events that led up to Vonnie's wedding due to begin a few hours from now. "But I think we should still go. You know, make the effort."

"She wants nothing to do with us now. You know that. Why did you go blabbing the truth about us all willy-nilly like that? We had a plan, remember?"

"Yeah..." I sigh, the weight of the world and this plan sagging into my being since its inception after we left Camden six years ago. The Plan, I think, in a sort of wistful/exhausted way as I admired Malik's excellent barbering on my edge-up, was a total shit show. I blew my cover with Von by telling her about our true identities as her blood brother and sister. I think I also blabbed about how I kept in touch with Mom, who I merely called once to check on. After that initial call, she'd ghosted me, and I took that as a sign to back off for fear of being discovered.

Shay, sporting her Hello Kitty pajamas and bonnet, paces behind me along the living room floor.

"What are we going to do now?" She asks, and I note her biting her nails as she wanders frantically.

"Calm down." I tell her through the mirror. "We're going to that wedding. No way in hell I'm letting her get married to the girl of her dreams with all that doubt that I put there. I won't do that to her. We just need to clear this shit up, and pray she understands."

"We lied!" Shay whined. "And you know Vonnie—stubborn like us! She'll never forgive us for this. We took it too far this time. I should have never agreed to this sham when we found out she lived here."

"Don't start that." I warn. "You wanted this, too. You even said it was best we don't interfere with her life by making her relive all those bad memories from before. Best to let her live in blissful ignorance. Those were your words, not mine."

She sank to the floor and hung her head in her hands. "You're right. I'm just as bad. I'm a monster. And now she's traumatized."

I met her in the living room, dropping to my knees and taking her hands in mine. "It's all right."

"No." she shook her head. "We're just like Mommy. Keeping the lie alive for the sake of our happiness. I can't stand this."

I'm not all too sure how to respond to that as I study her crestfallen state before me. Her nails, like usual, are perfectly manicured pink points, making the shining diamond more profound on her ring finger. Memories short circuit in my mind at the engagement ring Dev gave her before he left the farm. That damn ring, I think as several knots of pain twist my chest at just how it came to be on my big sis's petite finger this day.

"Take this, son." Mom said with teary eyes and out-stretched arms shortly before we left town. It takes me a full minute to register the tiny black box in her small hands. "It's my wedding ring."

"You're giving this...to me?"

"More like, getting rid of it."

"But why? What you want me to do with it?" I fire off my questions from somewhere deep in me. I don't quite understand the mixed emotions I'm feeling as I stare at the diamond that seemed ever-fixed on my mother's finger as long as I've been alive. In fact, it's only now that I'm realizing I've never seen her without it.

"Do whatever you like, Shamel. Keep it safe for the future girl of your dreams, or pawn it. Either way, it frees me. Understand?"

I nodded slowly, my eyes fixed on it and never meeting her eyes. Instead of withdrawing, she takes my hand and encloses it around the tiny black box of dreams. Perhaps, it was more like her nightmares she'd finally been able to wake up from. Her time as The Commander's fake wife coming to a final curtain close. I know it's good for her, I do, but I can't shake the extreme disappointment and sorrow that's taken residence in my hollow heart at the final chapter of Quincy. Somewhere deep down inside, I knew that I'd never see him again. Even though there were parts of me that ached for vengeance against the guy who tore us apart, there also lived smaller parts that longed for the illusion he sold us.

I was still a little boy, much like Mike, wearing nothing but pajamas and a bleeding heart hoping for a happy ending after all.

I had every intention of offering the expensive diamond to Jerica True, in all honesty, but recall how I fucked up any future with her the second I abandoned her at the Transportation Center. She warned me never to come back if I left her again. And I did. Embodying all the shame my name invoked, I even killed her brother and fled town. I didn't deserve the happy ended I secretly longed for. Which was why I ended up wagering the ring to DC in a b-ball game. I wove some lie together, explaining how the ring was passed down from generations and sacred in our family when it was the opposite. Was more like a tangible product of my mother's imprisonment and the beginning of our family's greatest stain.

Now it shined, bright and elegant on the finger of my big sis. Even though Devin left her high and dry and hurt her heart in the process, she still wore the ring he bet me for and proposed to her with.

"You're not Mommy. Or Quincy." I whisper as I hold her hand in mine. "Neither of us are manifestations of our parents' mistakes. All we can do is be straight up, take no shit, and try our best not to hurt those we love in the process."

"That's impossible." She mutters. "We'll always hurt the ones we love. It's unavoidable."

"But that's why we have tomorrow. As long as there's another day there's another opportunity to right our wrongs. Forgiveness can be a one-way street, and if it means we both get hurt in the process of making Vonnie smile at that altar today, then doesn't that make it worth it?"

"But what if she hates us—"

"Then she hates us," I finished. "That can't be helped and we can't be concerned about covering our skins anymore. We got to tell the truth, Shay. We owe her that much."

She nods and finally looks at me. "You're right. I want her to live and love out loud with Kimmy. I hope she's happy after this. Hope makes it worth it."

"Damn right." I chuff while pulling us both to our feet. "Now go get dressed."

My heart nearly skips a beat when she reaches over to throw her arms around me. At six foot one, we're both around the same height, causing our foreheads to slam into each other from the contact.

"Ouch, Shay!" I groan in pain, but freeze at the sound of her light sobs in my ear. "Shay?"

"I was wrong. And I'm sorry." She crooned. "You're no Commander. No 'Shame' either."

I gulp, all words escaping me as I listen to her soul shedding its tough exterior and making my heart race.

"You're nothing less than the best brother a girl like me deserves. Thank you."

I wrap my arms around her, and bite down hard to refrain from sobbing right along with her. Despite all that's transpired and added to the heaviness on my heart, her words make me feel light as air.

"We're all we got. Love you, kiddo." I say, squeezing her an extra second before we separate.

"I know," Shay affirms while wiping her face. "And I think I'm going to be honest with Dev when I see him today."

"Oh?" I asked, raising a brow. "What you gonna tell your lover boy?"

"Shut up!" She squealed in embarrassment. "And I'll be telling him the truth."

"What's that?"

A coy smile lights up her face just as her embrace lit up the dark corners of my soul. She gazes at the ring on her finger Devin presented to her all those years ago.

"That I'm ready now. To be his."

***

An hour passes by, and the familiar vibration from my phone in my pocket sounds. I don't bother checking the caller ID before answering to hear the feminine operator announce that it's the Camden prison calling or if I accept the charges. Though it wasn't exactly our scheduled time to talk this evening, I figured it was Milio calling to wish Von congratulations on her wedding like he promised.

"Milio, wassup?" I say real easy into the burner phone.

Instead of the grating Jersey Shore accent I expect, a cold, brittle baritone bleeds through the line and shakes my insides.

"Milio won't be calling anymore."

I pause, dead in my tracks at the brutally uttered words. I was in the middle of adjusting my tie in the bathroom mirror when the familiar voice growls the words at me I don't expect.

"Who is this?" I demand.

"He's dead, Shame." The voice repeats. "Heard you was sending that nigga money on his books and getting all snuggly with him. Y'all was getting too comfortable."

"All Bad?" I demand the voice, feeling my knees wobble as I listen on. "What you talking about man? Who's dead?"

He chuckles before snarling, "Come on, nephew. Don't play stupid. You know exactly what I'm saying. I got your bitch ass letter some months ago and made good use of it after writing down your phone number. Made for good toilet paper."

My entire body trembles and shuts down slowly as his words resonate in my gut. All Bad was grimy enough to carry out something like that without blinking if it meant justice or cash for him.

"Now you'll know what it's like to lose your closest homeboy for no goddamn reason. That's my gift to your snitch ass."

"Cuz, listen—"

"This the only call I'm allowed to make this month, and I sure as fuck would rather spend it talking to my woman. But she ain't answering and I know you got something to do with it."

"What the fuck I got to do with your woman? And where is Milio? Get the fuck off my line with this bullshit!"

"Bro, I'm telling you nicely. Respectfully. Not like the way I found out about how you capped Hector. You lucky I'm in here and you on the outs. I spared your life that day, when I could've easily snapped your neck after piecing together what you did. Not following through on that move and proposing to Sommer Rose will be my only two regrets left in this life."

I'm all but growling as he finishes and my fist flies through the bathroom mirror and slices skin. Blood isn't quite gushing everywhere like in the movies, but deep cuts from the thick glass wedged inside my palm make me see a little clearer. Insane that I'd needed this level of pain to force my thoughts not to skitter into grabbing my gun and making my last contract Shaheim fucking Dabney, but this was real. A very real threat that I couldn't afford to make light of, and though the agony surged triple fold in my mind at the thought of my LC homeboy dead somewheres, I had to set some shit in motion. Had to put together a plan of action that got me the assurance of knowing my mother and daughter weren't under the clutches of the Kobayashi's.

But first I had to deal with him.

"AB," I work past the tic in my jaw. "You been in contact with my moms?"

"Ain't you listening? I told you my girl been holding me down since I got locked up again. She usually pick up when I call, but not today. Sommer always answers for me. That's why I finally made use of that number you sent, to make sure you ain't done no stupid shit in these streets that could've gotten my Sommer hurt."

"I tried with you, bro. I really did." I tell him through gritted teeth. "Milio been telling me to give you time and give you chances and shit. But fuck that. I ain't that same little cousin from before. I'm all man, and this shit is the real deal."

"Whatever, nigga." He says before cackling laughter follows.

"If I don't get a call from Milio by tomorrow, then you can bet on never hearing from Sommer again. You hear me? If I find out you iced my dog for real, then that's the fucking end for you. Bet."

I ended the call by slamming it into the tiled bathroom floor and roared my anguish. *No. No!* That nigga was bluffing about capping Milio, I think frantically. It was my turn to pace the living room floor as hot tears cascaded down my cheeks. I'd eventually got around to telling Milio about Hector, that it was me who did him in under contract by The Commander. And my heart aches at just the mere memory of his response to that during our second ever prison phone call.

"I'd normally have you handled after learning something like that." He spoke. "But I'm in prison now and that shit is yesterday's problem. You are the only homie who's making the effort to rock with me through all this. So, consider us even. Life dealt you a blow just as hard as it's doing me, so let's bury that topic for dead. *Capiche?*"

"Milio..." I hiss in abject agony as the memories from our childhood rush back. He was always there to look out for me in his own way. That same poetry-spittin ass Italian LC fought his entire life as a Sicilian immigrant, and never asked a soul for shit he could hustle for on his own.

"Call me, bro." I whisper and pace at the same time as Shay rushes out from her bedroom. She's wearing a gorgeous evening gown I'm not too sure she obtained it from and scanning the room for the threat.

"What's wrong?!" She demands. "Why are you screaming out here?"

I struggle to slow down and find the words, but it's impossible. All I'm thinking of is my daughter and mother left out there in god-knows-where and my potentially dead homeboy.

"I'm tight right now." Is all I say.

"Slow down." She instructs, grabbing my bloody hand and examining it like the actual medical professional I often forget she's training to be. "Let's get this cleaned up, all right?"

I yank away from her. "Fuck that!"

"Shamel—"

"All Bad just called!" I blurted. "Told me he off'd Milio and that he's been talking to Mommy this whole time. The whole time! But now he don't know where she at and I'm scrambling tryna figure that out, too.

"I know she's gone." Shay mumbles in a tone so low it flies by my head. All I can think of is the wellbeing of my fam. Making sure they're all right and getting to them.

"We got to go."

"Where?"

"To D.C." I bark. "Apparently, Miss Pat is living with her oldest daughter now. You know, the one we never met?"

"I remember," Shay says in a tone so calm it only adds more coals to the fire of my wrath. "We can't leave the farm, remember? That's why we're here in the first place. To lay low. If you run off to D.C. there's no telling who you might run into!"

"Fuck all that!" I snarl. "You ain't even a little concerned about our mom? I know she hasn't been an angel, but damn. I want her to be all right."

"Me too!" She exclaims. "Listen to me for a second."

"Go get your duffel." I instruct her while walking towards the living room safe. We had an agreement to keep a bag packed at all times in the event we'd need to ditch town again. Mine was inside the living room safe and fully loaded with the only three things I needed in a pinch: money, passport, and a gun.

"We don't need to do that!" She shrieks. "I know Mommy's gone. I knew about All Bad, too."

"Whatever, Shay." I spit as I whip out my badly cracked cell. "This ain't the time for games."

She's yapping on some more, but I tune her out as I shoot off a desperate request to one of my most reliable homies.

> **ME**: *Yo, B. Don't got time to get into the details, but can you ride out to D.C. today to check on something for me? I'll pay you whatever you want.*

A few seconds tick by that had me typing another message to him before his text pops up in blue.

> **BONE**: *Where to?*

After forwarding him the address and names, I breathe a sigh of relief at his response.

> **BONE**: *Got you. That's about an hour and some change from here. We gonna head out now to beat the traffic.*

I don't linger on the confusion that arises at his use of 'we' instead of 'I,' since reaching Miss Pat and making sure my family was alive was my only priority in that moment.

> **ME**: *Just let me know what she says and if you can get a hold of her. Thanks, man.*

"Are you even listening to me?" She screeched just as I repocket my phone.

"I did. I'm not going anywhere. I know you don't want to miss Vonnie's wedding, so I sent Bone to Monica's instead to check on Miss Pat."

She shakes her head and I examine the red in her cheeks as she walks over to the couch and sink into it.

"I told you I knew Mommy was missing and that she and All Bad were in contact. And your response was to send Bone to D.C.?"

"Wait..." I sputter, pausing as her admission finally takes root in my brain. "What you mean?"

She hung her head in her hands. "I didn't want you to find out like this, Mel."

"Explain, Shay." I growl, stalking over to her.

Her next words send a bullet through my chest and makes me question the fabric of time, space, and trust altogether.

"Mommy and Lux are in England. I saved up enough from work and school to send them back to live with Mom's mom, our grandmother, in Leeds."

"Are you fucking kidding me? So, they've been in England this whole time?"

"Not the whole time." She whispers. "Jaimie and I have been working extra hard to get Luxury's travel papers together. But the second her passport came in the mail, we were able to work out guardianship enough to get them to Granny Dot's last year."

"Jaimie?"

"My lawyer friend. She's an immigration attorney I met a while back when we worked the clubs together. She's been a real gem through this entire process."

The sting in my palm brings me back to reality in that moment and makes me realize just how different our worlds were back then.

"And you knew about Mommy and All Bad?"

"Unfortunately." She sighs, and I note the frustration in her tone as she falls back into the couch. "And I thought our stubbornness came from The Commander's side of the gene pool, but Mommy's been addicted to All Bad like a moth to a flame. I got word all the time from my girl Truth that she was always sneaking around on the phone during the kids' naps or whenever she goes to work. This has been a tough transition for everyone, but I think everything's finally calming down. Mommy and Lux are living with Granny Dot and they're good. Far away from here. I've been meaning to talk to you about this, but thought this should be a conversation had after Vonnie's wedding. Especially since you went and blabbed to her about who we really are. Everything's a mess now."

"And what happened to all that shit about zero contact, huh? Sounds like you and Mommy been cahooting this entire time we've lived here. It didn't occur to you to consult the father of the little girl you been shuffling around first? Why am I just now hearing about this? This shit ain't adding up."

Shay fires off her response in a moment I'm not present in as her previous words finally hit home in my head. My mother and daughter hadn't been living with

Miss Pat in the Harlem hood house like I thought, but had been staying with one of her homegirls instead while Shay worked out a transition plan to move them from Jersey to the UK. As in, the United fucking Kingdom.

It's one of her homegirls they stayed with for the past three or four years. But not just any homegirls.

One called Truth.

I deflate from the shock and confusion swirling around my head and sink onto the living room floor.

"Shay." I grumble as the world spins. "That friend of yours. You called her Truth?"

Crossing her arms, she nods. "Yeah, that's her. Well, her name is actually Jerica, but that's what she goes by in the clubs."

"She still in Maple Shade?"

"Used to. Jaimie was able to help us get her into a nicer place since Mommy and Lux still needed a place to lay low. She's living in a nice townhouse in Trenton now with her two kids."

A charged silence crackled the atmosphere before any of us said anything.

However, Shay stands up suddenly and walks over to stand above me with a suspicious frown on her face.

"How did you know she used to stay in Maple Shade?"

Thirty-Two

TONIGHT

I never did receive that call from Milio, nor did we make the covert appearance into Vonnie's wedding like intended. Instead, it's total pandemonium erupting at the backyard ceremony where Jeremy, the previous annoying ass neighborhood kid turned extortionist, is lying in a pool of his own blood.

"Y'all shot my son!" Viv screams while wrestling with one of the many police officers swarming the place. Kimmy is fighting and screaming her anguish to reach her dying brother on the ground, and I even see Vonnie restrain her in efforts to trigger reason into the girl she pledged her love to.

I'm barely registering any of it, however, since all my focus is on the Asian man and beautiful Black woman who stole my heart some time ago.

"Nice seeing you again, Shame." Si, the lethal ghost from my past is really standing there. His cold eyes zeroing in on my probably-blanched face as he utters the words I'd done my best to avoid for five years. Five whole fucking years we lived here with our family we created by choice and trust for it all to end tonight.

"Jerica?" Shay exclaims in a voice that closely mirrors a frightened child's. "How are you here right now?"

"Y'all gotta come back to Jersey. Please." Jerica pleads after looking to Si for what looked like permission to speak.

There's an interesting cocktail of emotions starting in me at the prospect of Jerica in danger. I'm wrestling with the instinct to kill him for involving her in this, but I hold back. And not because of the way the light gleams off the handgun in his black pants pocket. Just how did he find us? We were so careful, bordering hypervigilant with every detail of our plan that involved living double lives. Shay and Xavier Rose were the runaway kids who had a bad go of it in their old city, and now were living honest lives with honest jobs to get by. That was us. Living. In peace for a change despite the haunting, dilapidated similarities of our farm shack to our Jersey one. Though I'd been in regular comms with Milio, I'd never revealed my true location. All he knew was that I'd been living on a farm down south. Other than that, everyone from my past, from Shame's life, were as dead to me as they thought I'd been. The rumor that I'd been gunned down by 8Roadz seeking revenge for their now imprisoned lieutenant was one I let fester. Irritating as it was, I took joy in Shame dying so that Zay could live. And make Vonnie's living a little easier, too. That made everything worth it.

The usual calm Jerica or even confident Truth has disappeared, and maybe it's my imagination, but she looks completely terrified as she wraps thin arms around herself.

I stare into my big sis's eyes, seeing all the shame and fear mixed in that mirrors my own. We don't need to speak to understand our next moves. The next moves we'd been on one accord about should this very instance arise, forcing us to flee to save our skins.

We sprint through the backyard, side by side, and run for our lives back to the cozy shack that's been home during our stint here.

Vonnie, I call to her inwardly, *please forgive us. This ain't your fault. But it's our time, baby girl.*

"Grab your duffel!" I holler as we stumble frantically inside the house.

"Got it!"

"We'll look up prices on flights when we get to the airport. Come on, let's go!" I bark the orders as she hastily packs a few items into her bag.

"Where are we going, Mel?"

I don't even hesitate or doubt the answer as soon as it leaves my lips. "Leeds."

"As in, England?"

"Yeah, where else we gonna go?"

"Literally *anywhere* else!" She yelps. "I have finals this week. I can't just up and ditch the country in the middle of exams. I *won't* do that."

We're already in the car, swerving through traffic as we hit the highway high-speed towards the airport. My head spins some more as I maneuver the car through several lanes of traffic.

"Shay, nowhere else is safe. He'll always find me. That's what he does. He'll find me sooner than later and shoot me dead if we stay in the States. Sending my daughter over there was a smart move. We might have a shot at this if we do this right."

"Mel, I can't go."

"Yes, you can!"

"I can't, all right!" She hollers. "We're leaving every-one behind again to deal with our mess. Mamma Dean, Vonnie, Mr. Eddie, and..."

Her voice trails off, but I understand the name that died on her lips unsaid.

"I get it." I said. "You don't want to leave Dev behind when you just got him back. I know that feeling. Leav-ing the love of your life behind high and dry, even though it's for their own good, is worse than dying."

Her lips quaver as she says, "Yeah."

"Shay, we're no good to anyone dead. You don't know Si like I do. He'll kill us without blinking twice about it. This is the only way."

"I'm so tired." She whines into her hand as I pull the car into the Richmond International Airport.

There aren't many cars like I expect lining the public parking area, but it doesn't really matter. They can tow it for all they want, I think, since this will be our last day in this country. We prepared for this, always keeping our cash and passports close to take off in a jiff if needed.

"How did he find us, anyways?" I asked her, my curiosity from before compelling me to do so. "I thought we were being careful."

"We were." She fumes. "Nobody knew."

"Nobody?"

"Yeah."

"Is that right?"

"Just what hell are you saying?" She demanded. "Are you trying to suggest this is my fault?"

I avert my gaze, unsure how to approach the subject of my suspicion or general lack of trust in her since this morning's admission.

"It's just a little convenient, is all I'm saying. That you been talking to this Jaimie person who's been helping you out where Mommy and Lux is concerned."

"So?"

"So." I start, shifting to face her. "You sure she don't know where we are?"

"Of course!"

"Shay, think about it. Come on, now. You've been in way more contact than I have with people from back home. You sure that info ain't slip at any point?"

She remains silent as confusion and fear writes itself over her face. "I don't know...to be honest. Maybe?"

"Maybe?" I snarl. "Are you kidding me? How could you?"

"I said I don't know, okay!" She cried. "I didn't talk to Mommy on a regular basis or anything, but..."

"What?"

"I may have...accidentally told Jerica. Fuck! I think I did...I was just so mad and lonely the entire time Dev was gone. I had nobody to talk to who could relate to me. All the bitches I work with are only interested in spreading gossip, so...I don't know. Maybe I called her a few times from my burner to vent a little. That's all."

"Shay...I don't even know what to say to you."

"I'm sorry!"

I shook my head. "It's okay. We just need to get out of here that much sooner, then. All right?"

"Um, okay. Right. You all right? You're taking this information much more calmly than I expected."

Though my voice was calm and controlled, it betrayed the true emotions raging through me. Sure, I was angry. Had every right to be considering all the facts that had us running again. But it's something else that makes me want to ball up in a corner.

Betrayal. I felt utterly betrayed by the woman I couldn't even lie about loving to death in spite of my lethal actions that led to her brother dead. If Jerica was the only person Shay confided our location in, then that only meant Jerica told Si. I wasn't well versed on the particulars, but knew deep in me that Jerica gave up on me. On us. She chose Takeo Kobayashi over me, and god dammit that made me want to kill again. But that's only a knee-jerk reaction to the cold slab of hurt solidifying in my chest.

"I'm all right." I lie to her before getting out of the car. The dark sky denotes something ominous in the air, as if not only rain was coming but another downpour of ruin. There just wasn't enough time to argue anymore. We had to get out of here, before—

"Did you fuck Jerica?" Shay's question nearly makes me stumble into the pavement. But I don't, in fact, I do my best remaining neutral as I turn to face her.

"Nah."

An 'ah-ha' look shined in her eyes as she jabbed an accusatory finger at me. "I knew it!"

"What's it matter?"

"It matters." She said plainly. "And explains a lot, too."

I hated the curiosity that immediately reared its head at that ambiguous statement. She betrayed me, but I still had to know.

"A lot, like what?"

She shrugs. "Oh, nothing. Just whenever I mentioned your name during a vent call, she'd, like, seize up. Get real quiet. What actually happened between you two?"

"This really ain't the time for social hour, Shay." I bite out as I pull the heavy steel door open.

"Oh, come on!" She whined trailing behind. "I'm missing out on some serious finals for this, and ended up spilling all my secrets to you today. Can't you tell me?"

I sigh. "Nah, man. Let's go."

A tense second passes with us just staring at the floor before she says, "Really, though. Are you okay? Didn't you say All Bad having something to do with hurting your boy? Was that true?"

My chest seizes at the mere mention of Milio's potentially dead body somewheres. All of this shit I didn't need nor wanted to think about. I forced a few scriptures from the Good Book into my brain, reminding myself to have faith that he was okay. Alive and well somewheres despite All Bad's threats. Have faith that my mom and baby girl really were thriving in England, where we'd soon join them. Have faith that Vonnie would be all right left behind, though my soul screamed at the idea of abandoning her again. I had to put stock in that mustard seed faith that all would turn out okay.

"Thanks, Shay. But I'll be all right."

I'm just about dragging her into the nearly empty airport as I rush to one of the available agents.

"Sorry," the older white lady grunts. "The next flight to Leeds Bradford Airport departs tomorrow night."

"Fuck!" I swear as our duffels fall to the floor. "There's no other flights to England happening in the next three hours or so?"

"Sir, I'm going to ask you to lower your voice." She warns, alternating her focus between me and her computer. "And no. The soonest flight is heading to London five hours from now. Would you like to buy tickets?"

"Whatever," I spit, my fists aching from how tightly balled they are. "How much?"

She studies the screen before reciting the number that made me blink several times to process it.

"How much?"

"A one-way, same day flight to London will cost you $2,390. This is the only same day flight available to England."

I swore, my mind blanking as I considered all the money I had left to my name: fifteen hundred bucks was what was left of my No-Touch stash. After purchasing that *Weapons from Zeldar* game for Von and refilling my latest stash of bud, my funds depleted to an all-time low. I figured working a few more farm jobs would replenish me enough to get by, but I hadn't banked on Si showing up. Not like this. Not ever.

I take a deep breath to steady my mind and reconfigure my thoughts. Just what the fuck was I going to do?

"It's all right." Shay cuts in, raising her hand in attempts to calm me and reassure the old bitch agent who was saying a combination of all the wrong things. "We can afford that. We'll take the two tickets for London, please."

"This is an information desk, ma'am." She drawls dispassionately to my sis. "You'll need to purchase those tickets online or over the phone with a ticketing agent."

"But why can't we just buy them from you? Since you're literally staring at them on your little computer?"

"This little computer is for information purposes. All I can do is reference the data and inform you of it. Nothing more or less. That a problem?"

I saw waves of patience funneling from my big sis as she ground her teeth and forced a large fake smile. The same fake smile she used for years towards our mother amidst a lie.

"No, ma'am. I just want to know why we can't literally hand you the cash. Then you spit out the ticket and hand to us. It's easy-peasy."

"Easy-peasy isn't policy. Sorry." She grunts again in that nasal voice of hers.

"Listen, Agnes." Shay started, making me notice her name tag for the first time. "We need those tickets. Right here. Right now. Please tell me how we can make that happen instead of a spiel about policy. Please."

Another long moment of Agnes glaring and flexing her jaw at my sis, as if she's considering calling security or not. "Let me speak with my manager and see what we can work out, okay?"

"Thank you!" Shay beamed at her short form scuttling away.

"You ain't have to do that." I tell her once we're alone.

"Newsflash: fuck yeah, I did. She wasn't hearing reason."

"Nah, not that." I say. "I mean, you don't need to pay for my ticket. That's not on you."

She frowns a knowing look at me before crossing her arms. "Mel, where is this coming from?"

I shrugged. "Just saying. I don't want you to feel like I'm your responsibility. I'm grown."

"Boy, bye." Her chuckles turned into full blown laughter, making her grip her sides. "You'll always be my responsibility."

"Ain't nothing funny about that." I growl, but it's ineffectual since she laughs harder. "Stop laughing!"

"Sorry, sorry." She sobers. "It's the look on your face. Chill out, Mel. We're always going to have each other's backs, okay? I have some cash saved up to afford this, so no worries. Okay?"

Resigned, exhausted, and a bit defeated, I sigh and nod. Conceding to owing her for the last time. "Thanks. I'll pay you back when we get to England."

"No, you won't."

"Yeah, I will."

"No, seriously." She says deadpan. "Us landing safely on our new home soil will be enough repayment. So don't worry about it." Her smile is large and infectious as she grins at me though a mask of unshed tears.

I can't resist the urge to pull her into my arms and hug her with the remaining trust and hope in me. Though this day has been insane, a warm feeling starts in my body, reassuring me that everything just might work out all right for a change.

I'm grinning like a goof when Agnes returns to the desk with a tiny black dude wearing a manager tag.

"We're happy to get those tickets printed for you two." He says while typing something into the computer.

"Oh fuck!" Shay yelps, sending me into high alert as I assess her rummaging through her duffel. "It's not here! Fuck!"

"What's wrong?" I bark, looking at the bag for the culprit that had my sis so panicked.

She cups hands over her face. "My god! I'm just stupid is all. I'm sorry, Mel."

"What is it?!"

"I forgot that I'd sent Mommy most of my check last week. Instead of the four stacks I thought I had there's only a little left. Not nearly enough for that ticket." Her chest quakes with the sobs of her frustration, and we're drawing some attention from the desk agents and bystanders as her sobs morph into howls.

"It's okay." I reassure her with a calm I didn't feel, yet again. "How much do you have?"

"About two hundred bucks."

"Shit!" I hiss, that amount was nowhere near enough for even one ticket. My heart and mind felt like they'd explode as I wracked my brain for what to do next.

"Sorry to hear about that, ma'am." The manager says. "But there are other options. A one-way ticket to Leeds costs less than a ticket to London. The flight leaves tomorrow night, but the ticket is only twelve hundred dollars plus tax. Is that a little better?"

"No!" Shay sobs. "That's still way too expensive for the both of us to afford it."

I could afford that ticket, I thought, considering the fifteen hundred on my person. It was just enough for me to get there and it was even enough left for me to potentially get a room somewhere for the night until the flight tomorrow.

But that meant leaving Shay behind. And from everything I've learned from that Good Book encouraged me against selfishness to receive grace and redemption from the almighty. I wanted so desperately to leave the underworld from which I was bred, and I knew abandoning my sis right now would only land me right back where I started. In a hell all on my own.

Releasing a weary, long breath from somewhere deep in my soul, I nod to Gerald, the manager in front of us.

"I'll take that ticket. For one."

"Sure thing." He affirms without question and begins to speedily tap away at his computer.

"What are you doing?" Shay asks, in a tone I recognized as the same level of hurt as when I aimed that gun at her back at the Dirty Kitten. "You're...buying the ticket? For one?"

"Take this, and make sure my little girl has the best life over there with the Brits. Okay?" I say to her in a shaky breath, extending the twelve-hundred-dollar ticket that exhausted the remains of my No-Touch stash.

She reared back, dropping her duffel to the ground. "What?"

"Take it, sis." I instructed, shoving the paper ticket into her hands. "Before I change my mind about staying behind."

"Mel, no!" She sobbed, shaking her head and holding onto me for dear life. "You can't stay here. You said it yourself that Si dude would kill you. You take the ticket!"

"No, thank you." I hugged her back, a large smile curling my face and a stray tear slipping past my cheek. "Everything will be okay."

"No!" She growled, slapping my head. "I'm your big sister! If anyone should be taking huge sacrifices like this, it's me! Besides, you have Luxury to worry about. So, go be her dad. Be the father The Commander never was with us. Doesn't she deserve that?"

"She deserves to be happy." I whisper in her hair. "Whether I'm there or not, I know you and Mommy will be the best family to make sure that happens."

"Mel, no!"

"It's okay!" I fume, not letting her go. Afraid that if I did she'd slip away forever. "Stop worrying about me and go live, all right? It's time you shine bright. I might not be there for your med school debut, but think of me when you make it to the top."

She's shaking but doesn't respond. Just holds me tighter as I do her.

"Please?" I whisper brokenly into her hair again. "I need you to promise me. Promise to make me proud."

"Okay." she sniffles as we separate. "You got it. Just make it back to me when all this clears, okay?"

I only nod as I fight the tears at bay.

"And Mel?"

"Yeah?"

Her watery smile lights up her face as she says the thing that elixirs my soul. "You're not the shame of our family's existence. You make us so proud, both mom and me, every day. You understand?"

Keep it together, Mel. This was for the best, I thought. It was time I faced these demons I dragged my family through for the past six years. In all actuality, it's been longer than six years. I'd been the shame of my family's existence for so long, or at least that's what I told myself. For real for real, they'd loved me all along, even when I occupied those dark corners of the streets and wrought havoc. I guess I was still worth loving after all.

I kissed her forehead. "Stay dreaming, sis."

"Stay *alive*, bro." She warned.

I opened my mouth to respond, to say something tender or quippy to send her off on a lighter note, but her eyes saucer at something behind me.

"Uh, Mel." Shay squeaks. "Who's that?"

My eyes follow hers to see a tall man with tanned skin walking towards us. He's wearing that familiar lethal looking all black getup: a leather motorcycle jacket paired with black jeans. His boots aren't the same as what Si would wear, but besides that minor difference, he looks damn near identical to the dude I called The Silence.

"Get out of here, okay?" I demand, gathering her exposed duffel and tossing it at her. I shoved the remaining cash in my wallet into her hands as I pushed her towards another exit.

"What about—"

"Just run!" I scream at her, and she pauses for an extra second before heeding my words and dashing away. A small crowd encircled us enough to hide her getaway, but not for me. It was time, I thought as I crossed the floor to meet the unfamiliar Asian man halfway.

"Shame, right?" He says in an unexpected Jersey accent.

I nodded.

"Let's not make this hard, all right? You kept the man waiting long enough."

"All right." Is all I say as I follow him to a parking lot almost a mile from the airport. The sky is darkening and there's nobody outside besides the obvious stretch limousine in the abandoned lot.

"Who you?" I ask the annoyed escort whose gun is so obviously bulging out from his jean pocket.

He scowls as we get to stand in front of the black vehicle.

"The only people who get to know my full name are six feet under. If Take wanted you dead, you'd have seen me twice over by now: once before you get buried and possibly another time after your spirit crosses over. Depending on what you believe."

My mind is racing with questions as he knocks on the passenger door. Just who the fuck was this gritty Jersey asshole? He was similar to Si in that metaphorical way he spoke, but grimier and more lethal looking like my brother-cousin who was really my uncle.

All my thoughts come to a blaring halt when I gawk at the passenger door swinging open. His black Jordans show first as he gets out the car, and I'm doing my best to control the shaking as I face Takeo Kobayashi head on, like I feared.

"Shame." Si says, his tone even and neutral like always. "Good to see you."

"Wish I could say the same." I say, deciding to hold nothing back for the first time. If this was going to be my last few minutes alive, then there was no use in any more lies. It was time I honored up, like Si always preached before his executions.

"Why did you run?" Si asks, cool and direct as he walks closer to me. "I'd really like to know."

"To protect my family, man." I say, nothing but the truth on my side as I spill the words easy-peasy. "Plain and simple. I didn't mean to steal your shit or fuck with your clan, but it was the only option I had."

"It wasn't the only option."

"Fuck yeah it was. You know I wouldn't have pulled some devious shit like that if I had any other choice. My sister's life was in danger. So was my kid's. And my mom's. I even left my woman behind to protect her. I cut ties with everyone in my corner to survive. You know how hard that was? How hard it still is?"

An emotion flares in his eyes that I don't recognize as he nods. "I do."

"Then hear me out." I start. "If you got to take care of me to settle up that debt with the Kobayashi's, then go ahead. I just came back to speak with you, man to man, to ask a favor."

His brows raise. "Go on."

"Don't hurt my family. Not my sis, my moms, or my daughter. Neither of them had anything to do with this.

Let it end with me. Just take me out and make it clean, all right? That's all I ask."

"You're wrong, you know." He answers, his tone gravel as he circles me. "You did have options."

"I didn't!" I roar.

"You did." He answered coolly again. "You could have come to me. Why didn't you just talk to me, Shame?"

"Because this was my shit to deal with, bro!" I holler, my eyes following his circling form. "This was my family. It was my time to take care of them. I dragged everybody into my messes all the time. It was just my time to do the cleaning instead of making it worse."

He stops suddenly, breathing heavy as he stares into my eyes. "You did this to protect your family?"

"Yes."

"To preserve the honor of men in your family line, in spite of Quincy Masters's actions to sully your name?"

"Yes."

"Even at the risk of owing my clan for the rest of your life? Or even dying at the risk of nonpayment?"

"Yes."

He's inches away from my face now, and we're both breathing heavy as the minutes tick by. My mind is surprisingly clear, clearer than it's been in years as I do nothing but rattle off truths to my executioner.

Wordlessly, he brandishes a semi-automatic gun equipped with a silencer the ten-year-old me would have drooled over. The cold metal touches my right temple at his hand, but I'm not afraid as his finger lingers over the trigger. This was it. My time in the sun, in Richmond with my chosen family, coming to an abrupt close at just a couple pounds of pressure.

I had no regrets, just concern for the stress the news of my death would bring my family.

"If awarded the opportunity to go back in time. To the moment before you called to ask me for that advance. Would you redo it, or choose differently? I must know."

I gulped. "Without a doubt, I'd redo it."

"What a shame." Is all I hear him say before he pulls the trigger. Though my eyes are closed, the squeak of the bullet firing through the silenced chamber coupled with zero pain confuses me. I should be dead, I realize, but after patting down random parts of my body, I open my eyes to the unthinkable.

Si is standing over the dead body of the nameless Asian man from before, the one who escorted me to this strange parking lot uttering strange threats.

He bends down to speak to the man in a voice so low I can't make sense of it. But his final few words project loud enough for me to interpret.

"I'd ask you to tell my brother hello when your souls cross paths, but hell is the most fitting destination your afterlife entails. And my brother won't be there. Good-bye, Yamada Shindo."

My jaw is on the concrete as I stare at the weird exchange. I'm not sure how to even make sense of Si's shooting this Yamada Shindo character, but whatever the story is, I'm sure it's a long one. A long one I wanted no part in, but a few answers to.

"What the fuck was that, bro?" I demanded as sweat poured down my forehead.

Si's breathing is heavy and uneven, and I have to squint to bear witness to the display I didn't believe: he's crying. And I mean huge sobs wrack his chest as he turns his back on me to wipe his face.

"Si?" I asked, unbelievably concerned for the dude who'd held me at gunpoint. "What's all this about?"

"I didn't come here to kill you, Shamel." He says, and I flinch at his use of my legal name. "I came to ask for your help."

"My help?"

He turns to me, and I note the tears falling in waves down his face. "Yes. You mentioned risking your life to protect your woman, and..."

"Yeah?" I gauged cautiously.

"And it's what I have failed to do. I risked everything and now...she's gone. My woman, my *Hanabi*."

I'm gawking at him in open awe as I watch the normally calm, cool, collected killer I've seen gouge men's eyes from their sockets, sink to the ground and crawl to me. On his knees, he stumbles over and wraps his arms around me like a wuss. No, not a wuss, but like a wounded child.

"Shamel, please help me find her. She's gone and I am not able to function without her by my side. I fear she's out there in danger and pregnant with a child I'll never see."

"Si, man." I start, in total shock but forming words somehow. "You came all this way to...*not* kill me? To ask me to help you find your girl?"

He nods. "Yes. And to assist me staging a coup."

"A coup? With who?"

His eyes revert back to that cold, soulless co-killer I knew from the gritty streets up north as he says his next words.

"My entire clan. They must be taken down. I need your expertise with this. To rid the world of the terrible clan that's done nothing but terrorize and destroy the lives of underserved populations with crippling debt. Aid me in taking them down so we can run the entire narcotic trade together. Like I always intended. But now we'll have total control of our product and investments. We'll be unstoppable."

"Si, I...."

"Don't answer me yet." He starts frantically. "I understand there's a lot of wrongs needing to be corrected on my end. Please, just sit inside the limo and give me your answer afterwards. Okay?"

I nod, sort of numb from the bum rush of info. I should be dead, I realize, and this death cheat should make me grateful, but I'm mentally stuck in a limbo of emotions as I climb into the limousine.

It's complete darkness inside, but a familiar, sweet musk assails me almost instantly as I shut the door behind me and sit.

"Shamel?" She calls.

I have to squint to see her, but I know it's Jerica True there. In front of me in the facing seat and calling out to me.

"Baby, is that you?" She calls again, her voice shaky. "Please, tell me that's you..."

"It's...it's me." I say, tears pouring down my face after all the holding back I'd been doing since this morning. "Fuck, Jerica, I missed your voice so bad."

Again, I don't see her, but feel her arms wrap around me in the dark. All the anger I should be feeling at her possible betrayal or disloyalty washes away as I melt in her arms. None of that shit mattered, at least not in reality. Same as Si from a few minutes ago, I embrace her tight, afraid she's been a figment of my imagination. Her lips find mine and in a frenzied next few minutes, and before I get the chance to tear her panties off in the dark, her warm hand stops me.

"Why do you keep doing this to me?" She pleads, but I'm not sure if the question was for me or herself. "I should be fucking mad at you. No, I am mad at you! You left me behind. Left me to rot after all these years. I loved you, and you left."

I squeeze her in my arms again, hoping they'd do the apologizing for me instead since my words didn't quite feel like enough.

"Shamel, you left me." She whispers, broken and meek.

"I had to." I croaked. "I'm sorry. You should be mad at me. Hate me. I can take it."

She shoved me. "Ugh! How can I hate you now when you say sweet shit to me like that?"

"I don't know." I whisper. "But I could never hate you. I'm just so glad to hear you're okay. You're alive and okay. That's enough for me. Even if you hate me for the rest of your life, I'll accept that. So long as you stay alive, my dying will be easy."

"Don't talk like that." She snaps, holding me tight again. "You left us, but I can't let you talk about dying. You mean too much to me for that."

"Us?" I asked, confused and touched at the same time by her beautiful words.

"That's right. Us. There's a lot we need to discuss, too." She breathes, before light floods the inside of the vehicle. On the opposite side of the limo, there's a sleeping child wearing a little red cap, overalls, and red long sleeved shirt underneath. He's snoozing so peacefully in his car seat, but stirs at the light illuminating the small space.

"Mommy?" He squeaks in a small searching voice before looking at me. I'm looking around for his Mommy, too, but freeze when Jerica climbs over and pulls him into her arms.

"Have a good nap, baby?" She sings, revealing bright white teeth through a beaming smile.

He nods, but frowns as he studies me from across the seat. "Yes, mommy. Who's that man?"

Jerica's smile vanishes as her eyes follow the little boy's finger jabbed at my shadowed presence. Her words send three thousand bullets flying through my skull as she cradles the kid with large brown eyes.

"That man right there?" She points. "Is your daddy, Khalil. Say hi."

EPILOGUE

SHAY

"I gotta go my way. Gotta find my voice. Make my choice in the light of day..."

My eyes drift closed as the made-up song sprang forth, allowing me to chant the words my heart felt as I washed the remainder of breakfast dishes my brother ritualistically neglected. Today was my first day off after pulling doubles at one of the only two nursing homes in town, and even though I needed every cent of overtime pay to go to savings, my aching body needed the break more. I should be resting, I know, but the rank odor of unwashed dishes from the prior night's dinner filled the cabin with a pungent smell I couldn't sleep through. *Shamel,* I inwardly scowled at my absent brother, *your ass is mine the next time I see you.* I'd gotten so sick and tired of reminding the unemployed sleazeball to wash a damn dish or sweep a damn floor. Resolving myself to exchange a few choice words for him upon his return from his homeboy's house, I polished off the final roasting pot and continued my idle dream song.

"It's all on me now...sweet spring, now...how will I find my way...?"

"When you gonna bake me another one of those cakes you're so famous for?" Devin Carlson asked after poking his head through the open window in my small cabin kitchen.

"Damn it!" I screeched, clutching my chest involuntarily from the fright of his sudden appearance.

His hyena laugh preceded him, making me hear him instead of seeing his entire body as he rounded the cabin to stand at the front entrance.

"My bad," He chortled, "Ain't mean to scare you."

I'd been so enveloped in the task of scrubbing the dirt and anxiety away that I'd lost myself in the idle dream song. Heat rises up from my neck and colors my cheeks in an embarrassed flush.

It's Devin, or DC the boys called him, standing at my front door. My wide-open front door that I don't even bother shutting these days since the farm is such a small intimate community of kindness. Unlike in Camden, unlocked doors were the norm.

I gulp, attempting to regain some composure and control of the upcoming conversation.

"You ain't scare me."

"Oh, for real?"

"No!" I yelped. "You scared the living shit out of me. Why are you sneaking up on me like that?"

He gripped his sides and hunched his six-foot four frame over to guffaw more of his amusement and teasing of me. The asshole had the nerve to laugh at my terror after showing up unexpected at my door?

At six feet, there aren't many men I look up to on the Virginian farm filled with miniature men by comparison. They're all mini (save for Bone, whose height had even Devin beat) and intimidated by me, well, all except the pretty boy jerk at my door.

Laughing at me.

I'm stomping over to him in a blink, and by the time my hand reaches out to smack him, he catches it and yanks me into his front.

"Hey, now." Devin warns, breathing hard and staring into my eyes in that intense way that heated strange parts of my body. "Play nice."

"Shut up!" I blurt nervously before shoving him onto the front porch. "And tell me what the hell you're doing here? Zay isn't here."

"I ain't come to see Zay." He answers while straightening. I note his shaved fade I could tell was a product of Malik's expert handiwork. Though an apprentice, he's been the best around for all haircut needs, pro bono, for mostly his friends on the farm. One of those tight friends included Devin, the eighteen-year-old D.C. explant whose little sister happened to be my little sister as well. It was a weird story, one I didn't care to linger too much in the weeds of as I considered the tan skinned teen before me. Wearing that silly grin I'd grown to secretly adore.

"Okay..." I muttered, an awkward sinking feeling weighing heavily on my shoulders suddenly. "Then...how can I help?"

"I told you. I wanted some cake."

"Well, I can't help you with that." I tutted petulantly while crossing my arms. "Too bad."

"Come on, Shay." He begged with that same pretty boy smile. "Von told me you baked her some yellow cake yesterday, but she left it here since she didn't want the whole thing. Can't you share some with me?"

I started back towards the house. "Dev, go find something to do. Or somebody else to bother. I'm busy."

"Busy doing what?"

"Uh, cleaning my house."

"Shouldn't you be resting on your only day off, though?" He asked, repeating the same question I'd asked myself earlier.

"How'd you know I'd be off today?" I asked, turning back.

His cheeks burn now as he casts a guilty look at me. "Your schedule ain't hard to pin down."

I only stare at him to say something along the lines of 'go away' or 'leave me alone,' but...

Caving, as I always did where it came to my secret crush, I shot him a droll stare.

"All right. Come in. But you can only stay for a little while."

"Damn, where's the rest of it?" Dev questioned as he stared into the fridge. We're both staring at the half a slice remaining in the Tupperware I stored all my baked goods in.

"Xavier Rose happened." I laughed. "He destroys all the good food in this house. Leftovers don't ever exist with him around."

"Damn, Zay." Devin breathes in weak irritation as a chuckle overcomes him, too.

We're soon laughing together, and I hated to admit the welcome mood change from the sad atmosphere stirred by my idle dream songs. I spent so much of my life alone, always keeping a strict line between home and the hustle that got me where I am today. I regretted nothing, especially as I look around at the quaint house that most might call a shack. The freedom and tight knit community of the farm residents filled me with a warm feeling I never knew before in my old home. But there were times, like now, where being all alone in this small house made me feel casted away. On an island far off somewhere and drifting without a paddle.

We sober after a moment, and that leaves us staring into the open fridge with fixed gazes on the plate my brother left behind where yellow cake used to be.

"Well," Devin starts, "I guess I'll let you get back to it, then."

"Sure." I say out loud, but inside I'm screaming for him to stay. To rid me of this lonesome loneliness my pride would never let me admit to feeling. "You should go."

He nods, scratching his mowed hair. "Okay."

"Hey, Dev?" I call after him, my heart pounding in my chest as I watch him turn back so quick the whiplash was visible.

"Yeah, Shay?" He asks eagerly.

"Um." I murmur. "Tell Vonnie I said 'hi,' okay?"

His face falls, sending splinters through my heart for some unknown reason. "I got you."

Why did this guy's every move I see so vividly? His every emotion I felt as if there existed an invisible cord connecting our separate hearts. The further he walks away, the harder he pulls on that invisible string and makes my breathing uneasy.

He's walking away, I observe, and scream inwardly for him to come back. *Devin, please don't go!* I holler against the pride writhing inside me. That bitter, stupid, pride that got me in so much trouble all those years ago. Was a part of the reason for our secret lives in this sleepy little farm town I couldn't live without.

I turn my back to him, forcing myself to resume my focus on the remaining dishes in the sink. I didn't bother closing the door like usual, and the evening breeze was welcome as it washed through the heated kitchen and splashed my hot face.

"Don't leave me..." I can't resist the idle dream song floating past my vocal cords anymore. Exhausted and defeated from letting him go, I allow my heart to do the talking. *"Everybody walks away...why won't you stay...the day with me...?"*

A pair of strong arms wound around my chest from behind, but this time I don't yelp from fear since I know the identity of this intruder. At least, my heart and body does as I grab onto his sinewy arms with frail force.

"I'm here." Devin groans in my ear, squeezing me tight to his body. "I ain't walking away."

A tear slips down my cheek that I'm glad he can't see. "D-Devin?"

"The cake was a front." He admitted in a throaty whisper. "I just wanted to see you."

"You did?" I ask, my heart flipping in my chest.

"No," he said. "Needed to see you. I don't know why, but I can't get you out of my head. I've been trying to ignore it, but just looking at you drives me crazy. Tell me I'm crazy. That I'm just a psycho for feeling all this shit for you."

"You're crazy." I answered behind the mask of tears while holding onto him for dear life.

He laughed. "Maybe I am."

The tears ebbed enough for me to feel confident to twist in his arms. Again, I'm tall for a girl, but he's even taller for his age, making us sort of fit perfectly into each other's arms. I reach hesitant arms up to wrap around his neck and revel in the feel of his warmth.

And strength.

He's amassed in pure muscle that meets my softer, fleshy front, and I'm suddenly conscious of the extra twenty-five pounds I've packed on since living off of Mamma Dean's southern fried cooking she called "homemade."

"Guess we're both just crazy, huh?" I say, staring into his burning eyes.

"It's your voice." He breathes.

"My voice…"

"Something about when I hear you sing…it makes me want to hold you."

A fit of rage poured through me at that sentiment. "So, what, this is sympathy? You feeling sorry for the overworked big sister of your homeboy that much to make up some excuse to bother her?"

"What? No!"

"So, I'm just a big joke to you?" I spit. "Just leave."

"You don't mean that." He growls.

A dark penetrating stare stabs me as I look up at him. His brown eyes are promising something I'm not emotionally able to handle right now. It's all a little too much. Too much realness in front of me as I glare at the guy I'd been lowkey drooling over since moving here. I knew it wasn't right to want him this bad. Knew it was morally fucked up to shiver with a wanton need whenever we occupied the same crowded room full of people for Mamma Dean and Aunt Stevie's Sunday Communions. I pretended to not notice the way his eyes lingered on me from across the room or how he'd always accompany Vonnie to our house whenever she'd come visit. Vonnie was a tough girl. Knew these fields like the back of her hand and could run away in a jiff if needed to find help. So, Devin joining her on her walks or drives here for "safety" purposes was purely unnecessary, but I never called him on it. Especially since I wanted to be around him, too. Craved his presence just as bad as I craved his strong fingers pressing into my curls and massaging my scalp.

The action is so unexpected that it diffuses any remaining faux anger in me as a deep moan escapes my throat from the sensation he'd caused.

"What are..." I hiss, eyes shut, "...you doing?"

His next words sent my soul soaring yet tightened that thread linking our beating hearts.

"Spending the day with you, baby."

***

"Devin!" I scream, waking in a terrified daze and scanning the dark bedroom. It's pitch black and I cringe at the pools of sweat sticking to my forehead and gluing me to the sheets beneath.

I don't even need to peer over to know I've kicked the covers off the bed again. My body feels heavy, heady, and my nipples are hard as fuck as my need makes me feel that much more agony. It's that same dream. *Again.* Every night for the past month I'd dreamt of that day between me and Devin. The day we first made love and confessed the truth of our feelings to each other after living with the agony of denying ourselves.

The memory of his hands roaming my body, holding me tight as he pledged to never let me sing another lonely sad song again. He said I drove him just as mad with desire as he did me, and our secret relationship began that lazy afternoon as he laid me down on the kitchen floor and entered my slick heat. Neither of us caring about getting caught or the emotional blowback we'd need to take care of if that happened.

To put it simply, we were...one. That day and every day after, until...well, he left. I couldn't forgive him for that, still couldn't get over the betrayal and utter loneliness that returned at his surprise departure. He fucked me the day of his deployment. But not in a good way. Not in the way my body craved. But the way that made me hit the ground hard with reality. The reality of living the rest of my life without him, since he couldn't care enough to consider me by leaving me behind as if I were a silly afterthought. Or a conquest.

A stirring beside me alerts me of another presence in bed with me. I flinched, surprised he'd gotten off work on time to sleep with me for a change since his schedule as a physician demanded him away most nights.

"You all right, love?" Landon asks in a tone groggy from a sleep I'm sure I interrupted.

I smile against the sadness in my heart. "Yes, babe. Go back to bed. Sorry to wake you."

"Righto." Seemingly satisfied, he shifts his position and sighs. His light snores let me know he's fallen back to sleep, and I use that moment to tip toe into the micro bathroom in our flat.

It takes me a minute to waddle to my feet in the pitch dark, but I eventually make my way to the toilet my bladder desperately needs.

Unable to stop myself, I roll the tight buds of my nipples between my fingers as I recall that nightly dream that won't cease to leave me alone. In all honesty, I welcome the hot visions from the past that often leads to me screaming to quiet orgasms in the middle of the night. I always see it as Devin's way of coaxing me to get the rest I need, especially now, since my body isn't truly my own anymore.

My pussy clenches and spasms with an orgasm that sends me over the edge. No clitoral stimulation was needed to send me cumming like a horny teenager in my flat's tiny bathroom. Again.

I stand up after finishing my business and study my curvier form in the mirror. My breasts are twice their usual double-D cup size, and the chub in my face can only be attributed to the extra lunches my Granny Dot packs me for work. All of it is just extra cushion, I can almost hear Devin say as I study the curvy goddess in the oval mirror that needed cleaning. I'll worry about it later, I tell myself, running shaky hands over the slight notch in my previously flat belly.

"It's you and me, baby girl." I sing to the child in my womb. The baby I still hadn't told Landon about, but would need to soon since my belly already began spilling over my scrub bottoms now. An incredible wave of longing and loneliness fills me as I cradle my barely-there baby bump. If things had just been different, I think, reflecting on the past two years of living in England. I missed my farm fam so much that breathing was a challenge just thinking about it. All the loss and scandal that lead me to this incredible loneliness. I'd give anything for things to just be different...

"Shayne?" Landon calls from the bedroom. He probably woke up and reached for me, coming up with a mere flat sheet in my wake instead of my body. "Are you coming back to bed?"

"Yeah, babe!" I call, shooting a final look of longing at the girl I barely recognize anymore in the mirror before rejoining my husband in our bedroom. "I'm here."

AUTHOR'S NOTE

Whew! What a ride. To say penning this eighth book has been a journey of emotions would be the understatement of the century. Thank you so much for reading Shamel's story of darkness and redemption. He truly touched my heart from his inception to the final chapter, and I am so stoked for you to see what's next in store for The REAL Series.

Love always,
Laura

About the Author

Since the age of twelve, Laura could always be found writing. She writes within a wide array of genres, including paranormal, drama, slice of life, and (her favorite) romance. In her free time, if she's not writing, she's reading or listening to a steamy audio-book.

Her most notable works include Something About Kyle and her ongoing, the REAL Series, which explores the narratives of various, interconnected young adults. Support her craft by purchasing from her bookstore.

OTHER BOOKS IN THIS SERIES

*written by Laurie Ross

www.ingramcontent.com/pod-product-compliance
Lightning Source LLC
Chambersburg PA
CBHW071441260626
47170CB00013B/2294